LEVIATHAN'S FALL

by Fergus Bannon

First published by Hartley and Truro in 2016

Chapter 1. *Diggs Town Virginia*

A dog growls in the cold night. Yao's hand flicks instinctively for his gun, but still nothing is moving in the darkened streets. His hand slips back out from inside his thick coat and down to his side.

The neighbourhood is poor, at least by US standards, and he checks the address again. The light from his phone washes over him and, sure enough, the map shows he's exactly where he's supposed be.

That a man with such an important job should live here, languishing with his family in a district of beaten up clapboard houses. He shakes his head in disbelief.

The dog growls again and this time he gets the direction. It's coming from behind the next house along and he gets a chance to appreciate the timbre of the animal's warning. In his own country one learns to be a connoisseur of dogs and their barks. Medium sized at most, he guesses this one is full of wind and piss, barking and growling from the safety of its own territory. Not at all like the evil, slavering hellhounds of his youth: straining to get at you, desperate to attack and rend.

As he passes by, the dog grumbles once again but he pays it little attention. He can see the lights of the bar a couple of hundred metres ahead, where the darkened residential district gives out and a garish oasis of fast food joints begin.

He's trying to look relaxed, at ease. An American going for a drink, loafing casually through his own too-familiar-to-notice neighbourhood.

But he knows he doesn't fit. He'd arrived from Africa in an Airbus only months ago, not on a slave ship hundreds of years back. His ancestors haven't interbred with slaves from other tribes or with the whites. His lineage is solid *Ewaga*: shorter stature, skin darker, body leaner and compact but with broad shoulders and well-muscled arms.

He crosses the road, only listening but not looking for oncoming cars, as seems to be the way with people in this part of town. Did turning their heads make them look uncool, make them look like they wanted to live? Or did they genuinely not care if they were mowed down?

Always at the heart of this country he senses an emptiness.

Not that there are many cars to run him down at this time of night. The only ones around are poking diagonally into the kerb running along the little strip mall. Most are parked in front of the bar. As he approaches this, he sees many garishly coloured posters offering beer and spirit combinations at what they assure him are rock bottom prices.

At the sticky handled door, he glances around for a final time, then takes a deep breath and enters.

It's noisy in here and the place reeks of beer and fried food. The Americans are roaring at each other as usual, confident their inane observations should be heard by the rest of the world. He threads his way through the tables to the bar.

He sees Wiggins further down the long counter. The man is alone, staring up at a baseball game on one of the big screens above the bar. Around these hang baseball pennants and autographed photos of sports stars.

He notices the barman is already looking at him, eyes fractionally narrowed. He will never look like anything other than a stranger in this country.

"A coke, please," he says then remembers the last word, like politeness itself, is considered unmanly in a place like this.

While the barman waddles away down the bar to ladle an iceberg into a frosted glass, Yao turns to his own reflection in the mirror. It does not do to be vain, but he knows his regular features make him attractive to women, though in this country his tiny ears are a problem. Evidence of his tribal purity, it marks them out from the elephant ears of the Westerners.

At least he never got the tribal scars. For a second, he

thinks of Zinzi, of gently tracing his finger across the undulations on her face, and an erotic charge arcs through his loins.

He shakes his head gently in exasperation at this self-indulgence.

The barman gives him the freezing drink and he pays. Leaning back on the bar, aping the exaggerated ease of North Americans, his eyes flick over the other customers. Many are middle aged and overstuffed. That doesn't mean they couldn't be counter-intel, but there's something downtrodden about them, something beaten. Believable denizens of America: the Land of Broken Dreams.

A young couple at a booth in the corner catch his eye. Nicely positioned so they can cover the whole bar and the entrance, they appear entranced by each other's company. The woman's chestnut brown tresses swirl invitingly as she shakes her head and laughs at something the man has said. She's in a stylish black dress and he's wearing the only jacket in the bar. This isn't the place for a pre-theatre drink but, on the other hand, surely nobody in the Great Game would draw attention to themselves like that. Unless that's what they wanted him to think.

He touches his forehead with his fingers. He isn't really cut out for this and he wonders for the hundredth time why Olomo chose him.

He keeps surreptitiously watching them and, in the end, is won over by how carefree they seem. Perhaps they're from one of the expensive colleges nearby and are slumming it for reasons incomprehensible to anybody other than privileged white people.

One can only trust one's instincts, so he goes back to examining the other customers. Only the tall black woman in her early thirties is of note. She's at a table and is talking volubly to her companion whose back is to Yao. All he can tell is that the guy is white, male and thickset.

That doesn't fit. America may pride itself on its racial tolerance, and elect black people to high office, but mixed couples are still rare. Especially black women with white men.

There's something else about her that increases his unease. Maybe she looks a little too...collected, too focused for a place like this. He wonders if she's really looking directly at her companion, or the bar's mirror over his right shoulder. Maybe she's looking at his reflection.

He turns back quickly but doesn't catch her out. He does see Wiggins' reflection looking at him from down the bar. The man's eyes immediately dart away.

Yao keeps looking around at the others in the bar and feels the paralysis of indecision that comes on so easily in these situations. Finally, he shakes his head once more, gives a bitter little grimace at his reflection then saunters down the bar. As he gets close to him Wiggins turns, smiles wolfishly and reaches out a fleshy paw to shake his hand.

"Long time no see," he says loudly.

"I'm surprised to run into you here," replies Yao softly.

"Don't live far from here. Almost my local."

He's short for an American but still has a couple of inches on Yao's five foot six. Yao hates looking up at these people but it's all he ever does in this country.

Wiggins may be off duty but you can never take the navy out of the man. No creases mar his freshly laundered clothes.

Neither seems inclined to break the ensuing silence. They've met before but there's nothing companionable about them.

"Well?" asks Yao finally.

"Well what?" Wiggins eyes below his balding head are cold.

"Have you come to a decision?"

"About what?"

Yao blinks slowly.

Wiggins takes a pull on his beer, blue tats of a scaly tail visible on a thick forearm where the short sleeve ends.

"What you're asking me to do is crazy. Dangerous, maybe even suicidal."

Yao nods wearily. "Have I made any secret of it being

dangerous? Suicidal: not so. Not if you are careful."

"How do you know it's not suicidal? What the fuck do you know about one of these things? Have you any idea...?"

"This is not a favour I am asking, it is a transaction. For multiples of what the navy would pay you in your lifetime." The man's pay is poor by rich world standards, making all this possible.

"Have you got it here?"

"Don't be foolish."

"But it would be in cash?"

"Would you prefer it be by bank transfer? After all, who would notice a seven-figure sum going into the bank account of a naval rating?"

"Yeah, yeah. Cash is fine."

"Why are we going through this again?"

The man ignores this but the hard eyes never leave him. "Before I say yes, I want to be absolutely clear on exactly what you want me to do."

Yao's stomach tightens and he struggles not to react. Casually, he glances over Wiggins' shoulder at the nearest window. *Lurie's Tavern* is etched on the glass so it's probably single paned. It's pretty high, but there's a bench seat right below it.

He puts one foot on the floor and pushes back a little. No resistance. The stool isn't bolted to the floor.

Not turning his head, he flicks his eye back to the mirror.

The black woman is looking at him.

He motions to the bar tender and soon another massive schooner of coke and ice is in his palm. It's reassuringly heavy.

"Well?" says Wiggins impatiently.

A crescent of liquid arcs out as the schooner sails through the air. It strikes the plasma TV and shatters, ice and glass showering down. People instinctively hunch down, covering their heads.

Grabbing a leg of the stool, he swings it round and hurls it crashing through the window.

Wiggins reaches out. Yao's stiffened fingers jab deep onto his eye sockets. The man roars in shock and stumbles back hard against the bar.

An explosive sprint takes Yao across the bar. Vaulting a table, his forward leg finds the bench seat and he's catapulted up through the window, like a high jumper over the bar.

Then he's tumbling. Hard silver things break his fall and he feels ribs go when he hits. The beer barrels clink together and roll like skittles as he surfs uncontrollably off them.

Up and sprinting despite the pain, he hears glass tinkling as someone follows him through the broken window. He spins and drops, the 9mm already in his hand.

It's her. She's missed the barrels and has landed better than him. He fires two sets of two and hears bullets *spang* off the containers.

She dives to the right and down, and he's off again. She yells "Federal Agents," then something else he can't quite catch.

He's vaulting the picket fence at the first house when she opens up. He can't even afford to flinch as the bullets zip by. Not that she has a chance. Not at a moving target, not at this range.

He angles diagonally around the house and towards the first real garden fence. It's nearly as tall as he is, so he launches himself up as high as he can and bangs over it. Popping up quickly, he sees she's already broken cover and is coming fast across the road in long, easy strides. He takes two more shots at her and she dives down into the gutter.

Engines roar angrily and a car comes round the corner from the front of the bar. She's pointing frantically in his direction. Steadying the gun on the fence top, his bullets star the windscreen and the car screeches to a stop.

The neighbourhood dogs are going wild and people are shouting. Nobody will hear him now. Ducking down, he runs along the fence, slithers over another fence at the end into a neighbouring property, then turns back through ninety degrees and climbs over the next one.

He's heading back in the direction of the bar and hears the woman and others scrambling over fences and thundering away on his original course, taking them deeper into the houses.

One more fence and he'll be back on the street where he'd gone through the window. He peers over and sees people milling around outside the bar. Two cars with lights flashing speed by.

He thinks he's trapped then he hears the clatter of a helicopter. Everyone turns away to look and he's quickly over the fence and across the street and down the alley behind the bar. Looking back, he sees the chopper, searchlight lancing down, chase after his pursuers.

He keeps to the alley, moving fast, avoiding the trash cans. When he gets to the end, he checks the street is clear then sprints across to the alley on the next block. And so he continues: ducking down in the shadows whenever he hears the chopper come close on its increasingly eccentric search pattern.

Soon he's well clear.

Chapter 2. *Norfolk, Virginia*

Coming to from the best night's sleep she'd had in many years, it took a while for the events of the previous day to percolate into her consciousness. When they finally did, Joey felt a surge of exultation.

She'd shot at him. Not only that but she'd been vastly pissed off when he hadn't gone down.

Pulling the sheet aside, she lowered her legs over the side of the bed. The bare pine floor was cold but she hardly noticed. Instead, she was zeroing in on his retreating back (*my, but the little bastard was fast!*) and feeling the kick of the Sig against her palm. Aiming for the midline, not fucking around. Always go for the thick bit: the torso. Trainers at MPD and then later at NCIS had drummed it into her. Anything more fancy, like a shot to disarm, was pretentious.

And in the cop dictionary of firefights, pretentious was defined as: 'wind up dead'.

How right they'd been. But sometimes...

The good night's sleep tempted her. Could she revisit the territory, that terrible place she'd managed to thrust aside for so long except when sleep came? Would it look different now? Would she feel different?

Still sitting there, the dim early morning light barely making it through the drawn curtains, she took the first tentative barefoot steps down the flinty path of her memories.

East of Rock Creek Park. DC had been the murder capital of the States back in the early '90s, but, by the time she'd joined the Metropolitan Police Department ten years later, it'd calmed down some. Still pretty meaty though. Ward 8, represented by Council Member the always entertaining Marion S. Barry Jr, had had the highest concentration of poverty in the city.

Though they were slowly being eased out, the Columbian gangs were still supplying the crack there. And Anacostia, with most of its shops and restaurants and movie theatres long gone, was the worst area in the Ward.

So there they were, she and her then-partner Dobbs; two black cops looking for a white woman turning tricks in a district that was over 90 percent black. Should've been easy. Finding her certainly was. Old Faithful had shown them where to drive and had pointed a withered finger at a row house near the river.

"She in the upper half," he'd said.

Joey had looked at the houses, front doors so close together they must be impossibly narrow inside. "That little place has multiple occupancy?" she'd asked in disbelief.

Old Faithful's wicked old face, pitted with bad diet and reddened with alcohol, had cracked open in a grin. "Sign of the times. You folks don't know you're alive. This is where the real people live. Tour finished. Money!"

"If she's there," rumbled Dobbs.

"Oh no! You're goin' to drag her out here so she can see me. She'll tell her pimp and I'll be a dead man."

"And her pimp would be...?" asked Joey, turning around to look at the scruffy old man in his ancient gabardine coat.

"That'll be another twenty bucks on top of the twenty you're going to give me now."

She looked across and met Dobbs' hard eyes, then waited; she was the junior partner here. Still couldn't even find her way round the Ward without a map.

Undoing his seat belt, Dobbs sighed and hitched his thick body onto one expansive buttock then fished out his wallet from a trouser pocket. Holding the twenty up at shoulder level, he didn't look back. "Fuck off!" he said.

Joey felt the air move as Old Faithful's hand whipped the note from Dobbs' fingers. She heard the door open then slam shut.

"Come on!" said Dobbs.

As she got out, she saw heads come up. People were

11

sitting on some front steps several houses down. They scrabbled their stuff together then slunk back inside. "Quick," said Dobbs, "some of them might start phoning."

Increasing his stride, he got to the door and banged heavily twice with his fist. "Maybe I should go around the back?" she said but he ignored her as usual. At least with him a few steps above her, she wasn't looking down on his sweaty bald spot.

The door cracked open and Dobbs barged right in, hand on holster. By the time she'd followed him in, an old black woman was already pushed back against a tattered divan. Dobbs wasn't so much being forceful, as trying to squeeze round her in the narrow space.

"Antonia in?" he barked.

The old woman, thick rimmed glasses askew on her face, just opened her mouth like a goldfish.

Dobbs finally got past. Joey saw threadbare carpets and one room in the front and one at the back, and she guessed it would be the same on the upper floor. The little house was less a shotgun shack, more an under-and-over. Between the two rooms a staircase rose to the right.

Taking a stance against the wall, Dobbs darted his head around the corner to look up the stairs then quickly withdrew it.

"Oh for fuck's sakes," he said.

"What the fuck do you want?" a hoarse female voice roared from above.

Dobbs turned to look at her. "After you, Joey" he said. "Woman's touch required."

She eased her way around his bulk. Looking up the stairs, she saw the woman called Antonia. Young, late twenties at most, she held a baby to her exposed right breast. She'd loosened the strap of her diaphanous shorty nightgown to let it in. Looking up at her on the stairs, Joey found herself peering straight at the woman's hairy crotch.

"You fuckin' shits," the words were drawly and blurred with drink.

"Take it easy Antonia. We got a search warrant."

Joey's sensitive nose could smell the milk, even over the whiff of the booze and Collard Greens stewed to death. She saw milk had leaked from both of the woman's engorged breasts and was staining the nightdress.

"Why can't you leave me alone? I ain't done nothin'!"

"We're just going to have a little look around. Now I want you to go into one of the rooms either side of you so I can get up the stairs." For emphasis she put her hand on the butt of her gun.

"Gonna shoot a mother and her baby? What kind of people are you?" She was swaying and the baby was having trouble keeping a lock on her nipple. The baby's jet-black hair and dark colouring were a deep contrast to the woman's pale, blotchy skin.

"Come on now, Antonia. A couple minutes and we'll be gone."

Joey started to edge up the stairs.

Red eyes watched her advance. The woman's blond hair might once have been fashioned in bangs, but now it was greasy and had clumped into rats-tails. Make-up, long since applied, had smeared out over eyes and lips.

"Fuckin' black bitch," she said but stumbled to the left and out of Joey's sight.

Quickly taking three steps at a time, Joey followed her. Maxwell had been stabbed to death so she didn't want to take chances.

Joey looked into the reddened eyes. "Antonia, I need you to keep your hands on the baby. At all times."

The stench of sour milk was overpowering and she cursed the acuteness of her sense of smell. Behind her, she heard Dobbs clumping up the stairs. She felt him shoulder his way by her and into the room to the right.

Two up/ two down they called these places, though she saw now that a small extension to the back gave onto a bathroom up here and, probably, a kitchen down below.

She couldn't even guess the function of the room she was

in now. Junkyard, maybe.

"What's this about?" asked the woman.

"First of all, what's your name please? Your full name."

"Antonio Lidell. Who wants to know?"

"Officer Beck, and this is Officer Dodds."

"You're skinny for a cop. Not much in the way of tits. With your height you ought to be a basketball player. A man basketball player!" She gave a grunt of satisfaction at her own wit.

"Do you know this guy?" Joey held out Maxwell's picture. The man was grinning smugly like everything in the world was peachy, as all middle-class guys seemed to when they had their picture taken.

"Nope. Should I?"

"You were seen soliciting up on the corner of 3rd and Whitney. Got a video camera there monitoring traffic and red light running. Shows you getting into his car at just before midnight last Wednesday."

"Wasn't me." She'd stopped swaying and the baby gave a contented slurping sound.

"Yes it was. What happened?"

The woman shrugged and the baby came off again with a whimper. "I was home with my kid. You got the wrong person."

"Well looky here," said Dobbs behind her.

Joey pointed a finger directly at the woman and, with the other hand, tightened her grip on the gun butt. "Now: you don't move, and I mean *at all*!"

Turning, she took one step across the head of the staircase and was into the midden of the bedroom. Dirty clothes and nappies were strewn across the floor but, beside the filthy bed, was a brand-new cot. Inside, a pristine pink teddy bear was smiling out at her. Joey swallowed.

Dobbs had been at a little chest of drawers on the other side of the room. He was holding up a wallet.

"Is it...?"

Dobbs' eyes went wide and he was scrabbling for his

14

holster.

Joey flinched down and stumbled forward, hauling out her gun and turning. Her momentum brought her against the wall with a jolt.

A deafening discharge and chunks exploded out of the wall by Dodds' head. He dropped down for cover behind the bed.

Joey brought her weapon to bear. Still with her kid on one tit, Antonia was waving a gun around unsteadily.

Then it swung towards Joey.

The kid's tousled head was inches from the midline. Bringing the gun down, Joey fired at the woman's legs and saw cloth kick.

Another roar and hot gas scoured the side of Joey's face. Chunks of plaster slapped the back of her head.

The recoil kicked the woman's gun up, but now it was coming down.

Back against the wall, nowhere to run, no cover available, Joey centred her gun on Antonia's left shoulder.

The trigger was impossibly heavy.

The crack of the next shot filled the universe. Something plucked at the side of her open jacket.

Fear made her jerk the trigger, pulling the gun down and to the side as it fired.

The bullet struck the woman's chest. Slamming back against the wall at an angle, she skittered sideways and down.

The baby flew out of her hands and back through the doorway. Hitting the wall above the stairwell, it bounced off and fell down onto the little landing, rolling towards the stairs.

Meanwhile something big had flashed across her vision, and she saw Dodds, arms outstretched, as he slammed down hard across the woman's body.

His arms jabbed sideways and out of her sight.

A long second, then the baby bellowed with healthy rage. Somehow, he'd caught it.

Without thinking, she'd moved forward and found she'd

pressed her gun down on the woman's forehead. Antonia's eyes were open but unfocused and blood was already bubbling out of her mouth. Gobbets of yellow fat and droplets of milk and blood were sliding down the underside of her jaw.

Joey saw the hand holding the gun, its arm trapped under Dobbs' thick legs. She reached down and tugged the weapon clear.

And now, years later, sitting on the side of her bed as the sun peeked through her boring brown drapes, Joey still felt the nausea.

But not the bone-gnawing despair.

Maybe the shrinks had done some good after all. They'd descended *en masse* right after it happened. For a while she wasn't sure they'd let her back. She wasn't even sure she wanted to go back.

And she'd been lucky: sort of. The media could have played it either way. *Brutal cop guns down nursing mother/ Cop traumatised after killing murderous whore.* They'd gone for the latter. Though if she'd been white and Antonia black...

The shrinks had her back on the range firing away at human shaped targets. Then on a live fire course with targets popping out at her. Finally, she'd been sent through a run where nearly all the targets were nursing mothers. Only on one had they stencilled a gun in the mother's hand. And she'd got that one midline, the slug going through the little sucker on the tit as well. Full marks!

But firing bullets into cardboard had never been a problem for her.

Even later, after she'd left MPD behind for NCIS, she'd never been called on to draw her gun in anger, never mind shoot at anyone.

Which left something of a doubt.

Then came yesterday and the African. She'd loosed off without a second thought. Missed the fucker sure enough but not through want of trying.

Just like the descendant of a genuine honest-to-God black cowboy should.

She realised how hungry she was, so she got up to make breakfast.

"Ears that small *are* unusual," said Grooms meditatively, "and that might really help us pin him down. Otherwise I might make a stab at West Africa. Short, compact stature, moderate flare on the nostrils...."

"It's funny though," Joey said. "At first glance, the ears looked freakish but then, after a while, they looked kind of nice and neat and all the rest of us started to look weird."

"Yeah, ears are pretty ugly. We just get used to them and stop noticing that."

She'd got some covert shots of the guy with her phone before he went into warp drive. Facial recognition software was even now chewing through the databases, but her hopes weren't high as he probably wasn't domestic.

"Did your informant Wiggins say much else about him?"

She shook her head. "Definitely had an accent. Didn't seem at ease, like this wasn't his country."

Grooms turned his eyes from the screen and perched his spindly frame on the edge of the workstation desk. "And how is Wiggins?"

"Sore, but he'll live."

Grooms was being paternal, working his way up and, sure enough: "And you... I hear it got quite intense."

"Look, some dipso rating wanders in off the street and starts in with wild stuff about being bribed by a foreigner. I couldn't call out the marines on the basis of that. Me and Harlan inside, Lester Symes and Breona Altman in a car down the road, plus the local cops alerted. That should have been more than enough."

His hands were up, the white of the palms contrasting

17

with his black skin. "Look Joey, I wasn't criticising. You should know that. Just as I know that your response now is classic deflection tactics."

She'd always liked Grooms, but she wasn't up for any more soul searching today.

She smiled. "' There's nothing more stimulating than to be fired at without result', someone once said. It's true."

"I know, it was Winston Churchill. And you're still deflecting, but I'll take the hint. So anyway, none of the good guys were hurt. What about the perp? Did you hit him?"

"Didn't even hit the planet, far as I know. Little fucker was out that bar and across the street like shit off a shovel. And he must've doubled back real quick while we charged on like assholes. Knew what he was doing. He's been in scrapes before."

He nodded. "Africa's renowned for its 'scrapes', as you put it." He brought a finger to a greying temple. "DNA?"

"He touched a glass and drank from it but that's broken into a million pieces. The techs are going through it, doing the best they can, but this wasn't a spotless joint. God knows what other sort of DNA's been tramped in. He grabbed a stool, leaving one set of prints amongst twenty or more. A lot of drudge work there which, thankfully, I don't have to do. Harlan's down at the lab right now trying to hurry them on."

"By the way, say hello to your partner for me. Haven't seen Harlan for a while. So anyway, is that why you brought me in? The last resort."

"Don't get precious with me. And now *you're* deflecting, trying to hide your modesty. Not many NCIS agents have a PhD in... what was it?"

"Don't you worry your pretty little head about that. It'd just make your eyes glaze over," and he gave a big laugh.

"Bastard! But seriously, it was something about racial facial characteristics, right."

"Racial facial? Are you listening to yourself?"

"Gimme a break, OK?"

"Classifying features by race. That do?"

"Yeah. I've heard your knowledge has come in useful on occasion."

He grimaced. "Usually only with the unidentified dead." He pointed to the screen. "Don't often get called in on a live one. Between you and me though, my PhD was written back in the Triassic. Field's moved on a bit since my day. My only expertise is knowing the people who are current in it now."

"Not what I hear. False modesty again."

"Whatever. I'll look into this guy."

"Thanks, Grooms."

He turned to leave but then it occurred to her. "Hey, Grooms!"

"Yes."

"Where do I come from?"

He frowned. "From your accent, I'm guessing mid-West."

"Not bad, but that's not what I meant."

"Every fucking where," he said with a smile.

"Seriously?"

"Don't you have any idea? Grandma didn't reverently pass down the knowledge of the generations."

"Not that kind of family. Stuff that was passed on you don't wanna know about."

"Tough, eh?"

She nodded.

"Well, tall, lean frame like yours suggests some Nubian, but there's been at least six generations of mixing since. As for those weird grey eyes of yours. North West Africa. Maybe. Perhaps even, dare I say it, a little bit of white."

"Get to fuck!"

He gave a big shrug and laughed. "Look at me. Wife reckons she married a white man."

"How come?"

"Can't dance to save my life."

The hotel receptionist, a buff young man with swept back blond hair, narrowed his eyes as she showed him her ID, then quickly gave her the once over. Men were simple to read on these matters and she could tell he liked what he saw. They pretty much all did at first, hard bodies being considered so hot in this age. But there was always a fine line between hard and bony and, sooner or later, they always fled back to softness. At least, that was the explanation she preferred.

"Naval Criminal Investigative Service," she said. Beside her, Harlan flipped his badge and the kid nodded. "I'm Special Agent Beck and this is Special Agent Weiss."

"What can I do for you, Special Agents?" The Saint Pierre was no flophouse and everyone was polite.

She showed him the photo. "Need to talk to this guy urgently. We know he's staying here." She didn't, but she wanted to cut through any crap. A car abandoned near the bar in Diggs Town had yielded a number plate but, even with number plate recognition, it'd taken a long time to run it through numberless old traffic cam feeds. Harlan had thrown in the towel after a couple of days and had gone back to one of their other cases.

But, dog with a bone, she'd kept plugging away until she nailed the car on a main drag eight days ago. Having a time and place, she'd been able to follow it from camera to camera until it'd pulled into this hotel. The car had re-emerged a day later but had taken a side road soon after and she'd lost it.

The kid shook his head. "Don't recognise him, but I can ask my colleagues." He took the photo and wandered off down the long counter.

Joey turned to take in the grandeur. The atrium was stepped as it rose higher, so it was like you were in a pyramid but the inside was made of air, the outside of marble. On each floor, doors opened out into corridors that looked directly down onto the tamed but luxuriant vegetation of the lounge.

"Must be a couple of hundred a night, minimum." Harlan sounded pissed. He didn't like it when the bad guys earned more than he did. Public sector pay being what it was, his annoyance was never ending.

The young guy came back with an older woman dressed in the same dark blazer as him. She smiled at them and started clicking at a terminal. "Can't quite remember his name ... Ak....something like that."

"But you do recognise him?"

"Pretty sure.... yes, here we are. Mr. Akwasi, room 612. Registered two weeks ago. Due to check out on Friday."

Harlan put a finger on the counter top. "We need a full printout of his registration details. And we need into his room."

"Is he there now?" Joey asked.

"Couldn't say," replied the woman. Behind her, a printer sprang to staccato life and the young man reached across to pick up the paper.

Joey took it then looked him in the eye. "I'd like you to come with us and bring the pass key." In theory they needed a search warrant but the big chains never made a fuss about these things. Not for a non-celeb like Mr. Akwasi.

Harlan leaned in and whispered in her ear: "We are going to get proper back-up this time, right?"

"Try not to be such a dick."

"I'm serious."

The young guy had started to look alarmed and was waving to a security guard.

"He's long gone. Sending a SWAT team crashing into an empty room would be embarrassing."

"Embarrassing? Since when..."

But she ignored him. "Lead the way!" she said to the receptionist.

By the time they got to the elevator, a gilded cage affair that ascended up a recessed groove cutting into one side of the pyramid, the security guard had joined them. An older man in a nicely cut suit and with no obvious firearm bulge in his jacket, he wasn't going to be much help.

"What's this about?" he asked.

"We're NCIS. Person of interest in the attempted murder of a federal agent is staying here."

The man nodded and pursed his lips, clearly wishing the receptionist hadn't caught his eye.

"The room's on the other side," the young guy was pointing across the atrium as they get out of the elevator.

"You both wait here. Give us the card. Activates at pull-out, right?"

"Green light, yes." He handed her the card.

"I've got to come with you," said the security guy. "Sorry, but it's my job."

"OK but keep well back. The room, how's it laid out? What's to the right and left?"

The guard wrinkled his brow a second. The doors were clustered in pairs, indicating adjacent rooms were mirror images.

"To the left are just the recessed wardrobes. To the right: first the bathroom, then it opens into the bedroom itself. There's nothing else."

"Lights?"

"You've got to the put the card in the slot just inside, to the left of the door."

They padded along the carpet until they got to the first corner. She checked back to make sure the receptionist was still by the elevator. His hands were clasped over his crotch, and he looked unsure of what he should be doing.

Coming up to the room, she noticed a 'Do Not Disturb' sign hanging on the handle.

"Me to the left, you to the right," she said, taking out her Sig and cocking it, but keeping it below the level of the balcony. Harlan did the same.

"You put the card in, but I'll go first. I'll do the bedroom, you get the bathroom, then the wardrobe."

Harlan got ready on the other side of the door. Both were close into the wall so they couldn't be seen from the spyhole. The guard was to her other side. She looked round at him. "Stay here 'til we come and get you."

He nodded.

Harlan and she looked into each other's eyes across the intervening space. She nodded.

Gently Harlan rested the edge of his hand on the electronic lock and slowly dipped the card down into its slot.

She nodded again and he whipped the card out and a little green light came on.

He pulled back as she grabbed the door handle and wrenched it down. Crashing her shoulder into the door, it flew open and she lurched in.

"Federal agents," she yelled.

Two steps forward, left hand back up and supporting the gun, she swung it round covering the empty bed. Behind her the bathroom door banged open.

Round the bed, checking the other side, then she launched herself forward onto the floor. She poked the muzzle into the coverlet hanging down over the side of the bed. It hit something solid. She yanked the fabric aside but, sure enough, there were only a couple of inches of clearance so no place to hide under there. "Clear!"

She heard the wardrobe's sliding doors being opened.

"Clear!"

She stood up and went back to the door and beckoned to the young receptionist who came reluctantly over to her. "It's OK, he's not here. Go back to reception and, if the guy should come back, phone the room immediately. Understand?"

"Sure," and the guy and was quickly away.

'Fat chance,' she thought to herself. 'After that business in Digg's Town he'll be long gone.'

She waggled her finger at the guard and he followed her into the room. She shut the door behind him.

She and Harlan holstered their guns and got to work.

The room was neat and tidy and the bed was made, yet

she found an empty bottle of water in the trash bin. This showed the *Do Not Disturb* sign had kept the room cleaners out, and so this neatness was all his. The clothes in the wardrobe were carefully folded, all restrained in style, mid-range in price and recently purchased.

She pulled off the coverlet and caught a faint smell. She stuck her sometimes embarrassingly sensitive nose between the blankets and took a deep breath. They smelled like the blankets of any man, but there was something more earthy as well. 'Is this what an honest-to-God African smells like?' she thought. It was kind of pungent but, ultimately, not unattractive.

Pushing herself upright, she saw the guard looking at her wide eyed.

"We all smell," she said. "Even you."

No phone or air ticket or passport. There was a safe anchored to the bottom of the wardrobe, and the guard used a pass code to open it, but it was empty.

Next to the TV was your standard post-it type notepad. Like the bottle in the wastebasket, she knew she should leave it for the forensics team.

"Ah," said Harlan coming up beside her. "Perhaps the old note pad tracing trick, as seen on every TV cop show since the dawn of time, might work here."

"Maybe they don't have any cop shows in Africa, or wherever the fuck this guy actually comes from." She looked around for a pencil.

"No!" he said. "Don't even think about it! Leave it for forensics and whatever hi-tech equivalent of a pencil they use nowadays."

She snorted impatiently, but then went back to the search.

Like the clothes, the man's suitcase was banal. Mid-sized, dark blue with two little wheels and a telescoping handle. Harlan hefted it onto the bed and started to open it but she held a hand out to stop him. Between one black wheel and its black recess there was something lighter.

Poking with a hotel pen dislodged a scrunched-up bit of paper. She took it to the desk. Gingerly, delicately, so it didn't tear any more, she slowly flattened it out.

By now Harlan was looking over her shoulder. "That, as I'm sure you're aware, could be any old piece of shit he ran over on his way from the airport."

It was only a fragment of a handwritten address, but at least she got the number and some of the name:

118 Roma...

"Roma, Roman, Romantic..." he said, but already she was tapping away. The map page on her phone app took wildcards and gave her only one choice in Norfolk.

"Romana Boulevard."

Harlan was shaking his head. "It' could've been picked up in the lobby or in the corridors. Dropped by another visitor."

"Why are you so negative? Any better ideas?"

He was on his own phone, hitting a single speed dial number. "No, just trying to damp down your expectations... Lester... It's Harlan. Got an address here. Need to know who lives there and what they do. 118 Romana Boulevard."

Arms folded, she stood and watched him. Eventually his eyebrows rose. "A Midshipman called Hierra, so navy," he said. "You know where to look now, Lester." He stuck his tongue out at her.

Her foot was tapping hard on the floor by the time Lester came back with the answer. "Attached to the *Sands* Battle Group," Harlan said and broke the connection. "Just like Wiggins."

He shook his head. "You are so fucking lucky."

It was well into evening and she watched dark things converging on the single storey house. They swarmed along the sides of adjacent buildings and over fences. At the back of the

25

house she knew the same thing would be happening.

Romana Boulevard sounded like it should be grander than it was. Deep within a typical blue-collar district, it looked no different, and certainly no wider, than any of the streets leading off it. Streetlights were sparse and the beams from the few passing cars did little to lighten the shadows.

"Sure you don't want to go point?" whispered Harlan sarcastically. They were peeping over the top of a car parked two houses down.

She wished she was. Maybe she'd look cool wafting in like Lady Bountiful when the hard work had been done, but she liked getting her hands dirty.

The black shapes stopped moving and it was like the night was holding its breath.

The silence was broken by a great splintering sound as the SWAT guys smacked the door in with one mighty blow. The black shapes funnelled rapidly into the hole left by the door and she heard stamping and yelling.

"Now that sounds like men enjoying their job," said Harlan.

The commotion soon died down and Joey and Harlan got up and sauntered down the sidewalk. By the time they got to the house, the sergeant was coming out. Covered in black armour, he looked like a two-legged beetle.

"Secured," he said.

They followed him back in. A corridor ran centrally down the middle of the house, rooms to the left and right. First right took them into a lounge, TV still yammering away. A man was face down on the floor and tie-wrapped to within an inch of his life.

"Roll him over," demanded Lady Bountiful and a couple of the SWAT guys obliged.

It was Hierra alright. Thick white hair carefully swept back from regular, lined features might have given him a distinguished look in better circumstances, but not right then. In the dark eyes, shock and horror were dawning.

She knelt down, her cold grey eyes only a few inches above his. "Where is it, Hierra?"

"What... what are you talking about? Why are you doing this?"

Drugs or explosives, it still wasn't clear, so she took a guess: "Because you're a fucking terrorist. Because we can do what the fuck we like with you."

"No...no it's not true, you've made a mistake."

She curled her lips up. "Last time. Where is it?"

"Where is what?"

But then, just like that, the tension went out of his body. Game over.

"In the roof space, above the kitchen."

Behind her she heard Harlan hurrying off.

"What're we going to find?"

" Look, I was just doing this as a favour."

"So what is it?" Somewhere further down the corridor there came some clattering and it sounded like Harlan had found a metal ladder.

"I don't know. Drugs I suppose. I never opened it up. Didn't want to know."

He seemed too embarrassed, too shame faced to be a terrorist. Which meant it must be drugs, and she needn't be so conscience stricken about letting the African get away.

"The man who gave it to you. Black guy, a foreigner, right?"

"Yeah."

"What's his name?"

"He never said. It wouldn't have been his real one, anyway."

"And what were you supposed to do with this package?"

"I just had to get it aboard and....."

She heard someone coming quickly down the ladder then rapid footsteps pattered down the corridor.

"*Explosives! Everyone out! Now!*"

She looked over her shoulder. Harlan was at the door, eyebrows raised in alarm and beckoning at her furiously. The SWAT guys were already slipping by him and out.

Nodding slowly, she flicked a languid finger at Hierra. "Is it OK if I bring my friend?"

Chapter 3. *35,000 feet above the continental US*

Far to the west, she could make out the steel and glass of Las Vegas.

"Why would anybody build a city in the desert?"

Beside her, Emison, his head buried in a file, didn't seem to be paying any attention.

She sighed. He'd made it clear that drink was off the menu, and the novelties of the navy's little executive jet had long since palled. He was her boss so there wasn't much she could do about it. She was also pissed off that he'd ordered Harlan to stay behind in Virginia.

She looked back out the window and had another shot at booting up a conversation. "It's ridiculous."

Emison looked up irritably. "What is?"

"Cities in deserts. Las Vegas, Phoenix, Los Angeles. Unsustainable. Trust me, the desert will reclaim them and sooner than you think."

Emison's broad, jowly face was showing puzzlement and irritation in equal measure. "Are you some sort of tree hugger? Can't ever remember seeing that in your file."

"I'm not being political. It's just common sense."

He sighed. "Why didn't you bring a book?"

"I don't read books. They put me to sleep!"

He shook his head. "That's reassuring."

Desert, the real deal, was speeding by beneath them, yet over the far horizon snow-capped peaks were rising. She pointed at them. "How does that work?"

Emison raised a finger. "Look, Joey. I don't mind you not working, but at least let me get on with my own stuff."

But he was putting his file down on the little coffee table. "This is a big deal, you do know that?"

"Yeah I get it. Don't get to travel much in little numbers

like this. It's been a long flight and I'm just a little bored."

Emison wiped a hand over his tired eyes and then back over the few straggling hairs on the top of his head. "And how are you going to be on board a ship?"

"We don't know I'll have to. Anyway, I've been on ships before." She smoothed the creases out of her dark trousers.

"For how long was that? A couple of months on a courtesy trip to a few pleasant South American ports. A carrier group like the *Benjamin F. Sands* is a different matter."

"Maybe the Admiral just wants to pat me on the back."

The stewardess, young but rounded, and looking matronly in her white dress uniform, appeared from the tiny galley. "Just to let you know, we'll soon be descending into Fallon. Perhaps you'd like to freshen up," looking at her when she said it.

Joey made her way to the miniscule shit-can. It was impossible to stand upright so she crouched like a penitent over the steel washbasin. The curved roof was pressing down on her hair but it didn't matter. Short and straight and, when cast in a particular style, her hair was bombproof. In the mirror, the pale eyes looked back at her, sharp and distant even to herself. Face too thin, too intense.

And why was that, she wondered?

They'd passed over the plain East of Denver an hour or so before, but she'd kept quiet as she looked down on Arapahoe County and all its memories. The high plains could be bitterly cold in winter with a wind that was like ice on bare flesh. But every morning before school she'd run, lung capacity boosted by the mile-high altitude, sparse frosted grass crunching underfoot. Towards one horizon were the Rockies, jagged toothed in the clean clear air.

Getting away from the house in Aurora. Father never good any morning, but at his worst when his week-long shifts in the Aurora Fire Dept were just starting. Mother fearful but always combative, trying to get ready for her domestic duties at Fitzsimmons Army Medical Center, not in the mood to take shit

30

from her monster of a husband.

Recipe for Bedlam.

So, she'd take off over the plain, sometimes thinking of her ancestor, name lost in the four generations since, who'd driven herds of cows over these same grasslands. The Black Cowboy.

And he hadn't been alone. Back then, fully a third of cowboys were black, though you'd never think it from the numberless westerns. The only one she'd ever seen at the movies, Cleavon Little's character in Blazing Saddles, had been there as a joke.

America liked its stereotypes and tended to edit out what didn't fit. Just like blue collar people nowadays. Watch movies and TV and it's like the States was full of doctors and lawyers. Nobody to run the factories or the farms, nobody to build the houses. The only blue collar main characters you saw were the cops. Otherwise, a whole class was edited out of cultural history.

But she'd had other thoughts on her mind that final morning when she'd come back from her run and he'd hit her one time too many.

At fifteen, she was already taller than him, though he was more solid with the full chest of a fire fighter. It hadn't even been a hard blow by his standards, just an open-handed slap to the side of her head.

Long legs like hers, with joints supple from long runs, could give her foot bowling ball momentum. Without thought or hesitation, she'd boosted his balls into high orbit then fled the house, never to return. Her last sight of him had him bunched up and heaving in agony, clutching testicles, she would later be reliably informed, that would swell to the size of grapefruits.

A fifteen-year old loose in the mid-West. Things had got pretty wild after that point.

But the thing with her father had awoken a taste for justice: had given her an intense high only beaten by sex. The worse the asshole she arrested, the more sublime the feeling was. And if they chose to resist arrest...ah, then that could be the sweetest time of all.

The downside was the ones who got away, whether in Norfolk or Washington or on TV. It made her feel like a snake was coiled in her guts. The drunken driver who ran over a child and got off on a technicality; the mugger who killed for a pittance; the dictator who terrorised an entire country.

So, some people thought she was too intense. So what?

After a freshening up the stewardess would no doubt have considered perfunctory, she went back to her seat where Emison was squirreling away files in his briefcase. They both strapped in as the jet banked over a desert so dry there was hardly any shrub.

"Some place for a naval station," she said.

"I think that may have been commented on before," said Emison. He was looking old and weary.

Ahead, she saw tarmac. Encroaching sand made a scalloping effect on what should have been a straight edge. The plane banked once more and then came in, thumping down noisily. Out of her side there was nothing for miles but, as the plane turned, she saw a couple of single storey buildings the sun had faded into near invisibility against the desert. Far off, a vehicle was approaching out of the shimmer.

The stewardess unpopped the door. Air so hot she thought it would burn her hair off, punched its way into the cabin.

Getting up, she took the holster out of the netting in the seat back and clipped it onto her belt. She shrugged on her plain black jacket while Emison was still huffing and puffing out of his seat.

She waited at the exit while a set of little metal steps extended down. The heat was overwhelming, but she noticed with dismay that the angry ball of plasma hadn't even reached its zenith yet. She and Emison hesitated rather than step out into the searing light.

Instead they watched as a Humvee, farting a cloud of dust, pulled up parallel with the plane and a lieutenant got out. Dressed in khakis, he filled his uniform out nicely. His eager face broke into a smile as he approached, his hand outstretched and up towards Emison. Rather than risking precariously leaning out to take it, Emison reluctantly climbed down the stairs.

"Good morning to you both. I'm Lieutenant Patterson of Admiral Macik's staff. You must be...."

"Supervisory Special Agent Arthur Emison. This is Special Agent Josephine Beck."

She took his hand. Either young Patterson was a lizard or the Humvee must be fiercely air conditioned.

"Welcome to Nevada. If you'll just get in, we'll take you to the Admiral." He swept his hand towards the vehicle.

Emison climbed in the opened back seat door. She was about to shuffle in after him when she saw the big transmission tunnel bisecting the base of the passenger compartment. Emison was making no attempt to clamber over it to let her in, so she had to go around the back of the car and in the other door. The door was functional, in that it opened and closed, but its elegance and smoothness wouldn't be putting BMW out of business any time soon.

As she'd suspected, the inside was cool. She watched as Patterson climbed smoothly into the front passenger seat. His khaki stretched over well-muscled thighs.

The Humvee took off, leaving the airstrip and moving out onto a sand filmed road cracked by the heat.

When it came to suspension, *military grade,* it turned out, meant *worse.*

"How was the flight?"

"Fine," said Emison.

"Been to Nevada before?"

"Only Vegas, but who hasn't been there?"

Patterson chuckled. "The Admiral has strong views about Vegas, so generally we all stay well clear."

"Tough customer?"

"I'm saying nothing."

Patterson seemed to have expended his reserves of small

talk. The desert stretched endlessly away to the east while, to the west, the big peaks rose into the sun-bleached white of the sky.

"So, where's the ship?" she asked brightly.

Emison turned to her and grimaced wearily. "Give it a rest, Joey!"

Patterson had turned to look at her and she could tell he wasn't charmed. "The navy has many aircraft and aircraft-based weapons systems. It's easier to test out the new stuff here. We also deploy land-based weapons systems, where required, and so again it's good to test them out on dry land. We're checking out one of those here today. Believe me, you'll find it interesting."

"What kind of weapon?"

"The future of warfare. You'll see. But that reminds me...." He reached for a briefcase and pulled out some clipboards and a couple of pens. "I'd like you both to fill in these forms for me."

Joey leafed through maybe ten pages of closely typed text with growing alarm. Everything seemed to be in triplicate with long columns of tiny tick boxes.

"What is this?" asked Emison. "The DDS did our PSI's. A long time ago. We have full clearance."

"Well the Defence Security Service doesn't actually do Personnel Security Investigations anymore; it's the National Bureau of Investigations who does it now. The DSS findings still theoretically apply, but we need the forms filled in as a ... refresh."

Emison's craggy face was becoming even more lined. "A refresh? And what's this about 'theoretically'. They still apply everywhere else in the DoD."

"The Admiral likes to dot the *i's* and cross the *t's*. Believe it or not, this is him being flexible. Normally he'd want the NBI to do the whole thing over, but time's against us."

"'Have you ever been a member of a foreign security service?' Forty years serving all over the DoD and I've got to answer this again?"

"Maybe you only started working for the Chinese last year," said Joey, but turned quickly away when he gave her a face like thunder.

Emison started leafing through the papers again. "And the SF 86 form isn't enough, apparently. There's another one here specifically for this base and dated for today where I've got to fill in all these details again."

Patterson squirmed in his seat. "Well the Admiral considers the SF 86 as rather too general. He's concerned that a smart lawyer could find an argument against it for that very reason. The DV 090 in your hand relates to specifics."

"No, it doesn't. There's not a damned thing here about what we're going to see that's so secret."

"There's another form there for that."

"This is going to take us hours. Couldn't you have sent this before so we could do it all electronically?"

"Sorry. It's got to be in your own handwriting, ink on paper, here and now. And we still have about a thirty-minute drive ahead. You should be able to get it done by then."

Joey had been going through her pack. "There's a whole bunch of risk assessments here. There's even one just for walking in the desert. Scorpions, snakes, sunstroke. Dirt bike strikes?" She glanced around at the yawning emptiness.

"Yes. Please read each of them, write personnel details in block capitals, then sign and date."

"And there's one here about what I feel about the visit," Emison's voice had risen in disbelief.

"Yes, that's for audit purposes. To be filled in as you leave." Patterson turned and gave a winning smile, teeth white. "You'll see there's one place where you have to rate me. Please be kind."

Emison gnawed at his lower lip. "You know, I've worked with more than a few admirals in my time. To a man, they hated paperwork but your guy seems to enjoy generating his own, like there's not enough already."

"The Admiral believes that to optimally control something as complex as a carrier strike group you need feedback, and you need people who have been provided with documentation describing exactly their duties and responsibilities. And how can anyone argue with that?"

For a second Emison, looked like he was about to try, but instead pulled the pen out from under the big clip and started to fill in the form.

Disappointed, Joey felt she had no choice but to do the same.

Pens scratched over paper as the Humvee droned across the interminable desert. As the sun approached its zenith, the heat haze dissolved away even the distant mountains. It would be like an oven out there, and she hoped that whatever they were going to would be happening indoors.

Somewhere to the west a hardy bird was banking in a turn. 'Rather you than me,' she thought but then noticed another and another. With a start, she realised they were much further away than she'd thought. Whatever they were, they were much bigger than birds.

The lead one swerved quickly now and was suddenly coming towards them.

She bent down so she could squint up through the Humvee's windshield. The thing was closing fast.

The Humvee wasn't too loud but she still couldn't hear the thing coming, even when it zipped over their heads. She whipped round, trying to catch a better view of the thing. All she had a sense of was some odd looking with down-turned back wings.

"If this was for real," said Patterson, "we'd already be dead. We just wouldn't know it."

"No cockpit," she said. "A drone."

"Not just any old drone. That's the daddy and it's directing the others."

She followed his finger and saw the other two drones wheeling in more slowly, their bulbous heads on the thinner fuselages making them look dick-like. Two hundred metres from the car, the drones split apart and, as they rolled away to either side, she could see the missiles under the fragile looking wings.

She narrowed her eyes. "You said it was directing. One machine directing another."

"Yeah, they're fully autonomous, a hunter killer drone pack."

"Are you saying they decide who to kill?"

"Under carefully specified Rules of Engagement, yes."

"Well, that's reassuring. What could possibly go wrong?"

"Forgive my companion," said Emison. "She's been watching too many Terminator films."

The lead drone suddenly shot over the car and she flinched down. Sneaky fucker had come out of the sun this time.

Patterson was smiling at her condescendingly. "There are operators, human beings, responsible for maybe three HK packs each. They can step in if things might go wrong."

She scanned around. "So where are these operators with their little remote-control radios?"

"They're in a secret location, a long way from here," said Patterson, flicking his hand airily.

She smiled. "You mean Creech Air Force Base. Everyone knows that's where the controllers for worldwide drone operations are."

"Well they shouldn't," said Patterson irritably.

"I can see how it'd be easy to pilot them when they're so close, or at least in the same high broadband rate country, but what about when they're on the other side of the world? From what I hear, the signals can take seconds to get to the drones via satellites. A lot could happen in that time, especially if you're trying to keep track on three sets of three."

"The smarter the UACVs are, the less oversight they need."

"UACV's?" asked Emison.

"Unpiloted Aerial Combat Vehicles."

Far ahead, she saw something forming in the turbid air. It was resolving into some sort of white building, like a small grandstand. As they got nearer, fifty or sixty neatly parked

Humvees and big civilian SUVs swam into view.

"Busy day," she said.

Patterson nodded. "Big chance for the manufacturers to show off their wares."

"An arms show?"

"Purely for internal consumption. Just for our military."

They came to a stop, but the kicked-up dust cloud continued on for a few metres ahead of them before subsiding back into the desert.

When they got out, she and Emison immediately took off their jackets in the scorching heat. Patterson led them through a side door in the structure and the darkened internal space gave immediate relief.

"This way," he said, stepping through a door and up some steps. There was more light now and, as they cleared the stairwell, the desert lay before them. On the banked seating were assorted high rankers in uniforms, their left breasts confetti-splattered, peering down like Romans into the arena.

Emison whistled. "Some audience."

She followed the audience's rapt gazes and felt her jaw actually drop. "What the fuck?"

They looked like sand creatures, things created Golem-like from the dust of the desert. Barely more than a man's height, they were impossibly stocky, their movements slow and implacable.

"Christ!" she heard Emison say. "They look like the Hulk."

"But yellow," she whispered.

The two creatures were advancing towards a small container city, like the temporary offices on a large construction site. A few old cars were parked amongst the containers but she couldn't see any people.

Something big with lots of barrels was strapped to the back of one of the monsters. Slowly, carefully, it reached back with a massive paw and pulled this over its shoulder. Beneath it, a thick metal container was revealed. This remained behind on its shoulder, tethered to the gun by a thick, swaying intestine.

"An M242 Bushmaster chain gun," said Patterson and you could sense his pride. "Usually mounted on an armoured car. Weighs 260 pounds, and that doesn't include the 25mm shells."

The way its thick arms manhandled the huge cannon with unearthly ease made her feel nauseous, like she was having a fever dream.

Then the damn thing took off at impossible speed and she nearly lost her breakfast.

And it shrieked. Her teeth felt like a grater was being run over them and she almost pissed herself in fear.

Despite the sickenly fast motion, the massive eight-foot gun came to bear in a leisurely arc. Then it roared and belched a fierce splash of fire. Huge holes punched up the side of a container. As they tore into the roof join, the whole container buckled upwards, tearing loose from its moorings.

The thing was strafing the chain gun sideways now, the container kicking across the desert like a cardboard box.

When the container came to rest it was like the wreckage of a high-speed car crash.

Only then, when the ear-splitting noise had subsided, did she think to breathe again. Emison was gasping beside her.

The second monster had stopped while the other one had messed up the container, but now it loped forward. Getting to one of the cars, it jack-knifed down into a squat and got its paws under the chassis.

A single easy movement brought it upright and the whole car came with it. Swivelling round, it faced the grandstand thirty metres away and leaned right back.

She heard expletives as the audience stumbled to its feet.

The thing's body jacked forward and the car sailed free. She ducked down, hands over her head.

The car came down well short, but was bouncing end over end towards them, coming to a stop less than ten metres away.

Trembling all over, she looked up at Patterson who hadn't budged.

Somehow, she managed not to claw the smug grin off his face.

Emison was getting back up from where he'd dived into the stairwell for cover. "Sweet Jesus! What are those things?"

Back on the desert, the things were waving and doing a cumbersome jig: slowly and carefully, like dancing geriatrics.

"Don't worry," said Patterson easily. "There're men in those things. ZEOS exoframes. Powered Battle Armour."

Perhaps he saw something in her eyes. He pulled his head back a little. "Want me to tell you more?"

Slowly unclenching her fists, she gave him a shark's smile and a small nod.

"Their skin, the yellow stuff, it's just fibre to keep out the sand and act as camouflage. Inside, there's a lightweight titanium and carbon nano-tube exoskeleton. That can take the weight and gives good armour protection to the operator. Operators in a haptic suit..."

"A what?" asked Emison.

"It's a thin fabric with surface contacts. The operator moves to do something, these sense it and fire up the computer-controlled hydraulics to make the suit move in the same way."

"And what does it all run on? Batteries?"

Patterson shook his head. "Would need too many of them. It's not the weight, it's the volume. No, that's where we have to go low tech. Internal combustion engine. They have to be small and lightweight which means they have to work very hard, the pistons firing at very high speed."

"Hence the noise," she said. "That shrieking sound. I thought it was just to scare people."

"Oh it does that as well. Would be better if we could do without it though. Damn things're not exactly stealthy."

"And with the engines, and the loads they're carrying, even with your nano-tubule things rather than steel plate, I bet they're pretty heavy. Not much use on frozen lakes for example."

Patterson nodded. "Weapons are like that: good in some

places, not so in others."

Emison seemed to have got over his shock and was becoming interested, like a kid with a Tonka toy. Soon he and Patterson were lost in a world of tech talk.

Ignoring them, she made her way down the steps to the front of the grandstand, threading her way through small knots of military talking excitedly. She noted that the Navy and Army were mixing, as usual, like oil and water.

Putting one hand on the wooden balustrade, she shielded her eyes with the other. The car had come to a rest on its side, underneath exposed to view. Dirtied up though it had been to look like the rest of the underside, she still spotted the two cross-members welded to the chassis. Just as she'd guessed.

She looked across at the Golems where they'd come to attention and were saluting the senior military in the grandstand. Looking down, she could track back their paths by the footprints they'd made in the sand. The footprints weren't deep, nowhere near deep enough for such heavy objects. Peering carefully into these footprints she could just make out something dark beneath.

The container was too far away to check. Big red signs made it clear that stepping down from the grandstand was both forbidden and extremely hazardous. Not that she had any inclination to get closer to these monstrosities. Nevertheless, she was willing to bet the container had been modified, a lot of the metal removed, and maybe thinner plating used. Cannon shells could rip it up all right, but it would've otherwise been too heavy to be kicked around like they'd just seen.

A lot of showmanship had gone into this. With zillions invested by whoever had manufactured these things, could she really blame them?

By the time she got back to them, Emison and Patterson where deep into power-to-weight testosterone bullshit.

"When will the Admiral see us?" she interrupted.

Patterson glanced around and his gaze came to rest on some tables set up at the back of the grandstand. "Come on, let's see!"

Judging by the exited huddles Patterson steered them round, the show had been an off-Broadway hit.

He came to a halt, hovering on the periphery of a group of middle aged men in Summer Whites, caps under their arms and drinking from frosted glasses. From the orientation of their stances, she had no trouble picking out the top dog.

While Patterson waited, trying to catch Macik's eye, she had time to give the Admiral the once over.

Mid-fifties, white hair cut short so it clung to his head like a skull cap. From the paleness of his skin and the freckles, she guessed his hair might once have been red. At just under her height, at about 5' 10", he'd weigh more at maybe 160 lbs and looked in good shape.

It took a while, but finally Patterson caught his eye. Macik nodded and took a step towards them, the men around him moving quickly aside.

"Admiral Macik, permit me to introduce you to Supervisory Special Agent Arthur Emison and Special Agent Josephine Beck."

Macik's white eyebrows rose a millimetre above cool blue eyes as they shook hands, no doubt in surprise at the strength of her grip.

"Thank you for your good work, Special Agent Beck." New England accent maybe.

"That's very kind of you, Admiral, but the guy did get away."

Macik nodded. "But you didn't let it go. You persisted, above and beyond the call they tell me, and you stopped a bomb getting on board my carrier. For that I am much obliged."

"Your thanks are appreciated," said Emison, "and we're glad to be here. Any reason to get out from behind a desk is good, but can I ask why you did bring us out here?"

As Macik turned slightly to address him, she drew the disturbed air slowly and steadily into her nostrils. Whatever he used to clean himself was unperfumed. In this heat everyone was leaking steadily, but his smell was still somehow inoffensive, unlike the notes of gorilla and goat she was getting from the other guys.

"Tell me. What did you really think of the demonstration?"

"It was scary but very impressive. Those guys in the suits looked like superheroes."

Macik turned back to her. "And you Ms. Beck?"

She shrugged. Holding stuff back wasn't her forte. "Impressive...superficially at least."

The pale eyebrows rose again.

"Whole thing was staged on a runway, something that can take heavy planes landing on it. Makes me wonder how well those suits would perform on real desert. Wouldn't move so quick or so steadily. If the sand was soft enough, maybe wouldn't move at all."

"Anything else?"

"That container they shot up. They messed with it. Must've taken out metal so it was lighter. Shouldn't have moved so easily, even with all those cannon shells.

"And that car: pure theatre! I'm guessing they'd taken out the engine blocks to make them lighter too. They'd definitely welded a couple of cross members to the chassis. Without those to grab hold of, that man/robot thing would've just torn open the side. The lifting and throwing would have been messier."

Macik smiled; still no signs of actual warmth, but clearly pleased. "Didn't spot that last bit but you're right. Though, even opening up the side of that car like a can opener would have been quite impressive."

"And more honest."

"I can see you're going to keep us all on the straight and narrow, Ms. Beck."

"How do you mean, sir?"

Macik turned back to Emison. "Mr. Emison, I want your Special Agent here to sail with us, a week from now." He paused and lifted his head a little. "It'd hardly be without precedent. Shore side investigations back in '02 stumbled on a heroin supply chain leading back to the *John C. Stennis*. A shore-based agent was seconded to follow through on board during the next tour. Similar thing on the *Carl Vinson* in '07."

Emison opened his hands. "Can I ask why you don't want to leave it up to your own NCIS Agent Afloat."

"From the transcripts of Ms. Beck's interviews with Midshipman Hierra and Midshipman Wiggins, it's clear that this...suspect..."

"We call him the African," she said. "For want of a better name, though in truth we're not even sure he is from there. So far he's really just a black guy with an accent."

"Right...the 'African' has apparently been attempting to suborn at least two of my crew for months now. Who knows what other members of the crew he's been targeting and for how long. Sadly, our Agent Afloat hadn't got a whiff of any of this. Sounds to me like we'd benefit from a new pair of eyes." He looked back at her. "Especially ones that aren't easily fooled."

"Of course we'd be happy to second Special Agent Beck, Admiral," said Emison with a nod of his head.

"And you, Ms. Beck," said Macik. "What do you feel about this?"

Nice of him to ask. He didn't have to. At least it all sounded interesting; make a change from Norfolk. "Your NCIS agent afloat might not like it. I mean, I'd have to work with that person."

"Don't worry about that. She'll give you her full cooperation. And if she doesn't...well, it'll be a long swim home for her."

That tepid smile again. "I'll assign one of my staff to work with you directly. Any problems, then just let him know."

"One question, Admiral, if I may?"

"Fire away."

"Have you any idea who might be behind this? Any idea why they might be doing this?"

"Agents, you know as well as I do that America has many enemies. So many that, as there is no specific threat we're aware of the moment, we're in the realms of speculation. A few years back the finger would have pointed at Libya but, since the end of Gaddafi, things have quietened down a lot. North Africa and the Middle East have plenty of internal worries to distract them at the moment."

"Well I for one can't help but speculate," said Emison. "Al Qaeda's cells are getting smaller and smaller and more and more isolated. Whenever they pop their heads up we take them off with drones, not unlike the one's that we saw driving in. ISIS is on the back foot and has a lot of other stuff on its plate at the moment. China and Russia...well things are pretty tetchy with them right now but well short of putting bombs on US naval vessels."

Macik nodded. "And, again, our role in the Atlantic would hardly mean much to China. Likewise, that would take us out of North Korea's narrow range of interests."

Joey pursed her lips. "Which leaves us with something from left field."

Emison shook his head. "Not necessarily. Could be the African is working alone. A one man Al Qaeda cell looking to make a gesture. That bomb we retrieved wouldn't be enough to sink a carrier."

Macik took a deep breath and looked around and she realised their audience was ending. "Like I said, we're in the realms of speculation."

He glanced at Patterson who straightened quickly. "I take it everything is in order."

"Of course, Admiral."

"Signed our lives away ten times and in triplicate," Joey said, but Macik had already turned and was striding away like he hadn't heard her.

"Play the game, Joey," said Emison irritably.

"The Admiral comes across as a bit chilly."

Patterson gave her a sardonic look. "I have absolutely no

comment to make on that."

"What's he like as a boss?"

"Highly effective. Hands on at every level, so leads by example."

"Stickler for process?"

Patterson ruminated for a while, no doubt looking for a trap. "Sure, all the best Admirals are. CSG runs like clockwork."

"What's his background?"

"Impressive, as you'd expect. Top of class at the Naval Academy, Masters in Aerospace Engineering, commander of an FA/-18 Strike Fighter squadron at 28, flew combat sorties in the First Gulf War. EO and CO on several Nimitz Class carriers. Made Admiral of the *Sands* Carrier Strike Group at 45."

She nodded. "That's right, isn't it? They only let fly boys become COs of aircraft carriers and Admirals of CSGs?

"It's what carrier groups are all about. The forward projection of air power."

"Didn't I hear something about Macik serving with the President?" asked Emison.

"They were midshipmen together at Annapolis and I understand they're friends..."

"That can't hurt," she said.

Patterson ignored her. "... though President Tridens left for politics after she'd served as CO on the *Vicksburg*."

"That's a Ticonderoga class guided missile cruiser, as I recall," said Emison.

"Correct."

Joey hadn't voted for Tridens. Admirable the way she'd worked her way up through the navy then politics but Tridens was too pugnacious, too ready to condemn. A hard-minded and intransigent women in a world of shifting complexity.

"So now what? Back to Virginia?"

Patterson smiled. "Yes, but first I have a present for you."

Chapter 4. *Liganda, Gulf of Guinea*

The beat up old 737 tilts gracefully to the side and tracks across the cobalt blue waters of the Gulf of Guinea and then back towards the land.

For hours the vastness of Africa has slid smoothly by below him. The fierce deserts and endless mountains of Algeria and Mali finally giving way to the forested Alani plateau: his country's highest point and where he spent his childhood. After that came the vast plains leading down to the sea.

The engines' roar lessens and he feels the plane begin its controlled fall towards the Tembe airstrip. Most of the bulbs in the seat belt signs have failed, so this is the signal for the passengers to start rummaging around for their straps. Clicks, as though from a forest of crickets, fill the cabin.

The stewardesses are behind their little curtain, passengers ignored, as they have been almost since *Charles de Gaulle*. Seated close to the cabin, he can hear their giggles and raucous gossip.

He shakes his head in exasperation. General Olomo still has much to do.

Blue flashes to yellow then green as they come in over the beach and palms, then finally they're over the grey of the runway. To both sides, acres of short grass flash by, fingers of taller jungle vegetation already invading it.

The plane, its fall not so controlled after all, hits hard and baggage thuds around in the overhead lockers. Beside him, the sleeping businessman's eyelids peel far back in surprise then he's grasping his seat as the plane slews to the left before fishtailing back again.

Yao has made this landing often enough but, even so, his shoulders hunch up as reverse thrust kicks in and the engines shriek. Some rogue resonance is making the nose bump up and down as they rumble across the tarmac. It damps down only as they come to a final, sudden halt.

Yao turns his head to the window and cranes back. Sure enough, they've missed the final turnoff on the short strip. It often happens.

People have started to grumble by the time some vehicle comes up behind them and starts to tug them backwards. It takes another quarter hour before they finally make it to the terminal.

He watches as a white haired old guy pushes the rusted stairway into the side of the plane and feels the thump as the door is opened. The curtain is whipped aside by one of the slutty stewardesses, her tight skirt and blouse accentuating her thrusting bottom and breasts. A little red pill box hat sits jauntily on her head above sullen eyes and lips.

Humid air piles into the cabin. Sweat immediately prickles his brow.

"You may disembark now," says the stewardess before disappearing again.

People ease themselves upright, tugging out clothing wedged into moist crevices. They sigh and stretch, then are reaching up for their hand luggage.

Yao waits as they struggle out then finally follows them down the rickety steps.

Making the short walk to the terminal, he admires the menagerie of planes painted in the colourful liveries of various African Airlines. It's disappointing there was only seven in total. This is, after all, the country's main airport.

Yes indeed, there is still a big job to do.

A couple of soldiers, sub-machine guns hanging loosely from shoulder straps, are lounging against the side of the building. Their heat stunned eyes are blank and incurious except for when the younger female passengers file by.

In the terminal, time passes as the passengers wait for their baggage. When it comes, it's all dumped onto time-served trestle tables.

Yao has no luggage, but already many of the other

passengers with only carry-on bags have formed themselves into two big lines. At their head, two officials, each performing the functions of both immigration and customs, are taking their time pawing through suitcases and leafing through passports.

Eventually he presents himself before one of them. Concentric salt stains from the man's sweat radiate from both armpits. Yao notes the heat can't be too bad: today's moisture has made it only half way out to the most extensive of the white halos. The man's sharp smell is almost welcoming after the chemical sterility of America and Europe.

"Baggage," says the official, a paunchy man with a dark curly beard almost up to his eye sockets.

"Just this," says Yao, lifting up a newly bought hold-all no bigger than a carrier bag.

The man's eyes narrow in suspicion then travel over Yao's body, taking in the new shoes and clothes.

"Hmm, unusual," he says. "Suspicious even. We must detain you, make sure you're who you say you are. Unless...perhaps..."

The nakedness of it makes Yao sneer.

Anger flashes in the man's eyes and he reaches forward to grab him but never makes it. A huge hand has suddenly appeared and grasped the man's elbow.

Both Yao and the official turn to look up at the big man dressed in battle fatigues, then at the two others behind him.

"Not your problem," says the soldier evenly.

The official is already nodding hastily but the soldier seems in no rush to let his arm go. When he does, the official thrusts the passport back at Yao with one hand and shoos him away with the other.

"This way," says the big man.

The city's entire fleet of taxis seem to be parked out front. Their owners, aggressively touting for business, nevertheless part like the Red Sea before Yao and the soldiers.

The parking lot holds a handful of dilapidated vehicles

and one mud-caked SUV. Inside this, a fourth soldier has kept the engine and aircon running so the air is suddenly cool again.

Yao wishes it wasn't; he likes the raw heat better than this fake rich world chill.

None of them bothers with seat belts. Many think African fatalism a sign of weakness, but to Yao it's a sign of strength. Even rich world soldiers, men paid to risk all, are too careful, too frightened to lose their precious lives in some random car crash.

The SUV takes off before Yao can even make himself comfortable. Tyres squeal in outrage as it takes the left turn out of the parking lot too fast. He sees heads swivel to follow their progress out of the airport. Soon, Yao reflects, drawing such attention to themselves will be fatal. Even now it isn't advisable. He opens his mouth to speak just as the big man stretches two fingers out and drives them into the base of the driver's skull.

"Slow!" he roars.

Rubbing his forehead where it had banged into the steering wheel, the driver slows to a speed still fearsome by western standards, but unremarkable here.

The road between the airport and the city is good, and they have an easy few miles before they swerve onto a bumpier track heading into the bush and their speed drops further.

Jungle around the coastal strip gives way to grassland, though stands of mahogany became more frequent. Finally, they drive under the canopy of one of these and find a rainbow coloured *taku* waiting. The little bus is empty but for a driver.

The big soldier points. "Now the Evil Birds will follow us and not you."

"Drones already?"

"Probably not, but the General said to take no chances. He is training us to always think this way."

"Yes, soon it will make the difference between life and death."

Grabbing his holdall, Yao climbs out of the SUV and walks across to the bus's passenger door next to the driver, but the man inside waves him to the back door. Sliding this open, he makes to sit at a window seat but the driver turns around and indicates the middle.

"Keep away from the windows," he says gruffly. "The Evil Birds must not see your face."

For a second, Yao is gratified by this show of prudence. Then he wonders if perhaps the drones are already here because he has foolishly left a trail for the Americans to follow. The thought that he may have disappointed the General is a bitter one.

The *taku* coughs into life and they turn and putter back the way he's come. Already the SUV is disappearing from view in the other direction.

A few hundred metres and they turn left onto an even smaller and rougher road. "You should make yourself comfortable. It is a long way."

"Where are we going?"

The driver's eye regards him coolly in the mirror.

"Nasengi?" Yao asks. That's where the General has his main compound.

"Of course not," says the driver. "You must have been away for a long while."

Now and then they drive through tiny villages and Yao drinks in the brightly coloured bands and diamond shapes of the womens' Kente cloth: a relief from the drab colours of the bush. Even in these hard times, as the nation gears up for war, the women still find money for that. Perhaps it keeps their spirits up, keeps them from going mad in this vast wilderness.

The sparse clumps of trees finally give out to dry plain. With fewer potholes to rattle their bones, the driver eases the bus up to 30 mph.

Stress and the endless travelling have exhausted Yao, and he falls into a deep sleep. When he comes to, the sun has shifted far across the sky and he can see hills ahead. Beside the road rises the occasional thorn tree and, further away, he sees baobabs, the hulking trunks making their branches and leaves look starved and underdeveloped.

It all looks so familiar and he guesses they are heading towards his beloved Alani Plateau, or at least into its approaches. And soon, sure enough, he sees the green line ahead, the sudden and mysterious demarcation between dry plain and forest. From the first straggling shoots, to trees at their full height and glory, takes barely thirty metres, and it's like plunging into a vast green wave. A curtain is drawn closed as the light vanishes beneath the forest canopy.

The driver quickly tugs off his sunglasses and leans forward, the better to avoid the thick trunks hemming in the meandering track.

Memories drift back. On cool nights in his childhood, scrambling up one of the small hills that break through the tree canopy then lying for hours staring up at the glittering sash of the Milky Way blazing across the night sky. Stars beyond number: the countless eyes of God.

And Africa's stars are something he's sorely missed in the all-consuming light wash of American cities. 'Why put a veil on something so beautiful?' as the General once asked.

A nation that would shut off the sky from its own eyes has lost its soul.

As the sun goes down, and the gloom under the canopy deepens even further, the driver turns on the low-slung headlights, making the potholes ahead look ink-filled. The incline becomes more obvious now and in a few miles they turn into what he knows to be a steeply wooded valley cutting into the hillside. Far ahead, through the trees, he begins to catch the flickering lights of wood fires.

A barrier, a thin tree trunk resting on a couple of metal stands, blocks the road and they come to a halt. "Raise your hands," says the driver.

Yao looks round, trying to pierce the dark to the sides of the track. Something small and white is floating to the right. This resolves into the white of a single eyeball staring straight at him down the barrel of a gun.

Shapes come quickly out of the darkness. His door is opened and he's pulled out of one side of the bus, the driver the other. Arms haul him round and push him back against the *taku*. His head is pressed down against the warm metal of the roof. Hands roughly grope around his belt, up and down his legs, into his crotch and armpits.

It goes dark as someone finds the switch for the headlights. As his eyes adapt, he sees a red firefly, its light unflickering, moving around the vehicle then down over the snub nose of the engine compartment.

A voice comes out of the darkness. "Nothing."

The hand lets go of the top of his head and he's able to stand upright. A light shines full in his face, but he resists the urge to bring up his hands to cover his eyes.

"Who are you?"

"Special Commander Yao."

"Sure enough," says a deep voice he knows too well.

He still can't make out their faces but he feels all the hands release him.

"Obeng, open the barrier!"

The door opens and he's gently shoved back in. The driver's door clunks shut and the lights come back on. A tall, lean man in battle fatigues gets in beside Yao.

"Hello Justice," says the driver.

"Frederick," replies Justice absently.

"Why the rough stuff? It's not like you didn't know we were coming."

"You're early."

"I'm a good driver. I make good time. You know that."

Justice doesn't reply. Ahead of them a soldier has grasped one end of the barricade and is walking it round, clearing the way ahead.

The *taku* mutters into motion and Yao settles back.

Beside him Justice lights a cigarette, the match's light

flickering over a long pock marked face.

"Hello, little brother" Justice murmurs in a voice deeper and more chilling than Arctic ice.

"I'm not your brother."

"You're still not one for irony are you?"

Yao doesn't say anything.

"Or humour for that matter."

"It's strange to hear you say that. I don't remember you making anyone laugh."

"You'd be surprised what I make people do."

Beside them, a little clearing in the mighty trees shows dark shapes sitting round a campfire.

"Is that a present you brought me? What about those for your wife and her family? Surely all their presents can't be in that one little bag?"

"I had to leave quickly."

"Ah, I remember now. You made a mess of things. Back with your tail between your legs."

Yao hisses air between clenched teeth. "It was a high-risk operation. Sooner or later something would go wrong, one of the sailors on the *Sands* would tell the authorities. We knew that."

"If you say so. Does that mean the whole plan has collapsed? The General won't be pleased."

Yao tries to tamp down his anger. "No. Wiggins, the man who betrayed me, did not know of any others."

"But their counter-intelligence will suspect that there may be others. They will look."

"I left no tracks. They'll never find them."

"So you say."

Another clearing, this one larger, the firelight making the flat green and orange camouflaged sides of some trucks stand out against the black of the tree trunks.

"The women in America. Are they nice?"

Yao ignores him.

"Do they fuck?" prompts Justice.

"They are unclean," says Yao. "I would not touch them."

"The white skin. You don't find it fascinating because of the contrast?"

"I find only my wife's skin fascinating, as should you."

"Oh I do find your wife's skin fascinating," says Justice, and laughs.

Yao grits his teeth. "*Your* wife."

"My wife was killed," says Justice harshly. "What few possessions I had were seized. All I have left is what I wear. With everything taken from me, would God really begrudge my dreams of milky skin?"

"Forgive me if I'm not won over by your sad story. You've had many 'wives'. It's hardly surprising one of them might be dead by now."

"You are such a self-righteous little prick."

They are several miles into the Cleft now and have passed two more sets of guards. In larger areas of cleared ground, moonlight glints off trucks and small lorries: some flat bed, others with tanks for water and petrol. Many tents and some cabins can just be seen amongst the tall trees.

Finally, they turn off the track and drive into a clearing, then pull up at a large wooden bungalow with a veranda running around it. Justice gets out and beckons Yao to follow.

A dozen soldiers lounging on the floor of the veranda spring to nervous attention when they see Justice stalking towards them. He's quickly up the steps and through the open door, Yao hurrying behind him. The main room is large but, to the right, he can see several doors to other apartments. A couple of old mahogany tables, carved by the ancient hands of colonial artisans, are in the centre with a dozen chairs scattered around them. Bare floors and walls testify to its long abandonment even before Olomo had reclaimed it.

The General is at one table, handsome head down and reading. A camping light casts fierce illumination over his short black hair. As Yao gets closer, the General looks up then stands and comes around the table to greet him, long arms held out.

Yao comes to him and the General envelops him. For the first time in months he feels a sense of ease.

The General kisses him on the top of his head then releases him. Yao stands back, head down, hands clasped over his stomach.

"My son," says the General kindly. A simple metaphor, but how Yao wishes it were true. "Sit down and tell me of your adventures in America." The General lightly eases his lean six-foot frame back into his own chair. Without being invited, Justice grabs another chair and brings it to the table.

Yao takes a seat at a more respectful distance but still keeps his head down, too shy to look into the great man's eyes.

Olomo chuckles. "Look at me, Yao!"

He glances up but can't stop looking back down again. Steeling himself, he finally brings himself to meet the warmth of the General's eyes.

"You must not be so in awe of me, Yao," says the General gently. "I am just a man. Always remember that!"

"I owe you everything," says Yao simply.

"And you have already repaid me many-fold. America...?"

Yao nods. "I am sorry about Wiggins. All was well otherwise."

"Don't worry about him. I am just pleased you emerged unscathed. You came under fire?"

"Their shots did not even come close."

Justice snorts, but Olomo ignores him. Instead he nods sagely. "Fat and lethargic no doubt, their people would be no match for someone as fast as you."

The American woman had been neither, but Yao does not even consider correcting the General.

"And your other targets?"

"Weaker than Wiggins. Too concerned about money or their secrets. I think they will do what we ask."

"I have read the reports you made on these people. You

were very thorough."

"It wasn't just me as you know, General. With the money you provided I was able to make use of private investigators. They were able to find most of the ...ways in."

"Yes, with money. We have so little, so what we have we must use effectively. Leverage: emblematic of everything we do."

The General's gaze is unwavering and Yao struggles again to meet it.

"You spent a lot of time there, in that terrible country. You saw all their sins. Were you ever tempted?"

Yao shakes his head firmly, his mouth grim. "Never!"

Olomo smiles. "And that's why I chose you instead of others," the flick of his eyes towards Justice would have been like a lash if directed to Yao, but the man seems unperturbed. "God was guiding me the day I found you. God knew this day would come."

And Yao feels like the silent seven-year old again. Crouching by the burnt out remains of his home for days, no longer even smelling the stench of death, too shocked to eat, too shocked even to drink despite the harsh rays of the equatorial sun. Holding on to his mother's hand; at first this had grown cold and stiff, then later becoming softer and with decay bringing back warmth.

He forces his mind back to the present. The General is nodding sadly. "There is a reason for everything." He spreads his arms. "Do you like our new home?"

"Is it my failure in America that made you move here?"

The General shakes his head. "Don't be so hard on yourself. What happened was not unanticipated. Aside from your goodness and faith, you also have the advantage of being unknown, untraceable. Even if they have pictures of you it will get them nowhere. No, we did not move because of what happened in that godless land. You see only one strand of the tapestry. There are many others."

"Forgive me, General, but I thought we were not anticipating a response until after the rainy season."

"Things are going better than imagined. Much better. Come! I will show you."

By the time they are out the door and down the steps, a dozen men have again scrambled to their feet, this time forming a phalanx around the General. Olomo strolls easily, one hand hooked into his belt near his side arm. With the other, he indicates high into the night. "This valley is good for us. My adviser says it is an old volcano which blew a side out countless years ago. It forms a valley whose sides are steep and easily defensible. But it is the trees in the valley, growing huge in the fertile soil here, which will be our greatest allies. They give us cover, even against infrared. The high, sharp sides shield us from forward seeking targeting from most directions. If the Americans come for us it would have to be from one direction only," and he points towards the valley entrance.

"Not that they even know we are here and hopefully that will remain the case. Electronic trackers are what we must fear. When you came in, did they check for such devices?" The softer the General's voice becomes, the greater the import.

"We checked, General," says Justice quickly. "Believe me, we checked!"

For a second Yao thinks Olomo might look to him for corroboration, but he doesn't. Always he treads a careful path between what he calls his Black and White Knights.

"What about human intelligence?"

The General nods sadly. "Ours is a poor country. Empty bellies make people easy to corrupt. But we do what we can. Everyone comes here in the dark. Only the drivers know where we are for sure, and they've been hand-picked almost as carefully as you."

Yao has gained an inkling of the size of this encampment, and the many drivers it must take to keep it supplied and to ferry men back and forth. Despite what the general says, when trouble erupts it will not stay hidden for long.

A zephyr brings the smell of roasted meat and his tongue

becomes wet with saliva. The drive has been long and he hasn't eaten anything since the plane passed over the Mediterranean. Ahead, he can just make out a large circular hut, a conical roof disappearing up into the canopy. Several soldiers at the entrance come to attention when they recognise Olomo.

He waggles a finger and two soldiers quickly open the door. Yao ducks down to follow the General inside.

The interior is poorly lit by an oil lamp. It takes a while for Yao to see the twenty pairs of frightened eyes looking up at him. The people are seated on the ground against the inside of the cabin, hands tied to ring bolts in the wall.

Slowly he scans them, taking in the hunched, wretched bodies and the whiteness of their skin, and he understands the dice have been well and truly cast.

Chapter 5. *Bito Village, Liganda*

The dogs, of course, hear him coming.

Hiking out from the Cleft, he'd flagged down a *taku* taking its meandering course towards Tembe, where all roads in this country lead. The *taku* dropped him where the dirt track forks off from the road, a kilometre short of the village. The quarter moon's pale-yellow light is all he needs for he knows the way well enough.

There had been no question of providing advance warning. The wave of cell towers, touted to sweep over the country, had broken barely fifty miles out of Tembe, and poor maintenance has brought it back in a stuttering retreat. Even in that city itself, cell phone coverage is very patchy.

It is the ultimate kindness on Olomo's part to let him come at all. All journeys to and from the Cleft are a risk.

But now here he is on the outskirts of the village and the hounds are barking angrily. Light starts to flow out from under doors as lamps are lit. The owners may not venture out but they may well loose the dogs.

"I am a son returning," he calls and waits for the first brave soul to investigate. The huts, baked clay walls and thickly thatched roofs, lie in a three-quarter circle where the track ends.

Khimo, of course, is the first to stick his head out. Holding back a frenzied black hound by the scruff of the neck with one hand, he has a lantern in the other. Yao blinks in the sudden direct light.

"Well, I'll be damned," says Khimo. "Back from your whoring at last."

Yao sucks in his breath. "May God have mercy on you, Khimo. You and your filthy tongue."

Khimo is shaking his head. Around him, other doors are opening and he can hear dogs being beaten into silence.

"Is she here?"

"Of course she's here. But why should she have you back? A pretty woman, alone for so long. Why should she wait for you?"

Khimo has always wanted her. Yao is glad he has not brought a gun for he might use it now. Instead he turns off the track and makes for her hut across ground beaten flat by generations of feet. Cooking smells, still hanging in the airless night, are those of home.

All the time he is praying. Her love is all that has kept him going.

Getting nearer, his heart leaps when he sees the door open and a head peer out. He falters.

She's in his arms before he knows it.

Kissing deeply, clutching each other, their tears intermingling, seconds turn to minutes. Then, breaking free, she's pulling him away, between the huts and towards the trees.

"But..." he says.

"My parents are asleep. Let's not awaken them." His heart feels like it will burst from his chest.

The swollen trunk of the baobab rises out of the night, blocking the stars. To him their girth has always been obscene, like the elephantiasis swollen legs of some poor old woman, but tonight he's grateful for it as she pulls him round the trunk. Safely hidden from the village, Zinzi takes his head in her hands and kisses him.

He brings a hand up and gently runs his fingers over her cheek, feeling the undulations of her tribal scars. It inflames him, as always. Without thought, his other hand finds her breast.

She shudders and he draws back. "I'm sorry, please..." he starts.

He can see the flash of her smile. "I was just startled: it is so long since you laid a hand on me. You are my husband. You must do as you wish."

His hands come up to her shoulders and pull down the straps of her shift. He catches his breath as he sees her breasts in the moonlight, the nipples already hard. Thoughts of this moment have made for agonised yearning in countless dead hotel rooms.

His tongue runs wetly over a long nipple, and then he's sucking on it, trying to drink her in. Her hands, at the back of his neck, are pulling him harder towards her, trying to make their flesh one.

Then they're kissing again and he's tugging the shift down over her slender thighs. Feeling her wetness, his desire rages uncontrollably. Roughly grabbing her shoulders, he turns her towards the tree and fumbles himself free of his military fatigues.

Entering her, he gasps in ecstasy.

Like an animal he bites her, little nips to her neck and shoulders. Her whole body surges up and down as he thrusts deeper and deeper into her.

She's sobbing and gasping now. His head at her shoulder, he can see the parallel scars on her cheek etched by moonlight. Glancing down, he sees her tender breasts rubbing across the tree's rough bark.

Too much.

He roars as his seed, dammed by a year of celibacy, at last bursts forth.

Perhaps he faints. Somehow, he's on the ground and she's on top of him. She's crying and he feels her tears falling on him.

"I love you so much," she's saying.

"You are my life," he says simply and holds her tightly against him.

Throughout the long night they cannot leave each other alone. When dawn comes, its light glistens on thighs made wet with their juices.

"Please don't leave me again," she whispers.

"You know that I must."

"I cannot live without you."

Trawling his hand through the thick stemmed grass, he

feels the faintest of dews forming.

"I must go back soon."

"To the General?"

"Of course, he is the only thing that could take me from your side." Now the dew is forming in the corners of her large dark eyes.

Cradled in his arm she's looking up at him, timidly. "I know he is like a father to you. I know you love him. But he has so many men to follow him. Why does he need *you*?"

He looks at her face, at the high cheekbones tapering down to an elegant jaw and framing the lusciousness of her lips. Lips he could drink from for eternity.

"I am part of the plan. The General has trained me over many, many years. My English, my education, my skills in... other things."

"Fighting," she says. To anyone else this would have sounded matter-of-fact. Only because he knows her so well can he detect a hint of something bitter underlying her meekness.

"No, not so much of that. That I learned in my early days with the Divisions. No, once I came to the general's attention, he showed me other things...hidden things."

"Not fighting. What does that leave? You are no clerk, Yao, and I do not see you cooking for the soldiers. Olomo would never use someone like you for things like that." Hesitating now, she touches his hand. "You spy for him, is that not right?"

His oath of secrecy to Olomo has been absolute and he's already said too much, but he has been apart from Zinzi for so long. He burns to tell her everything.

"Not like that." The dark eyes peer deep into his soul. "Not quite like that."

She shakes her head sadly. "My poor Yao. Such a truthful main yet made to do dishonest things."

He grasps her hand. "Some things are so important you must go against your natural inclinations. You may wish for peace but sometimes it is necessary to go to war. I must do whatever I can to help the General. He is a great man, a military genius. His vision is... magnificent."

"For it to keep you away from me, it must be. From the way you first took me tonight I can tell that your need is as great as mine. At the time it felt there could be nothing more important in the world."

"But there are more than just us. Across this vast land there are countless other lovers who have been broken by poverty or parted forever by war or disease. Africa could be a great continent. If we could unite, if we could work together, we could outstrip the rest of the world. The American Century is already finished and even they are beginning to see this. China has risen, and India is following close on its heels, and soon they will lead the world. Yet look at them compared to what Africa could be. We too have over a billion people but have double the land of both combined. Compared to Africa their natural resources are..." and he clicks his fingers dismissively.

She looks weary; she's heard this before. "But we are nearly 60 countries and all we do is fight."

"That is the legacy of the colonialists. Fighting their wars by proxy. Dividing and ruling. The Belgians, the British, the French; they raped this continent then left us snapping at each other's throats like a pack of hungry dogs."

With his free hand he tangles his fingers in her long beaded hair. "It needs a strong man to unite us. And there are no longer 57 countries, already there are only 54 in all but name."

"The General's puppet governments."

He nods; this is hardly a secret. "Africa does not deserve to be poor. The continent has everything we need. Nobody needs to go to bed hungry. Nobody should be homeless. We should have hospitals and roads and railways like the rich world."

Zinzi is suddenly smiling again. He stops uncertainly. "You think I am being funny?"

She shakes her head. "You are not a fierce man, Yao, and I love you for your tenderness. But I like to see you so worked up like this, though I know it will take you away from me. I might be jealous of that but I know there is one other time when your eyes burn so fiercely."

Freeing her hand from his, she trails it over his thigh and cups his genitals.

"Have you any passion left for your wife?" she whispers.

Chapter 6. *USS Benjamin F. Sands, Western Atlantic*

She looked down on a brutal, shrieking scene from Hell.

Yet something about it was so... medieval.

She watched as a knight appeared, baggy flight suit flapping in the breeze, colour coded serfs hurrying behind. The serfs eased the knight up and onto his charger, tugging at straps, the ear-splitting noise forcing them to bend in close and yell into his helmet.

Once their liege was secured, the serfs scurried away as the Super Hornet inched forward, its engines adding to the cacophany. As the plane slowed to a halt, and the blast deflector angled up behind it, green-liveried serfs appeared as though by magic from out of the deck and ran forward to lower something from its underside.

"The 'holdback'," intoned Lewis.

The men were still rummaging under the plane and then were lowering something else, the end of which went down into a nubbin on the deck.

"The 'towbar' is lowered into the 'shuttle'." She liked ironic deliveries but it was all Lewis seemed to able to produce and it was getting old. No wonder he'd been given the shit detail of being her minder.

Now all the serfs were running like fuck and diving down into metal gullies at the sides of the deck, though one stood his ground and held up a chalkboard. In response, the pilot made some weird hand gestures. He wasn't the only one. All around her people were making these frenetic gestures, like the Flight Deck was a school for the deaf.

The reason, of course, was too much fucking noise.

The man with the chalkboard sprinted to the side and disappeared below the deck. A few metres aft, a hand rose from a pit and the pilot saluted back. Intense acetylene-like fire howled out of the back of the plane, raping even their defended eardrums.

She must have blinked because, like a magic trick, the whole thing was gone. Looking down the metal runway, she just caught sight of the plane being tossed off the deck and into the sky.

"The steam catapult," said Lewis gravely.

"Knock it off," she said. "You sound like Carl frigging Sagan."

"Aren't you interested, Josephine?" already aware she didn't like being called that.

"In the deadpan delivery: no. In conversation between two normal human beings: yes."

"Normal," he said thoughtfully. "I've heard of that."

The noise made them act like lovers necking, their heads having to keep dipping close together. Sometimes the plastic of their ears defenders clicked annoyingly as they contacted. She was getting a closer view of his face than would otherwise have been polite. Good complexion, though way paler than her natural preference, but with his black hair giving his jaw a twelve o'clock shadow. He must have to shave twice a day in this man's navy. At near six foot, and with a rangy build, he was like the positive to her negative.

Out the corner of her eye she caught movement and turned to see blue suited men swarming over the parked planes. There wasn't enough room for the eighty or so planes to be parked below deck at the same time, so there was always plenty littering the flight deck. Now they were being shifted to the forward main take-off runway, to clear the angled extension runway. That was used for landings.

"That's unexpected," said Lewis. "Someone must be in trouble. They weren't due to re-spot the planes until that last Hornet was due back."

She scanned the grey cloudy sky. She'd learned that if the visibility was good you'd always see a plane somewhere around: out there circling, looking for trouble.

Lewis pointed and she saw the Hawkeye arcing around and coming astern of the carrier, its radar disk tilted over so she could see the odd candy swirl design on the top and the four vertical stabilisers on the tail. It made the otherwise standard two prop plane look outlandish, like a bird with a knapsack, something that shouldn't be able to fly.

"Must've developed a fault. Those things should stay up for years," Lewis roared in her ear. "Now's your chance to see a controlled crash close-up."

They watched as the plane came out of its gentle curve to line up with the angled deck. Her sharp eyes even picked out its landing gear and tail hook descending. She glanced across at the now cleared deck and the four steel cables stretched across it.

"The third one's considered the best to catch, less deceleration on the aircraft, plus less chance of a ramp strike."

"Ramp strike?"

"Hitting the fan-tail."

"What the hell are you talking about?"

"Remind me again what the N in NCIS stands for?"

"Jesus! I wasn't hired for my sailing skills."

"The back end, the bow, that's what the fantail is. Number 1 arresting wire is too close to it for safety. Wire 2 is OK, 3 the best because, if the hook hits short and bounces over the wires, they can still max the power and get into a climb before they get to the end of the angle. But the pilot shouldn't be aiming for the 4 because if they miss that then they're almost certainly going to take a bath."

The Hawkeye glided in, slamming down with a shocking bang that made the deck kick up under up her feet. Immediately the engines surged, straining for full power.

Had it missed the wire?

No, she could hear the stretched wire's high keening note as the plane thundered to a stop in an impossibly short distance before the engines were suddenly cut. A green suit rushed forward to undo the tail hook, allowing it to zip back across the deck as it straightened out.

She found that she was grasping the rail as though for dear life, suddenly aware of the sticky coarseness of the salt on the metal. She eased her hands off.

"Why did he do that? Go to full power just as he landed."

Lewis' blue eyes came close as he leaned in. "In case he didn't catch any wire at all. Maybe he doesn't swim so well."

Once freed, the Hawkeye had wasted no time and was already taxiing to its parking bay where blue suits were ready to tie it down to the deck.

"Had enough fresh air for one day?"

She nodded and he led her off the little balcony and back into the Island. She'd only seen the whole thing from the outside once when she'd come on board at Norfolk. For the first three storeys the Island, sticking up proud from the Flight Deck, was pretty featureless but then you came to three more storeys for the bridges and flight controls. Above these, aerials spouted like a fungal growth out of a rotten apple, and a huge radar dish rotated.

Lewis opened the hatch and stepped over the 'knee-knocker' and down onto the knurled bare metal. As he shut the hatch behind her, the nauseating stench of jet fuel was mercifully cut off. The smell of lubricating oil and concentrated humanity was suddenly almost fragrant.

"Where to now?"

"Cup of coffee. Nice little ward room on the third deck. Below the water line. You'd get a lovely view of the fishes but for all that steel plate. I'm supposed to brief you a little more. Then I could take you to meet your colleague."

For the two whole days since embarking she'd been confined to the tiny rec room on the fourth deck. Her present from Patterson had been reams of electronic paperwork and endless nannying safety videos. There were, apparently, endless ways you could get killed on board a carrier even without actually going to war. One fifteen-minute segment had been about how to safely make it down the stairs.

Anything would be better than more of that. She nodded quickly and Lewis led the way, pattering down the steep stairs in a distinctly cavalier manner, she noted. Not even holding the rail with one hand, never mind both.

She shook her head, trying to clear this pervasive Health and Safety nonsense. This whole thing was a war machine, for Christ's sake.

As they progressed through the labyrinth, she was reminded again that a carrier was like Dr. Who's TARDIS except in reverse. At well over 300 metres in length and weighing over 100,000 tons, from the outside it was a vessel so big it had two runways on it, but inside it was a rat run: everything was cramped. Sure enough, her NCIS training had taken her aboard several navy ships but inside they were palatial compared to this. It was the passageways that really did it. Always you were touching metal, sticking to the bulkheads like you were afraid of something. People were constantly scraping by carrying everything: food and drink to the various messes, documents to offices, tools to broken machinery.

She'd begun to feel like a drone in a hive.

Ahead of her, Lewis suddenly turned and flattened his back against a bulkhead, revealing two senior offices in khaki bearing down on them. Joshing with each other, the one in front kept looking back over his shoulder at the other. They didn't even seem to see Lewis though their shoulders brushed his chest.

She stood her ground, shoulder leading. Nobody was brushing against her chest, at least not without an invite. The leading man's shoulder glanced off hers, and he struggled short-sightedly to focus on her, but was passed her before he could. The second gave her a disdainful look but took avoiding action, sliding along with his back to the bulkhead, before resuming his stately advance.

She watched as they steamrollered on, never looking back, ratings and lower officers parting before them like water before a bow.

"Fucking Camelot," she said quietly.

"What?" asked Lewis.

"Nothing, keep going!"

It was like making your way through dense jungle, just a lot more hard-edged. Fire extinguishers and fire points sprouted like orchids, door latches plucked at your sleeves, bulkhead mounted monitors seemed to swing at your head.

Many jinking turns through the maze brought them into one of the pair of quarter mile central passageways on deck 03. But for the myriad knee-knockers, and the bobbing heads of the scurrying crewmen, it gave her a long view in one very restricted dimension. Being able to walk in a straight line for more than a few metres had become a luxury, but you still had to avoid the steady stream of worker ants humping their assorted loads in the opposite direction.

One feature of these long passageways was the absence of the otherwise ubiquitous TV monitors. In the rest of the ship they hung over every corner broadcasting network news, stuff from the carriers own station, plus the 'plat cams' showing real time activity on the flight deck. Without them she felt strangely unplugged.

Another turn and they were back in the steel rabbit warren. Three more turns and they were suddenly in a room large by these deprived standards. Several tables and benches held small huddled groups of officers and enlisted men. Lewis led the way to the end of one table and pointed for her to sit down.

"Coffee? What do you take?"

"Black, two sugars."

As he ambled away she glanced around. A few snack dispensers, a couple of video game machines and three TVs flickered away, their remotes hanging off them on chains. All were silent.

She registered a few casual glances from both men and women, perhaps because of her black boiler suit: the uniform of government civilians. She wasn't the only one on board not in the navy, the place abounded with civilian contractors here to maintain much of the technology throughout the tour. They wore boiler suits of many different colours and replete with industrial logos.

Lewis was soon back with their coffees and he sat down across from her. He too glanced around, no doubt making sure there was nobody else within earshot. That there had been a plot to get at least one bomb on the *Sands* was not common knowledge.

"What do you think of it so far?"

"Oppressive, claustrophobic, smelly, loud. And, apparently, you chose to serve aboard this nightmare."

He laughed. "Don't hold back. Tell me what you really think."

"So why *are* you here?"

"You know, I've been asking myself that quite a bit recently. I guess the novelty's really worn off."

"And before it did, what was the big deal?"

He screwed up his eyes. "It's like being in a football team: dedicated, focussed. Something greater than yourself. 'Cept the team isn't twenty or thirty, but six thousand on this boat, ten thousand in the whole battle group. All with a defined, unquestioned goal. That can be very compelling."

She decided not to deploy the ant analogy; she wasn't quite sure yet how he might take it.

"So comradeship, that sort of thing."

"And power. Big time power. Enough for this Battle Group to fuck with nations. Waste their radar and air defences, send cruise missiles into their bunkers, sink their ships and, when they're nice and soft, the Amphibious Ready Group takes in the marines to mop up. We've got everything. Penetration missiles, cluster bombs, you name it. Nobody ignores us when we sail by."

"So, the CSGs are America's big stick."

"Every President, whenever some hot spot flares up, first question he asks is...."

"'Where are the carriers?'"

"Yup. We've been kicked off nearly all our airbases around

the world over the last fifty years. In terms of forward projection of power, we're pretty much it nowadays."

"And are their nukes here on the carrier?"

"Sort of, two nuclear reactors at least," and he pointed at the deck. "Deep down. But no nukes on the carrier. The public have got used to nukes on subs, or in ICBM silos, or on the big bombers. Otherwise their attitude can get a bit problematic which is why the carriers themselves aren't allowed to carry them. As for the Aegis Class Destroyer and the Guided Missile Frigates that accompany us, the official position is a bit...vague."

"I see. So those three top heavy ships I can sometimes see wallowing away on the horizon, they're up to the rafters in nukes,"

He shrugged and spread his hands.

"And are there any submarines?"

"Sometimes we have one mooching around. Depends where we're going. We're heading for a ceremonial visit to Cape Town right now, so we don't need it this time. Maybe it'll join us later, depending on how the tour develops."

"And there are ten CSGs, right?"

"Yeah, ten Carrier Strike Groups. Usually only three deployed at any one time, on six-month cruises. Persian Gulf, Western Pacific and the Med/Atlantic. The rest are back home. We work on a 2:1 basis. A year in or around port or on friendly visits, six months deployed."

"Sounds kind of soft."

"Maybe, but there's plenty of training during port time. Especially for the pilots; they never stop."

"And this CSG. Does it always patrol the Med and Atlantic?"

"Usually." He raised his eyebrows at her. "Looks like we're going to be working together for a while, so tell me about yourself!"

"You first."

"Ocean City, Maryland, born and bred. Sea and sand, crab and lobster. Big for college vacations. Can be wild."

"And were you wild?"

"More than a little. Got in the usual scrapes, smoked too much dope, didn't pay much attention at school. Teetered on the lip of a downward spiral but managed to take a step back before it was too late."

"What made you do it? What saved you?"

He pursed his lips and lines showed on his face around mouth and eyes. She guessed he couldn't be much more than mid-thirties so she wondered where these came from. Too much sun in Ocean City? Too much slit eyed peering into stormy weather? Or maybe he was just born with skin like a saddle bag. Some people were. Wasn't all that bad to look at, though.

"Had a bit of an accident. Got into trouble with the cops. Local Sheriff had a word with my dad..."

"Military or jail. Heard that one before often enough. What kind of 'accident'?"

"Mail box hockey, except we didn't have a convertible. It's much easier without a roof on your car. My pal Phil was leaning right out the window to take a good swipe. I was drunk, we hit a parked car and Phil broke both his legs."

"Navy as atonement. You're a walking cliche, Lieutenant Lewis!"

"It wasn't atonement. Phil mended good enough and, anyway, he'd been as wasted as me. We're still good pals. The whole thing just made me realise I had to get a grip."

That's wasn't what she was seeing now. In dress, in attitude, he lacked a certain sharpness. Not something you'd notice back on land but, in this clenched ass milieu, it was obvious.

"You reckon you've still got a grip?"

"I hope, when it's your turn, you'll be as forthcoming as you expect me to be."

She spread her hands. "Open book."

He snorted. "We'll see. As for me: two years and I'm out."

"Why? Wife and kids? Too long away at sea?"

"Haven't got any of those. You know what they say about

sailors? Port in every girl." He smiled weakly. "Least that's what I aspire to."

"So why?"

He shook his head. "Navy's going to hell. Has been since the 70's but, since the big budget cuts after the Meltdown in 2008, it's got so much worse. The Senate had to keep a check on naval expenditure somehow. Control and accountability, that's what it's all about. The Admiral can't take a shit without getting orders in triplicate. And it's a trickle-down thing, especially with Macik. Everything's driven by straitjacket protocols. Nobody is allowed any professional initiative. And the checks and audits! Endless paperwork. You see all those people working at computers all over the ship?"

She nodded.

"Electronic paperwork. Every action logged, every decision referenced to some bullshit protocol. It's stifling."

"I think it's sort of like that in most lines of work nowadays. What are you thinking of doing when you get out?"

He waggled a forefinger. "Oh no, Josephine. Your turn."

She sighed and glanced away then back. "Got into trouble when I was young, like you. Killed a man."

His eyes widened.

"Bastard called me Josephine."

"OK, OK, 'Joey'."

He waited.

"Brought up in Denver," she said finally. "Left home at 15, lived with some friends while I finished school and earned enough to get to college..."

"No help from your parents?"

"We didn't get on. Anyway, I was always good at sports, running mainly. When the time came, turned out I got a sports scholarship to Villa Julie, as it was called then, in Greenspring Valley."

"I know that place. It's Stevenson University now. So, you were in Maryland for a while. What did you think of it?"

"Greener than Denver, that's for sure. Never seen so many trees in my life. But the main thing was the ocean. Dated a midshipman for a while. Took me sailing down the Chesapeake and out into the Atlantic."

"You can't get much further away from the sea than Denver."

She nodded. "The ocean was a revelation. Anyway, got into law enforcement. Philadelphia first then Washington DC. NCIS job came up in Norfolk and it seemed like a good medium. Liked the water but didn't want to spend all my time on it."

"Law enforcement suggests a need to right wrongs. How come?"

She shrugged. "Too many cop shows as a kid. Sort of expect the guilty to be punished. Get upset when they don't."

He raised his eyebrows. "Shot anyone?"

"No," she said.

"But you loosed off a few at this African guy."

"Oh yes."

"And what happened to the midshipman? Don't see a ring so I guess you didn't marry him."

"Scared him off. Tail between his legs. It happens."

"I'll bet." He looked amused.

For a while there was silence. She took a sip of tepid coffee. Had the version of his life been as sanitised as hers?

He tapped a finger on the desk. "I guess it's time I took you to meet your colleague. Not sure she'll be keen to see you."

She started back. "Well, I never saw that coming," she said.

He shook his head. "And you have the nerve to call *me* ironic."

Another scurry through the rat run but at least she was starting to get a sense of direction. Trending forward and down, they shimmied round ratings carrying kitbags like engorged white slugs. The air was becoming even hotter and more humid.

Rumbling and hissing sounds grew louder. Then, through an open hatch, she glimpsed the hell that was the laundry. The white kit bags were being emptied, dirty clothes tipped into the open maws of huge washing machines. Steam presses opened and closed like the jaws of crocodiles. Thick air con ducting and pipes made the place look like the gastrointestinal tract of some fabulous beast.

"Nice," she said.

He nodded. "Prestige address." And, sure enough, the last door at the end of the laundry passageway had the sign: *NCIS: Special Agent Afloat Marceline Lundt.*

Lewis tapped at the door and they heard a muffled 'Yes'. He pushed into the compartment and lent forward to shake Lundt's hand. "Hi. Don't think we've met. I'm First Lieutenant Ivor Lewis, attached to the Admiral's personal staff. I'd like to introduce you to Special Agent Josephine Beck. I believe you've been expecting her."

Lundt was short and dumpy with close cut brown hair and rather pale blue eyes. Joey reached in to shake her hand. Lundt's handshake was limp and she didn't get up from behind her desk. Joey found herself looking down on her, probably not the effect Lundt had been shooting for.

"Take a seat." Lundt's tone didn't suggest that 'no' was an option.

"If you don't mind, Special Agents," said Lewis edging back out of the door, "but I have other duties to attend to." He hesitated for a second. "The Admiral is most interested in Special Agent Beck's investigations, so be sure to keep me informed. I sent you my email address."

Joey eyes locked onto Lundt and she didn't bother to look back as Lewis left. His dropping of Macik's name, then running away like that, wasn't going to soothe these troubled waters.

"Lundt and Beck," said the Agent Afloat. "Good old Germanic names. That explains me but not you."

Starting right in with how descendants of slaves got their

names. Excellent!

Lundt waited but, when it was clear no response was coming, she picked up a file from the desk. "Not much detail in this. Got to say I feel like I've been kept in the dark."

"Macik called the shots on that. He took the view that making this stuff common knowledge would make any potential saboteurs cut and run. Also, this way, they'd be less likely to see us coming."

"OK, but on the other hand disclosure might make whoever's behind this abort the whole thing. No bombs go off. Nothing sinks."

Joey shrugged. "It's Macik's call."

"And you found two saboteurs. Any indication there may be others?"

"Wiggins was on our side, it turns out, so really only Hierra was a potential saboteur. On the other hand, there was also the case of Harley Leeman."

Lundt's rather bushy eyebrows rose. "I know about that. Guy had a torrid love life, turns out. Not such a surprise he wound up shot dead."

"Could well be. Or maybe he made it clear he wouldn't play ball with the African. Maybe he was stupid enough to say he'd tell the Navy about it. Leeman's lovers, the ones we know about anyway, have rock solid alibis. Same for their husbands and significant others. Leeman was in debt. Enough money might have got him out of all his entanglements. Nice new start somewhere else.

"But if Leeman *was* involved, we're talking about attempts to suborn three of the crew. So why not even more? It's something we've got to seriously consider. The African was offering big money."

Lundt gave a frosty smile. "He should have asked me. What did this guy you call the African want Wiggins to do? Hierra, I know, was supposed to bring explosives on board."

"We don't know: the curtain came down before he

revealed that."

"Unfortunate! And then he got away."

Joey licked her lips. "And what about you?" she asked. "The last cruise, plus the year you've just spent port side. Notice anything suspicious at all, while our African friend was suborning your fellow crew members?"

The woman's eyes narrowed slightly. "It's a big ship, a big Strike Group. With the best will in the world, I can't keep tabs on ten thousand people."

They stared at each other as the seconds ticked by.

"Look," said Joey leaning forwards, "we can just keep poking away at each other, and both get tossed out if anything bad does happen, or we can work together and both come up smelling of roses."

Lundt gave a thin smile. "Oh, I'll help. Been made clear that's what I've got to do. Doesn't mean I have to like it." She pointed at the folder. "You call him the African. Are you sure he is? Couldn't he just be an American?"

"There's no certainty in this but, according to experts, he has racial characteristics and DNA which point to him being of the Ewaga tribe. They hang out half way down Africa and towards the west. African Americans tend to show dissipation of tribal characteristics. And he spoke with an accent."

Lundt wasn't looking convinced. "People emigrate. Maybe he was brought up in Yemen or somewhere. Islamic fundamentalism is our biggest threat, so something like that would make sense. "

"Could be, but I'm afraid that's all we've got to go on." Joey looked around the compartment. "I've served as a trainee Agent Afloat on smaller vessels for short stretches, so I have some idea what your work entails, but maybe you could run through it. There's a lot more crew for a start."

Lundt nodded. "Yeah, but the business we do is pretty much the same. Drugs and alcohol are always problems. The guys bringing it on board are the ones I go for. Might seem strange people can get away with taking stuff like that, living on top of each other like they do. But they still manage, somehow.

"Fights as well. Carrier people have a code of politeness. Have to, the way they scrape by each other in these rat hole passages. Sometimes people don't show the right degree of politeness, the right degree of ..."

"Respect," said Joey.

A wan smile. "Yeah, just like in the ghetto. You don't get what you think you deserve and you get angry." Joey thought back to the two seniors who had steamrollered by her. Maybe the cult of politeness only extended so far up the chain, despite what Lundt and others might have her believe.

"Sexual relationships, that's another cause..." Lundt held up her hands. "I know. How do they find somewhere to do it? You'd be surprised."

Joey bit her lip. "I'm not wanting to be disrespectful but..."

"All low-level stuff, yeah, but I haven't finished. Death pretty much always makes an appearance, even when we're not in a shooting match. Those runways and the hangar deck are lethal. Aircraft handlers blown clear off the deck and out over the safety nets when an engine starts and they're behind it. Or they get sucked into the front. Or squished by all sorts of other moving machinery. And as for those poor guys on the arresters! One of those lines snaps and everyone winds up in two pieces.

"None of this can be construed as death from disease or natural causes, so I've got to investigate, photograph the carnage, write it all up."

"Any espionage investigations at all?"

"Of course! I'm supposed to go through everyone's file on each trip. Get the folks back home to follow up on anything catches my eye. Ten years afloat and I haven't found a damned thing in that line, yet here you come and pick up on two cases without even trying." Lundt shook her head.

"And, of course, shore side's always sending me things to follow up. All these people, some are bound to have got up to no good on their last leave. It all catches up with them. Civil stuff usually, like abandonment of a spouse, but quite a bit of criminal stuff ranging from affray up to...well just about anything,"

"You have cells?"

"There are compartments that can be used as brigs."

"And the other ships in the group? Do they give you much work?"

"Not so cramped, so more room to get up to mischief. And then there are the marines. Crammed in like this with nothing to shoot: they're never going to be trouble free. I guess I have to be choppered across to all the ships at least a couple of times a cruise. Like the sheriff riding into Dodge."

Joey couldn't imagine someone with Lundt's overstuffed frame chasing down a marine. Then again, on a ship even as big as this, there was nowhere to run.

"Clothes," said Joey.

"What about them?"

"You're wearing some, proper ones I mean. Shirt, trousers, not this damned boiler suit they've got me wearing."

"That's what comes of joining a boat when there's already an Agent Afloat. They had to put you with the rest of the crew. That little locker you've got can't hold much. T shirts and knickers, you can change as often as you like, but each boiler suit has to last you a week."

"And where do you sleep?"

Lundt waved her arms around the cabin. "Fold-down bed in that big locker, clothes and personal possession in that smaller one. Civilians usually travel in style compared to the sailors in their racks. Comfortable?"

"Lovely, but for the noise and people always coming and going."

"You get used to it, or so I'm told."

Chapter 7. *The Cleft, Liganda*

The creaking of a rusty hinge, and the blast of light, shocks him back to consciousness. He keeps still but for one hand that creeps slowly to the gun under his pillow. Muffled by the material, the hammer still makes an audible click.

"Whoa!" says a voice in alarm. "It is just me. Altukhov."

Yao cracks open an eye and makes out the blurred shape silhouetted against harsh sunlight.

He eases the hammer back down and rolls over. Lowering the tough soles of his feet onto the splintery wooden floor, he yawns and tries to blink away the sleep.

"Good morning, Special Commander Yao." The Russian accent makes the words richer, fuller bodied. The man steps into the room. "I have a little errand for you." Fifties, black curly hair turning white, the man is too shambling ever to have been a soldier. In this light Yao can't see them, but at other times he's noticed the fine lines around his nose and eyes and ears. Altukhov has had extensive plastic surgery at some point.

"Since when do I do errands for you?"

"I am sorry. What I meant was that the General wants you to do an errand for him. I am just the messenger."

Altukhov has always been a puzzle. Why does the General need him?

"He wants you to bring one of the prisoners to him."

Yao lowers his brow and the Russian holds up his hands. "I know, it sounds demeaning for one such as yourself, but there is more to it than that."

The man shuffles over to a table and tentatively hoists a buttock onto one end. The table creaks alarmingly but he doesn't seem to notice. For a fleeting second Yao has the pleasant image of the man crunching to the ground.

But...if the General trusts him then so should he.

The sun, slanting in over the tops of the trees and through the door, catches myriad dust motes in its hard light. The Russian absently wafts a hand, sending them in swirling trajectories. "You see, we don't know which one. It has to be a leader, or at least someone senior."

"Don't we know that already?"

The man shakes his head. "Their original entry submissions are back in Tembe, no doubt lost in some filing cabinet somewhere. They were picked up in Tigali just a couple of days ago. Tied up and bundled into a couple of *takus*, then a long journey over bumpy roads. It seems to have made them uncommunicative. You speak their language very well. The General wants you to identify the leader."

"What if that person won't talk?"

"The General wants whoever it is to be in his main cabin by midday exactly. Use whatever means are necessary."

"Isn't this sort of thing more in Justice's line. He speaks English just fine."

Altukhov shrugs. "The General's instructions were for you, not Special Commander Nyere." He eases himself upright and begins to lumber towards the door but then stops. "One other thing. By 'leader' I mean the most senior of them who is both white and male."

"Why?"

"It is all part of the plan," says the Russian with a smile. He waddles back out of the door.

Yao reaches down for the khakis he's left folded carefully on the chair by his bed. Getting back late in the evening from seeing Zinzi, he'd been dog tired but, somehow, he always has time to be neat; a result of the General's deeply ingrained discipline. But as he pushes an arm through the sleeve of his shirt, his hand comes close to his nose and he smells her. Looking round, making sure he's unobserved, he brings his fingers right up to his nose and inhales deeply. He's fully erect in an instant and has to struggle not to grasp himself to ease the terrible pain of his desire. He forces himself to think holy thoughts. Minutes pass until his vision of the Holy Mother, black as he is himself, gently calms the savage yearning.

Outside in the clearing his boots kick up dust; the rainy season is late. A month ago water should have been drilling down into the canopy, hitting the leaves and turning to a fine spray, then drenching everything below in a heavy, all pervading mist that turned the earth to mud.

Yao knows the General will be worried. Everything is part of his plan, not least the coming of the rains.

The natural background noise is muted. Birds still sing in the trees but, with all these soldiers, any monkeys have long since been shot for bush meat.

The earthy smell of cooking cassava comes to him. Over fires dotted amongst the trees, cooking pots plop as thick bubbles break the surface of the gruel. Around each fire a squad of men are clustered, eating from bowls or cleaning their weapons.

His stomach growls at him. When had he last eaten? The walk back from Zinzi's village was a long one, and he'd finished the food she'd given him whilst still on the road.

A movement catches his eye and he sees Nafari getting out from under mosquito netting. A miniature bull of a man, he's a similar height to Yao but even more muscular.

Yao walks up to him as Nafari scratches his bottom and winces up at the light.

"Hello, old friend."

Nafari squints, then a smile comes to his face. "The traveller returns."

They kiss each other's right cheeks as is their custom. Nafari smells of hard working days and long nights sleeping on the ground with little water for washing.

"Are you well?"

Yao nods.

"Have you had a chance to see...?"

Yao's smiles and Nafari runs a hand through his cropped hair. "She is far too good for you."

Yao signals at the cooking pot. "Have you lost all your manners? Letting your guests starve while you feast."

Nafari glances doubtfully at the simmering pot. "That would be a favour, not a slight."

"It smells fine to me."

Nafari shrugs and, limping slightly, goes over to the pot. He grabs a fired clay bowl from a pile which may, or may not, have been cleaned. He thrusts it at the soldier tending the fire who reaches slowly over and grabs the ladle. Thick porridge slops into the bowl.

Nafari steps over to a large bunch of blackened bananas, automatically poking it with his foot to dislodge any inhabitants, then picks two. Squatting down, he whips the skins off and unsheathes the knife on his belt. The finger thick dark brown slices hit the surface but hardly made an impression on the porridge. None of this stops Yao shovelling the contents of the bowl into his mouth, relishing the solid, lumpy consistency.

"Apart from cadging food like a beggar, what are doing back with us?"

"I heard you fools needed help. Something about not being able to find your bottoms with both hands. But, today, I have work to do with the prisoners."

Nafari grimaces. "Evil people, telling terrible lies" he says. "Our men," he indicates vaguely with his knife, "wanted to cut their tongues out."

"It's not what the General wants. He has plans for them."

"The General has plans for everyone."

Yao nods. "Where I have been there was little news of Liganda, or at least nothing that wasn't lies. What has been happening?"

"We've been busy. Nthanda has been cleared of colonial whores and unbelievers. Now, all are in their graves."

Yao nods his approval. "It was well defended. How did you do it?"

"The General," says Nafari simply and it is enough. Yao has witnessed other campaigns: has seen the stark brilliance of Olomo's military mind.

"We are blessed that he came to us."

Nafari smiles. "I liked Nthanda," he says. "Many rivers full of mountain water. Cool to bathe in even in summer. The *Land of the Star*, indeed. And now," he smiles, "very few men."

Yao raises an eyebrow. "Surely even Nthandan women wouldn't be desperate enough to take you as a husband?"

"Give them time," says Nafari.

Yao likes to see him smile. As with so many of Olomo's longest serving officers, Nafari's wife is long dead, his children killed along with her while he was being tortured nearly to death by the *Katlegos*. The 'Boiling Stare' soldiers, cats-paws for the multinational oil companies that had been syphoning the riches from Nafari's land for the past twenty years, had used murder and rape as unreflectively as a mechanic uses his tools.

"Anyway," says Yao, "some of us have work to do. I'll leave you to your daydreams. Thank you for the food. It was most delicious."

Nafari snorts. "Ah, Yao, such simple tastes. Perhaps one day you may come to appreciate the finer things in life."

Before he goes, he thinks to ask: "Has all White Squad work been halted?"

"Yes, no more digging wells and harvesting crops for a while. The General needs all hands for the great plan, whatever that is. Don't suppose you'd...."

Yao shakes his head. "Have faith! Olomo knows what he's doing."

Nafari reaches over and runs a finger over Yao's palm. "I've felt breasts that were harder," he says. "No White Squad work for you for a long time, I'm guessing."

"It is my brain that is required for the work I do."

"God save us all!"

Yao glances at his watch. He claps Nafari on the shoulder and wishes him well.

His stomach full, and feeling much the better for it, Yao continues on his way through the forest to the makeshift prison. Though he does not recognise the guards, they must have been expecting him for they let him in unchallenged.

The interior is not much dimmer than the tree shrouded ground outside, so he's soon able to see clearly.

There are barely twenty of them and many are young, perhaps students taking a year off from their studies. Two of the men have dark brown skins, but the rest are white. Seven are women. Shirts and shorts, now grubby, are common though a few wear jeans.

Hands behind them and bound to the ringlets, they form a circle round the cabin. The smell of shit coming from a row of buckets over to the side is awful.

Flies buzz around his head but he stops himself from swatting them away.

There isn't much time left before midday but Yao is confident. Language will not even be necessary. The eyes will be the test. The prisoners are fearful, but it's clear from their faces that some have already slipped into that incurious state of accepting their fate. He has seen it so many times before. In his own village when the *Katlegos* came. Then, many years later, when the tables had turned, he had seen it on the faces of the same men just before they were put to death in their turn.

Dead or fearful eyes are of no interest to him. Yao turns slightly to look at the door then glances quickly back. He sees hatred in one pair of eyes, though the man looks quickly away.

A guard has followed him into the room. "Him," Yao says, pointing. The soldier steps forward, a knife appearing in his hand to cut the bindings.

Yao walks back out into the fractured sunlight as he hears the man dragged to his feet. He hears cuffs clicking into place.

At the bottom of the veranda, he walks a few paces further before turning. The soldier, his hand round the scruff of the man's neck, pushes him out into the sunlight. The man takes a first tentative step down, but the soldier hooks a foot round his leg and shoves his neck, sending him thumping down onto the steps.

The man groans in shock and pain, his head down in the dust with his legs slanted back and upwards.

Yao sits on the steps beside the prone man "You stay like that," he says in English, "while we have a little talk."

The man turns his head sideways and looks at him but says nothing. He has a short beard, blond like his hair but whitening with age. His face is lined but Yao doubts it is with the hardships of the world. Westerners always look younger than they are. Only age finally chisels its way into their skin.

And the man is well fed, of course.

"What is your name?"

The man's blue eyes narrow but still he says nothing.

The soldier raises a foot in the air to slam it down on the back of the man's ankle, but Yao signals him to stop.

The man gulps.

Yao leans forward, just a little. "Really, it is better if you talk to me. One way or the other, you will."

The man hesitates for barely a second then sighs in resignation. "O'Grady."

"Christian name?"

O'Grady looks puzzled. It's not like they're ever going to be friends. "Thomas," he says finally.

"And what is your role? What is your job title Mr. O'Grady?"

"Volunteer," but Yao catches the slight hesitation.

"You're not just a volunteer and my patience is not limitless."

A goat wanders out of the undergrowth beside the track, sees the man on the floor, and stops. Men and goat look at each other for several seconds then it turns and ambles off.

Yao turns back to the man and raises an eyebrow. "Project Leader, right?"

"No," says O'Grady. "He's away in Telu."

Yao glances at the soldier. The man takes one step down with his left foot and drives his right boot between O'Grady's legs. The white man yells and his body skitters fully down off the steps, his face scraping across the dusty ground.

Yao waits patiently for O'Grady to recover.

Eventually, the man's body loses some of its stiffness.

"Project Leader?"

The man shakes his head. "We don't have project leaders," he gasps. "Team Leader."

"I'm sure there's a distinction, but shall we just say you are the boss of all the others back up there?"

"Yes."

"Get him to his feet!"

The soldier grabs O'Grady's shirt and the back of his pants and hauls him upright, the blond man wincing as the fabric cuts into his bruised perineum.

"Follow me!"

Yao checks his watch again then sets off, taking his time while O'Grady shuffles painfully along behind him.

The delicious coolness of the morning is already evaporating. It is going to be a hot day. Everything needs the rains.

"Why are you doing this?"

Yao doesn't bother to turn around.

"We were only trying to help." The man sounds pitifully aggrieved.

Yao shakes his head. "Africa does not need your poisons."

"Vaccinations aren't poisons. They prevent disease."

Yao ignores him.

"Can't you at least let the women go?"

"Are men and women not equal?"

"Not in a situation like this."

Yao smiles. "They either are or they are not equal. You

Americans pay only lip service to equality."

"God save us," O-Grady mutters. "Being lectured to on sexual discrimination by a man who thinks an ointment can ward off bullets."

Yao turns quickly, palm open, his gesture freezing the soldier whose rifle butt is raised and about to come crashing down on the man's skull. Yao doubts the soldier has really understood what O'Grady has said, but he will have recognised the disparaging tone.

"How easily you fall for your own propaganda. What you are talking about is simply a metaphor. The ointment is made from the Oranda root, a plant that grows only in Africa. It is an essence, a sacred anointment, a token of our heartland."

"And do all your soldiers understand it's only a metaphor?"

"There are many soldiers. I cannot speak for them all."

Yao signals and they continue along the dirt track.

Olomo's dilapidated meeting hall begins to appear through the trunks of the tall trees.

"What happens now?" asks O'Grady, his voice breaking embarrassingly.

Many men with sub-machine guns stand guard. One of them standing by the door beckons to them and opens it. As they file into the large single room, Yao is surprised at how full the place is. All the chairs are arranged in rows and are full of middle aged men and women facing forward. To the side sits the General and two of his senior military. Colonel Sylla, who has fought by the General's side for twenty years, is appraising O'Grady with his hard little brown eyes. Beside him Colonel Conteh, round shouldered and almost matronly despite her battle fatigues, is talking animatedly to Olomo.

All chatter ceases as the General rises and points to a spot in front of the audience. As Yao leads O'Grady towards this, he notices two cameras at eye height secured by aluminium poles to the aged timbers of the roof; both are centred on the spot indicated by Olomo. Some curtains have been opened to let in the greenish light, emphasising how ramshackle the place is.

As O'Grady looks at the audience, Yao sees Olomo signalling to him and he makes his way over.

"His name?"

"Thomas O'Grady. Team leader, he says."

Olomo indicates the rows of chairs. Making his way amongst them, Yao spots a couple of spare seats on the end of the back row.

As he settles himself, the General begins.

"Fellow Ligandans. Today we meet at the tribunal of the man called Thomas O'Grady who is charged with espionage and murder. His will be the first of twenty-one such trials as the State seeks justice for the terrible atrocities committed. As the Team Leader of the accused, he is the first before us.

"For the sake of the defendant I will explain, in English, how Blessed African justice functions. Its essence is simplicity. No lawyers or appeals or torts or any of the paraphernalia of so-called developed world justice. All are simply elaborations designed only to make the lawyers and judges rich. There will be no references to previous judicial investigations, no quoting of precedents from other trials, and no legal loopholes available which might allow the guilty to escape. The focus of our justice is that each case is special and must be considered as such. There will be no generic assembly line justice so common in the rest of the world. That is why each case is referred to as a tribunal, not a trial."

Yao smiles. Despite the battles and hardships and all the other horrors of the last twenty years, Olomo is still a lecturer. Thrown into prison and tortured, the military historian had died and the soldier been born, but still some trace of the pedant remains.

"Essence is the key. Witnesses can be bribed, evidence can be tainted. So, we judge the man and how he handles himself before the questioning of our investigator, Major Sayon," and he indicates a slender man, as carefully dressed as the conditions allow, at the near end of the first row of chairs.

"Mr. O'Grady. You are neither stupid nor intellectually handicapped in other ways, is that correct?"

O'Grady has been watching all this with mounting disbelief written across his face. "Is this a military court? I'm a civilian. I should be tried by a civil court."

Olomo sighs. "Mr. O'Grady. You are in Liganda. Tribunals here use *our* legal rules, not yours. It is true that senior, well respected civilians usually serve on this triumvirate," and he indicates Sylla and Conteh at his sides, "but we are at war. Circumstances have forced us to use military personnel."

"What war?" asks O'Grady, cocking his head.

"With the West which, of course, means with the Americans."

"There's no war!"

Olomo shakes his head. "Undeclared, perhaps, but a war nonetheless. Drone strikes may make fighting so clean for Americans that they do not perceive it as war at all, but to those on the receiving end it can be seen as nothing else."

"I don't know anything about drone strikes." The man seems genuinely mystified.

"There have been drone strikes all over Africa. Yemen and Somalai and Libya are the most well-known, but in many other countries as well. However, we are already getting away from the essence. The point is whether you are not sufficiently intelligent or articulate to make your own defence. I think it is obvious to all that that is not the case. However, if you insist, we can appoint a mediator. I should point out that they, like the investigator, are neither solely on your side nor against you. We seek the truth and will not have it made hostage to the skills of either. When the expertise of legal officers becomes a factor, then we see the travesties of justice so common in the West."

He points to the opposite end of the row at a thin man in civilian clothes whose brow is heavily beaded with sweat. "Mr. Nwosu has agreed to act for you this way, if you wish."

O'Grady doesn't appear impressed. "I'll represent myself," he says tightly.

"Major Sayon, please begin." Olomo sits back in his chair and crosses his legs.

Sayon stands up and pulls the bottom of his tunic down to smooth out the wrinkles. Tough but usually urbane, today his intensity is unnerving: no doubt aware of the tens of millions who would come to see this. "Mr. O'Grady, when did you and your colleagues come to Liganda?"

"Just over a year ago, most of us anyway. Some just a few months ago."

"And who do you work for?"

"The Saving Africa Foundation, a non-governmental agency."

"Who funds the SAF?"

"Public subscription, usually. Governments make some contributions but have no say in the running of the Foundation."

"So you say. What about drug companies? Do any drug companies fund this so-called NGO."

"A company called Celeris has donated the vaccine we've been using."

"An anti-malaria vaccine?"

O'Grady nods.

"Has this vaccine been approved for human use by the Food and Drug Administration in the United States or by the European Medicines Agency?"

"Not as yet."

"Why not?"

"Too many regulatory hurdles to be negotiated, taking many years. But people are dying now, in vast numbers, and early trials show the vaccine to be very effective. Look, I'm sure we could get experts in to explain this better."

"Essence," says the General simply.

The man shakes his head in exasperation. "None of us here are experts in vaccines. How can you make any sort of judgement without that?"

"Let me get to the essence, since you seem keen to avoid it," says Sayon evenly. "Vaccines which are not considered safe enough to use in the United States or Europe, are being given to Africans. In the parlance of Big Pharma, they are participants in a Phase II trial. A trial which doesn't even test efficacy of a drug but simply determines how safe, or otherwise, the drug is. In other words: testing how safe a drug might be is done *before* you test to see if it works."

"I'm not an expert, as I've said. I just work for a charitable organisation."

"What are Phase I trials?"

O'Grady doesn't answer and Yao gets the impression he's beginning to see where this is all going.

"Trials on animals. That comes first," says Sayon turning to look at the audience. "After that comes trials on Africans, both Phase II and Phase III. And if all that is successful...well then, and only then, will it be used by people in the Western world."

O'Grady is shaking his head. "It's not as simple as that. Malaria is more prevalent in sub-Saharan Africa than anywhere else in the whole world. There's no point in testing whether a vaccine works by giving it to someone who's never going to be exposed to it anyway."

"Really," says Sayon, "I thought malaria has made its way as far north as New York. Why not use your own people for these tests?"

O'Grady is becoming exasperated. "Over ten thousand people die a year of malaria in this country alone. A handful die in the States, and usually from contracting the disease during foreign travel."

"Was this explained to your African guinea pigs? In fact, did you fully inform them of what you were going to do to them."

"Of course," says O'Grady.

"You know that is not correct. Your people told hardly anyone anything."

O'Grady takes a deep breath. "Clinical trials are extremely complex, as is this disease. The education system here is..."

"The people were too ignorant to give what you would call 'informed consent', is that not right? So, you... what is the expression you would use... glossed over it."

"We were just trying to help. Just trying to save thousands of lives. Lives of your countrymen."

"Very laudable. But tell me, what were the results of this trial? How many people died from malaria, how many suffered serious after effects from the drug. How many did the drug itself kill?"

"There were no such additional significant side effects that I know of in the Phase II studies."

"Hair loss, ulcers, psychosis, liver disease, neurological degeneration, heart problems, teratogenesis..."

"I'm sorry," the General interrupts. "We cannot have essence without clarity."

"Induction of birth defects, General. Also, induction of abortion..."

O'Grady shakes his head. "All anti-malaria drugs produce some side effects like that. The incidence of side effects is low and must be balanced against the effects the drugs have against a potentially fatal disease."

Now Sayon is the one shaking his head. "But, in order to see if it does help against the disease, you do large scale Phase III trials. Which may reveal, if the drug is not as effective as you would hope, that it may do much more harm than good. Correct?"

For some reason the American's eyes settle on Yao. He finds himself unable to meet them. Instead he runs his eyes over the termite roughened log walls.

"Please answer," says Sayon.

"Yes, that is how our knowledge of medicines advances."

"And if the drug does more harm than good...well it's only Africans who will get hurt. And, of course, it is even more outrageous than that. Phase II is only an approximate indicator of safety. Larger scale Phase III trials often show ill effects Phase II studies don't. For example: the drug may even make people more susceptible to malaria. Isn't that possible?"

O'Grady shakes his head but doesn't answer.

"Five years from now, perhaps a statistician looking at the nationwide incidence of malaria might be able to say one way or the other. But not you, not now."

Olomo leans forward.

"The *essence* please, Major."

Sayon nods. "This man is accused of supervising the administration of a drug, considered unsafe for Americans or Europeans, to over ten thousand Africans. And, of course, this is not the first time this has happened. Most of the major drug companies, Big Pharma as they are called, test their new drugs in this way. Even for conditions like heart disease that are a developed world problem, somewhat giving the lie to Mr. O'Grady's assertion that drugs are tested where the prevalence is greater. Quite simply, they are tested here on poor people who do not have the regulatory protection to ensure standards are properly applied. If they are injured or die because of the medicine, expensive legal action against such rich western companies is impossible for these poor people. In fact, using Africans is even cheaper than using animals in Phase I trials. In the descent to the 'bottom line', how long before Africans replace even laboratory rats?"

Sayon turns to look at Olomo. "This degradation must be stopped. That, General, is the essence."

Yao feels a tinge of sympathy for O'Grady. Perhaps by his own standards he has not been acting badly, perhaps he really has no perspective on the brutal racism inherent in his position. He wonders how American blacks, so called African Americans, could let such things happen. Or how they keep gorging themselves while their brothers starved in Africa? Or sit by while their companies raped the continent of its natural resources.

"This is crazy," O'Grady is saying. "We're a charity, we're

volunteers. We came to do *good*. The vaccinations were only part of it. We sank wells, bought livestock, provided medical care. We helped."

Sayon waves a hand dismissively. "It was the British who first invaded us and, when we fought for our freedom, labelled us 'terrorists'. They executed hundreds, starved thousands. They set one tribe against another. Then you, the Americans, the bastard successors of the British, came to plunder our wealth. Not with soldiers but with men wearing business suits. Your country has taken billions from Africa in oil and copper and rare earths, has exploited us and toppled our governments when they tried to object. And now here you are, testing your drugs on our people and trying to tell us you are giving something back."

He snorts in disgust and, turning his back on O'Grady, he goes to resume his seat.

Olomo and his senior officers bend their heads together to confer and the audience begins quietly chatting. Yao, junior in this company, keeps silent and instead watches the blond man struggling to comprehend.

"Is that it?" says the American disbelievingly. "You can't be serious. Where's your evidence?"

The tribunal ignores him.

"Don't I even get a chance to put my case?"

And as they are paying no attention, he tries to do just that, his voice rising to a shout until, at a signal from Olomo, a soldier punches him in the kidney. O'Grady arches right back and starts to topple over, but a couple of soldiers catch him and keep him upright until he gets his breath back.

The decision doesn't take long. Olomo suddenly clears his throat and there is immediate silence. Outside and from high up, a bird, hidden amidst the canopy from the hungry soldiers' gunfire, caws loudly.

"Mr. O'Grady, you are condemned from your own mouth. You have used Africans as little better than laboratory animals. For this you will be executed."

"Come on! You can't do this. This wasn't a trial, it was a witch hunt. I've done nobody any harm."

Olomo looks over at the guards. "Take him away!"

"Don't I get an appeal? I didn't understand my life was on the line. I didn't understand your system. I want a lawyer."

"That would not change the facts Mr. O'Grady. May the Blessed African forgive you!"

O'Grady's mouth flops open as he's pulled to his feet but no sound emerges. The soldiers drag him backwards, heels scraping over the rough wooden floor.

Olomo stands and, behind him and to one side, Yao notices an ancient grandfather clock for the first time. On its face is a gilt crescent moon with what appears to be a cow jumping over it. It's odd to see something like that in this place.

Distracted, he almost misses what Olomo says next.

"We must all bear witness," and with this, Olomo follows the soldiers out.

Yao hangs back as the older men and women file out then follows respectfully in their footsteps. A short walk through the towering trees brings them to a small clearing. By the time he gets there, O'Grady's arms have been pulled back and secured around the trunk of a tree. "No," he keeps repeating.

A firing squad has already been convened, eight men standing in a raggedy line three metres from the American. To the side, a camera crew is setting up.

"Can't I have a phone call? Just one to my wife and kids in the States. Please!"

Yao notices Justice standing to the side of the squad. A grim little smile is playing across his long face. The big scar beneath his beard is not visible in the high sun.

A sergeant, over six-foot tall and a giant in this company, steps forward with a rag. Yao doesn't hear what he says to O'Grady but the American shakes his head. The sergeant walks back to the line and looks across at Olomo.

Olomo himself is looking at the cameramen who are

making final adjustments. Then one of them looks back at Olomo and nods. The General glances across at the Sergeant who has now turned to face the American.

"You shits," says O'Grady. "You fucking shits. You frightened little fucking shits."

"Take aim," calls the sergeant.

"Oh sweet Jesus," wails O'Grady.

"Aim."

"No, for God's sake, no!"

"Fire!"

The bullets kick a hole in O'Grady's chest. His head and torso fall limply forward. Yao can see shattered ribs protruding, like sideways rows of teeth in a gaping bloody maw.

He looks across at the General's stern face.

They have goaded the lion and must now await its wrath.

Chapter 8. *USS Benjamin F. Sands, Eastern Atlantic*

It was only 9am but already they'd been sparring for two solid hours. Joey's eyes ached from all the files that had flitted across the monitors, Lundt usually dismissing them before she could get a proper look.

"Put that one back up! What do you mean you can vouch for him? Every file you say the same thing. You can't know all ten thousand people."

"I've been on this boat forever so I know plenty of them. And when you sail with someone, believe me you get to know them real well."

Joey was sick of Lundt's whining, defensive tone."Gimme a break! What about Hierra? How well did you know him?"

Lundt's nostrils flared. "I didn't say I knew them all. Anyway, his money troubles were recent."

"Look, this so-called 'sense check' you're applying is eliminating everyone. No crew is this clean." She knew this wasn't quite true. Now and then Lundt hadn't immediately given a clean bill of health to someone, perhaps by way of throwing her a bone. Joey was beginning to suspect that even those few were just people who'd rubbed her up the wrong way. Whatever. Her colleagues back in Norfolk could dig deeper, though she'd heard that her partner Harlan wasn't available. Apparently, he was off chasing a lead on the African in Scotland, of all places.

The telephone warbled. Lundt took the call and listened intently.

"Right now?" she asked.

Whatever the response was, it was short and to the point, leaving Lundt surprised and looking uselessly at the phone in her hand.

"Joint Intelligence Centre. They want us up there right

now."

"They?"

"Orders from Macik himself."

Joey pursed her lips and nodded. "Can't wait."

Back into the labyrinth again. Joey tagged along, following Lundt's ample bottom as it wobbled up the steep stairways towards 'O3'. In the starboard long passageway, oncoming sailors were forced to flatten themselves against the bulkhead as Lundt squeezed past. Joey saw a few give little smiles. People on the boat were young and generally pretty lean; it was like being in a sports college. Matronly Lundt in her civilian gear was an oddity.

They passed doors with signs indicating squadron ready rooms. One open door showed a space densely textured with trophies, banners, photos and plaques: like some kind of antique shop for military nuts. Fly boys in their aviation suits were already lounging around and doodling on pads. One or two checked her out desultorily as she passed, the black boiler suit hiding whatever skinny charms she might have to offer.

Then a series of open doors to port revealed the biggest compartment she'd seen on the ship, at perhaps half its width. Massive cylinders thick as oil pipelines lay forward to aft.

"What are those things for?"

Lundt turned ponderously and made her way back. "Hydraulics for the arresting gear. Got to absorb vast amounts of energy very quickly to bring one of those birds to a stop."

The place smelled of lubricating oil but the gleaming metal of the cylinders, and even the floor itself, were spotless. The whole ship was navy style clean but she hadn't seen machinery this pristine except in museums.

"Why's it so...?"

"Clean?"

"Yeah."

"I know a guy works here. Says the floor is clean enough to eat my breakfast off it, though I've always politely declined. It's something to do with leaks. They show up better if the place is clean. Hydraulic leaks apparently are a bad thing when you're trying to stop a 30-ton Tomcat so quickly that the pilot's eyes pop out on stalks like in a cartoon."

Joey wondered if breakfast was the only thing Marceline had been invited to eat but cast the thought aside. Not because it was cheap, though it was, but because she still couldn't figure out how anyone could find the privacy to fuck in this ant farm.

Starting off again, the central passageway and all the corridors leading off it suddenly changed in appearance. Dull Navy grey gave way to sky blue. Joey usually didn't have much time for aesthetics but any change from the monotonous background was like seeing colour for the first time.

"Blue tile country," said Lundt over her shoulder. "This is where the big boys play."

Lundt turned off the main passageway and, after a few more corners, they came to a door saying simply 'JIC'. As they entered, to a room full of the usual jumble of workstations, the first thing she noticed was that everyone was wearing sweaters, the next was the aircon cold that struck her like a bucket of iced water. Goosebumps rose on her exposed flesh. From an open door at the back of the compartment a beehive of servers hummed away.

Important people change a room's centre of gravity. Macik, off to the side near a big wall mounted screen, was exerting the gravitational influence of a black hole. Crewmen with clipboards or electronic signature devices formed a line leading away from him. Macik seemed intent on dealing with these supplicants. Meanwhile, several senior men hung about uselessly, like punks on a Baltimore street corner. One thinner, slightly stooped guy had the insignia for CO, so this must be Larsen. He looked unimpressive for someone in direct command of such a massive vessel and its crew.

While they waited for something to happen, Joey cast an eye over the other crew in the room who were beavering away at a dozen or so workstations.

"Busy place," she said.

"Yeah. Information nexus. Nerve centre if you will. Just about everything of import gets routed through here."

"I got the impression this summons was quite urgent."

"Me too."

"So what are we waiting for? Why's Macik still doing his paperwork. Doesn't he have an XO for that?"

Lundt pointed at a doughy white guy who was sitting on the edge of a desk, arms folded. "That's Essen there."

Joey watched as crewmen entered and left, Macik's line of supplicants not getting any smaller. Essen pursed his lips and looked fixedly at the floor.

"Delegation issues?"

"Uh huh. We could be some time."

But eventually Macik checked his watch then shooed those in the line out of the JIC. After the door was closed on them, he looked round and nodded at Joey and Lundt. Then he turned and raised his eyebrows at a guy sitting at a desk further down the room. "Commander Terni?"

Terni was thickset and, unlike the others, was wearing a short-sleeved shirt which showed hairy arms. He stood quickly and made his way to the other end of the room where the largest of the flat screen displays was positioned. He motioned to another guy who started clicking away at a console.

Meanwhile Lewis had squeezed in behind them.

"We've got an early heads-up on this, but it'll be on the networks within the hour," said Terni. "It comes from Liganda, a country in west Central Africa."

The display came to life and a room full of black men and women were staring balefully at a blond white man whose hands were cuffed behind his back. Terni pointed at him. "Thomas O'Grady. US citizen. Aid worker. Employed by a charitable foundation devoted to good works in Africa."

Now he pointed at three beribboned figures. "General Olomo, essentially the President of the country. The woman next to him is Colonel Conteh and the other guy we can't yet put a name to. What happens next is, as you'll see, self-explanatory."

They watched the kangaroo court take its inevitable course. After sentence was pronounced, the camera panned to follow the prisoner out of the door.

Joey sat bolt upright. "Whoa!" she shouted. "Stop!" and she started forward, hand outstretched towards the screen. "Take it back just a little!"

The picture froze and started to rewind. "Stop!"

The end of a row of chairs. "This man! Can you zoom on him?"

The picture expanded and got a little grainy, but it was enough. "It's him," she said excitedly. "The guy in Norfolk! The guy we've been calling the African."

Macik was nodding his head. "Another piece in the puzzle. Continue!"

A decade of web-available execution footage had, thankfully, not dulled their outrage. The sense of suppressed anger was palpable in the room as they watched O'Grady meet his end.

"Commander Terni. Background if you will!" Macik's command was almost a bark.

Terni was nodding and spreading his hands. "Some have called Olomo the Black Gaddafi, but that's a dangerous underestimation. Gadaffi may have been crazy and self-indulgent but, all said and done, he also wasn't that bright. He managed to get by pretty much on brutality alone. Olomo does plenty that looks nuts to us, but he's also unquestionably brilliant.

"Guy majored in military history at the University of Edinburgh, Scotland, then did a postdoc at the University of Birmingham, England. Demonstrated a remarkable tactical insight for wars already fought anyway. Could have had a cosy life as a military historian in the developed world but made the mistake of going home.

"Back then the Brits were giving it all away. The sun had pretty much set on the Empire and they were getting out. The

USSR was always stoking things up in Africa back in those days, so the Brits at least exercised some discretion. They tended to favour tribal leaders further to the right than the left."

Terni shook his head. "That didn't always work out. And it wasn't just the Brits, pretty much all the European nations did the same, even little ones like Belgium. What they did in the Congo while they were there beggars belief. Ten million died and then another five million inter-tribal killings afterwards. Without the colonial powers keeping tribal rivalries in check, it all got very nasty.

"Mamadou was the thug the Brits left in charge of Liganda. Guy was a beast and from a different tribe than Olomo. Olomo comes back from the UK full of hope now the British are gone. Wanted to build his country up. Jailed and tortured for his pains, like most of his family and friends, but fled to the bush before he wound up in the usual mass burial pit.

"Then twenty years of civil war: outgunned, outnumbered, nobody to help him, not even the Russians who had more meaty pots to stir."

Terni smiled grimly. "But eventually he won and on several fronts at once. Founded resistance movements in the neighbouring countries of Niassa and Bukana. Governments overturned, Olomo's puppets in place.

"Gotta hand it to him there. Niassa and Bukana: different colonial masters, different languages and, here's the rub, different predominant tribes. Yet they all now dance to his tune. That's a neat trick to pull off in Africa."

Macik inclined his head. Though he'd hardly moved, they all looked at him. "That's an important point. Olomo had some sort of wilderness conversion, or so the story goes. A vision of the 'Blessed African' who now guides him. This God-like creature supposedly has no tribe or, rather, is of all tribes."

Terni was shaking his head. "And maybe that's where Olomo's real craziness lies. In the West we talk of Africa like it was a country, but nothing could be further from the truth. They're not like the individual States back home. Africa is nearly sixty quite separate countries made up of something like three thousand different tribes. Uniting them under one banner, as seems to be Olomo's vision, is never going to happen."

Macik was smiling. "Not so sure. Empires are never born fully formed. They get built up by uniting disparate peoples and cultures. Roman, Greek, Chinese and, even today, look at the European Union. That's the only one not brought about by war and suppression, not directly anyway, but it's still a form of empire. I'm not saying that Olomo hasn't got his work cut out for him, but it's not beyond the bounds of possibility. What we have here is a potential Black Napoleon.

"Anyway," he continued. "Commander Terni, perhaps you would describe the General's latest shenanigans."

"The forces at Olomo's command are, frankly, trivial by our standards. We have nothing to fear from him militarily. However, what he does have he uses extremely effectively. Whether Olomo's crusade to unite Africa is madness or not, he has managed to destabilise the whole region. Civil wars are breaking out like brush fires along the Gulf of Guinea.

"One point worth emphasising is that the State department has been advocating all US citizens should leave the region, but unfortunately that's easier said than done. Ever since China became cagey about letting other nations buy its own Rare Earths, this region of Africa has been the place to go, so we have a lot of our mining people there. Add in all the aid work being done, plus citizens of our allies working there, and the numbers of westerners climb into the five-figure range."

Joey put up her hand like a school kid. Terni nodded at her.

"Rare Earths?" she said.

Terni smiled slightly. "Produced by supernova nucleosynthesis." Several people gave mocking whistles and there were even some chuckles, though she noticed Macik wasn't joining in.

106

"I know," said Terni, milking it," here in JIC we speak of little else. Seriously though, all the matter on this planet is made from the debris of stars. However, Rare Earths aren't just produced in any old exploding star, which is why they're so rare. Stuff like coltan and tantalite are used in everything from cell phones to tablets. They're formed where molten rock crystallized out, a long time ago and deep down. Needs the covering crust to have been whittled down by long periods of wind and time.

"Sub-Saharan Africa, especially in Niassa and points north, is now second only to China for the stuff. Until recently China supplied 95% of Rare Earths but then got pissy about it. Everyone's been scrambling to find alternatives ever since."

Macik stood and again easily commanded their attention. "So what we have here is a clear and present danger to the twenty remaining hostages, plus potential danger to many more. And that's where we come in. There's nothing like a CSG to calm things down, so the President has ordered us to steam there and help get the foreign nationals out asap."

He turned to look back at the screen and at O'Grady's frozen, dangling body. "This doesn't fit," he mused. "This is a provocation, pure and simple. And it's madness. What have they got by way of air cover...?" he held up a hand to stop Terni who had gone to answer.

"Two Czech Aero Albatros," said Macik, answering his own question, "one of which was grounded, last we heard. A couple of Aermacchi trainers and five transport helicopters at most. They're all a joke, not even worth batting aside if it came to a shooting war. We could almost just ignore them."

Joey didn't bother to put her hand up this time. "Can I speak freely? About the events in Diggs Town."

"This is the JIC," said Macik. "They're all cleared."

"Maybe he's put his faith in his saboteurs."

"Maybe, but that would be more from hope than judgement. One small bomb isn't going to stop a CSG."

"Maybe there's more than one."

"Of course," said Macik. "That's where you and Special Agent Lundt come in."

Chapter 9. *The Cleft, Liganda*

Yao awakes with a start. Something big is crashing through the foliage. There's a thud and a volley of explosions, then all is silent.

Clambering from the bunk now musty with his sweat, he grabs his AK and staggers to the door.

But it's darker outside than in and he hesitates at the threshold. Around him he hears confused shouting. A couple of torch beams split the darkness.

"It came from over there," someone shouts.

"Where? We can't even see *you*," Yao yells, his head turning towards the head of the valley. "Keep shouting and we'll come to you."

A steady ululation marks whoever it is as a north westerner, from the dusty Lialan plains. Yao can hear others homing in towards the sound, crunching through the dry leaves and twigs. Torches cast dancing cones of light in the faint early mist as it clings to the trees.

The light helps but the beams come and go too quickly. Crooking his arm for protection, he holds it out in front of him at eye height. Leaves and branches flick at his skin and he jams his eyes closed as they brush over his head.

Then his forearm slams into a tree and he only just manages to stop before his body crashes into it.

Ahead through the trees he sees two torch beams converge and fix on a single waving man.

Now he can move more quickly and soon catches up. "Which way?"

The soldier, teeth bright in the lights, jabs a thumb back

over his shoulder. "Not far," he says. "Maybe it was just a monkey falling."

"Yes, exploding monkeys are a problem round here," says Yao. Other soldiers are joining them. "Give me your torch!"

The man hesitates but then hands it over. "Do you think it's Special Forces then?"

Yao ignores him. "You," he points to another torch holder. "10 metres to the right, I'll take the left. Keep your torch pointing ahead. And hold it away from your body as far to your left as you can. That way, if they take a shot at it, they'll miss you."

The soldier doesn't look pleased.

"The rest: in a line between the two of us. If it's Special Forces they'll have automatic weapons so they'll have to hold them close. Aim for the muzzle flash."

Striding to the left, he hears the men shuffle into a ragged line behind him.

As the men move slowly forward, Yao's beam flickers over odum and ebony, the trunks casting black shadows into the mist.

"Oi, just ahead!" a soldier several positions along the row whispers. Yao tracks his beam to follow the man's gesturing arm.

There's a mass, like a boulder on the forest floor. Try as he might he can't quite resolve it: its bulk transected by shadows cast by the tree trunks.

The soldiers have gone into a crouch, pulling back the slides, guns aimed forward and ready to fire. He signals them further down until they're all stretched out on the dusty ground. Fixing his line, he flicks off the torch and starts to crawl forward.

Coarse fibred grass and spindly ferns brush at his cheeks. To his right he hears faint grunts from men propelling themselves forward on their elbows.

All else is silence.

Then he hears them coming. From somewhere ahead, somewhere low down, comes a scratching sound. Risking it, he raises the torch above his head but points ahead and down. The light flashes over the forest floor and into the red eyes of the scuttling things.

The light is a trigger, kicking the creatures into urgent motion. Surging forward they're upon the men before they can struggle up.

Men scream in terror and something hits his face, hard little legs clambering over his head. One pokes deep into his ear. Yelling in alarm, he flicks his head, trying to dislodge it. Scrambling upright, torch falling from terrified fingers, he feels the thing lose its purchase and drop away.

His AK roars and the muzzle flash casts a brutal flickering flame, dirt exploding upwards where it meets the earth.

But the thing is already gone.

The other man's torch comes on again and flicks across the grass and ferns, populating the ground with malevolent shadows. Guns explode into life all around but the creatures have disappeared, lost in the spindly vegetation and the dark of the forest floor.

"Is anybody hurt?"

"I think I shit myself," says a surprised voice. "What were they?"

"Rats, I think," says someone else.

"Or spiders," says another.

"We go forward again," says Yao. "But we won't crawl this time."

He picks up the torch and soon the line of men is moving through the trees, scooting for cover from tree trunk to tree trunk.

A movement to the left makes him jerk the torch round. A thick black tail, with a slow sinuous thrust, is disappearing into a clump of azaleas. "Don't shoot," he says. "It's just a snake."

"A big one," says a soldier. "Bigger than I've ever seen round here."

Yao brings his light back to bear on the boulder-like object. Close enough now to make out its boxy shape, it looks like a grey cube with many black circles stuck to it. Yao and the other man with the torch push ahead and around it, their triangulating beams

111

not finding anyone lurking behind.

The object is draped in a spider's web of thin lines. Following the lines up with the torch he sees the parachute canopy high above them, hopelessly entangled in the branches.

Coming closer now, he sees the sides of the crate lying flat on the ground, and guesses they'd been impelled off by explosive bolts. That would have been the firecracker sound. The black circles resolve themselves into cylindrical holes drilled all the way through. The crate is a matrix, like a honeycomb.

"Do you think that's were those things came from," says a voice beside him.

"I think so," says Yao.

"It's the Americans. They have sent in plague rats to kill us."

"Nonsense," says Yao, trying to keep himself calm. "Perhaps it was a food drop from one of our own planes. Maybe rats got into it and ate everything."

"What food drops? Supplies come in by lorry."

Brighter lights begin to flash through the trees. The men watch, shielding their eyes as they come closer.

Through his fingers Yao can make out the tall figure of Olomo leading his squad of body guards. Without hesitation he walks up to the cube box and thrusts his lantern at it.

"What was in this?"

"Plague rats," says a soldier.

"We don't know that," says Yao and the General turns his light on him.

"Ah, Yao, good man." He sounds pleased. "Tell me what happened."

"An airdrop crashing down through the tree canopy woke us up. As we approached many small things, perhaps rats, were scurrying away from it."

"They attacked us," says another soldier.

Yao sighs. "There was no attack. We were just in the way. Nobody was hurt."

"Don't forget the snake," says the soldier.

"What snake?"

"A big black one, thicker than a mamba, slithered into the undergrowth over there."

Another light, held by a soldier, is approaching and behind it, bobbing in and out of view, is the white face of the Russian. As he gets nearer they can hear his hurried breathing.

Catching sight of the box he slows to a stop and puts his hands on his hips.

"It has started," says Olomo.

He hears them baying, like banshees lost in the forest, before he even hears the rumble of the trucks. The afternoon sun has already disappeared beyond the valley's craggy sides, but the heat is still high. Few breezes can find their way into the heavily wooded Cleft.

The first truck has a flat bed with uprights nailed to the sides. Over this spreads a mesh of chicken wire, already half chewed off by the slavering hounds.

As the truck jerks to a halt, the heavy dogs thump against each other, growling savagely.

Five more trucks pull up higgledy-piggledy across the small clearing.

"Boerboels," says someone just behind him. It's Justice and he's nodding his long face appreciatively. "This should be fun."

Olomo strolls out of his cabin, his bodyguards springing to attention as he passes. Reaching the first truck he goes to the driver who is untying the binding wire of the makeshift gate. "Let me!" he says.

The driver steps back. "They've been travelling for hours in the sun. Be careful."

But Olomo is already curling back the chicken wire and thrusting his hand under the nearest dog's nose. Its big square head sniffs daintily around the outstretched fingers. Olomo claps his hand on the scruff of its neck and tugs it back and forth. Soon the other dogs are trying to hustle each other out of the way to get their turn to be mauled.

Olomo and the driver begin hauling the great beasts off the truck. They thud to the ground and begin stretching and yawning. The other drivers are quickly unloading, and soon twenty or so mastiffs are sniffing at the crotches of the soldiers who've gathered round to watch the show.

"They're smart fuckers these dogs," says Justice. "Good at telling friend from foe. Best not make any sudden moves though."

Olomo looks back at the cabin and waves. The Russian hobbles out, carrying some cloth. As he gets nearer, he becomes hesitant and slows.

"Not a good idea," says Justice sucking his breath in through pursed lips. "Got to be confident with these monsters."

Hackles are already rising so Olomo strides over quickly to the Russian and puts his arm round his shoulder. He grabs the cloth with his other hand and, tugging the Russian along, makes his way back to the dogs.

The Boerboels are still giving the Russian the evil eye but the cloth is distracting them. To Yao it just looks like an oily rag. They sniff at it then draw back, not pleased with the smell.

Letting go of the white man, Olomo strides into the midst of the dogs and makes a far-flung gesture with the arm holding the cloth.

The dogs scatter like a grenade, lolloping away into the trees.

"Get the meat," Olomo calls over to one of his bodyguards. The man drags a case from the passenger seat of one of the lorries and starts to open it.

Angry squawks erupt from the trees but these turn quickly to alarm and soon the first dog is back, blood spotting the chicken's white feathers. Right up to Olomo it comes, the bird limp in its jaws. The General leans down, grabs the two webbed feet and brings the flat of his other hand crashing down on the dog's

114

head.

Stunned, the dog lets go of the bird and shuffles back.

"Brave man," says Justice.

Olomo thrusts the rag at the dog and again makes the all-encompassing gesture. The dog looks hungrily at the chicken but then whirls round and is gone.

All around the forest chickens are dying loudly and, when the next dog bounds into the clearing, Yao is expecting more bloodied feathers.

But what the dog drops at Olomo's feet is no chicken. It looks like the biggest beetle Yao has ever seen. On its back now, the creature can't get purchase so its six black legs, single jointed but each segment perfectly straight, are waggling frantically in the air. Then one leg rotates through an impossible one eighty degrees and stabs down into the ground, flipping the black body over and onto its front.

Its legs already frantically pumping, it hits the ground running, but Olomo's big boot comes smashing down on its back.

Some of the legs are still kicking but, broken backed, it isn't going anywhere

"What the fuck is that?" whispers Justice.

Olomo tosses a big lump of meat at the dog.

More dogs come lolloping into the clearing, all carefully skirting the first dog tearing ferociously at its meat. Some bring chickens but others come with the machines. Soon the ground is littered with the broken bodies of both.

Yao kneels down by one of the crippled creatures. His eyesight is good and he can make out the tiny lens on each quadrant of its body. He guesses the little nubbin on its matt black carapace is a pinhead mike.

"The antenna is in the carapace," Yao feels Olomo's hand on his shoulder. The big man kneels beside him, takes out his knife and drives it into the thing's midline.

With a twist, it's suddenly in two parts and Yao can see wires and a tiny printed circuit board.

"Those tiny things are servo motors," says Olomo pointing with his knife tip. "And that…" the tip comes to rest on a silver lozenge, "is the battery."

The Russian has ambled over. "There will be a drone up there acting as a relay." He's pointing to the little bit of sky visible above them. "It'll be sending and receiving signals, boosting them, allowing communications with Niger."

"Niger?"

"Nearest US drone base."

"Snake!" someone shouts.

Looking quickly round, Yao sees the mastiff, tail waggling, dragging the swirling black thing into the clearing.

Always hating snakes, he's instantly on his feet and ready to run. But then he sees the snake's sinuous movements are too slow, too machine like. This is no flesh and blood creature writhing in agony.

The dog drops the snake at Olomo's feet. A thrust from his knife pins it to the ground.

The Russian comes forward and puts on his glasses. "That looks like something the Israeli's were up to. It can even get up steps. Can rear up like a real snake so the camera at the head can look in through windows." Putting his feet on its head and tail he pulls out his own knife then slits the thing along its length. Finding the battery, he prises it out and the writhing ceases.

The Russian shows the soldiers what to do and soon the batteries are being hacked out of the machines the dogs bring them. They're kept busy for a while, but finally the dogs are bringing back neither machines nor chickens.

"General," says Yao quietly.

Olomo looks at him and smiles for him to continue.

"I see these things are here to spy on us. That is clear. But why have they used these two different types, the spider and the snake?"

The Russian laughs and Olomo smiles.

"Because, my friend, we are an easy target. We are weak

and the American's know they will win. So, they can afford to test out their new weapons. It's like with the vaccine. We are just guinea pigs again. Everything is tried out first on the poor African."

Chapter 10. *Edinburgh, Scotland*

The brooding castle, perched bleakly on rock made black by the drizzly rain, looked down on Harlan Weiss as he made his way through the chilly city. Tourists, disappointed and bedraggled in the rain, jostled each other on sidewalks too narrow for comfort.

It'd been a mistake to let the taxi drop him off on Prince's Street, the main thoroughfare, rather than take him all the way. But he'd never even been to the UK before and the agency wasn't going to let him stay here for long. He'd wanted to see the sights.

Checking his phone again for directions, he took a right across a bridge next to the main station then, between ancient buildings towering over nine stories above him, he found a street rising steeply in a half spiral. But for the endless coffee shops and the cars, he could have been back in Charles Dickens' time but with added gothic overtones.

Reaching the top of the street, he crossed the Royal Mile, canned Highland music playing from a string of tartan tourist shops leading up to the castle. Then the phone took him down a long flight of narrow stairs into a valley between long rows of these tall, ancient buildings. In winter, with the sun always low in the sky at this high latitude, this place must be in perpetual gloom.

Coming to a narrow little road, Weiss spotted the plain clothes cop right away. More upright and outwardly more severe than the ones he was used to, nevertheless there was that certain air of confidence about the man. He would be used to telling members of the public what to do.

He watched as Weiss approached. "Special Agent Weiss?" he asked, the pallor of his skin showing just the faintest touches of redness in his cheeks.

'Do they never get the sun in this country?' Weiss thought.

Weiss nodded and stretched his hand out.

The man looked pleased. "I'm Sergeant McMillan, your liaison, which makes it sound very official." He was smiling, the freckled hand shaking Weiss's in a firm grip.

"Mind if I see your documentation?" asked McMillan apologetically.

"Sure," said Weiss showing his wallet ID and passport, fished out from the inside pocket of his long black overcoat.

McMillan gave it all the once over but didn't seem to be trying too hard. "Nice flight?" he asked.

"OK," replied Weiss. "Cattle class, of course."

"Of course. Our bosses aren't made of money, or so they say. Have they put you up somewhere nice?"

"The Primrose Hotel, over on Lothian Road. Know it?"

McMillan squinted a little. "Not what you're used to I'll bet."

"I've been in better. Look...do you mind if I ask something before we go in?"

"Nothing," said McMillan emphatically. "Scotsmen wear nothing under their kilts."

It took longer than Weiss would have liked to admit for him to realise this was a joke. He smiled but maybe a little tightly. He liked to think he had a good a sense of humour, but work was work. The Brits just didn't seem to get that. Everyone he'd met in this damp little country seemed determined to inject quips or wry observations into any communication. Almost like they were afraid of anything serious.

"No, that wasn't what I was asking. It's to do with guns. You don't have one, right? We're going into a ..." he indicated the dirty grey building looming over them, "...low rent multiple occupancy building where a terrorist may have stayed, and we're going to do it unarmed."

McMillan was looking back at him in disbelief. "Mrs. Anderson's over seventy. Don't worry: if she cuts up rough I'll protect you."

"That's not what I meant."

"Isn't it?"

A scuffed panel by the door had names scrawled on little bits of paper stuck next to a stack of buzzers. McMillan checked for Anderson's name and buzzed.

They waited, glancing back at the rain slick cobbles as a car rattled over them.

"Hello," said a woman's tremulous voice.

McMillan leaned into a little grill where the sound was coming from. "This is Sergeant McMillan of the Lothian Police again, with Special Agent Weiss from the United States. He's from the NCIS, like on the telly."

"Third floor left, as you know, Sergeant. I'll be waiting." The door buzzed and McMillan pushed it open.

The entranceway ceiling was high, fading white distemper covering the walls. White painted pipes, clinging to the crevice between ceiling and wall where a cornice might once have been, looked suspiciously old and possibly made of lead.

It was chill and damp like the grave.

McMillan led him up long flights of stairs, at each landing a little window, dirt blackened strands of spider's web in its corners, gave rising views of the opposite tenement barely fifteen feet away.

They came to a landing where the right-hand door was festooned in blue and white police tape. The door to the left was open and Mrs. Anderson was waiting for them. She was a little stooped perhaps, but her demurely dyed light brown hair and unlined skin made her look late fifties at most. Weiss doubted she could have lived in a place like this all her life.

"Come away in," she said, leading them into a better furnished apartment than he had been expecting. Straitened circumstances brought about by death or a divorce, he guessed.

"Tea, coffee? Can I get you a nice wee bit of shortbread?"

"That would be very nice. Tea for me, please" said McMillan, settling into a well stuffed armchair near the window.

"Coffee for me, please. Cream and sugar."

Mrs. Anderson looked a little taken aback.

The two men sat watching each other as Mrs. Anderson left the room. They could hear her pottering about in the kitchen.

"That'll be her gone to fetch her sidearm," said McMillan.

Weiss sighed. "Give me a break, OK!"

McMillan shrugged. "I don't suppose you'll give me any more information about why you want this man."

"Can't. National security."

"OK, but no waterboarding Mrs. Anderson, mind. She might get onto her MP."

"Military policemen?"

"Member of Parliament, of the British parliament to be precise. Like one of your senators, or representatives or congressman or whatever. I'm a bit hazy on US politics."

"So I gather."

Weiss had begun to tap the faux leather armrest before Mrs. Anderson finally returned with a tray of drinks and biscuits.

"It's not really cream," she said apologetically. "Semi-skimmed milk is the best I can do."

Weiss could smell the coffee was instant but smiled bravely. "That's fine," he said.

After she'd settled into her seat, he asked: "I believe Sergeant McMillan has told you why I'm here. He's shown you the picture of the man called Yao. Yao is someone we're very interested in back home. We've been trawling through databases of photos and found a picture that matches, on a student visa for the UK, for someone coming to study here in Edinburgh."

"That must have been a helluva wide trawl," interrupted McMillan, his brow furrowed and his tone perhaps a little surly. "Lots of photos on lots of databases and, by the sound of it, not all of them American."

"But then we are allies, Sergeant. And, yes, it took a great deal of time. Not only that but facial recognition isn't anywhere near as good as you see on the ...telly... so it produced thousands of supposedly near matches." Matches that sometimes didn't even look remotely like the African. "And then I had to spend days

121

looking through those." He waved his hand. "Anyway, to cut a very long story short, the guy who stayed here was definitely our person of interest."

He'd lost the thread but then Mrs. Anderson chimed in. "Yes," she said glancing across at the McMillan, "the Sergeant told me you were after the young man, but he didn't tell me why."

"It's a security matter, for us in the States. It would be very helpful if you could answer a few questions."

"Of course." She picked at the hem of her skirt nervously.

"When did you first meet him?"

"As I told the Sergeant, it was five years ago. He took the flat across the landing, sharing with two other foreign students. They were all studying at the university: Edinburgh University that is. They were all very quiet, very studious." She shook her head a little. "People staying in that flat change all the time. I've long since given up going over to introduce myself unless they make too much noise. That wasn't the case with Yao and his flatmates, by the way. I heard their door opening and closing now and again, but that was it."

"But you did know this man called Yao?"

She nodded. "Yes. One day, a couple of months after he moved in, I had a problem with one of my doors. We had a very hot May..."

Weiss must have looked doubtful because they both laughed.

"It does sometimes happen," she said. "Anyway, the door to my flat must have warped a little in the heat, just enough to jam. I needed someone to get it open. Luckily, I was outside trying to get in, not the other way around as that would have been more serious. I would have had to phone the Fire Brigade, but I'm sure they would have had better things to do."

McMillan shook his head. "You shouldn't worry about doing something like that, Mrs. McMillan."

She smiled at him. "Anyway, my daughter and her husband, who live over in Morningside, were away on their

122

holiday, so I just knocked on the students' door. Yao answered. And he was very helpful. Pulled it open right away then went and bought a woodworking plane and shaved off enough so it never got stuck again. Can be a little draughty in the winter, though."

"And what was he like?"

"Very nice. Quiet, shy, respectful. The sort of son a mother would be very proud of."

"And his flatmates?"

"Never really talked to them?"

"And they're not still there."

McMillan shook his head. "They come and go in these student flats. No, they're long gone. Far as we can tell, they headed home to Mali and Zimbabwe respectively, once their courses had finished.

"I can take you to look at the flat later, though our forensics people have been through it and I can assure you they're thorough. But with that kind of occupant turnover, it was more like archaeology than a crime scene search."

Weiss nodded. He looked back to Mrs. Anderson. "And did Yao have any friends?"

"He didn't mention any, not that we talked a great deal. We'd meet sometimes on the stairs and I'd have him in for a coffee...oh...and once I had him in for Christmas drinks, though he didn't touch alcohol."

"So he didn't go home to Liganda during the breaks?"

"No, poor wee man didn't have the money, not like his flatmates. He didn't like staying here during the winter, not one bit."

'I'll bet,' thought Weiss.

"And his course," he asked. "did he tell you anything about that?"

"Military History it was, I think."

McMillan sat forward a little. "Don't know what it's like in the States, but here they do lots of subjects, particularly in the first year. Psychology, politics and IT were his other mains. Some of his

123

fellow students were doing postgraduate work and are still in Edinburgh. We'll be talking to them tomorrow."

Weiss had never had much hope for this trip but maybe these others would have more of interest to tell about Yao than nice Mrs. Anderson.

"You didn't see any strange people lurking round in those days, nothing suspicious?"

"This is the Old Town," she said, wearily. "Look around you. Junkies, prostitutes."

Weiss nodded. "Is there anything else you can remember about him? Something that might be useful?"

She hesitated: a blaring siren for anyone in law enforcement and both he and McMillan leaned forward. "What is it, Mrs. Anderson?" asked McMillan softly.

"You're going to think I'm a silly old woman, Sergeant. It's just when you were here last time I was rather nervous. I've never had a policeman in my flat before. I can't even remember the last time I talked to one. When you're nervous..."

"You forgot something," said Weiss gently. "I'm like that myself. If I'm out of my comfort zone, maybe talking to a lawyer about buying a house or whatever, I can even forget my own name."

She nodded gratefully, lie or not. "It was the biggest thing Yao and I ever did together and yet I forgot to mention it." She took a deep breath.

"I was a witness at his wedding."

"What!" McMillan had sat bolt upright.

Mrs. Anderson was looking alarmed. "I thought you'd get angry."

Weiss reached out and touched the back of her hand where it lay on her lap. "We're not angry. Really! Please tell us about the wedding. Which church was it in?"

She shook her head. "No church. No registry office. Did it right there in his flat."

"He married someone here?"

"No."

Weiss and McMillan glanced at each other.

"He did it over the phone. She was back in Liganda."

McMillan tilted his head back a little, like he'd remembered something.

"Muslim, is he, our little friend?"

"No, what he believes in was a mystery to me. It sounded like a mixture of just about everything."

McMillan seemed to be getting excited. "It's just I've heard of this sort of thing before, at least for African Muslims when they're over here. They can get married *in absentia*."

"You're kidding me!"

"Nope! Colleague of mine acted as a witness for one. All he had to do, over the phone to the priest or whatever back home, was testify that the groom was present and willing."

Mrs. Anderson was nodding. "I think when the men are away from home for a long time, they can start worrying someone else back home might snap up their girlfriends. I think it preys on their minds. Taking this kind of step makes them feel better, more secure. Gives them the strength to carry on with whatever they're doing."

"Do you know whereabouts in Liganda the bride was when this happened?"

"He told me the name, but it was an African name I didn't recognise at the time. And this was five years ago, after all."

"So you don't remember?" Weiss couldn't hide his disappointment.

"No," she said quickly, "but there is something else. Yao wanted me to have a memento. He gave me a picture of the two of them, before he left Scotland."

"And have you still got it?" asked Weiss quietly.

From the pocket of her cardigan appeared a postcard sized photograph. She offered it to Weiss and McMillan got up quickly and came to stand so he could look over his shoulder.

Weiss worked inwards from the background. There were

some huts with a cleared space in front of them. *Maidan* were such spaces called, or was that only in India? No writing he could see, but in the far distance, in the space between two huts, a single peak reached into the sky.

Yao, smile blazing, was next to a pretty little black woman. Her head tilted a little away from the camera, he saw the three parallel scars high on one cheek.

"Zinzi is her name," said Mrs. Anderson.

Chapter 11. *The Cleft, Liganda*

The incline is more obvious now as they make their long climb out of the valley. The camphors and yellowwoods are becoming more stunted and their cover sparser. Between them, he can look back over the green roof covering the valley floor. It is still early morning and the cool easterly breeze makes the air feel pleasantly chill against his skin.

There are eight of them, all in battle fatigues but for the Russian who, despite a cool looking safari suit, is florid with the exertion.

"Maybe you should turn back," says Yao. "It will get much steeper soon."

"Thank you for your consideration, young man, but I need the exercise. And the heat down there..." he indicates the valley, "...well, I just need to get out of it for a while."

Soon the big trees, struggling in the chilly air, give out completely like a green wave that has crashed into the valley and left behind a high-water mark. A few hundred feet further up he can see the start of the bamboo, the light catching the regular, upward angled leaves and making the stand look like a series of tyre tracks ascending into the sky.

The other Africans keep quiet as they stride steadily, their movements fluid though their packs are heavy. Yao is glad none of them are having to carry weapons: those would be waiting for them up on the lip of the valley.

"You have been with the General for a long time?" asks the Russian.

Yao nods. "Almost for as long as I can remember, Mr. Altukhov."

"Matvei," says the Russian. "Just Matvei."

"And how long have you been with the General yourself?"

"Ah," says the man, "I shouldn't really say. The General likes to keep things as compartmentalised as possible. The right hand not knowing what the left hand is doing. Only he knows everything, like a spider at the centre of a web."

"So maybe you shouldn't have asked me how long I've been with the General."

"Maybe you're right," says the man who calls himself Altukhov. "But I think the General trusts both of us. And he's obviously proud of you. Some of the things he says about you, it is almost like you were his son."

Yao feels foolish as his cheeks flush with blood and his throat contracts with pride. Struggling to keep the muscles of his face relaxed, he makes no comment.

 Far up and to the left is the volcanic peak, a huge blemish on this vast plateau. In times long gone, one side has collapsed under the pressure of the magma, creating this whole valley. The big trees have triumphed in the rich volcanic soil, forming a deep green delta descending into the Cleft.

The group slows as they enter the bamboo. In some ways it's nasty stuff. Useful though. In Hong Kong, he'd seen it growing up the sides of twenty storey skyscrapers and his first thought had been that it was reclaiming the city. But then he saw it was really just scaffolding. Better than iron some say, though he imagines it must flex mightily as the Chinese scampered over it, or when the typhoons blew.

What he doesn't like about it is the speed it grows, and he's pleased to see the men hacking away at the new growth with their machetes. Already it's sprouting from the floor of the little track that has been cut through the stuff. Watches are changed every three days, so it hasn't been long since the stuff was last pruned back, but already the new growth is standing proud.

The Russian keeps back from the hacking blades and stares in wonder at the older, arm-thick bamboo tubes hemming them in.

"Hard to believe I'm in Africa," he says.

"Africa has everything," says Yao. "That's why nobody will leave us alone. Everybody wants something from us. Arab slavers, colonialists, multinationals. .."

Yao lets the obvious question hang in the air. The Russian is no soldier: no simple mercenary. There's nothing tempered about him; whenever he looks at the man the word 'soft' springs unbidden to his mind.

"So," says the man after a few seconds, "you are wondering what *I* want out of Africa."

Yao shrugs. "Money?"

"No, I'm an old socialist. Money means little to me."

"Then why?"

"I want the General to succeed. David against Goliath. There is always something compelling about the underdog."

Yao feels himself bridling. "Does that mean you think he will fail?"

"His path is difficult but I would not be here if I didn't think he had a chance. I am no admirer of lost causes. No, I sense here in Africa a fulcrum about which monumental events might pivot. A little effort at the right place and right time could move the world."

They move slowly through the bamboo stand and the air, stilled by the denseness of the thicket, becomes hot again. He hears the Russian begin to pant like a dog.

Then further ahead, at the end of the green channel framed by the bamboo, he sees brighter light. Soon the men are out on rockier ground and the jagged lip is looking closer, more reachable.

The land is sloping steeply now and little soil can cling to the rocks. Reaching a scree slope, and aware of the man's clumsiness, Yao holds back and lets the Russian ahead of him. Sure enough, he's soon tottering around and pin-wheeling his arms, struggling to keep his balance on the sliding stones.

"Try to relax," says Yao. "Walk more slowly but in bigger strides. If you feel the ground sliding away below you, go with it. Don't try to fight it. Three steps forward, two steps back, but you will get there."

It takes a couple of tumbles, but eventually Altukhov seems to get the hang of it, aping the slow, languid strides of the others.

Finally, the scree gives way to solid rock and, after a final steep scramble, they're over the edge. On the other side, where the volcanic cone is still intact, the slope is less severe. A huddle of tents, all nicely camouflaged against the grey of the rock, lie just twenty metres away.

"Come... and... see... my... beauties," says the Russian between gasps as he recovers his breath. "The box tent... over there."

"Your beauties?"

"My idea!"

Men are crawling out of tents and squinting in the sun. Greetings and banter are exchanged. Apparently the rations on the ridge are less than savoury.

The handover is swift and soon the relieved men are heading back down to the camp for some decent food.

The Russian walks over to the box tent and grasps a flap, gently pulling it back and signalling for Yao to look in.

Always cautious, he leans just inside the entrance. All he sees at first is darkness. As his eyes adjust, he suddenly finds himself looking at cruel, hooked beaks and the unwavering regard of ten cold eyes.

"Beautiful birds," he says uneasily.

Carefully taking his head out of the tent, he turns to look up. Over to the west a bank of clouds is moving in and is already covering nearly half of the sky.

The Russian follows his gaze. "Now would be the time," he says. "First cloud cover in weeks."

"So that is why you came up today. It wasn't just to get away from the heat."

The Russian shrugs. "As good a time as any. My pets have been trained well, so of course I want to see what they can do."

"How long have they been keeping watch up here?"

"A week, since the hostages arrived."

"Was it the beetles and the snake that prompted this?"

The Russian laughs. "You mean the Autonomous Biomorphic Hyper Redundant Robots."

"Do I?"

"You do. That's what the Americans call them, but we'll just stick with robot beetles and snakes. They are a prime example of the risk aversion that has seized the US military and intelligence forces. They have retreated behind a wall of technology. Where once they would have used humans to gather intelligence, now they use little machines. Or try to, anyway.

"The snakes they got from the Israelis, the beetles from a Department of Defence contract with MIT. They cost countless millions to develop and a lot of people made a lot of money."

"You seem to know a great deal about this."

Matvei smiles. "So perhaps now you see why I may be useful to the General."

He slaps his belly. "It has been a long time since breakfast. Let's get settled in then see what all the fuss is about these combat rations. After that...well, we watch and wait."

Stevens stared at the blank screen, his fingers gently and unconsciously caressing the cock-like joystick. Every now and then the airframe would shudder and objects would rattle as they ploughed through denser regions in the clouds. His headphones managed to attenuate most of the noise, but the comments of his colleagues were still sometimes difficult to catch: their tones scratchy over the electronics.

"Nearly there," he heard the Captain say. "Five minutes. In and out, that was the deal."

"I'm doing the best I can," Stevens heard Dreyfuss mutter. "This damn catch is stuck."

Stevens imagined Dreyfuss directly below him, flat out in the tiny hold, desperately poking away at the technology in the low light.

Keyed up, he glanced round in exasperation, taking in the

cramped space. The plane had once been a Lear Jet but had been heavily modified by the military. Modifying an AWAC for this job would have been overkill, like using a B-52 to drop a pine cone. Once, however, they'd have designed a plane just for this type of mission but after the cutbacks it was all make do and mend.

Three other operators sat at workstations in the cabin, dark but for the strings of fairy lights in the electronics.

'First time in anger,' he thought.

He heard something click and Dreyfuss yelled: "Got it. Activating!"

It may have been his imagination but he thought his screen lightened a tad.

"Get back up here now!" The Captain didn't sound too pleased.

Stevens heard the trapdoor in the raised floor slam open. He didn't look as Dreyfuss crawled back out, but he felt the man get behind him and look over his shoulder.

"Just in time. Release module!"

There was no sound but the plane pitched a little as the Lear's new cat flap slid open. This time there was definitely more light in Steven's screen and he grasped the joystick hard.

A little red light on his console blinked on. "Chute deployed," said Dreyfuss.

The faint grey patterns on the screen shifted as the module swung back and forth on the parachute lines.

"MAVs deployed," he heard the captain say as his screen flashed to white. Trained to within an inch of his life, Stevens was already using the joystick to alter the pitch of the blades, stabilising the machine even as the camera compensated for the sudden light change.

The little camera, peering through an inverted hemisphere of perspex, began to show rock spiralling across the screen, outcrops and ridges boiling up and down in the peripheral distortions of the lens.

"Better hurry, not far to go," said Dreyfuss unhelpfully.

Stevens ignored him, already bringing stability to the downward descent and gently increasing the rotor speed. He had to slow the descent quickly. He needed to thread the Miniature Unmanned Vehicles down *through the trees, not crash into them.*

"Not too shabby," whispered Dreyfuss.

The trees were already resolving themselves into the bigger branches. Now that he had control, Stevens activated the target icon. Culled from AWACS overpasses and infrared signatures it was still only a best guess. The trees bottled up most of the radiation but stuff from the hot truck engines sometimes peeped through.

Just a few hundred metres south and down the valley and he'd be pretty much there.

It was all about battery time. Military grade though the batteries were, he had an hour at most. Getting through the canopy without getting snared would take a good ten minutes. After that it was jinking round the trunks, mapping the camp and trying to find out where the hostages were stowed.

Then, battery near depletion, he'd fly the MAV into thick bush never to be found again by man. Olomo and his men would know nothing about it.

He moved the joystick, angling the rotors, and the MAV, still descending gently, was now moving towards the icon superimposed on the tree canopy.

As he got nearer he began to check for a way down. Already he could make out the bright waxy green leaves of the tops of the camphor trees. Bushy damned things: getting down through them would be a nightmare.

"What about there?" Dreyfuss was stabbing a stubby finger at the screen.

Annoyingly, the fucker was right. Stevens brought the rotors almost to horizontal and the view gently skated towards the gap in the foliage.

"Plenty of room..."

The tree tops leaped up at them. Curved bars slammed down across the screen.

"What the...?" said Stevens, already increasing the throttle. As he did so the view tilted, valley wall coming into view over the trees. Everything started to recede.

"Is this thing working?" Gently he altered the rotor angle and sure enough the thing seemed to climb, but faster than it should have done.

Then he saw the view was moving up and down: slowly, rhythmically.

Behind him he heard Preslaw yell: "Something's wrong with my controls."

"Me to," he called. "It's like something's fighting me."

"Christ," said Preslaw, "I'm already over the ridge."

Stevens saw rock sliding into view and realised that's where he was going as well. By now he'd tried everything but throttling down to zero. If he did that the thing would just fall.

Suddenly he understood. "Cut power," he yelled.

Yao has long since become bored and he wonders why Olomo has ordered him to come. The other soldiers have pretty much taken to their tents, not used to the lower temperature at these higher altitudes made worse by cloud cover shutting out the sun.

A few of the men are playing cards but he has refused to join in. To him gambling is a stain on the soul.

A conversation with the Russian might even be welcome, but the man gets up late. Yao can hear him snoring away.

Up since early morning himself, he's getting cold and is tired of pacing the rocky terrain. A discrete little shower of cold rain blows across the ridge and passes over him, so he retreats to his tent. He'll try to get more sleep. Tomorrow he will climb to the top of the volcanic cone and spell one of the lookouts there. The climb won't be so bad, but it'll be even more cold and windy up there.

What a sight it will be, though: a full 360 view of the country around.

He must have fallen asleep because he comes too at the

crackling sound of a walkie talkie conversation. Checking his watch, he sees that it's a quarter past. The lookouts radio in every hour, on the hour.

Something's up.

By the time he's crawled out of his tent, the Russian's head is poking out of his tent flap. The man says something but he can't make it out.

Men from the other tents are already heading towards the box tent. Matvei follows, his safari suit even more crumpled now. The faint shadows of the ridged cloth give his body a zebra like appearance. Tugging at the bunched-up cloth around his groin, he's able to get to the box tent just as a man emerges with the first bird on his forearm.

In daylight the damned things are even more impressive and even bigger than he'd thought. From the top of its head to the end of its long black and white striped tail, it's longer than his leg.

The raptor is already scanning the sky.

"Quickly!" shouts the Russian.

As each man retrieves his bird and emerges from the tent, they unclip the traces and thrust their forearms high. The birds take off with a mighty flapping of wings and Yao, metres away, feels the wind pluck at his hair.

He shades his eyes as he scans the sky. Other than the climbing hawks, it looks clear.

He sidles over to the Russian. "What's happening?"

"The watchers on the ridge. They thought they heard engines but didn't see anything. It could be a false alarm." But he sounds excited nevertheless.

The hawks are struggling into the thin air, following long upwards spirals.

Yao's eyes drift away to the east but then flick back as he sees movement high above the top of the cone.

"What's that?"

The Russian follows his pointing arm and scrabbles in a side pocket. Soon he's holding some little fold-out binoculars. "I see it. It's not going to come down anywhere near here."

He swings the glasses back to the hawks. "Oh yes! They've seen it too."

Yao sees there are more dots in the sky now and he follows their tracks down.

Then the hawks are diving.

"There!" says the Russian, pointing with one hand and thrusting the glasses at Yao with the other.

By luck, he gets it as soon as he brings the glasses to his eyes. Descending gently, the object seems to be made of four black saucers round a central hub. It's a drone of some kind. As he watches, the angle of the saucers changes and the object begins to drift in a direction towards the middle of the valley.

Beguiled by the object's gentle, stately journey, Yao's shoulders jump with surprise when the hawk hits it, making it plummet.

He follows the path down, seeing the hawk unfurling its mighty wings and thrashing frantically at the air. Its claws are closed over the short cross members connecting the saucers to the hub.

Then the fight begins. Whatever is controlling the device is making it twist back and forth, and Yao sees the hawk's legs suddenly bend as the drone kicks up. The bird's tail feathers dip into one of the saucers and are shredded, but it still doesn't let go.

Glancing up from the glasses, he sees other hawks struggling and then he hears men falling to the ground beside him. Looking down, he sees two taking aim with long barrelled assault rifles. Two others are still on their feet, shotguns ready.

The wounded hawk is already near them, unsteadily dragging the thing through the sky. One final shrug by the device and the hawk loses control, making it bank over and slew down onto the rocks. The hawk hobbles clear just in time as the shotguns open up, fragmenting the drone and sending its remains cartwheeling into oblivion.

Two more hawks in clumsy dives bring the devices to

within a few feet of the surface before letting go. The devices hit the ground with the clack of plastic on rock and the hawks bank away. More crashes of gunfire shatter the objects like clay pigeons.

One more bird still has something in its claws. Barely fifty metres away, it seems to have gained the upper hand and is heading towards them, but then it suddenly drops like a stone, its wings flapping uselessly above its head.

"Fire!" shouts the Russian.

The assault rifles roar and the bird and device dissolve into fragments of plastic and flesh.

Yao realises his pulse is racing and he's been holding his breath. Looking round, he sees that two of the birds have already made it back to their trainers' forearms. The one without the tail feathers is hopping around twenty metres off. It looks like it's broken a wing in the fall.

The Russian is already making for the most intact of the downed devices and Yao hurries after him.

One rotor is still spinning though, as they watch, even that comes to rest. The whole device, including the rotors, is barely thirty centimetres across. The rotors are constrained within guard disks, the saucers he thought he'd seen. The guards would stop the rotors fragmenting if they touched a tree branch on the way down. Luckily this also meant the raptor could grasp the body of the MAV without danger of losing its legs in the chopping rotors.

"You trained the birds well," says Yao.

"Yes, and you know what I used?"

Yao shakes his head.

"Childrens' toys, just like this!" The Russian smiles. "Available in a good toy shop near you. The only difference with these is the military grade battery. Gives them the much longer life they need."

"And the people controlling them? Like with the big drones, are they back in Niger?"

"No, a radio receiver good enough to send a signal that far would be too heavy. They are up there." His finger is pointing directly up into the clouds.

Yao sees these are getting heavier, promising more rain.

"I wonder what else the Americans have got up their sleeves," he says.

Chapter 12. *USS Benjamin F. Sands, Gulf of Guinea*

Down in the bowels of the ship the air became hotter and denser. One thing missing, though, was the all-pervasive smell of diesel oil found on other warships.

"Certainly doesn't smell like an engine room," Joey said.

Lewis nodded. "Well, of course, that's the reactors for you. There are no big diesel engines or generators for powering all the systems. A few drops of lubricating oil are all they need."

Ahead she saw two marines armed with assault rifles either side of a door. "This it?"

"How could you tell?"

The marines came to attention as Lewis stopped in front of them. "First Lieutenant Lewis and NCIS Special Agent Beck. You'll have heard we were coming."

The marine on the right nodded as he checked the photos on their IDs against the real things. Then, turning, he zipped his own ID through a reader. "Step right through, please."

Once over the knee knocker, they were in an area of nondescript lockers. A slightly pudgy white guy in a white boiler suit was waiting for them. He saluted. "Yeoman LaTrobe, here to escort you."

Lewis smiled. "You pulled the short straw, eh? Enginemen and the Techs too busy?"

"Naturally, sir." LaTrobe seemed to have the same dry delivery as Lewis. She figured they'd get on fine.

Lewis was looking at her. "Yeomen in the Reactor Dept tend to do all the paperwork."

"And the machinists and the techs and the mates do the real work," said LaTrobe, shrugging.

"How many work here?"

"Four hundred."

"What? Four hundred just to work on the reactors!"

LaTrobe shook his head. He was in his early twenties, like

139

so many on this ship, but already he was losing some hair at the front. She imagined that might feel devastating to a young man hoping to find a mate, but he seemed cheerful enough. Good for him!

"They don't all work on the two reactors. The reactors just produce the steam. Remember there are four steam driven main engines further aft, plus we're responsible for pumping most of the fresh water round the ship. Well...perhaps describing it as 'fresh' might be shooting a little high."

Joey nodded. Her sense of taste may not be as sharp as her sense of smell, but even she caught two unusual flavours in the ship's water. Rust, and something Union Carbidey, she guessed.

"But four hundred still seems high."

Lewis and LaTrobe looked at each other. Lewis hesitated for a beat. "You raise a delicate point. Warships at sea are over manned. Can you work out why that would be?"

"Is this a quiz?"

Lewis raised his eyes to heaven. "War brings death so you need to build in a certain level of redundancy."

Now it was her turn to hesitate.

"If you're worried by the numbers, because you were thinking you'd need to check them all out individually, it won't be so bad," Lewis said. "They split down into reactor-dedicated and the more conventional type of engineers."

"You want to talk to the reactor crew?" asked LaTrobe.

"Maybe," she said. "I'm just here to scope things out first of all. I've never been near a reactor before. Don't know what to expect."

"Well, I guessed you weren't here out of idle curiosity. This is a secure area, so we don't run tours. You need a good reason to get in here, but orders from the Admiral work like a charm too. As you're NCIS, Ms. Beck, this must be about security. I'd have a better idea what to show you if I knew what you were looking for."

She looked at Lewis who just shrugged. "You're right.

Security obviously, potential sabotage specifically."

LaTrobe didn't seem surprised. "Never going to happen!" he said, "But I'm happy to go through the motions."

"The reactors can't be sabotaged? You're confident of that?"

"Like the Lieutenant says, I'm just a paper pusher, but I know enough to be confident, yeah. Anyway, we can talk about this more after you've changed. Ms. Beck, through the curtain is where you do it. Down to underwear, then on with the boiler suit you'll see in the wrapping on the bench."

A plain black curtain separated the locker room into two halves. She stepped through and started to undress.

"Are there many women in the Reactor Department?"

"No need to shout, Ms. Beck. I can hear you well enough through this thin cotton. There's about ten. Big girls most of them. Didn't know what your size was so...sorry."

Joey checked herself in the mirror. The boiler suit made her slender framed body look like a sack of shit, yet still managed to be tight at the shoulders due to her height.

"Are you guys decent?"

"Never more so," said Lewis. Stepping through the curtain, she couldn't help noticing how well his boiler suit fitted him. He could look rangy at times but he had a broad chest and a nice straight back.

LaTrobe handed her a bit of blue plastic. "Attach this to your lapel area. It's a radiation badge. Want to make sure you don't get a dose, so to speak."

"Is that likely?"

"Not a chance. Even if it did happen, it wouldn't matter anyway. It'd mean the primary circuit had gone and the steam would have scalded us red like cooked lobsters."

"So why wear the badges?"

Lewis was smiling. "Ionising radiation. Heap powerful medicine... little talisman - he ward off evil!"

LaTrobe grimaced. "It's actually standard Health and

Safety practice when you work with radiation. For example, if you were dishing it out in a hospital, say in an x-ray department, you might get a range of doses though hardly anyone would get anything big. With us it's more either/or. Either you're totally screwed or you aren't. The badges are just for posterity if the worst happens."

"That makes me feel a lot better."

"Glad to be of service. This way!"

The hatch this time was more substantial and, as she passed through, she saw the thickness of the door frame. "Steel and lead," said LaTrobe. "This is our containment area: if radioactive steam is ever released then it stays in here."

"Radioactive steam?"

"I'll get to that."

They'd entered a larger room with banks of controls and twinkling lights. On a quick tour of the bridge she'd seen controls for some of the more modern weapons system and they'd looked like standard issue modern day high tech. The electronics in the rest of the carrier, however, seemed to come from a different age, seventies probably. Dials here were as prevalent as digital readouts, and even the latter had numerals made from dots big enough to be individually resolved. The surfaces of the equipment were clean, but tiny scratches and scuffs made by generations of servicemen gave it a slightly shabby look. Much like the rest of the ship in fact.

Shabby and *old* were not words you wanted to associate with nuclear reactors.

"This stuff is older than I am, isn't it."

"The reactor itself is newer, it's changed after twenty years, but the controls stay pretty much the same."

At least the two other white suited guys in the compartment were tapping stuff onto tablet computers and the few monitors around were flat panel and HD. Several showed different views of heavy, convoluted piping like air conditioning ducting but obviously much thicker walled and heavier. Others showed what looked like a robot head wearing a fright wig.

LaTrobe was smiling at her. "That's the reactor. Those things sticking out are the control rods. They suck up all the neutrons which would otherwise split the atoms. You drop them in and the reaction stops. Slows anyway."

"So if you wanted to mess things up, you'd pull out the rods, then damage the controls so they couldn't be pushed back in. The reaction would heat up and you'd get a ..."

"Bucket of sunshine?" said Lewis helpfully.

"No," said LaTrobe emphatically. "The rods are held out by electromagnets. Smash the controls, shut off the power or whatever, and the electromagnets turn off and the rods fall under gravity into the core. Bucket of sunshine turns into a dying ember. Anyway, the core isn't atom bomb pure. It can give off a lot of heat and radiation but it can never be a nuclear bomb."

"What about this radioactive steam you were talking about?"

"This is a pressurised water reactor..."

"And you have two, right?"

"Right, in completely separate compartments. This one is starboard. Water at very high pressure is pumped through the reactor, picking up heat from the core. If that primary circuit was breached, the pressurised water would turn to superheated steam. If that got to us in here, radiation would be the least of our problems, as I said before."

"And this radioactive water powers the turbines so, if they were damaged, say in an explosion, all that radioactive steam would get out into the ship."

"No, we have a heat exchanger. The superheated, irradiated water gives its heat to other water in the completely separate secondary circuit which then turns to plain, un-irradiated steam. It's that that drives the turbines."

"People have thought of these scenarios before, you know" said Lewis patronisingly.

"Humour me," she said. "A fresh pair of eyes. Who

knows?"

Neither man looked convinced.

"OK," she said. "What about if the pump in the primary circuit failed or was deliberately damaged. If the water didn't take away the core's heat, wouldn't it melt down?"

LaTrobe lowered an ass cheek onto the edge of a console. "Well, we'd drop in the control rods."

"And if they weren't working for whatever reason?"

"Well the pressurised water is itself a moderator...what I mean by that is the water slows down the neutrons enough for them to interact with the fuel atoms and split 'em apart. Without the water they can't do that and the nuclear reaction is actually slowed."

"Slowed but not stopped."

LaTrobe nodded reluctantly. "If the control rods weren't working, and if the water was lost, then the core would still be live. Not enough for a meltdown, though. Not for a while anyway."

"Not for a while. How long?"

One of the other white suits had come over by now and was watching them all. LaTrobe lifted a hand in his direction. "Senior Engineman Spadaro. He's your man for this stuff." He made the introductions.

Spadaro was about her height and pretty skinny but she noted the thickness and definition of his thighs even through the boiler suit. Keen cyclist perhaps. Not much of a hobby even on a vessel as big as this. Not if you didn't want a jet landing on your head.

"With all due respect," said Spadaro and she picked up a faint Texan drawl in his accent, "we know the reactor would be the target if anyone wanted to sink the carrier. All of us who have access to this place are security cleared to within an inch of our lives. Agent Afloat Lundt has been through my bank account more often than my wife. And believe me, my wife's a suspicious woman.

144

"Don't let the easy way you got in here make you think it's always like that. What the Admiral says goes; anyone else trying to get in here unauthorised would be shot down like a dog."

She didn't like feeling outnumbered. She took a breath. "But, getting back to my original question, if the rods were out and the cooling water lost, would the reactor build up enough heat for the core to melt down? And if it did, how long would it take?"

Spadaro shook his head. "Days probably. Enough time for us to get a coolant supply connected up."

"But if the ship was sinking, you'd have to abandon it."

"In which case being at the bottom of the sea would be a great place for it to happen. But the Sands is never going to sink, so this all academic," said Spadero, like the case was closed.

Joey looked at the other men but they seemed to be taking all this at face value.

"It's big and heavy and made of steel. Steel sinks, even in this navy."

Spadaro was looking at Lewis. After all, he was the one who'd brought her here.

Lewis sighed in exasperation. "Carriers like this may be made of steel but they're almost impossible to sink. As well as steel there's lots and lots of air. All trapped behind bulkheads. Even with many of the bulkheads breached, and with most of the compartments filled with water, she'd still float."

LaTrobe and Spadaro were nodding sagely.

Joey put her hands on her hips. "One word..."

"Titanic," said LaTrobe and Spadaro simultaneously. Spadaro's smile was now frankly condescending. "Yeah, we get that. A lot. Hey, Yeoman! You've been to college more recently than me. Remind me, do we get many icebergs here in the tropics?"

"Not sure," said LaTrobe, deadpan. "Don't think so."

Spadero nodded. "Now I'm trying not to be a nervous Nelly," he said, and indeed it didn't look like he'd ever had a nervous moment in his life, "but I can't help sensing a sub-text

145

here."

She looked at Lewis.

Lewis shrugged again. She'd noticed it was something he did a lot. "These guys are cleared so high they probably know what's stored at Area 51."

"Yeah," said LaTrobe. "Sometimes we even get to change its diaper."

She folded her arms across her chest. "Clear and present danger," she said.

"To the reactor specifically?"

"No, no specific target known."

She still couldn't see any signs of concern. Was this macho bullshit or just plain arrogance? Did being part of the deadliest naval weapon system on the planet numb them with complacency?

"Look," said Spadaro. "Even though we're going into a war zone, you're safer here than in just about any city back home. Nothing can touch us, and definitely not anything that Olomo loser could afford."

"Yeah," said Lewis. "A hundred or so cruise missiles might do it, though the anti-missile systems on the picket ships would get almost all of them. A couple of them hitting would spoil our day but it still wouldn't be enough to sink us. Which is all mute anyway, as our friend the General doesn't even have a pot to piss in by all accounts."

"Basically," said Spadero, "he's fucked. Pardon my French!"

"You people need a kick up the ass!"

Lewis shook his head in disagreement. He was leading her as usual and the conversation was disjointed as they jinked one way and another to avoid the countless obstacles along every passageway. Sometimes it was like the ship itself was deliberately trying to impede her progress.

"The bomb Hierra had might've killed a few people but it

wasn't anywhere near big enough to sink the carrier or any other ship in the CSG. They're just too big." He held up a hand even though he couldn't see she'd been about to make a retort. "And, yes, I know there could be more than one saboteur, more than one bomb. Believe me, it doesn't matter where you put them, you couldn't sink something this big with little firecrackers like that."

"There's got to be leverage. One little bomb having a big effect."

"Didn't Spadero and LaTrobe convince you? The reactor's a dead end."

"Come on! Use your imagination! Fuel depots for the jets, armories full of their bombs and missiles. One little bomb there could set off something bigger."

Lewis slowed to let a sailor get by. The passageway ahead was now clear so he turned back to face her, hands on his hips. "And do you really reckon we hadn't thought of that. Macik's had men crawling over the whole ship looking for bombs and *especially* around the fuel and armaments areas. Thirty extra marines have been shipped in to guard these. That's over and above the existing guard details."

"Why's Olomo doing this then? Why's he going to all this trouble?"

"Maybe because he's an idiot. Maybe it's just a gesture. The little dog barking at the big dog then running away. How would I know?"

He waved a hand. "Anyway, that's your problem. C'mon." He turned and started back down the corridor heading towards the NCIS office.

But then, one level down, he stopped and held up a hand. Peeking over his shoulder she could see the wall mounted monitor he was looking at. It was set to the internal information feed and was showing the usual list of crew call outs. Then she saw that one was for her to go to JCIS.

"I'm guessing this isn't going to be good news," he said.

This time it was a woman. Blond hair rat-tailed by dirt and sweat, she made a pathetic sight as the kangaroo court went through its deadly business. They listened to every terrified response and watched each tear track down over the grime on her face. When the time came, her legs seemed to have stopped working and the soldiers had to drag her from her seat and carry her out.

Much more slightly built than O'Grady, the bullets kicked harder at her.

Everyone fell silent in JCIS.

"What a piece of shit!" hissed Lundt behind her.

Others started to murmur and Macik held up a warning hand. "Let's be professional about this, people!"

Joey struggled to unclench her jaw, the pressure in her chest almost unbearable. Beside her she could hear Lundt's rapid breathing.

That fucker Olomo wouldn't escape justice if she could help it.

Macik was looking at them all, his eyes scanning back and forth across the compartment. "It's a clear provocation. Olomo wants something and these executions are just to soften us up, or so he thinks. The guy's a loose cannon. Commander Terni, bring us up to date on theatre status!"

Terni came forward to stand by him. "After the first execution, the President and JCS ordered us to the Gulf of Guinea, as you know. Already we're in strike distance and, by midday tomorrow, we'll be stationed within 30 miles of the coast. A thirty-mile exclusion zone around us will be policed by high density patrols.

"We're to supply air cover for any ground-based actions if diplomacy fails. On the diplomacy front things are not going well. Olomo is talking but not listening. The strategists back home think this may just be a preamble to nationalisation of industries equipped and run by US and European commercial interests. They think he's using this..." he indicated the screen showing the dead woman's freeze-framed body,"... as just the excuse."

"What does that leave us to bargain with?" asked Lewis.

"Nothing. That's the problem. If these 'trials' are just theatre then it's not obvious why he would stop."

Joey self-consciously raised a hand. "Could we buy him off?"

"I imagine that's being tried. God knows he's poor enough but nationalising the oil and gas and mining would net him billions."

He shook his head. "It looks like there'll have to be a military solution if we're not to just stand and watch this happening day after day. The folks back home are throwing everything they have in the way of surveillance at Olomo's camp. That's up north on the Alani plateau in a valley they call the Cleft. It's well defended and well covered by dense forest so success so far has been limited.

"If we had to get sticks of parachutists in it wouldn't be too difficult but, for the big birds that'd carry them, the nearest airbase we could use is in Europe. With mid-air refueling we could do it. Also, the President is putting pressure on some African States further north for us to use their main runways. Good luck with that! Anyway, the real difficulty is that, even if we got the hostages out of the Cleft, then how would we extract them? The nearest usable runway is near Tembe, the capital city. Even if we could take that, the rescuers and hostages would need to get there by road through a hundred miles of hostile territory."

"Choppers," said someone.

"Yeah, but this CSG has only a Seahawk and Nighthawk, so we'd need more. The Pentagon's working on getting more helos to us right now."

Macik shifted and immediately everyone's eyes turned to him. "And, if we need to do any form of airlift, then we'd first have to suppress their air support and communications. But for us, of course, that bit is easy. Their air support is minimal and their radar stations and comms are essentially undefended."

Terni was nodding his head. "The number of cell towers they have is so pitiful we could take out every single one within a couple of days, tops. And that would be it for them. Liganda, like so many poor countries, never had effective land line communications and they were hoping to take the big technological leapfrog straight to cellular networks. With so little wire in the ground, and all their cell towers smashed, then we could pretty much destroy the country's entire telecommunications network."

"Olomo must be out of his mind," Lewis was whispering. "We could wreck his whole fucking country."

Lundt grimaced. "Pretty wrecked anyway, far as I can tell. Would they even notice?"

"You know what I want next people!" Macik wasn't asking a question.

"Risk assessments," chorused the JIC staff.

"On my desk by 0800. Lundt, Lewis, Beck. With me!"

Macik led them into the server room and shut the door behind them. He raised his voice to be heard over the fans. "So now we know what our little African friend was after. He wanted to slow us down so we couldn't project our military power the way CSGs are supposed to.

"Time was, we'd have been spoilt for choice which airbase to use, but over the last few decades we've given them all away. African countries stick together no matter how appalling their governments. Take Mugabe and Zimbabwe. We should have taken him out back near the turn of the century but the other African countries stood by him.

"No, the truth is we'll not have a friendly strip available for us south of Europe. We can do mid-air refueling but it'll still cramp our style and limit how many boots we can put on the ground. This carrier *has* to be in Olomo's face.

"And that means it's all down to you. You three need to make sure nothing stops the *Sands*. How's your investigation going?"

Macik was looking at her and she caught a look of disgruntlement on Lundt's face.

"Nothing obvious yet, but we've still got a long way to go. We may soon be able to give you more information on the African, though."

"Redouble your efforts! The President herself is taking this very badly: she's never off the phone to me. Don't screw up!"

Opening the door, he was soon moving comet-like across the JIC, a long tail of flunkies with clipboards and pads trailing behind.

"No pressure then," said Lewis.

"Oh, I'm with him all the way," Joey said. "Anything to get a cruise missile lodged in Olomo's gullet. I'm sick of seeing tyrants get away with things. Gaddafi, Saddam Hussein, Bin Laden lived far longer than they should have done. Idi Amin lived out his days in luxury, Kim Il-Sung died in his bed."

"I think I can guess why you became a cop."

"And what's wrong with that? Why should the bad guys get away with it?"

"And what gave you that quaint idea? Cop shows? In the real world, who's bad and who's good? I've read enough about Olomo to know what he went through under Mamadou. Now there was a real butcher! Olomo is anti-imperialist and with good reason. The British may have gone but now the Americans are back mining their minerals and with their Big Pharma using Ligandans as test subjects. I'm not saying he's right, but most people have reasons for doing things. There but for the grace of God and all that."

"Boy," said Lundt, "it really is time you got out of the Navy."

Chapter 13. *Bito village, Liganda*

Clomp, clomp, clomp. A sound from his childhood, it brings him out of a peaceful slumber. For a while he lies and just listens as the rest of the village comes to life.

At last, cracking open an eye, he sees light creeping in over the top of the door.

The thudding of the long poles down into the pots means the women are grinding corn, and it must be well past dawn, yet nobody has woken him. Listening carefully, he hears first Zinzi's gentle snoring but then the quicker breaths of her parents. How long have they lain awake, not wanting to wake him? Such concern for a son-in-law is rare.

Yawning and stretching ostentatiously, he sniffs and stifles a sneeze from the dust rising from the floor as his mat shifts. Zinzi and her parents are using the three beds: flat boards covered with mats and held up on forks lopped from older trees. His mat on the floor is harder, and the insect bites more numerous and irritating, but the alternative is worse.

Little villages like this have a hut set aside for the single men. Mostly young and all confined together in the heat of the African night, the scent of maleness is like a wave you could drown in. Worse even than in the military camps of his youth.

But there have been times during the night in her parents' hut when he's wished he'd been with the men. Close enough to catch Zinzi's tangy scent, hear her gentle breathing and imagine her breasts rising and falling, yet not able to reach out and touch, not able to gorge on her sweetness. The ache in his loins has been almost too much to bear.

Orphaned while very young, he has few memories of hut

living, but he knows of the unwritten rules when a husband and wife live with parents. It was true that some can and do make love while the parents can hear. But in most cases, countless little accommodations are made, periods left in the day when older or younger couples can be alone to show their love.

But even with these accommodations it's something he can't do. Old man Hadgu might clank his pail as he goes to milk the goats, and Tawia can complain about how long it will take to plait her friend Danquah's hair, but he never takes the bait, no matter the look of yearning in Zinzi's eyes. Their lovemaking is too precious a thing to share with other eyes, even if the sight is by forgetfulness or accident.

Late evening behind the baobab is all he allows them.

Shuffling to his feet, he unhitches the plaited reed chord that latches the door and steps out into the bright light. To some, the bank of clouds and light rain on the day of the hawks presaged the coming of the rains, but they've all been disappointed. Instead, the pounding of the tropical sun continues and the air is heavy in everyone's lungs.

Beating with the regularity of pistons, but ill-matched in their phases, the tall poles, taller than the women who work them, oscillate up and down like the flags of an advancing army. Many of the women have already brought out cooking pots from their huts and smoke is curling up into the still air.

As he emerges, the women turn to look at him. Eyebrows rise and the smiles are lascivious. A few whistle. Blood rises in his cheeks and he casts his eyes down while the women laugh at his discomfort.

Becoming suddenly aware of the pressure in his bladder, he makes his barefoot way to the south and out of the village and to the bushes behind which lies the village's latrine. Down wind and at the opposite side of the village to the well he helped dig years before, it can be a companionable place, but first one must check the company. To the right of the entrance the bushes have been trimmed back a little to allow a glimpse. If there are women there then he must wait.

There's only one man and it's Khimo. Yao hesitates a second but then goes in anyway.

Khimo is squatting down unselfconsciously. Yao thinks back to the high-end hotels he's had to stay in during his travels for Olomo, of the bathrooms sealed behind two sets of lockable doors, and he smiles to himself. The West's thinking, in so many ways, is about denying nature.

But he has to admit that there are some natural smells that he could do without. Yao takes up his position a few feet along the trench from Khimo and wrestles his cock out of his fatigues and starts to piss.

"So, she took you back," says Khimo, looking up and across at him. His face is broad and uneven and one eye is nearly closed. He takes some pains to keep it that way but once, in a moment when Khimo was surprised by a snake, Yao saw the mess of the pupil the man was trying to hide. A high-spirited game of chase amongst acacia bushes when he was a child had brought a thorn across his eye, making it look like a fried egg slit with a knife.

"Of course she took me back. She is my wife."

Khimo is cleaning himself with water he has brought in his wash pail. "You do not deserve her. You should be with her always. You should protect her."

Yao zips himself up and turns to face the man, legs a little apart, hands loosely by his side. Ready.

"Protect her? Who from? You!"

Khimo takes a deep breath. "I should thrash you for saying that," he says. "I would never hurt her."

"It is perhaps not hurting you have in mind."

Even Khimo's mutilated eye opens wide and Yao can see his jawbone working under his cheeks. He takes a step forward, a finger pointing at Yao's chest. Yao's hands bunch into fists.

But Khimo's finger never quite touches him. Instead his good eye locks onto Yao's in a glare like a bush demon's. "I would *never* do that to another man's wife. No matter how much he did not deserve her."

Yao's heart, soft as ever, melts before such genuine anger and he does not know quite what to say.

Khimo stalks away, the now empty pale tapping against his leg.

Yao waits, giving the man a head-start so it won't look like he's shuffling along behind him. Glancing round he sees the baobabs and feels a stab of desire. Night is a long way away.

In the time he's been away at the latrine, some of the keener housewives have got their washing out. Amongst the pale yellow thatched conical roofs and the brown of the dried clay and dung walls, multicoloured *kangas* hang out on lines to dry. The big squares, which the women wind around themselves to form ankle length dresses, hang motionless in the still air. Tawia is attending to one, white swirls set against a pink background with a black border surrounding it all. It's one of Zinzi's. Along the longer edge is the *jina*, or message, saying: 'The Black Messiah will protect us all.'

"*Desibah*," she says shyly when she sees him.

"*Desibah*," he replies automatically. Good though the morning is, what they really need is rain.

"Is there anything I can do, *teatu*?"

"You bring a smile to my daughter's lips, young man. I ask no more. And please, for the hundredth time, call me Tawia. Mother-in-law is too formal. And please don't tell me I am like most other Ligandan *teatu*."

"You are not. And for that I am thankful and *I* ask no more." Ligandan mother-in-laws are legendarily intrusive and overbearing, especially when they live with the young couple. In Tembe's only newspaper, the main advice sought in the agony columns is how to deal with your *teatu*. Tawia, however, has never complained about his absences, or criticised anything he does. If anything, she seems quite proud to have him as a son-in-law.

Life on the plateau has taken its toll on her. Skinny and a

155

little bent from working in the fields, her face still retains the elegant tapering cheekbones that make her daughter so attractive. A ready smile is marred by several blackened teeth: a mark of her only weakness, her craving for honey. Hadgu claims he has more bee stings than hairs from years of pandering to her. If Zinzi is anything to go by, Yao is sure Hadgu gets his own kind of honey in return.

"But I do want to help. Can I fetch some water?"

"From your well?"

"It wasn't just me..." but she's already waving his modest response away. She goes up the step that keeps the smaller ground crawlers out of the hut and disappears inside. She returns with a dusty plastic drum.

Taking this, he's heading off when she calls out. "Tonight, remember! You and the men will meet. They will make you one of us at last."

He nods and sets off again, thankful that Bito doesn't practice some of the hair-raising initiation rites of other places on this continent. Waving away the fermented honey they would press on him would be his biggest challenge of the evening.

The little paths and shortcuts through the village have been worn to the bare earth, and only a few patches of dried grass cling to the edges of the huts where feet cannot naturally tread. Scruffy little yellow dogs sniff at his heels and yelp for scraps. Little children, most naked, run by shrieking in mock terror in their neverending chases. Some dive for protection under the *kangas*, to the vast exasperation of the women.

The well is just outside the village and is still a source of great pride for him. Pickaxes had made short work of the impacted dirt but then the going had got harder as they'd hit rocks.

Yao and his White Squad of six from Olomo's army had been sent into Bito to deal with the water problem. The nearest river, tumbling through a steep ravine full of sharp rocks, was a mile away. Broken bones were the worst that came from using this, though the walk back in high summer with a big plastic drum full of water bearing down on your head was also unwelcome.

Bito's water problems weren't common though. In other villages they usually had their own water supply and the problem was a slowly lowering water table. Mostly his team dug to make the wells deeper.

But here at Bito there had been no well at all. Though guided by a dowser they had been doubtful they would ever find water. His team soon became discouraged and he'd had to lead by example, digging like a man possessed.

And what a prize it had brought him! Climbing back up the ladder at the end of one day, the sweat dripping off his compact but well-muscled torso, he'd seen Zinzi for the first time. She'd been looking at him but had cast her eyes quickly down as soon as he'd spotted her.

He could hear his men still down in the well complaining away. Above ground there was only him and her, alone under the broad sky.

"Can I help?" he'd asked.

She'd shifted uncertainly from one foot to the other and couldn't seem to find any words. When she did, her voice caught and she had to repeat herself.

"You have been working very hard."

"We are here to serve God. And the villagers are God's children."

"Yes, but it is still kind of you," she'd said and, glancing up to meet his eyes, had changed his world forever.

Now here he is, years later, back at the well that is still as full as his love for her.

He'd had the sense to start the excavations between two trees. Once the well had been dug, they'd lopped these off just above their first forks. Laying a thick branch between the forks made it act like a pulley over which the dipper bucket rope could be run. Once they'd done that, they'd built up a circular clay wall around the well so nobody would fall in while they were raising or lowering it.

Bringing up the water with your own hands seems somehow much more honest than just turning on a tap.

And how much better it had tasted after he'd pulled that first bucket up and trickled a chill mouthful onto his tongue.

Three buckets fill the container. Afraid the container will fall and burst if he tries to carry it on his head, he holds the handle in both hands and shuffles forward into the early morning sun.

The Sands' AWACS E-2C Hawkeye had picked out the car and a dozen others as they came out of the Cleft. Circling at 30000 feet, with the volcanic peak at its centre, the plane's radar tagged and automatically tracked the vehicles.

Handovers were made to the surveillance drones as the vehicles moved out. Drones were still sparse so coverage wasn't complete and some vehicles were lost. Over the next few hours some were tracked to smaller military camps around the plateau, some to Tembe, some down to the ports, others to warehouses. The one which went to Olomo's palace, a colonial mansion on a rise above Tembe overlooking jumbled buildings flowing down like lava to the sea, excited the most interest.

One vehicle was something of an anomaly. It went out only twenty miles from the Cleft to a small village where it stopped for less than a minute before heading back. The short length of time suggested a drop-off rather than a pick-up.

It wasn't a man that noticed this, but rather a machine. A machine schooled to recognise anomalies amongst the swarming targets of that day. Lifeless itself, it made no value judgements, just tallied up the indications until a single digit became a one rather than a zero, tipping it into a higher category. It suffered not a microsecond of hesitation before transmitting this change.

For the next few days, drone packs coming in over Mali had chased targets with higher priority numbers. But finally, a drone leader, stripped of weaponry so it could be stuffed with radar and infrared and high-end optics, finished its mapping of Olomo's valley. As usual, the trees made a jumble of everything in all frequencies but for the harder, hotter targets of trucks with their engines running.

What targets there were had been identified and now only its accompanying weapon drones, underslung with their Hellcats, might be needed for the Cleft now.

The leader was suddenly available for the single anomalous track that as yet hadn't been followed up. Sweeping low over the endless plateau, the drone was at the village in minutes. Aware of local time to the nanosecond, it calculated the position and height of the sun. Banking in a wide arc, it tracked in along a north west vector so the sun would be behind it and blinding any human eyes.

Slowing now to reduce camera blur, coarser forward-looking optics captured the village of small huts spread in a large arc around a central hard dirt centre and with a single track leading out. Pattern recognition algorithms picked out the vertical elongated shapes that demarcated people from the squatter outlines of the huts and the animals. Tiny servos whirred to bring the finer optics to bear on the tops of these thinner shapes and hi def shots were taken.

Then, before it reached the village and became visible, it swung to the west, heading back to rejoin its pack before they flew back over Mali to land and refuel.

The thirty-eight images uploaded to the AWACs were transferred via satellite uplink to the Pentagon where they were lodged in a mainframe. Facial recognition software immediately discarded twenty of the images; the faces were too oblique or the shadow of something nearby was too deep on them. However, the other eighteen provided plenty of food for its linear, electronic thought.

The mainframe was powerful and relentless but, even so it took over a day to find three matches from all the databases it could access. Job done, it sent them down the line to the first human eyes that would see any of this.

To the owner of the eyes it was another day, another dollar. A lowly analyst in an anonymous, windowless room in Langley, there were *times she felt like an assembly line worker. Compare two pictures and, if they look like they may be a match, then look deeper. And how often did it pan out?*

Like looking for a ruby in the proverbial mountain of rock.

The first one from the drone was a joke. The matched image didn't even look close, as usual. Separation of eyes, width of mouth, all the stuff that could be put into nice discrete numbers; 'Bingo' the computer would say, but to the human eye it was like chalk and cheese.

The second was a so-so. Enough to check on the match's file. Drug dealer in San Diego suspected of supply cocaine to the Pacific Fleet. Drives a Maserati but now, the mainframe would have her believe, he was holidaying in a shit hole village in Western Africa.

The third match looked pretty good though. She checked the match's file, something tasty about attempted sabotage, then an addendum from an NCIS guy called Weiss. A marriage to a woman in a village called Bito.

She glanced up at the header info for the location of the drone's picture.

'Ah!' she thought.

This time she felt bits of exploding breast actually hit her on the shoulder. Pushing her hands up for protection, they hit something unyielding just above her head. Opening her eyes, she saw her hands hard against the coffin lid.

She opened her mouth to scream just as something touched her shoulder again.

A woman officer, unrecognisable in the low lighting, had pulled her curtain aside and was crouching down beside her. Joey lowered her hands quickly from where they'd flattened against the bottom of the bunk above.

The woman was whispering something: "...Beck. Admiral Macik sends his compliments. Says to come to the JIC right away."

"Uh, right," she muttered, but already the woman was gone. Joey levered herself around so she could get her legs on the floor. Leaning forward, she looked to the right and left down rows of stacked bunks, all with their curtains drawn. Used to tons of protesting metal being hurled into the sky, then landing again in controlled crashes, all just above their heads, the advent of a tiptoeing officer had had no impact on the slumbers of their occupants. Or of hers for that matter, until her shoulder had been shaken.

She'd thought the nightmares had gone but the execution of that woman in Liganda seemed to have triggered them again.

Hastily putting on the black overalls, she smoothed down her hair then made her way aft.

They were all waiting for her: Macik, Lewis, Terni and Lundt. Patterson was there as well. She hadn't seen him since the weapons demo in Nevada. Even Captain Larsen had been dragged down from the Island.

"Special Agent Beck," said Macik. "Just in time! We've found your little friend."

Still befuddled from sleep, she didn't get it.

Lundt seemed to notice. "The guy Wiggins put you onto. The one your colleague Weiss tracked back to Edinburgh, Scotland."

"The African," she said. "Got you."

Macik nodded to an analyst who clicked up the picture of a man struggling with a large white plastic container. Next to it, a zoomed-out image showed the track he was walking on. This led into a village of circular huts with conical thatched roofs.

"A little village called Bito," said Macik, "which is where the woman he married *in absentia* comes from. We picked him up leaving Olomo's stronghold and tracked him there."

She checked her watch. Midnight. The image showed broad daylight and the time stamp was days ago.

"And he's still there now?"

Without prompting, the analyst switched views and a red scale image flashed up. Something large was flickering in the centre and she realised it was a fire. Around it dots were being alternatively consumed and then spat out as the flames wavered.

"Real time infrared view from another drone. It's been up above the village since late afternoon. Looks like we've chanced on something of a meeting. Men only, so almost certainly soldiers, having a pow-wow east of the village. Saw your man join them but then it got dark. He'll be one of the fireflies you can see around the campfire." Macik's usually earnest tones were betraying a hint of excitement.

Joey glanced round slowly and felt something cold forming in the pit of her stomach. "And what happens now?"

"We take him out," said Macik evenly, but she saw his jaw working under his skin. Fire beneath the ice.

"But what about the village? There'll be women and children there."

"Seventy yards to the nearest hut. We'll knock a few over, sure enough. But it's not like the huts are made of bricks or breeze blocks. Injuries yes, but fatalities unlikely, except for this bunch." His fingers pointed to the fireflies. "Looks like we've got a high-level meeting here. Worth the risk and well within our Rules of Engagement."

He cocked an eyebrow at Patterson who immediately began to nod rapidly. "No doubt, sir."

Joey shook her head, trying to clear away the sleep. "But what about the hostages?"

Macik screwed his lips up in dismissal. "Washington thinks Olomo hasn't got the faintest idea what he's got himself into. He's a bush warlord. Machine guns mounted on the backs of Toyota pickups are his speed. If we surgically remove one of his main men, the same one who tried to sabotage the *Sands*, then he may get second thoughts."

"But there sounds like a lot of assumptions are being made. Is he one of his main men? We don't know what the African means to him at all."

Terni came in smoothly. "Not much else we can do. Olomo

doesn't seem to want to negotiate. We can't get enough troops in to even attempt to take his stronghold. Nearest landing strip is over a hundred miles away and he owns it. That might change, but right now we can't let this target of opportunity go."

"What about all your marines?"

"We're a littoral force. We can command the sea and the land close to it, but Olomo's valley is five hundred miles in country. We might be able to give our guys air support, so they'd get there in one piece, but Olomo'd sure as hell see them coming and kill all the hostages."

Even Lundt, the only other civilian, had the same hardened look as the others.

Joey felt like an ant watching an elephant start to charge. She was just as powerless to stop it.

Smiling grimly, Macik picked up a microphone. "OK Commander. Let her fly."

Helpfully, a smaller screen had been set up to show the frigate. She watched the column of fire rise into the sky.

Chapter 14. *Bito village*

First sweet, then savagely bitter, the honey drink is full of surprises. Then the long taste comes in and it's like sucking on iron nails.

"Goats blood," says Hadgu. "Just a little. Men need the strength it gives."

"Yes," says Samson, "and it makes the shit our women serve us taste good by comparison."

All the men laugh and even Khimo, whose deep-set eyes have hardly left him all evening, manages a smile.

The stars are spinning above and the sparks are rising from the swirling flames to meet them. Everything is in motion. The only thing anchoring Yao to the Earth is the goat meat sitting like ballast in his stomach.

"My son-in-law is a well-travelled man," says Hadgu proudly. "He has been to Germany and America and Great Britain."

That had been for Zinzi's ears only and he feels a stab of disappointment that she has shared it with her parents. But she's a simple honest woman and it is not in her nature to hold things back. Besides, what else was there to talk of in the vast black night.

"The women have small breasts, they say. In America, I mean." The old man, cheeks caved in where teeth have long decayed away, is making his first contribution of the night.

Yao tries not to slur his words. "No, old father, it is that African women have big breasts." The men roar their appreciation and he marvels at how loose his tongue has suddenly become.

Hadgu claps him on the shoulder. "How dare you even notice the American women's breasts."

Despite Hagdu's swimming eyes and his drunken leer, Yao can't stop himself apologising. "Oh, I do not like white women, father-in-law."

"Why not?" asks the toothless old man.

Yao absently takes a sip of the mead and instantly regrets it. This time he catches a hint of violets, like from a chocolate he'd once been given when staying at a guest house in Zurich. He remembers the little piece of sparkling purple candy adorning the chocolate's black top.

What else have they put in this drink? Probably anything to hand.

"Well?" says the old man and Yao realises his thoughts have wandered away. He'd better leave soon otherwise he will disappoint his wife. Their late-night lovemaking behind the baobab is what they both yearn for all day.

"The Americans, men and women, are not a happy people. They have much but are always striving for more. They can never be satisfied."

"That's old news. Tell us more about the women!" This comes from a younger man further along the ring and almost hidden by the sappy, resinous wood smoke. Yao has already forgotten his name.

Yao shakes his head. "I was warned the men of this tribe thought of little else."

The young man gesticulates, pointing a single finger at the sky. "And that is because we are real men. Plateau men. Mounting our women is our job and we are very good at it."

"Oh really," says Samson, the head man. "And who exactly of our women have you been mounting, young Kosey?"

Kosey leans back a little so he's hidden by the man next to him. There is no answer to that question that won't cause him trouble.

Yao takes pity on him. "The American women are afraid of everything, even of their own smell."

"I'm afraid of my wife's smell too," says Samson, and they all laugh.

"But you still can't leave her alone," says Hadgu.

165

"It's her or the goat."

A large log cracks loudly in the fire, making their laughter stutter, and a swarm of embers take flight.

"We are letting our new member get off too easily," says Khimo slyly. "It is not like in the old days."

"Ah, the old days," says Samson. He's a tall man with large knobbly knees which stick out from under his leather skirt. "The old days, when the women walked far to get water. Before this young man-made life easier for them. It would seem a shame to repay him by chopping a bit off him."

Yao swallows and Hadgu claps him on the shoulder again. "He is too good looking."

"And if we took something off his ears," says Khimo, "he'd have nothing left."

Now they are rolling around in their drunken laughter. Yao feels his face go red.

"But we can still mark you," says Samson, drawing out his wooden handled *seme*, the blade glinting in the firelight. Leaning over, he runs three fingers from Yao's ear to his nose.

But Yao isn't too worried, despite the general drunkenness which might make anything possible. It's true most of the older men have the cuts, though it's sometimes difficult to see them against the wrinkled, sagging skin, but the younger men are all unmarked. The custom is still universal amongst the women, however. He had not liked such mutilations when he was younger, but Zinzi's tribal scars have changed his attitude; they arouse him mightily.

"I am not afraid of your knife, Samson, but it would make my job more difficult. I would arouse too much attention in my travels."

Samson pinches the skin on the back of Yao's hand. "Oh, I imagine you can't help getting attention in America."

Yao shakes his head. "There are many black men in America, but none have tribal scarring. One look and they would know I am African."

166

"And why would that be a problem?" asks Khimo.

Samson leans forward and glares at Khimo, who holds up his hands and sits back quickly.

"So, this is all we're going to make him do? Get drunk?" says someone.

"For now," says Samson. "But when he makes Zinzi with child then we must really make him one of us."

"Too late to cut anything off then," says Khimo and doesn't seem to like the laughter this provokes.

"We'll think of something, when the time comes," says Samson nodding in his way to signal the discussion is over.

"Welcome though the young man's well has been," someone says, "isn't it about time the village bought something to haul the water back and forth? Even a little two stroke."

Yao hears Samson sigh and he guesses this is an old argument, so his eyes drift away from the fire and beyond to the huts where the yellowed grass of the thatch can be seen in the light of the flames. The women and children are safely tucked up there. These meetings always get a little out of hand, and it's easier to deal with the men when they've returned alone to their homes. The women are well versed in bringing them back down to size.

Surreptitiously he checks his watch and is relieved to see how late it is. Zinzi might already be waiting.

By now the conversation has cycled back to cattle and where they graze, as it always does. Voices start to rise as disputes, generations old, resurface. Even Hadgu, whose cattle herding days are over, is intent on this long running saga.

A careless comment sends one skinny guy rocketing to his feet. One eye socket is empty and, as he shouts his curses to the sky and shakes his head back and forth, the light cast by the fire makes it look as though a black hole is being stamped in and out of his face. It is an arresting sight and gets everyone's attention.

Yao slips easily away. Even if Hadgu has noticed he's sure he'll pretend not to. He was young once.

The long grass brushes his bare legs, the odd wayward

167

strand getting up under his skirt and tickling his balls. Already he can feel his heart thumping against his ribs.

The engorged trunk of the boabab rises like a mighty pillar into the night, its bark flickering with the faint light from the fire. Edging round it, his eyes try to pierce the stygian shadows cast by its bulk.

Hands come over his eyes and he feels the softness of her breasts pushing against his back. "Who do you think it is?" she whispers.

Pulling her further into the blackness, away from even the sharpest eyes back at the campfire, he grasps her head and tilts it back. Her mouth is already open and their tongues slither over each other like mating snakes. He feels her hand come up under his skirt and cup him.

The first time is always driven by desperation but she never seems to mind. Pushing her back against the tree, he pulls up her shift and brings his fingers up between her open legs, making sure she is ready for him.

Putting his hands under her bottom, he lifts her and she quickly grabs his cock and slips it into her. He lets her go, her weight bringing her down, impaling her on him. For a second, she hangs there, hands by her sides, mouth open in a rictus of sexual agony, then he is driving his tongue between her lips, his hands pawing her breasts through the thin cloth.

He's a gentle man, but at times like this he fears he will hurt her, that his thick cock will tear her apart. But, somehow, it never stops him.

And, God be praised, her slender body can withstand his muscular force, though pain and pleasure war across her face.

And as he comes, almost fainting with the release, her body too goes limp and they slide down the trunk until he's on his knees, her legs splayed over the tops of his thighs.

"I'm sorry," he says through thick breaths.

Her hands come to his cheeks. "You must never apologise my husb..."

The trunk of the baobab becomes a thick line of dark in a world of piercing light. Sound and fury tear at his clothes and his lungs feel like a giant is using them to breathe.

White turns to red as a cloud of flame roils into furious existence.

As the echoes of the blast die away, she's squirming off him and then onto her knees, crawling around the trunk. He crawls after her.

On one side, the thatched roofs are already alight; on the other, the long grass too is blazing. Between these there is nothing but a hole.

"Mother!" she yells and is already off, sprinting away between the clumps of burning grass. He follows as fast as he can.

Drawing nearer the village, the flames from the thatch reveal everything. The huts here have been flattened. Further in, some are still standing though all their roofs are burning. Dazed women and children are struggling out of the wreckage.

Tawia's hut is no more, the walls facing the explosion have tumbled back, while most of the roof has blown clear and is blazing in a heap further away.

The explosion, rather than breaking the clay walls into big chunks, has pulverised them. Getting Tawia out will be more a matter of digging. They stand there befuddled, not sure where to start, then something long and thin moves and they're clawing at the dust around it. It's a roof support and it has swung down across Tawia's upper arm. As the arm becomes revealed, they see jagged bone fragments sticking out of the skin.

He gently lifts the support and they pull her out of the remains of the hut and onto some grass, Zinzi cradling Tawia's arm as best she can to stop it moving.

"You will be alright," he says, knowing it is a lie. There are no ambulances or hospitals, not within a hundred miles. Villagers tend their own injured, but hundreds of years on the plateau have never prepared them for a catastrophe like this.

"You must find Hadgu," says Tawia gently. "Make sure he

169

is well and bring him to me."

Zinzi is looking at him, her feelings clear.

Reluctantly, already knowing what he will find, he turns back towards the burning grass behind the village and makes his way between the mounds of the demolished huts. He sees women and children, battered and bruised, but no men. He sees two bodies, shapeless, dirty and ragged in death.

Where the campfire has been, a giant has stamped a heel print deep into the earth. All combustible material has been blasted clear and there is nothing left to burn. Like the negative image of a funeral pyre, all around it the grass flickers and smoulders.

Chapter 15. *USS Benjamin F. Sands, Gulf of Guinea*

"That's the kind of game we're playing," said Lewis dismissively as they both followed Lundt's stately, bulky progress down the corridor, crewmen flattening themselves against the bulkheads to let her pass.

"A fucking cruise missile...on a dirt poor little African village. It's obscene." Riled by his complacency, she almost grabbed the back of his shoulder so at least he'd turn around and look at her.

"That Command Meeting was way back from the village. The villagers would have survived."

"'Command Meeting'. A bunch of men means a 'Command Meeting'. Since when?"

"Context."

"What fucking context?"

"The African. The bad guy you were chasing. He was there, remember? Clear target of opportunity and maybe our only chance to get him. If he does have other operatives on this boat then maybe it needed a signal from him to activate them. Or if there were bombs, a signal from him to set them off. We've eliminated those possibilities."

"But there were women and children in that village. And if you say 'Collateral Damage', God help me I'll drop you!"

At this he did stop and turn to look at her. His eyes narrowed when he saw the bunched fists.

"Look," he said placatingly. "Seventy metres. They'll be fine. And even if one or two weren't, then it has to be weighed against the six thousand lives on this carrier."

"But the people on this ship are military. The women and children were civilians. If the African had been just outside a little village in England, would we have used a cruise missile there?"

"Well no, but..."

"Of course we fucking wouldn't. But those villagers...they were just Africans."

"Children, children, play nice now!" Lundt had stopped and come back to them. "Look, none of us has any say over what this CSG does. I suggest we get on with what we do have control over. Specifically: the matter at hand."

Lewis ignored her. "If it'd been in England we'd have used other means."

"OK, what about a village in Russia?"

"Obviously we wouldn't want to maybe start a war with the Russkies."

"Fine, so admit we did it because any 'collateral damage' would be amongst poor, and by that I guess I mean powerless, Africans."

"Look, I wish it wasn't like this but it's the way of the world and always has been."

Lundt raised her voice. "Would you two knock it off? And keep moving; we're holding everyone up."

Joey could see a line forming behind Lundt and, glancing back, she saw six guys waiting behind her. They all looked pissed.

She turned back. "OK, keep going!"

As they shuffled forward, Lewis said: "Hey! Why don't we just ask this guy to come to us rather than go to him?"

Lundt shook her head. "Because we don't want to alert him. If the African has got to him, he may be tempted to do what he was paid to do. Not on my watch, thanks."

Lundt's Sig was in full view in a belt holster and it oscillated with the movements of her considerable ass. Joey had hers under her boiler suit but above a thin armless tee shirt. The shoulder holster had risen up, the leather strap chaffing against the bare skin of her armpit.

The shops of the Aircraft Intermediate Maintenance Division were far aft. The *Sands* had recently run into a swell, the ripples from a big storm far to the south. Over three hundred metres long, and at over a hundred thousand tons, the *Sands'* stately motion had been so smooth she hadn't really been aware of it, but now the pitching was evident, particularly at bow and stern. She had to drag a hand along the bulkheads to keep steady.

The Chief's office gave out on the entrance from the passageway and he saw them coming and quickly came to meet them. He was still quite a young man with a clean white shirt and no signs of oil under his fingernails.

"Lieutenant," he said, holding out his hand to Lewis.

"Nice to see you again, Chief. Chief Brown, these are NCIS Agents Lundt and Beck."

"Does Trask know we're coming?" asked Lundt, too keyed up for niceties.

"Of course not, just as the Lieutenant specified."

"Where is he now?"

"Well, that's the thing. He's out on the fantail. Be easier all round if I just sent for him to come here."

Joey looked at Lewis.

"The fantail's off limits to all but the specialist engineers," he said.

Before Joey could ask why, Lundt had bulled in. "Can't take the risk. He could do a lot of damage back there."

"Why would he do that? Why are you after him?"

"Let's just say we have good reason."

Brown was looking perplexed. "Trask's a sound worker."

"Doesn't matter. Will you take us to him?"

"Sure, but first you'll need these." He went to a locker and pulled out some bulky ear defenders. Once they were on, he started down the corridor taking them further aft, but then he turned and looked back. "Lieutenant, you stay behind us please."

Lundt following Brown and Joey followed her, Lewis bringing up the rear. The corridor took a few dog legs, seemingly to access all sorts of different sized compartments, each full to the brim with lathes and drills and fume cupboards and much else she didn't even recognise. She wondered how people could move around in there.

In some compartments, whole jet engines were opened up, whether for surgery or autopsy she couldn't tell. Every section of bulkhead, if not filled with racks of drill bits or tools, was plastered with posters showing component breakdowns or providing dire safety warnings.

Over the reek of the jet fuel were chemical smells like someone had smashed all the display bottles in an old-style pharmacy.

The unearthly shriek slashed through her ear defenders and had her crouching down in a sudden panic. Even doughty Lundt flattened herself against the wall. The noise was rising in volume and becoming almost unbearable, but then it suddenly cut out, leaving a fierce ringing in her ears.

Brown had stopped, arm back and palm towards them. He looked at his watch then signalled with three fingers. Joey glanced round, trying to work out was happening as the seconds ticked by, then the sound of a klaxon came reverberating at them off the metal bulkheads.

Brown signalled to follow and they went around a final turn in the corridor.

Joey froze in the natural light, bringing her arm up to ward it off. As her eyes adapted, they widened in surprise at the size of the compartment. After the cramped corridors and tiny compartments, something this wide just didn't seem like it should belong in the universe.

And she could see the Atlantic, its waters a delightful deep blue against the paler sky.

It'd been days since she'd last set eyes on it, when she'd slipped guiltily away to catch some fresh air and sun up on 'Vultures Row. The metal balcony there overlooked the flight deck and was just about the only place you could see it during operations if you didn't work on the bridge. She loved the place but she knew there were crewmen who spent days, weeks even, without ever seeing the sky or the sea or getting a breath of fresh air.

But here in the AIMD the sky wasn't above; it could only be seen through a large open section in the aft bulkhead. Above her, and roofing the compartment, would be the underside of the flight deck though it was too dark to actually see it against the natural light washing in. Along the bulkheads on either side were catwalks, all terminating in two huge assemblies at the stern. In the centres of these, constrained by metal struts and buttresses, hung the sleek grey shapes of two engines.

Brown was scanning round the compartment. Suddenly he pointed to the starboard assembly. A tall, thin black guy was stooped over a control panel. He was too far away for her to make out his face but Brown seemed in no doubt.

Lundt signalled to Brown and Lewis to stay put, then crooked her finger at Joey. It'd been Lundt's determined digging that had unearthed Trask's Ligandan ancestry, so Joey couldn't argue with her being point on this one.

They crept along the bulkhead, benches and tanks of fuel and liquid oxygen providing cover.

Trask seemed intent on his readouts, but then he turned and walked over to an equipment cart and started rummaging in a toolbox.

Getting close now, Lundt eased the Sig out of her holster, and Joey was reaching for the zipper in her boiler suit when a plane suddenly dropped into view and was roaring straight towards them.

Liquid scalded her eyes and she staggered back. Her hands came up for protection but something batted them aside and pain exploded in her jaw. Knees buckling, she crashed to the deck.

Above them the plane smashed down onto the carrier and the engine noise was shatteringly amplified.

Blinking, rubbing at her eyes, trying to clear them, she rolled onto her side. Beside her a beached whale was sluggishly twisting.

"Christ! Fucker got my gun!" It was Lundt.

Joey's hands were black with oil. Trask must've thrown it while they were distracted by the landing. Coming in low over the fantail, it'd looked like the plane was going to hit them.

Joey struggled to her feet and could make out Trask pelting towards Lewis and Brown. They had their hands up and were backing to the side to let him through.

Without thinking, she was already into her long-legged stride. Lewis stepped forward, like he might try to stop her, but she stiff armed his chest and sent him down on his ass.

Scrabbling her gun out, she slid to a halt at the first corner and jacked one into the chamber. Double handed and stiff armed she swung round it.

Nothing.

He might have slipped into one of the workshops and be waiting to clip her as she went by. But she figured he'd panicked. Why else run when there was nowhere to go?

Calculated risk. She started sprinting down the corridor.

Doors flew by either side but there were no gunshots. Out of the AIMD shops, she turned right into the long passageway, convinced he'd be heading forward, not wanting to get trapped in the last bit of corridor before the stern.

Sure enough, there he was ahead. Those that couldn't get out of his way into side compartments had gone down flat, covering their heads as he leapt over their bodies. Running fast, she was soon gaining on the lanky, ungainly figure.

Twenty yards ahead of her, he stopped suddenly and swung back, firing wildly. The bullet ricocheted, little explosions of sparks coming towards her along either side of the bulkhead.

Then he was off again.

Sprinting, she was soon bearing down on him. She saw fear on his face as he turned into a side corridor and she slowed down, more careful now. Sooner or later he'd be trapped and he'd have no choice but to try an ambush.

But she heard his running feet so she barrelled round. Down two more short corridors then suddenly there was diffuse daylight and another huge compartment. This one was full of planes scattered higgledy-piggledy, the ends of their wings uptilted to form a thicket of metal.

She dropped to a crouch and scanned round. She flinched at the sound of the shot and the bullet dinged off the fuselage of an F-14 just above her head.

She went flat now and saw him to the left amongst the jumble of wheels. They both fired, but her shot was closer. He scrambled to his feet and was jinking in and out of the undercarriages and away from her.

Getting through this place quickly was a fucking nightmare. A couple of hundred feet long and half as wide, the place was a maze of undercarriages. To her left she could make out the huge oval opening that was letting in the light.

Ahead, under the fuselages, she saw the crouching shapes of crewmen, hands over their heads.

But one figure was upright and running determinedly towards a hatch about twenty metres forward.

She was after him again and saw him jerk the hatch open and stagger through. She barged through, almost tripping over the knee-knocker.

He was there, not twenty feet away, and coming back towards her.

Guns up, they started firing. Ricochets make the corridor flash like lights on a Christmas tree.

A bullet struck her forehead and she fell.

Chapter 16. *USS Benjamin F. Sands, Gulf of Guinea*

She was still consciousness but things were very blurry. She heard the sound of the trolleys wheels when they clacked up as they went over every knee-knocker. Spring loaded, they thudded back down as soon as they were clear.

This, and no doubt the endless drills the orderlies were put through, got her to the hospital in no time at all.

She didn't get the number of fingers right and saw the medic's dismay.

"Can't seem to focus," she said, but her swollen jaw, from where Trask had punched her, thickened the words.

Then they were poking at her head, eyes creased with concern.

Then: "Non-penetrating," said someone triumphantly and she could see relief wash over all their faces.

She felt a pin prick. "That'll help," said another.

And it did just that, the drug sanding off the sharpness of the pains, eroding their confidence, turning them into the most diffident of aches.

She may even have dropped off for a while because the next thing she knew she heard familiar voices and found she had to open her eyes.

"How are you, Joey?" Lewis looked frightened and she felt his hand on her shoulder.

"She'll be fine," said someone. "Nasty bruise on her forehead, but we x-rayed and her skull's intact. Same with her jaw. Looks worse than it is."

"Guy could punch." Lundt hove into view, her face still smeared with the black oil. "Think he loosened a couple of my teeth," and she brought her hand up tenderly to the side of her face.

"What happened to him?" asked Joey thickly.

178

"You did," said Lundt. "Won't be punching girls around anymore."

"So, I got him?"

"Need an autopsy to be sure, but I counted three holes."

"But he got me as well."

For the first time, Lundt smiled. "Hate to rain on your parade, sister, but I think you got you. Bullet didn't go through your skull so must have lost a lot of energy first."

"A ricochet?"

"At that short range it'd take quite a few of those to leave only a bruise. My guess is when you fired down that corridor you hit it midway along. Bullet followed a diamond shaped trajectory, bounced of two bulkheads and a hatch, bringing it right back to where it started."

"Ah."

"Three out of four ain't bad, though." Lundt was sounding almost warm.

"He was coming back at me, in the corridor."

"Hatch at the end was locked. Rat in a trap," said Lewis. "Sure to happen. Can't understand why he ran in the first place."

"I've seen it before," said Lundt. "Panic."

Joey got herself upright, shooing away Lewis' attempts to help her.

The young medic was shaking his head. "You should rest."

"Why, you said no serious damage was done?"

"That was a big shock to your system. Plus, those meds we gave you were heap powerful medicine."

"I'm fine. Besides we need to find out what Trask was going to do, or what he's already done."

"You'd be better here," said the medic. "Beds not bunks. Sheets changed every day."

She felt herself weaken. Those racks with their unchanged sheets were purgatory for her sensitive nose.

'Toughen up,' she thought.

"I'll be fine." As she was a civilian, they couldn't order her to stay.

But the walk back to the office was an odyssey. Residual wooziness, and the pitching of the ship, stoked each other up until keeping 'one to the wall' became an absolute necessity.

At one point she nearly went over and Lewis reached out to grab her.

She snatched her arm away. "Leave me the fuck alone!"

He backed off, palms up.

Taking a seat in the NCIS office seemed like a lifesaver until everything began to swim around, making her close her eyes for a second.

She was grateful neither of them made a comment.

"This thing with Trask isn't good. God knows how many of the jet engines he could've got to," said Lewis.

"Maybe it's not as bad as all that, at least as far as the engines are concerned. I managed to get a word with the Chief while they were looking after...while you were busy." It was nice to see Lundt was treating her with kid gloves as well. "On this boat every bowel movement is logged and every piece of work on the aircraft is independently checked. So, he knows which engines were being tested in the bay since Trask was on board. Most go straight back on the planes after testing, some get stored.

"Trouble is: he also had full access to the Hangar Deck. It's a big place to search if you're not really sure what you're looking for."

"Yeah and we'll have to start the whole search again. He may only have started planting any bombs in places after they'd been looked at," said Lewis glumly.

Joey gave a very gentle nod. "True, and it's not like we're looking for a black ball with 'bomb' written on it. It'll be disguised as something. This place is full of stuff you could hide something in. I guess we'll just have to heave to and go through the whole place," she waved a hand to indicate the *Sands*, "with a fine-tooth comb."

"Never going to happen," said Lewis firmly. "The *Sands*

has a job to do. A fingertip search would take us out of the games for days. We can do a basic search but we can't stop what we're here to do."

Joey opened her mouth to speak but he cut her off with an emphatic sweep of his hand.

"Yup, it's risky but putting ourselves in harm's way is what we do."

"And anyway," said Lundt. "We may have got him before he did anything. All those gases for the torches, the liquid oxygen and God knows what solvents they use down there: plenty of chances to start a fire without a bomb."

"But could that really do much damage?" she asked. "I mean you can't move in this place without tripping over fire-fighting apparatus. It seems like every day there's a drill. They talked of little else on that induction video they showed me. I mean that bit where they showed the whole flight deck being washed down with..."

"AFFF?" said Lundt.

"... whatever. It was like the whole deck was covered in waves." It'd looked weird, like a fast running stretch of ocean had been lifted 60 feet up and deposited on the deck.

"Slight problem there," said Lundt. "AFFF is the best. Not only does it wash most of the burning stuff overboard, but it floats on the surface of the burning fuel that remains, putting it out. But it's not eco- friendly, so they withdrew it. Back to the old protein foam bullshit. Stuff isn't much better than water. I guess they haven't updated the induction video for a while."

"Fire's the worst," said Lewis. "Places like the Bomb Farm, starboard of the Island, really need AFFF. A burning fuel spill could cook-off the ordnance. Hangar deck really needs it to. One burning plane could set them all off. Political correctness getting in the way of war fighting, yet again."

Lewis seemed to be getting into his stride, weary cynicism being replaced by an unexpected earnestness.

"Fire is what does for carriers, whether by ordnance from

the air or by accident. During World War II, big carriers like the Lexington, Yorktown and Franklin were hit by bombs sure enough, but in the end were lost because of fire. Since the war there's been well over twenty major fires killing hundreds of men, mainly in the fires on the Bennington and Forrestal. So, after each fire we 'evolve'. We try to plug up what caused the fire, but they just keep coming. For example: the Bennington fire that killed over a hundred men was because of the hydraulic fluid in the catapults. Under pressure it can spray out into an explosive mist. So, we moved over to steam catapults.

"So, we keep evolving, but with a hundred thousand tons of ship and equipment and with thousands of people, this still leaves plenty of opportunity for fire to start. And that's not even counting when people start shooting at us. Or sabotaging us."

She liked this glimpse of a different, more committed Lewis. "And I'm guessing carriers haven't been shot at or sabotaged in the last fifty years or so. So, they haven't really been put to the test since man first went to the Moon. You're not making me feel too confident."

Lewis pursed his lips. "Carrier fleets are there to project power. Their presence alone can be enough. Sure enough, we can attack, like in Libya, but the truth is carriers really haven't had to defend themselves in generations. If we did come under attack, by war or sabotage, then it's possible the results might be...surprising."

Lundt raised an eyebrow. "How come you got so high up the chain, Lieutenant, with a negative attitude like that?"

"What have I said that isn't true?"

"It may be true, but the finest minds in the navy know it too. They'd have modelled all those scenarios on the best computers around."

"Have they? If they have no example to go on, not for fifty years anyway, and the systems and weapons have evolved in complexity beyond any single person's ability to comprehend in totality, then are you sure they can predict every scenario that's possible now?"

Lundt smiled grimly. "Let's just say finer minds than yours have worked on this, Lieutenant. That's good enough for me."

Joey shook her head but it made eyeballs feel like they were rattling around in her skull. "Whatever. We've all got to do what we can. Search his stuff for a start. Why don't I take his bunk and locker, you take whatever personal storage he had in the workshops. They all seemed to have lockers there as well."

Lundt nodded.

"Can you check for explosives? Can you do swab tests for residue?"

Lundt and Lewis both laughed.

"On a warship?" said Lundt. "Waste of time. Even the chaplain'd end up in Gitmo."

It turned out Trask's berthing space, shared with sixty others, was further aft than her own but otherwise it looked identical. Bunks, or racks as she'd learned to call them, were stacked in threes down either side of the usual narrow passageway found on the *Sands*. Each berthing space had a head containing showers and shitters.

Mid-watch, crew were either in their bunks with curtains drawn, or in the tiny common room chatting or watching the TV there.

Before indulging herself, she checked around to make sure she wasn't being watched. Leaning down and into the lower rack of the three, she smelled Trask's sheets. Disappointed, but unsurprised, she found nothing of the African in his odour. He may have been of Ligandan ancestry, but Trask had been born in the US and throughout his life would've consumed the same high protein, high fat diet as his compatriots. Plus, he'd been on the carrier for over a week. People worked hard on a carrier and needed big calories.

So, their sweat, as they tossed and turned in a sleep that was rarely deep, had a thicker but blander quality than the earthy tones of the African.

Below the bunk was a stowage bin but it contained only the man's most recent cast-offs. Next to the head of the bunk were the three upright lockers used by the men in the stack. Trask's name was on the right hand one. Even as she looked at it, she realised belatedly that, in the excitement caused by her downing, nobody had thought to search Trask's body for his locker key. That should have been Lundt's job but, as Joey had lain on that gurney, she'd seen real concern in the woman's eyes and couldn't find it in her heart to blame her.

Her head was already feeling better but she couldn't be bothered to go back to the hospital and its refrigerated mortuary to get the key. One or two deaths from accident per tour weren't unheard of, the flight deck with all its movement being one of the most dangerous environments to work. The little mortuary could handle that. But if they got into a real shooting war then the freezer spaces used for the food would be called into service.

She remembered reading how in the old days, when corpses were buried at sea, that they'd be wrapped in sailcloth which was then coarsely stitched around the body. And how the last stitch, by tradition, would be straight through the nose. They'd figured that if the person could still be woken, that would do it.

Would they still do that now? Would it be there as a line in a process document detailing, step by excruciatingly detailed step, what to do with a death at sea?

Realising her train of thought had wandered off, that she'd been standing there like a dope looking at the locker, she turned and headed aft towards the common room. Several crewman were sitting there, arms folded, looking at Fox news on the TV. The sound was turned so low she wondered if they were just following the strap lines.

"Special Agent Beck, NCIS," she said, flashing her badge.

They all turned to look at her, blinking in surprise.

"Any of you got a screwdriver I could borrow?"

"Not here," said one.

184

"A knife then?"

The men looked at each other. One pointed at a small cupboard attached to the bulkhead. "There's a knife in there, but it's not sharp."

Joey was sure they'd be checking out her ass as she bent to open it, but she didn't really care. The cupboard's little drawer had all sorts of stuff, mainly pens and some stationary, but there was also something that looked like a butter knife. Should be enough.

"Did any of you know Trask?"

Blank looks.

"What does he look like?" said one acne faced young guy.

"Did", she said. "He's dead."

"He racked here?"

"Yeah. Black guy, thirties, tallish." She stepped back into the corridor and pointed down it. "Four stacks down, lower rack."

She was finding their blank stares annoying. Sixty guys bunked here and on different watches. Not surprising they didn't know him.

"How did he die?" asked one of the others.

She didn't answer. Back at the locker it was more of a struggle than she'd have liked and the noise got several angry comments from behind the little curtains. Finally, the latch squeaked up enough to give. Hinges were oiled to within an inch of their lives in the sleeping areas, so the door came open without further disturbance.

Uniforms, underclothing, sunglasses. Rummaging underneath, she found some books. 'Africa: The Colonial Legacy' was one. 'The Rape of Africa' was another. She flicked through the well-thumbed pages. No handwritten notes or marked sections of text that she could see. On the inner side of the locker door were photos of black women, but not the gleaming fashion shots of sleek, toned African-Americans. Instead these showed real women going about their business in mud hut villages. Their clothes may have been poor but they were well covered, not even a breast showing. Despite their clothes and their surroundings, despite the wear and tear of their lives, the women were still somehow beautiful.

A faint unease made her shiver. Who, exactly, had she just killed?

Again, she must have drifted away and didn't hear him coming until he cleared his throat. Startled, she only just tamped down the impulse to punch him.

It was acne face. "Special Agent Beck, right? You're wanted."

"What?"

He beckoned and she followed him back to the common room. He pointed to a smaller screen beside the big TV showing messages relating to the *Sands*. Beneath something about a choir practice was: "Special Agent Beck to report to JIC."

"JIC," said the boy, apparently impressed.

"Home away from home," she said.

More women, but the same dishevelled hair, soiled clothing and frightened eyes. Bigger firing squad this time as there were three to be executed.

"Missionaries who were helping out with the vaccination program," said Terni. "You missed the trial but it was the usual bullshit."

Joey saw Macik's eyebrows twitch at the expletive but for some reason he let it go.

An old guy, a shock of white hair deeply contrasting with the blackness of his skin, was reading out the charges. "Terrorism, murder, crimes against humanity." His voice was deep and forceful and it was like Moses himself was talking.

"Who is that guy?" she asked.

"We don't know. Probably a local judge in their quaint judicial system."

Macik turned. "I think we can do without the irony today, Commander.

Terni nodded. "Sorry, sir. Justice is tribal, village level

186

even. There's something more formal in the big cities but it's still not what we'd recognise as justice. The police or some other authority states the case and the judge decides. Sometimes he might take the trouble of interrogating the defendant and any witnesses, but sometimes not. The judges may be absolute in their own courts but if Olomo tells them to jump...."

As the soldiers lined up, two of the women started to wail in terror and thrash against their bonds. The third, a tall woman with fair hair cut severely short, stood as straight as she could and stared contemptuously at the men.

"Who's she?"

"She's a medic who works for the missionaries. Dr. Tori McAdam. Devoted her life to the poor. Married to an engineer with two grown up kids. Rest of the family's back in Kenya where they've settled, though they're all originally from the States. Wyoming."

"Tough old bird," said Joey.

"This is terrible," said Lewis.

They didn't catch the command but the soldiers suddenly brought their guns up. For the first time she noticed they were AK-47s. Didn't they use rifles for executions? Must have them on single shot mode like before, she thought absently.

But maybe Lewis had better eyes because he was quickly on his feet. "They're not going to...!"

The crash of the automatic fire drowned out the women's shrieks. Bullets tore into their bodies as the soldiers emptied their magazines over what seemed like an eternity.

Then the shattered bodies just hung there like bloody rags on a laundry line.

On the *Sands*, and in that cold, cold room in JIC, Lewis finally whispered: "Barbarism."

"This...is...just...not...comprehensible," said Macik slowly, and Joey thought she could just hear the faintest flutter of alarm in his voice. "It's like he's deliberately provoking us. Shooting women. Missionary women at that. It's as though he's wanting us

187

to kick his miserable country back into the Stone Age."

"There's only one way out of this now," Lewis said to her quietly.

Macik must have heard. He nodded. "I'm betting the President's already on speed dial."

He turned away from the grisly spectacle on the screen. "So, let's get ready. War footing."

"I just cannot believe this." In disgust, she threw the stack of documents across Lundt's desk where they came down in a pretty fan shape. She blinked in surprise but then the anger and frustration swept back. They should be out there helping look for bombs, not filling in incident forms about what had happened with Trask, but Macik had been emphatic.

Lewis was supposed to be helping but he wasn't.

She's always hated paperwork but this wasn't just the usual criminal reports. It included a whole slew of Health and Safety bullshit. Even worse, it was boiler plate stuff, as though the complexity and wealth of incidents could be covered by standard forms.

"And how exactly do I construct an audit to check whether measures I put in place (what measures?) are enough to ensure this doesn't happen again?"

Lewis shrugged.

"Thanks for the advice."

"Sorry," he said. "This stuff makes my mind go blank. But you've got to put something down otherwise the Health and Safety Police will be on to you."

"So what? What can they do?"

"They can go to Macik. And he can do what he likes."

"Surely Macik doesn't bother with this stuff?"

"How little you know! Macik makes micromanagement look like surgery with catchers' mitts. Says you can't run something unless you have an intimate knowledge of it."

"But what about the bigger picture? That's what Admirals are for. That's why he has Captains and XOs to run the fleet. What kind of bigger picture can he have if he's always diving into the minutiae?"

He shrugged again. "Good question."

"So, you're not going to help me fill this in."

"Look: just put something down! Something smudgy. 'Six monthly serial assessments', 'Review committee', that sort of thing. Health and Safety will file it away and it'll all be forgotten. You'll be long gone if there was ever any comeback. Just don't put my name on it."

"And this injury form. There's more boxes here than in UPS. Which ones do I tick? I mean, look at this! It wants to know if my injuries and the incident had a racial or sexual component."

"That actually says 'sexist'."

"Yeah, thanks for pointing that out, it really helps. Let's see: a black American woman citizen shoots herself while in a gunfight with a black man who is also an American citizen but is actually working for an African dictator who clearly hates Americans. Exactly which fucking boxes am I supposed to tick?"

They looked at each other for a few seconds.

"Useless!" she said finally.

He nodded his head in acknowledgment.

She started to quickly tick boxes at random.

"That's the spirit," he said.

"That business about 'War footing'. That sounded impressive."

"Less so than you might think."

"Yeah?"

"We were due to do our routine tour of the Atlantic and that's what we're geared up for. Nobody expected us to get involved in a land war, not at the moment anyway. North Africa is still bubbling away with all sorts of Islamic insurgencies but no President is going to want to get dragged into that. Even if they were it would be the Mediterranean Fleet that would do the heavy

189

lifting. So we don't have our amphibious group with us, and that's what we'd really need if we wanted to bull in and rescue the hostages."

"But it has been sent for now, right?"

"It'll take time. Anyway, what with the cuts, the amphibious groups have taken a big hit. After all, under what circumstances were they anticipated to be used nowadays? So even with redeployments, we'd be pushing it to manage to get a few thousand boots on shore. Olomo's army, or at least the armed support he can call on, may be in the six figures."

"But what about in Iraq and both wars with Saddam? Troop build-ups were in neighbouring countries. Huge numbers went in."

"Yeah but Saddam wasn't that popular with his neighbours. In fact, they were more than keen to see him squished. Here on the Guinea Coast, Olomo has a lot of traction with his neighbours. And even where he hasn't got that, they fear him. Using their countries as a beach head would be like declaring war on him. And if we didn't succeed in squishing him...."

"They'd be afraid that public opinion back home in the US would find any losses unacceptable and eventually we'd leave, as we pretty much always do, and then they'd be at his mercy."

"Yeah, we don't have a great track record there."

"So, what can this CSG do?"

"Bomb the bejesus out of them, shoot them up."

"But here in Africa, insurgents, or warlords, take your pick, seem to use Toyota pickup trucks with machine guns mounted on the back. Hundreds, maybe thousands of them. How many of those could we shoot up?"

He just smiled.

They were alone in the office. Lundt, at least, was doing what they should all be doing and was out looking for signs of Trask's handiwork.

The NCIS office was small and they'd been sitting side by side as they went through the forms. It had been a long day.

There'd been bursts of fear and a lot of running about and neither had had a chance to shower. Whatever deodorant he'd been wearing had worn off. The smell she was getting now was the real man. A connoisseur, though not necessarily always a fan, of man sweat, she had to admit his wasn't bad. Slight tang but nothing oppressive: slightly leathery in fact. Sort of calming.

Out of the corner of her eyes she'd seen him checking her out a couple of times when he thought she wasn't looking.

"You married, Lewis?" she asked.

"Not anymore. Good job my name isn't John."

"Why?"

"'Cos then it really would have been a 'Dear John' letter."

"Sorry to hear that."

"It wasn't so bad. We'd grown apart, the usual."

"Kids?"

"Nope. She was keen on her career. A librarian...."

"You got a Dear John letter from a librarian?"

For a second, he looked angry, but then relaxed and gave a reluctant smile. "I used the term librarian because it's a word even you would understand, but she's actually a data archivist. She takes a meta view of the whole process of information storage and retrieval."

"Ah, now I see. Not like a librarian at all."

"How sweet you are. So, what about you?"

"Never married. Men come, men go."

"And when they go, is it voluntarily?"

She looked into his eyes and gave it a few beats. "Not usually."

"Eat 'em up, spit 'em out?"

"That's been said, once or twice."

"Scary!"

"Don't worry, a pasty white boy like you has got nothing to fear."

He laughed. "You should've ticked that racism box."

"'You try black, you never go back'. Isn't that what the

191

white women say?"

"I'd be the last person they'd tell. Best keep that trenchant little dictum to yourself. Macik would not be amused."

She shuffled the papers together. Maybe she'd get back to finishing them sometime. "I'm going to hit the rack. I've had enough of this day."

He stretched, the material pulling tight across his chest. "Me too."

They edged round their sides of the desk. As she turned, he must have got a full view of the side of her face where the punch and bullet had hit. She'd been feeling the bruising develop. He blinked in surprise and unthinkingly reached out to touch her forehead. His touch, though soft, was excruciating; the proverbial blow upon a bruise.

Without thinking, she slapped his arm down and barged into him, driving her left arm behind him as she turned, grasping his left arm above the elbow. Pushing back against the bulkhead, she was squashing his right arm behind her back. She felt a stab of pain in her skull as their bodies crashed back, but she held her grip and pushed hard with her feet, trapping him.

Their faces were close. The shock and alarm in his eyes almost broke her heart with their sudden vulnerability. Before she could stop herself, she'd locked her lips on his and was trying to force her tongue between them.

His head tried to jerk to the side, but her right hand was still free and she used it to pull it back round. She thrust her tongue against his teeth.

Her cheek was hard against his nose and she felt his mouth come open for breath. She drove her tongue deep. He tasted of coffee. He tasted good.

Her right hand was dropping down to grab his balls before she realised what she was doing. Easing her body back, letting go of his upper arm, she let him wriggle out of her embrace.

In a flash he was at the door and pulling it open. "Jesus!" she heard him say. Then he was out the door, slamming it behind him.

She waited as her breathing slowly returned to normal. 'Whoa,' she thought, 'Where did that come from?'

Chapter 17. *Tembe, Liganda*

It has been a long drive and Justice is weary. Infinities of red dust and straggly grasslands, desperate for the rains, have finally given way to the ragged outskirts of the city. The road becomes lined with shacks that are both shops and homes, precarious stacks of shabby goods spilling out of them. Sun stunned men and women superintend them, huddled in what little shade is available.

Even here the roads are deeply rutted tracks, like lacerations in the skin of the planet.

The driver is using his horn almost continuously now. People stand aside smartly enough but carts and donkeys have to be dragged out of the way of the motorcade. A few SUVs back, some of the other drivers are starting to sound their horns out of boredom and frustration.

The noise is like a clarion call for the curious and soon the streets are lined, people waving and cheering and thinking it might be Olomo himself, though the tinted glass keeps its secrets.

It makes Justice think about how special Olomo is. Unlike like the woeful tide of other African leaders, Olomo does what he can for the people. He doesn't construct palaces or divert national funds into offshore accounts. No art treasures or foreign properties are salted away; no mistresses in fine apartments languish on the Cote d'Azur.

That's why the people love him so much. Poor and not always with enough food, yet still they'll turn out in the brutal sun and wave enthusiastically at the possibility of his mere presence.

And when his beneficence doesn't work, when people impede his plan, sometimes not through malice but from misplaced adherence to rigid ideals, well then that is where Justice comes in.

In the early days the problem was with the remnants of

the old dictator's forces. Skulking back to their villages in the bush, pretending they'd been farming all along and had nothing to do with the outrages. Eyes wide with their innocence, trying to disappear on the endless plains.

But Olomo was thorough. Even when Mamadou's palace was stormed, it wasn't the armoury Olomo's troops made fast right away. Instead it was the records, mildewed in rusty filing cabinets though they might be, and indecipherable to the illiterate troops.

Mamadou, catamite of the British, had absorbed his master's love of bureaucracy. A wealth of records was accumulated over his long-dissipated reign. To Justice's security team it was a gold mine.

Mamadou's influence had been tribal, mainly amongst the harsh lands to the east. Villages there were sparsely spread and communications were poor. And so, when Justice made a few vanish from the face of the Earth, it was as if they'd been reclaimed by the inhospitable plains.

Once the dictator's dregs were sorted out, the next problem had been here in Tembe: the lecturers, the civil servants and the intellectuals. Justice knew Olomo could not be shackled by their finicky sensibilities, that his plan needed strength and single mindedness. Democracy was a luxury that would come later.

Justice remembered The Point. An old fortress of crumbling sandstone, Portuguese it was said, on a headland to the west of the city. The dungeons still intact and cool whatever the heat. A place of ancient horrors.

That is where he brought them. Them and, sometimes, their well-fed women.

The motorcade rumbles onto tarmac at last and, ahead, the ground rises to the English District, as it is still called. It is indeed like crossing a border into another country. Wrought iron fences, painted black but always popping with bubbles of rust, enclose gardens shaded by magnificent old trees. The houses, absurd alien imports from a different climate, shine with sunlight reflected from myriad windows in their stately facades. Windows that let heat out when you want to keep it in and let it in when you would give anything to keep it out.

But now, below the stately windows, hang the rainbow colours of drying clothes. Built by the British for the British, ownership had seamlessly changed to the ministers and generals of Mamadou.

The cavernous rooms, in the past silent but for the sounds of a single family, are now brimming with noisy life. Now full of the extended families of Olomo's friends from the old days, they give the buildings more use than all the previous owners combined.

The motorcade turns into the long, ascending boulevard that takes them to the Pink Pustule, as it is known by the latest inhabitants of the English District. Even now it makes Justice' skin crawl with the shame. Mamadou's palace, its brick the same colour as the skins of the old oppressors, should have been dynamited but Olomo has kept it. Supposedly it is a reminder of centuries under the heels of the Europeans.

Which is why, in Justice's personal opinion, he shouldn't have let his wife Meelo and her children stay there. Love may be blind, but Meelo's greedy embrace of luxury is not fitting for one so ascetic as Olomo.

The ten SUVs are expected, so the guns are still just hanging on their straps from the guards' shoulders. Sloppy, but at least they don't open the gates. Instead a guard mooches over to the driver's side and peers in as the glass slides down to admit a fist of boiling air. One glance across at Justice is enough, and the guard is signalling frantically for the gate to be opened.

The heavy gate slides back, then the SUV is crunching over pink gravel in a wide arc to take it round the building and to the main door on the opposite side.

Justice climbs out, sliding on shades and his khaki baseball cap. He looks away from the house and over the view down across the city to the sea. A few rusty freighters anchor in the bay, patiently waiting their turn. The river, disgorging fine red silt, hasn't been cleared for years and few berths can still take them.

He should go straight to the main door, its dark imposing oak looking like a distended orifice in the pink of the facade, but he can't help but scan the skies.

It's going to be difficult. The non-reflecting paint and what colour it has will be dull, neutral. Only its movement might give it away so, though he stares straight ahead, he's hoping to catch something in his peripheral vision.

He's still for several minutes while he hears the drivers shuffling uncomfortably on the gravel behind him.

And finally, there's the faintest tickle in his peripheral vision and he waits, unblinking, until it drifts more centrally.

Now he knows where it is, his eyes can move to follow it. It's a shade too grey for the blue sky but if you blink you can lose it.

And eventually he has to do just that, and it is as if the Evil Bird was never there.

The drivers are exiled to the old stables for the night, but Meelo begrudgingly lets Justice have a room on the ground floor: a study with a chaise-longue which gives him more softness than he is used to.

Dreams of the red dust, to which he has returned so many, keep his sleep light.

It's still dark when he comes to, sweating despite the cool air gusting out of vents in the floor. He feels a presence. Beneath the sound of the far away generator and the clanking of the air conditioning, something nearby is rustling.

Reaching carefully under his pillow, his hand closes over the knurled butt of the 1911 and he deactivates the safety.

Bringing the pistol slowly out and over the blankets, he eases himself upright. Something blacker than darkness is moving towards the foot of his bed. Sighting carefully, he starts to pull the trigger.

"Hello," says a tiny voice.

Sighing, Justice eases the safety back on and hides the gun under the blankets. Reaching across, he finds the light on the table next to the couch and turns it on.

A little arm comes up to shield dazzled eyes.

There are too many to be sure but he thinks this one might be Ayesha. Wide spread eyes over a cute little chin, two bunches of hair sticking up like antenna, each secured with a red bow.

"You should be in bed."

"I wanted to talk to you about something."

"What?"

"You work for Daddy, don't you?"

"Yes."

"Why isn't he here with us?"

"He's busy. You'll see him tomorrow. We're leaving early. That's why you should be in bed."

By now his eyes have adjusted and he can see her better. Five years old, perhaps, a necklace of what look like shells around her neck. A tiny tick of a scar under one eye. A pretty little thing, despite the pout.

"Want to see him now!"

"Come on," he says, getting out of bed. "I'll take you back to your room. But you've got to be quiet." If Meelo found him with the kid then God knows what she'd suppose.

"You're Ayesha, right."

She seems very pleased he's got it right and Justice suddenly remembers she's one of twins. The other is called Siana and they're identical.

Lucky guess, but it works like a charm, and he lets her lead him back to her bedroom.

"What do you want to be when you grow up?" Not used to children, this is his only conversational gambit.

"Super model," she says with implacable certainty, like it was just a matter of time.

"Of course," he says.

She climbs into bed and he clumsily tucks her in.

"We will see Daddy tomorrow? You wouldn't be telling a fib."

"You'll see him."

"Promise!"

"I promise. Now go to sleep!"

"Daddy says I am his little princess. He likes me more than Siana. You must kiss me goodnight!"

The disjointed information has him at a loss for a second, but then he leans in and kisses her gently on her forehead.

Without a word, she turns away from him and burrows under the sheets.

He shakes his head sadly. For a second, doubt creeps into his mind.

He won't find sleep again tonight.

Six children, six harried nannies, one mouthy wife and mounds of luggage beyond belief. The ten SUVs are barely enough and the loading takes forever. Every time they seem ready to go, one of the kids breaks away and rushes back into the building. Justice, the only one who dares touch them, has to traipse back across the extensive red marble of the entrance hall to fetch them back.

He's desperate to get out of the place. The sun is halfway to its zenith and they still have a hundred miles to go. They have to be there well before sunset.

Ayesha and Siana, as the youngest, get to sit with Meelo and one nanny in their Landcruiser. Justice is the most senior officer there, so Meelo feels it only right they share the Toyota with him.

Finally, they're off and are soon out of the city. The kids aren't too bad but they seem to be going through a stage of fighting against their identical appearances. He meets all requests to judge who is the prettiest with a stony silence.

If these weren't Olomo's kids...

"When do we get there?" Meelo is fanning herself with something turquoise and shimmery like a butterfly's wing, though the air conditioning is doing a good job.

"Perhaps four hours. The road gets a little better soon."

Outside, the vegetation seems to be melting away in the heat. Even the acacias are wilting, making the malevolent thorns more evident. A few strands of brown grass survive precariously.

"I never liked the farmstead. Will there be cooks? Should we have brought our own?"

Justice has noticed this about her before. A neurotic questioning of decisions long after the possibility of changing them has passed.

"Everything is arranged. You have no reason to worry."

"I don't understand why he's seeing us. He's safe on the plateau, in his camp there. The Americans hate him. They will want to kill him."

"Perhaps he misses you very much," he says softly.

"Then why don't you take us to the plateau?"

"Because that is where they may attack, to free those human experimenters we arrested. If would be dangerous for you and the children."

He turns to look at her. Motherhood may have taken its toll, filling out her elegant, high cheek-boned features, but she's still a beauty with flawless skin that has never needed make-up. The daughter of one of Olomo's original bush soldiers, she's adapted to her new life quickly and effortlessly. That she has ever carried water from the well is beyond imagination.

Once she gives reign to her neurosis, it's difficult for her to stop.

"And that sow Mary and her litter?"

Justice sighs. "What about them?"

"They won't be there, at the farm?"

"Of course not. Not after what happened last time."

A reconciliation, an attempt to get both Olomo's families

to live under one roof, rapidly degenerated into literal warfare, nannies included. A score of soldiers, terrified of hurting any of them, were needed to drag them all apart. One of Mary's savage little brats kicked Justice on the shin. It ached for a week.

Mary's parents had both died of Aids and she was brought up in a missionary run orphanage. They were brutally strict Lutherans, according to Olomo, which explained why Mary is often wild and given to eye-wateringly frank outbursts.

If Justice was in Olomo's shoes, he'd settle for the more generously proportioned and less temperamental Meelo. But, somehow, Mary has Olomo in her thrall.

And that is not good for Meelo.

Olomo has chosen the place well. The farmstead is timber built with a red tiled roof and a veranda that goes all the way round. A stable block near to the house is a more recent addition. Leading away from the buildings is the paddock. An ill-considered plan by the original British owner to breed horses had foundered. Flies and worms, and the diseases they often carry, devastated the beautiful creatures. The stables had been converted to a storehouse, and the farm went over to rearing the local breed of sheep that were more resistant to just about everything. After the civil war, Olomo took it as his own home. It was modest accommodation by any other African leader's standards. The stables were converted again into rough and ready conference facilities for his high command.

As the circus noisily disembarks, Justice goes to the back of the SUV and digs out the Sony camera. High end, and with a huge memory, it can take an hour or more of Hi-Def video plus some exquisitely detailed stills. Standing to the side of the crescent of parked SUVS, he begins to take footage of the kids. Let loose from the long car journey, they chase each other around drivers struggling with the heavy luggage.

After one final pan over the buildings and the paddock, he lets the camera hang from its lanyard round his neck and goes back to the SUV for the satellite phone. There's only one speed dial number. As he holds the phone to his ear, his eyes automatically look up to the sky as though trying to find the satellite.

It takes a few seconds. Perhaps the rumbling of the tyres on the rutted roads make it difficult for them to hear the warbling phone.

"Yes?" says a voice at last. It's Charles, his second in command.

"We're here. You?"

"Two hours."

Justice terminates the connection. Two hours would leave barely three hours of daylight. Would that be enough?

Having no stomach to face the family again, he begins to pace the property, checking security. The land, fed by several rivers, is greener here. Once the place was marshy and even more fever ridden. The white farmers had taken the credit for damming and redirecting the rivers nearly two hundred years ago, making the land more productive. Except, of course, they'd not actually done the work. They'd only directed whilst people like him had laboured in the flies and the sun; had suffered the lassitude of malaria, only to be labelled as lazy *kaffirs* by the whites. As ever.

His guts feel like they're coiling up like a snake. The anger eases his conscience.

A few hundred metres to the side of the house is a row of tall fig trees and he seeks shelter there from the sun. Sitting down, his back against the trunk, he watches wispy clouds forming over the far hills and thinks of rain. Everyone did this when the rains came late.

The call comes an hour later. "Fifteen minutes," says Charles.

Justice gets to his feet and starts to walk quickly, grasping the camera to stop it banging against his chest.

Seeing him coming, the guards on the veranda struggle to attention. By the time he's got to them, all six are waiting. "Lockdown," he barks, "Nobody in, nobody out."

He tries the door and it's unlocked. He turns around to the nearest guard. "Once I'm back out, this gets locked."

Inside it's cooler. The floor is bare boards but the house is well furnished with stuffed leathers chairs and couches in the large lounge area. To the right he hears the cooks at work in the kitchen and, from above, come the thumps of the children running around upstairs. No TVs or other electronic diversions. Olomo is strict about this for his family.

Meelo, on one armchair, is looking at him over the top of a magazine.

"Don't you knock?"

"There's a problem," he says calmly. He sees her tense. "Men were seen, down by the river to the north."

"Americans?" Her eyes are wide with alarm.

"Probably not, but we'll take no chances." He points to the entrance. "This door gets locked. Whatever you do, keep the kids in here. You've got guards all around and your husband will be here with even more soon. They'll go straight to the stables."

"Can't I see him before...?"

"There'll be time enough for that later."

She looks uncertain and he doesn't wait for her to think up anything else to say. Taking the key from inside the door, he steps out onto the veranda and gives it to the waiting soldier.

"Locked, whatever happens!"

To the south, where the road runs, he can see the advancing cloud of dust and he starts walking to meet it. Fifty yards from the house he flags the six SUVS down. He goes to the passenger's side of the third and watches as the tinted glass slides down.

'Not bad,' he thinks. Close up the eyes are yellow and the skin is more saggy. Build's the same, but the man's sitting so he can't judge his height. Uniform's perfect.

The guy blinks against the light and coughs. Whisky smell.

"OK?" he hears Charles ask from the front passenger seat.

"Yes. Quickly now, then return to the Plateau. You are needed urgently." He sees Charles nod repeatedly, overdoing it.

Justice steps back and the SUVs crunch away and are soon by the stables. He takes out a small set of binoculars from an inner pocket and watches as the men disembark. He hisses in disapproval. These guys are shambling fuck ups: nothing military about them. From a distance the smart khaki, the nearest thing in Olomo's army to dress uniforms, might carry it if you didn't look too closely.

The tall figure climbs slowly out of the third SUV.

Something streaks into his vision. A child, Ayesha or Siana, is running pell-mell towards the gangly drunk. From far away he can hear the shrill excitement in her voice.

But then her head jerks back and she tries to stop. She skids and loses her footing, falling back on her bottom. She looks up at the man in disbelief.

Charles grabs her up and carries her back to the house, her head peeping over his shoulder. Justice sees her puzzlement.

Looking back, he sees the men ambling into the stables.

He begins to pace backwards, back across the grassland and away from the buildings and paddock. He unslings the camera and begins to shoot. Zooming first on the stables, he sees a driver lock the door after the last of the uniformed men goes in.

At the house a guard unlocks the door and Charles is shooing Ayesha/Siana in. He notices the guard has to pull against the door to close it, as though someone is trying to stop him.

Charles is walking back to the cars now, too quickly to be casual. Justice looks back at the guards, worried they might be becoming suspicious, but the two he can see are looking incuriously away across the paddock.

Charles makes it back to the motorcade. The engines start and the cars do an ungainly 180 across the grass of the paddock and then head back down the road.

Justice looks up from his camera, checking his own distance. A hundred metres maybe: too close still.

Lengthening his backward stride, he looks again through the viewfinder and zooms in on the veranda. Faces are at the window nearest the door: Meelo and one of the twins. He notices a soldier crouching below the window frame and guesses this was where Ayesha had climbed out.

Some editing would be required.

He looks up again. Two hundred metres. That should do it.

Keeping the camera running, he can't help but look around.

There was always the worry they would only use a Hellfire. The Evil Birds hunted in packs nowadays so Hellfires were always available. Would they opt for the immediacy of...?

The blast wave kicks him off his feet. His mouth foolishly closed, he thinks his eardrums have burst. Dust pulses into his nostrils and makes him sneeze and gag.

But sounds begin to trickle back as he spits out the dust. Getting unsteadily to his feet, he shades his eyes and looks back at the farmstead.

Too much smoke and dust, though he sees flames flickering within it.

Too big for a Hellfire. He waits in case they send in a second cruise missile.

He starts filming.

He'll stay where he is until the motorcade gets back. They would have been waiting a couple of miles away, waiting for the attack.

Eyes still stinging, he finally hears the crunching of the tyres and starts forwards.

A faint breeze is clearing the smoke. The stable is a crater now. The house has been pushed over but at least not vaporised. He's dismayed to see some of its timbers in flames.

They'll have to work fast.

He keeps the camera running, but makes little attempt to aim, as he lopes back to the remains of the house. The motorcade has already got there by the time he arrives, and men are frenziedly scooping at the wreckage.

A tiny bloodied arm protrudes from a pile of roof tiles, and the men quickly clear away the rubble around it, but it is to no avail. A roof timber has fallen across the child's chest, caving it in.

"Meelo," says Charles. "Last I saw her she was by the window which would have been...there."

They dig again. Justice only recognises her by her clothes. She must still have been looking out of the window. The fragments of glass have flayed the skin off her face, gouging out her eyes and scything off her lips and nose.

Justice catches it all on the camera: the feverish excavation, the fine dress, the mutilated face.

"Hey," says someone. "I think this one's alive."

Sure enough, a little leg is slowly flexing from under wooden wall blanks and broken red tiles. The men begin to scoop the debris away more gently now. One even begins to brush dust from the leg.

When the fabric above the knee is revealed, he knows it is Ayesha. When her face is finally cleared, he's ready.

Perhaps her mother's body has shielded her from the glass rain; her face is hardly cut at all.

But something more solid has hit her shoulder, and the broken collar bone has forced its way out of her skin. The shoulder joint had been smashed and the arm has come out of its socket, held on only by a few sinews.

"Help me," he hears her whimper.

He quickly brings up the camera, framing the shot.

Chapter 18. *USS Benjamin F. Sands, Gulf of Guinea*

"Hey," said Lundt. "Check this out!"

Joey looked up from her terminal to see Lundt open her desk and start digging amongst the junk in there. Fishing out a remote, she pointed it at the office's smaller wall mounted TV. Usually showing only internal ship messages with the sound turned off, it now showed a CNN anchor woman. A strap line at the bottom of the screen said 'Olomo taken out'.

As the sound came up she saw some buildings surrounded by fields of yellowing grass. One second the structures were there, the next they were gone.

"What you are seeing is a cruise missile strike on one of Olomo's headquarters. Pentagon sources indicate that Olomo and his senior staff were in conference in the single-story buildings to the right of the picture. Let's see that again."

This time the strike was in slow motion. The low building erupted and was gone, while the building a little further away looked like it had been pushed over by a cloud of bats. Then Joey realised these were roof tiles taking flight away from the blast.

"'With a huff and a puff, I'll blow your house down,'" she murmured.

"What?" asked Lundt.

"Doesn't matter. Olomo must have been really dumb to break cover like that. Look what we did to that Yao fucker. He must've known we'd do the same thing to him, especially after he executed those poor women."

"Maybe he thought rubbing himself with *juju* juice would protect him."

Joey decided to let it go. The news had been full of stuff about Olomo's bizarre beliefs. His Black Messiah group seemed to think that specially prepared herbal ointments could ward of bullets, that killing snakes would offend God, that eating black feathered chickens was unholy. She'd been digging around on the web and suspected that sloppy journalism had conflated some of the excesses of the Lord's Army, a rag tag group of armed terrorists who specialised in chopping off the hands of men and women and children in South Sudan, with Olomo's Black Messiah movement. The two groups had no linkage, as far as she could see, but it made good copy and it played well with Olomo's boogieman image.

But something was nagging at her. Olomo had had to be thinking well ahead when he'd targeted the CSG. The African had begun his dirty business over a year ago, long before Olomo had grabbed the hostages and the CSG had been sent into harm's way. That didn't sound much like a man who put his faith in the ordnance protecting capabilities of ointments. Or of someone who'd break cover when he knew the US was using all its surveillance assets to find him.

"How would they know he was in that building? In JCIS I got the impression their recent intel on Olomo was poor, not that the analysts are that forthcoming."

"That's because they don't know you. Pohost, Terni's deputy, is in my church group here on the boat and we sometimes have a coffee together after the Sunday service."

Joey arched her eyebrow.

Lundt sighed. "Church group. You do know what that means don't you?"

"Absolutely."

Lundt shook her head. "Anyway, it seems they were trying out some new surveillance gear. Latest tech. Miniaturised stuff, remotely controlled."

"Like what?"

"He didn't say, but it didn't work anyway."

"State of the art military equipment that doesn't work. My, my!"

Lundt patted the bulkhead. "Now this old girl: they've got most of the kinks out of her. Took about twenty years, mind."

"Then how come there seems like more civilian contractors than sailors on this tub if everything works so well now?"

"Upgrades. That's a cuss word, by the way. New stuff seems to work two times out of three, if that. When it's really new, it seems to me it usually doesn't work at all."

"You're starting to sound like Lewis."

Lundt leaned forward a little, as though to impart a confidence. There'd been a thaw in their relations. With the bruises on their jaws, they both looked like they'd been in a bar room brawl.

"I've seen whole exercises halted at sea, where we were testing new weapons systems, or at least new upgrades. Seen ships just bobbing away for days doing absolutely nothing. And you know why?"

She didn't wait for an answer. "Because something goes wrong late on Friday or Saturday. We need a part or a specialist from on shore but we have to wait. Guess why?"

"Dunno."

Lundt's voice was rising. "Because the contractors are on overtime, and it wasn't budgeted for in the original contract. A whole CSG has to cool its heels because one engineer might go onto double time."

"That's ridiculous!"

"No kidding. Inviolable budgets, powers taken away from the man on the deck, mountains of paperwork...the modern navy's in a straitjacket."

"Are you related to Lewis, by any chance?"

Lundt smiled wearily.

"OK, so that messes up the exercises. What about now when we're at sea in a sort-of war? Would that kind of bullshit cause trouble here?"

Lundt shrugged. "I think we're going to find out. You know the old saying: Battle plans never survive exposure to the enemy. Something like that anyway. Well what that says to me is that flexibility may be the most important thing a military can have."

"And you're saying we haven't got that?"

"Been squeezed out over the last twenty years, like juice from an orange."

Just then Lundt's terminal pinged as an internal email came in. She reached out and clicked the mouse.

"Post mortem results back in on Trask. Turns out he was shot."

"That would explain it," said Joey, deadpan.

Lundt nodded her head sagaciously. "Another mystery solved."

Lewis hadn't shown his face since she'd pounced on him. That was something to be grateful for.

She'd replayed the scene like a touchdown at the Superbowl. Either she was going nuts or coming so close to death had messed with her in some strange way. Only 32, she hadn't been to too many funerals, but she did remember something that happened at one in particular. It was for her old station sergeant, retired two years and dead from a heart attack. Hames was her partner then, and he hadn't stood a chance. She'd fallen on him like a lion on a wildebeest during the car ride back from the funeral.

A couple of her friends had admitted to similar feelings when she'd broached the subject after more than a few drinks. Life and death: the ultimate pair. The closer you get to one, the more you thought of the other.

Maybe that explained it. Or maybe she just was a desperate spinster grabbing for the nearest man.

Lewis had emailed her a couple of hours previously wanting to set up a meeting. Macik was too busy to attend himself, but he was after a summary of Trask's background and he wanted Lewis to report back.

The meeting was due any time now. She noticed her palms were moist.

A polite knock at the door and then he was with them. He smiled and glanced at both, but his gaze came to rest on Lundt.

"Looking very pretty today, ladies."

"Very funny," said Lundt. "Take a seat!"

Again, his eyes flicked to Joey but went quickly back to Lundt.

Lundt leaned as far forward as her stomach would allow. "How's this business with Olomo going down with the crew? We've been cooped up here going through Trask's files."

He nodded and smiled. "'Exultant' covers it pretty well. People are partying."

"I don't suppose you know where exactly."

"If I did, you'd be the last person I'd tell." Booze on board was forbidden. Not a problem to the great majority, but amongst six thousand there'd always be some who just couldn't live without it during the long months at sea. Agents Afloat had to be like Elliot Ness during Prohibition, and Joey knew that alcohol, its detection and the apprehension of its possessors, was a big part of Lundt's job.

"So, what have you got for the Admiral?"

The switching glances again. Joey sat forward, taking the lead, forcing him to look at her.

"Trask was like an iceberg: everything hidden below the surface. Second generation immigrant from Liganda: political asylum for Trask's father whose own father was beheaded by Mamadou. Trask's father crossed the desert through Mali to get away. Wife and kids didn't make it. Buried them in the sand with his bare hands. Then, several dunes away, he made the mistake of looking back. Saw the desert foxes digging up the bodies.

"According to his accounts, which as you can tell were pretty detailed thanks to a CIA interrogator he had later, he became delirious then got lost. Somehow wandered into Libya and was captured as a spy. Gaddafi's men did bad things to him as a matter of course. He survived and eventually they lost interest. Meanwhile Gaddafi had arranged a pan-European exchange to repatriate his scumbags who'd been causing ructions in the Libyan communities across the continent. Trask Senior was put in with some sort of prisoner exchange to bulk up the numbers.

"Finds himself in Brindisi, an Italian port on the Adriatic. Reagan was President then and we looked kindly on just about anyone who was Gaddafi's enemy in those days. Inseela Olugalulu, his original moniker, got a Green Card. Figured life might be a lot easier all round if he changed his name to Anthony Trask. Records don't tell us how he came up with that particular name."

"I can see why he changed it," said Lewis. He couldn't meet her eyes for long and kept glancing down into his lap.

Maybe she was being paranoid, but she got the impression Lundt was beginning to look curiously at both of them.

"Elder Trask settled down. Had been a lecturer in West African history and managed to get a teaching job at Olmhurst College near Dartmouth. Married a local girl, two kids. Trask Junior, named Elias, and a sister."

She waited until he met her eyes again. "Young Elias did OK at school. Graduated college but was never going to be an academic. Good with his hands, good with machines. Ends up in the Navy."

"Any connection with Liganda now?"

"Not until Olomo got rid of Mamadou. Until then, travelling back home as the son of a dissident wouldn't have been wise for Trask Senior. The grandfather had been a close colleague of Olomo. But after Mamadou gets chopped up and fed to the jackals, not a figure of speech by the way, Anthony/Inseela returns and gets a hero's welcome. Over the last ten years he makes many visits back, Elias and his sister in tow. Weiss, my colleague back home, has been checking Anthony's bank account, especially round the times of these trips which we got from Immigration. No payments we can find to airlines or travel agents."

"So Olomo bankrolled the trips?"

"Looks like it."

Lewis' eyes had narrowed. "So this supports your idea that this has all been planned for a long time?"

Joey shook her head. "Not quite. From when Yao first approached Hierra, we know that this has been going on for at least a year. CSG deployments are a matter of public record, so predicting which one might be available if something flared up in this part of the world isn't difficult. Longer than a year and it gets a little more unpredictable. Military policy changes, or a war starts up elsewhere, or some bright spark of a politician decides to increase or decrease naval leave and all the schedules are thrown out."

"So, are you saying this goes higher? Up to the people who assign crew to vessels? Olomo somehow got to them, got Trask assigned to the *Sands*?"

"Weiss is checking through the chain, but I've got to say the idea doesn't sit well with me. Does a single person make these decisions? And if they did, might an outsider looking to affect those decisions even be able to identify who it was?"

Lewis pursed his lips. "Not sure myself. But if it wasn't someone working for Olomo...?"

"Then maybe it was just chance that Trask was on the *Sands*. That's my guess at the moment."

"But if you're wrong, then there could be others like Trask on board. Shouldn't you be checking?"

"Why didn't we think of that?" said Lundt dryly.

He glanced down again. "Sorry."

Later, sipping on a soda in the little common room up from her berthing space, she'd been watching cable news when the first video came in. Some of it was jerky but it also had some good quality still frames. The anchorman made it clear that even more explicit material could be found on sites all over the web.

It started with Olomo. Ramrod straight, breathing heavily as though trying to constrain his emotions, he was facing the camera.

Beneath his image, the cable news strap line read: 'Brutal dictator issues statement'. Looking directly at the camera, the skin over his jaw taught, he drew in a deep breath then quietly said: 'The Americans killed my children today.'

Joey froze, the soda only halfway to her lips.

"My sons Duante and Bello, my daughters Eshe and Dalila. Ayesha and Siana, my youngest, my twin five-year old daughters. What harm had any of them done the Americans that they would murder them? They were just little children."

Joey swallowed, her mouth achingly dry.

"Is this revenge because a constitutionally mandated court found some human experimenters guilty of murder? Because they were executed according to the law of the country they were in?

"What trial did my children have? What court found them guilty?

"I ask the people of America one simple question. Who are the sinful here? My children or the government of the United States?"

Cut to video of the debris. A broken doll that was once a child, a tiny arm raised in mute supplication.

Chapter 19. *Liganda and beyond*

They were everywhere. In the bush, they tended the sick and educated the young. Some brought the Bible, others the Economist. They dug the wells in the northern lands that were always being menaced by the desert. In the south they taught the farmers how to treble the yields of their crops. They taught in universities and hospitals. In the bigger cities they were the bankers, bringing in foreign investment.

On the seas they manned metal giants standing proud on legs 500 metres high. In the jungles to the East their mighty machines drilled deep in the Earth or carved out vast hillsides hunting for the Rare Earths.

Many had settled and made the countries of Liganda or Niassa or Bukana their homes. Often loving Africa, but sometimes finding her challenges too much, many needed to return temporarily to Europe or America to recharge their batteries. Relentless poverty, grotesque tropical illnesses, thoughtless brutality; Africa had it all. No matter how kind and good hearted most Africans might be, Central and Western Africa was always a bracing experience for thin northern blood.

And they all went about their business, oblivious to what was coming.

It was like being an ant on the rippled sandy shore of a beach, though this was no beach and the sea was a thousand miles away. On the top of a mighty dune, he watched the setting sun turning the sand's pinkish tint into a lurid crimson.

Wildemuth-Travis put his hands on his hips and stared across the immensity. Even after so many years, the desert, implacably encroaching onto the fertile lands here at the northern tip of Niassa, thrilled him. A memory of Surrey flashed into his mind and he laughed.

"Twee!" he yelled to the desert winds, "Frivolous! Cucumber fucking sandwiches!"

Far below, down towards where the hard rock still protruded from the advancing dunes, some of his men who were already heading back down to camp had turned to look back up at him.

"Cosy! Comfortable! Cool! Con-fucking-strained!"

The men were shaking their heads. Wildemuth-Travis always went a bit nuts after the Desert Sunset Appreciation Society had made their pilgrimage to the top of the nearest dune or craggy hill. It always marked the end of a long day of drilling; a self-imposed pause before they got wired into their sundowners and the rest of the night became something of a blur.

"And green," said Wildemuth-Travis to himself, more quietly now. "Nothing but fucking green."

He could already see the first stars, still a little blurred from the heat of the day. As the night wore on and the air became chill, they would become needle sharp.

The desert always wrong footed you and he smiled to remember his first night in one. Newly graduated, he'd joined his first geological team as they'd surveyed the north of Niassa. He'd sweated his nuts off during the day and couldn't bear the thought of the stifling tent at night. "I'm just kipping down out in the open," he'd said and not a fucker had said a word.

He'd woken at three in the morning, hunched up like he was in the womb, his hands frozen into claws.

Deserts are hot in the day but cold at night. You'd think they might have covered that in his geology course, but apparently not. He wondered how many of his lecturers had ever been out of the Home Counties.

The shadow of the dune was already an ink stain advancing at walking pace towards the drilling rig, a reverse circulation and diamond setup. The rock here was old and hard and not ready to yield its secrets without a fight.

He walked along the dune's ridge until it fell away at its steepest point. He loved taking the big steps, the sand yielding under each footstep, amplifying your descent so you strode down the mountain of sand like a god.

Getting ready to take his first giant step, he took one final look round. Far away to the South, over the rocky plain, he saw something black and sinuous coming towards the drilling site.

Just for a second, the continents ancient atavism always ready to pounce, he had a nightmare vision of a massive serpent come to hunt them down.

He shook the nonsense out of his head. And sure enough, as he continued to watch, he saw the lights of the convoy come on.

'Strange,' he thought. 'Who the hell would be coming out here?'

Strauss looked out of his office window and down at the grid-like arrangement of bungalows receding into the distance. At six storeys high, the Bukana National Bank was the tallest building in Jumada, Bukana's capital city. He could easily see his own house from here, the red tiles contrasting with the green of the well-watered lawns surrounding it.

Beyond the bungalow district the houses became less substantial and their order became chaotic.

He looked at his watch. 5:30pm. Time to go home. He checked his screen, and the application form it showed, for one last time. He imagined the farmer painstakingly filling the form in by tapping slowly into one of the customer terminals here at the bank. The farmer was an enterprising chap, and had consolidated a swath of smaller farms, but he was in his fifties. Like many of the entrepreneurs of his age, he'd benefited little from what had been an almost non-existent education system when he was younger.

Bukana was better now. Even with Olomo pulling the country's strings by proxy, you couldn't fault his commitment to education.

But for the older guys, whip smart though they often were, their first language wasn't English or Portuguese or French. Lower end stuff, loans for the purchase of land or equipment, could be done in any language, but for the big stuff, and this farmer was asking for a substantial sum to build a soy bean processing plant to produce oil, language became key.

For that sort of deal everything had to be in English, even for Strauss. The translation software helped: it had glossaries for all sorts of tribal languages and it could supply helpful suggestions to the customer with words it didn't recognise.

The guy was asking for eleven million bucks, a tad higher than Strauss's approval limit. He'd have to pass it back to London.

He logged off and was getting to his feet when he heard the sirens. The office window was floor to ceiling and he could see the streets below were as log jammed as ever with the city's short but explosive rush hour. Several police cars, and what looked like army trucks, were trying to edge their way down the streets. Car and buses and donkey-drawn carts were reluctantly making way.

Another flashing light in the periphery of his vision made him glance over to Bungalow Land. On the far southern side, where the other entrance to the gated community was to be found, a convoy of police cars and trucks was coming through.

He felt his stomach shrivel. Something must have happened. The kids would be back from school. He'd better phone, make sure Hilda kept them inside.

He was reaching behind him for the phone when he heard the door open.

There'd been no knock and he turned around in surprise.

Tembe airport was full with white faces.

Ex-pats living nearby in the city had already made it out of the country, for the most part. As soon as Olomo started executing the hostages, all but the most stupid or booze-addled had figured the game was up. International flights going anywhere had been full for days.

Today, however, the concourse was teaming with those from up-country who'd only just now managed to get to the airport. International radio bulletins said emergency flights had been arranged by western governments and that some may

218

already be on the way.

Sam kept her kids close. For once there was a chance they might be lost in the throng, their white skins no longer the exception. They were becoming tired and fractious. She'd only kept them going on their disjointed bus journeys (that bitch Aretha had nabbed the school's only car for her own brood!) by lying to them about what they'd find at their destination, but now the wonders promised were losing their power.

Around her all the westerners were showing signs of long travel. Dark rings of sweat radiated out from armpits; faces were lined and often dusty. Women and children stayed in little family huddles while the men were off fruitlessly trying to find out about flights.

Gerry had disappeared an hour ago. He was convinced he had an 'in' with Ethiopian Airlines. One of his old pupil's brothers worked here at the airport and he seemed to think he could call in a favour.

Gerry was a good enough teacher, she thought, but maybe a little too strict, too distant, to excite much loyalty. But at least it was keeping him out of their hair. Fear made him a little pompous when he was backed into a corner, as if by looking down on something that scared him he could diminish its power.

The aircon had always been crap in this place but now it wasn't coping at all. Delayed flights weren't uncommon but the planes were generally small; not many wide bodies with room for hundreds plied these central African routes. So the airport usually wasn't busy, but now the place was full of many hundreds of people not going anywhere.

Behind her she heard a sudden clacking sound. Turning, she saw all lines on the departure board spinning through the combinations then blinked in surprise as the status indicators alighted on: 'Cancelled'.

Every single one of them.

"Mommy?" said Paul, uncertainty cutting through his petulance.

She looked round the sea of faces gawping up at the board.

Had there been an emergency, like a crash?

Very tall, she could see over everyone's head out towards the airstrip. A single runway, with a wide semicircular strip of tarmac at the side to allow planes to get to and from the terminal, it was all completely clear.

Only one plane was at the terminal itself, a dowdy East African Airways 737, but, even as she watched, the crew came down the aircraft steps talking volubly amongst themselves. That plane was the one they'd been about to board.

She felt Gerry grab her arm. "Nobody knows what's going on. None of us'll be leaving here for a while," he whispered in her ear. "We'd better head back into town and try to get some decent hotel rooms before they're all taken."

She put her palms on Paul and Laura's heads, their hair slick with sweat. "We're going for a little walk, kids," she said.

They started to protest but she hardly heard them. Already the crowd was starting to move *en masse* towards the exits and the taxi ranks. Like some terrible feedback mechanism, as everyone became aware of what others were thinking, they all started to surge forward faster.

Suddenly she could hear raised voices ahead. "What's going on?" asked Gerry.

For once not cursing her freakish gangly six-foot six-inch height, Sam could see it all. Men in battle fatigues, rifles and sub-machine guns unslung, were standing shoulder to shoulder blocking the exit. Glancing back at the boarding gates which gave directly out onto the tarmac, she saw a line of soldiers moving across them, barring these as well.

The voices got louder at the main exit and then came the sound of something solid hitting flesh.

The crowd went quiet. Thudding sounds: boots on ribs, she guessed. A woman started to scream.

The crowd edged back as one and, around her, she saw

people turn, only to find all their exits blocked.

She looked down at Gerry. Overcompensating for their height difference, his expression was often patronising, almost supercilious. But now he was looking up at her like the kids: wanting the parent to tell them all what to do next.

Chapter 20. *USS Benjamin F. Sands, Gulf of Guinea*

Joey watched as the Sea Hawk rose into view from the Hanger deck. With its rotors bent back it looked like a broken dragonfly and the yellow jackets nursed it forward off the elevator and quickly secured it to the deck. Without restraints, the swell from a far-off storm in the Azores would have sent it skittering across the flight deck and into the ocean.

"And I just use a little Volvo to get to work," she said, glancing at Lewis who was next to her on the balcony. The day was overcast and a light rain was coming down, driving even the most determined of the open-air lovers back below deck.

Lewis nodded but didn't smile.

She should be down below at work on the crews' files, but Lundt's departure had made a good excuse to get some fresh air and even Lewis had agreed.

The dragonfly's broke backed tail was being lowered and its main blades jacked up. Within a few minutes the scrunched-up insect had become a helicopter.

Finally, a blue shirt began to make signals and a dumpy figure wearing a big white flight helmet waddled out of the superstructure and towards the chopper. The flight suit and life preserver bulked Lundt up until she looked like the Michelin Man.

"Wyatt Earp getting the fuck out of Dodge," said Lewis.

Grey sea, grey boat, it was like Norfolk in the winter though not nearly so cool. On the heavy swell were streaks of foam, 'white horses' as they were called, which meant a wind speed of at least Force 4.

Lundt, with a little rearward assistance from the pilot, managed to get into the helicopter and the pilot quickly scrambled aboard after her. Soon the rotors started to turn and all but two of the deck crew retreated into the metal ditch along the far side of the deck.

At a signal from the pilot, the remaining crew released the shackles and the chopper was quickly airborne, lest the pitching deck lurch up to whack its underside.

They watched as it lifted astern before tilting to starboard and heading away towards the south and the Merrivell, an Aegis class destroyer bristling with cruise missiles and God-knows-what else.

"She didn't seem too enthusiastic about this," Joey said as they turned to get back into the superstructure.

"Yeah, sound like a bullshit job. Crew get into fights all the time. High density living, bound to happen. Usually it's forgotten, but it sounds like the one who came off worse this time is something of a mess room lawyer and wants to bring charges. That means interviews and a lot of paperwork. After the business with Trask, it's all going to seem pretty lame."

"At least she gets to fly in a helicopter."

"Maybe," said Lewis reflectively, "but the landing pad on the Aegis is about a thousandth the size of the *Sands'* flight deck. And the ship's much smaller so it'll be pitching a lot more. You have to sit there hoping they chain you down before you go for a swim."

The sudden notion of Lundt trapped in a metal box and falling into an angry sea flashed through her mind. Distracted, her heel came down close to the edge of the narrow step. It slid off the end and cracked down hard on the next step, making her wince and stumble. She felt Lewis grab her upper arm to stop her falling down the steep stairwell.

It hadn't been necessary; her other hand had gripped the railing firmly at the first hint of trouble. Any of other time, any other person, she'd have felt demeaned and offended.

But now she turned to look back up at him. "Thanks."

He was a step above her and for once they weren't eye to eye. She caught a softening in his countenance. Not a full defrost exactly, but maybe he suddenly felt less...

She sighed. Threatened men were the story of her life.

223

Men, or at least the more masculine ones she found attractive, liked to be the strong one, the tall one, the decisive one. It was wired into their genes. A woman with her physicality they could take, but only if she was suitably demure.

She didn't do demure. She'd always been forceful and athletic and tough.

So, the strong ones just didn't seem to like her: didn't like not making the running, didn't like not being the boss.

And the soft men, the ones she didn't like, always buzzed round her like flies. Wanting to be eaten up and spat out. And sometimes, when she'd been lonely or it had been too long since she'd had a man, she'd obliged. Riding them to within an inch of their gutless lives then tossing them aside like used Kleenex.

And now here was Lewis, an odd mix of the two. He was a man all right, tall and strong, but she sensed a weakness about him, and when she'd pounced it'd scared the hell out of him.

She turned and they began descending again. "So now what? What exactly is the Fleet going to do?"

"Depends on the Rules of Engagement."

"Wanna try explaining those to me?"

"I'll give it a go. In a nutshell: US armed forces have to comply with the international law of armed conflict or LOAC, plus we're bound by the Geneva and Hague Laws, of course."

"Of course."

"OK, OK. Details don't matter, but it's worth mentioning we've got to comply with US Law as well."

"It's beginning to sound like you'd need to consult a barrel load of lawyers before you could fire a shot."

"With Macik, that's not too far off the mark. Some say that's why he's risen so far so fast: safe pair of hands, plays by the rules. When you're in charge of the world's most powerful conventional weapons system, and you're a long way from Washington, and things are getting a little rough, well ...."

"It can go to your head. You go off message. You go rogue."

"'Lose perspective' is the phrase I was searching for. Don't have the bigger picture, which is the preserve of those super smart politicians back home."

"You're a bitter man."

"Really? I was trying hard not to let it show."

"Epic fail."

"It's a truism that 'no battle plan survives contact with the enemy' as Field Marshall von Moltke said in the mid-1800s. Everyone knows he said that but..."

"Back in Denver, we spoke of little else."

She was still leading the way so she couldn't see him, but she heard him snort.

"Look, you asked me to explain this."

"I'm sorry. Go on."

"What most people don't know is that von Moltke *also* said: 'Strategy is a system of expedients'. And, before you get snippy, that means that the purpose of strategy is to give the commander lots of options, so he can adopt the best one for the inevitably changing circumstances. Rules of Engagement by definition constrain a flexible response, so they need to be as light touch as possible.

"But with our present administration..."

Joey thought of the pompous, driven Tridens. Like Macik, but in charge of a whole nation. The navy had been savaged by cuts under the last incumbent, and Tridens wanted to keep the lid on that bottle.

"Can you give me an example, something a little more concrete so I can see what you're getting at?"

"Proportionality for one thing. 'Nature, duration and scope of force should not exceed what is required'. So Olomo has executed a few civilians. Does that mean we can go ahead and destroy his army?"

"Can we destroy his army?"

"Not unless they kindly all get together in one place, but we can kill lots of them and destroy whatever pissant equipment they've got."

"OK, so we can't respond by wiping out his army, but we would be allowed to defend ourselves if we came under attack, right?"

"That's usually a given except if, for example, your enemy has a treaty with a big power like China. Big picture, see?"

"But Olomo doesn't have any treaties."

"Yup. He's all on his ownsome, so not a problem there."

"So, does that mean we're restricted to killing just a handful of his men in response to the handful of hostages he's killed."

"Well, proportionality can be a bit of a movable feast, but there's other stuff as well. For example: we're not supposed to kill civilians unless they are directly involved in attacking us."

She thought back to Zinzi's village and how Macik had seemed determined to identify the group of men as terrorists.

"But what about the Bito village cruise missile strike? It must have at least injured women and children in the huts nearby. And Olomo's family at his ranch, civilians were killed there, assuming it wasn't staged."

"There's a sort of a get-out though. The use of the term 'Proportionality' in the ROE says we can do that, as long as the incidental loss of life or injury wasn't excessive in terms of the military advantage."

"But what was the military advantage of taking this man Yao out? Once we'd identified him, he was finished in terms of any further espionage he could do. We'd have arrested him as soon as he tried to get back into the States."

By now they'd got to the office and Joey was using the key Lundt had given her.

"Good point."

The door was open now but she turned to face him. "So, what does this all mean?"

He shook his head. "Let me finish off about the ROE. A document is produced with over 140 rules, some of them multipart, which describes the use of everything from naval mines to cluster munitions.

"And check this out." He brought out his wallet and extracted a laminated card, turning it so she could read it. It was headed 'Self-Dense Card'.

"That's one of the ROE cards we get. If we go into action we get another."

She screwed her eyes up to read in the dim light. "It says here: 'You have the right to self-defence'. OK. But it also says you should fire only aimed shots and 'to take all reasonable precautions not to injure anyone other than the target'. That's got to be a total bullshit box-ticking exercise. It would only make sense to someone in a comfortable committee room on the Hill, but in a real firefight? Every shot aimed? Really! This isn't a Rule, it's an aspiration. At best!"

"Welcome to the modern US military," he said.

Shaking her head, she went around behind Lundt's desk and took her usual seat to the left. Lewis sat down beside her.

"Now I'm really confused."

"Same here, but what it comes down to is this: despite history showing that flexibility is the key advantage in war, the US government relentlessly clips its military's wings. Drowns it in paperwork, constrains it with Disney Land ROE. But that's not necessarily the end of the world. A great military man could exploit whatever flexibility there was in the rules or, more likely, have the guts to totally ignore them where necessary."

"And you're really saying that Macik isn't that man?"

She waited but Lewis didn't answer. Instead he started logging on so she followed suit on her own terminal. So far, they'd got to *Efraim, Albert: stores clerk* on their alphabetical trawl through the crew list. Lewis was dealing with the crews' HR files, Joey the bank statements and government records that Weiss and others had trawled from the big on-shore databases.

The Rules of Engagement lecture hadn't been amongst the most thrilling of her life but at least he'd been talking. Now the silence began to stretch.

"Anything?" she asked.

"Jewish," he said. "Clean record. Ten years in. Not married."

"No criminal records. Bank account...the Navy doesn't pay well, does it?"

"So I've heard."

"A Jew in the armed forces. Isn't that unusual?"

"Why?"

She hesitated. "Actually, I don't know."

"Could that be a little, well, racist?"

"White people just love to accuse people like me of racism."

"Maybe, but I'm not letting you off the hook. Why shouldn't a Jewish man go into the military? You ever heard of Israel?"

"OK, OK, gimme a break! It was a stupid thing to say. I wasn't thinking."

Grumpily she went back Efraim. Every which way they looked he came up clean.

A thought came to her. "Wait a minute. Earlier we were talking about putting a cruise missile up Yao's ass. About proportionality. So how could Macik justify killing all those men and God knows who else?"

He sat back in his chair and this time looked directly into her eyes. "What do you know about Macik?"

"A few things."

"Came in as an aviation cadet at Pensacola..."

"Yeah, a fly boy."

"To run a CSG you pretty much have to be. The 'bird farm' is the centre of the whole Group and its sole purpose is to get wings into the air. And, sure enough, he did his share of command tours in strike fighter squadrons on the 5th Fleet. Plus, some handy flag lieutenant assignments to the Chief of Air Warfare Operations to raise his profile amongst the desk bound. Father was a naval captain which may have greased some wheels, but I can't fault the man's energy. He would have risen to the top, but maybe not so quickly without help."

He took a deep breath, his blue coveralls for a second outlining his broad chest and flat gut, and then he sighed heavily. "Shouldn't be telling you this."

"Not that I'm complaining, but why are you?"

He smiled wryly. "It was a bit awkward yesterday."

"I know. I'm sorry, I'm a slut, I couldn't keep my hands off you."

"You're not being fair on yourself. It was a helluva day. We were all keyed up. You nearly died. Not the time for decorum."

"Maybe you're right, but I'm sorry I made you uncomfortable." Without thinking it through, she reached out and touched the back of his hand.

For a second neither seemed to know what to do, then with his other hand he touched the back of hers. "I was just a bit startled. I guess you spooked me. I'm used to calling the shots."

She wasn't sure this really meant acquiescence, but it was enough for her. She leaned forward to kiss him but he drew his head back.

"The door," he said. "Warship: 6000 other people."

Smiling, she got Lundt's keys from her pocket and went to lock it.

He'd stood up by the time she got back to him. He started to reach up as though to gently cradle her face in his hands, but she wasn't having it. Instead she pushed him back hard against the wall and crushed her lips against his.

He tasted as good as he smelled.

It'd been far too long. The blood roared in her ears as her heart went into overdrive. With her right hand she cupped his balls, and with her left she grabbed his ass, urgently kneading the hard flesh.

He tried for her breasts but she was too close against him.

He turned his head aside, freeing his mouth from the assault of her tongue.

"Clothes," he managed to say.

She stepped back and was out of hers in seconds. He took longer, so she had a chance to check him out. Chest smooth, but a nice thick pubic bush and a good-sized cock that was already getting hard.

He was bending to get his socks off but she didn't give him a chance. Pushing at his shoulders, she got him against the wall again. Grabbing his cock, she stepped in close and went up on tiptoe. With just enough extra height, she managed to slip him into her, her pussy already wet.

Their heights were just right. She had real purchase and was able to ride him hard.

"Jesus!" he whispered.

Wanting to consume him, her teeth went hungrily for his lips. As she bit down, his mouth opened in dismay and pain. God knows what she'd have done next but for the jolt of orgasm. She threw her head back and yelled.

She was barely aware of being pushed back, but then felt her ass against the cold of the table top, tipping her backwards. This time he had the purchase and could drive into her. Just a few thrusts then he was dragging his cock out and coming over the thick black hairs of her crotch.

It had all happened so fast that they weren't even breathing heavily. She got up on her elbows now and their eyes locked.

"Christ," he said. "Where did you come from? The fucking zoo? What happened to dinner? What happened to a movie?"

"I'm a woman," she said smiling. "I have needs." Then: "You didn't have to pull out. I'm on the pill."

"I'll remember that for next time. If..." he looked at her archly.

"We'll see," she said.

"If there's some doubt, then I'd better do this while I have the chance."

With the gentlest of touches, he brushed his middle finger across a black nipple. They'd always been large against her small breasts, but now they were engorged as well. It felt nice, what he was doing.

"I'm a breast man. Normally it's the first thing I go for but you didn't give me a chance, beast that you are."

Bending down he took the nipple in his mouth and gently sucked it.

She lightly pushed his head back. "Don't start something you can't finish."

"Oh, I'll finish, but you're right. Better let the batteries recharge."

The seats were hard plastic with no cushions they could use. All they could do was lie down on their coveralls to keep their skin from contact with the cold deck.

"That was a little scary," he said.

"What can I say? I am what I am, and I've been through a long, dry spell."

"Same here. Normally I can take my time. Really!" he said as she smiled.

It was nice to hold someone again and they just lay there listening to the sounds of the ship. After a few minutes, there was a knock at the door and they grinned sheepishly at each other. After a second knock, whoever it was went away.

"Probably just a murder," said Lewis.

She stroked his smooth chest then ran her hand down over the sexy undulations of his delightful six-pack.

Lovely though this all was, she started to feel guilty about stopping the work.

"Where were we? You were saying something about Macik. Proportionality or something. Oh yeah, and why you're telling me all this."

"You want to do this now?" he sounded surprised. "Well, OK, if you insist. I guess it was because, for some reason, I trust you. I forgot that when you pounced on me."

"Thank you. But anyway, back to Macik. Don't tell me the squeaky-clean Admiral has a dark side which made him go disproportional on Yao's ass."

"Over and above the guy's ambition and drive, the man's a patriot and wouldn't do anything against the US. It's just that he's the product of a system that has within it the seeds of its own destruction. Well, perhaps not destruction, but at least defeat."

"Really?"

"It's all about control, about controlling complex systems. Governments, militaries, big companies think they can do just that. The think that by controlling each system more, by doing audits and ticking boxes and setting up all sorts of administrative systems, by getting huge amounts of information back, that they can understand and control the monster."

"Monster?"

"Complexity. A CSG is a complex creature. Its power comes from its technology, sure enough, but it also comes from its flexibility. A CSG in war is a complex organism responding to the most complex of environments. Rules of Engagement, and all the other administrative paraphernalia, constrain it. And if you try to constrain a complex system it will sooner or later fail."

"Yeah, you sort of said that before, but what has that got to do with proportionality?"

"Because Macik suffers from the delusion that he can control it all. He's the archetypal control freak. If in doubt, he wants more information. If something goes wrong he puts it down to a lack of information, and that's why the poor XO gets it in the neck all the time."

"He certainly doesn't look happy."

"Sidelined, marginalised. 'Too fine a filter' is how I've heard Macik describe him. Guy can't do anything on his own initiative.

"Washington has tied down the fleet with political initiatives. Health and Safety, career development, racial equality, sexual equality, environmental pollution, 'Public Focus and Public Involvement', zillions of ionising radiation regulations, non-ionising radiation regulations, data protection, freedom of information and God knows what else. All of them need forms to be filled in, all of them need boxes ticked. Every fucking thing we do needs a risk assessment. On a warship! It's madness.

"I once did a back of the envelope calculation. About how much time the crew spent pandering to these politico/bureaucratic mandates. Twenty fucking percent!

"And all of it eventually migrates up to the XO. By short circuiting the XO, by not letting him take most of the administrative strain, Macik has overloaded himself."

"So, he's under great pressure."

"Yeah, and when push comes to shove, my fear is that it'll get in the way of the business of fighting. Which is what we're supposed to be doing."

"OK, one last time: I still don't get the proportionality thing."

He laughed. "Sorry, I keep slipping into rant mode. Plus, you keep distracting me," he indicated their naked bodies. "Still haven't answered you, have I?

"Macik can't see the wood for the trees. He's got this whole battle group but what can he do? The potential battle ground is the worst sort of combination of bush and urban warfare. We don't have the troops or political will to go into a ground war and, believe me, getting these hostages back would soon degenerate into a shooting war. We could blow up his air force and sink his navy, sure enough. Trouble is: he doesn't have any of those, not to speak of. So, what can he do?"

"Yao," she said. "And Olomo's supposed war conference."

"Right! If it's all he can do then that affects proportionality. Can he really let the most powerful weapons system in the world just float here powerless? That would be a statement in itself and not a good one for the US projection of power. Who knows what terrible long-term effects this would have down the line? Just about the only thing the world respects us for anymore is our force. If that was undermined then that wouldn't be good. Perhaps worse, it would undermine the respect we have for ourselves. That's some heavy stuff Macik's weighing against a few lives."

"So, it makes him trigger happy." She pursed her lips. "There's nukes on this CSG, aren't there?"

He shrugged. "That's supposedly an official secret, but it's widely known the only nuclear stuff on the *Sands* itself is the reactors. Washington legislation, many years back, banned a carrier from ever carrying nuclear weapons."

"But the Aegis and the frigates...the cruise missiles. Nuclear tipped?"

He didn't answer but his silence was evidence enough.

"And does Macik have control over them? Surely he couldn't launch at will?"

"Hypothetically..."

"Oh, come on!"

"I'm sorry, but we've all taken oaths. I may be cynical but I won't break my promises."

There were a few seconds of silence.

"OK, hypothetically.... no forget it!" she said, "Maybe I can think this through myself.

"All nuclear weapons can only be fired if launch codes are used, and only the President with her, what do they call it...football...or whatever, can send those. But the launch codes only sanction the use of the nukes. It's someone up in a bomber, or on a nuclear submarine, or down in a missile silo who actually fires the damn things. So once the codes are given, the President is effectively devolving this, giving her commanders in the field some optional control over using them.

"So, if that were done, and if the CSG has nukes on it somewhere, then it would be Macik who'd make the final decision."

Lewis shrugged.

"And you reckon he's nuts?"

"That's not what I said. Overloaded. A control freak. The weight of the world on his shoulders. Not the same as nuts."

"Christ, that fucker Olomo doesn't have a clue what he might be getting into."

She felt him brush her nipple again. "Can we change the subject?" he said. His finger traced around the dark areola. "Like I said. I'm a breast man. Let me show you what I can do."

She lasted for five minutes of delicate caresses by fingers and tongue until, unable to stand it anymore, she climbed hungrily on top of him.

Chapter 21. *Near Tembe Airport*

How old is this kid? Arm outstretched in supplication, he stands out from the youngsters milling around him simply by virtue of his height.

Surely that shouldn't be enough?

Yao puts an arm on the shoulder of Corporal Diop next to him on the back of the flat-bed truck. The skinny little man is already reaching back for the next gun.

"Wait!" he warns.

He turns back to the kid standing there in the filth of the shanty's town's single dirt road.

"How old are you?"

"Seventeen," says the kid without hesitation, meeting Yao's eyes fearlessly.

"If not him, then who?" asks the corporal.

The boy's hand, outstretched above the heads of the other kids, opens and closes entreatingly.

In his heart he knows this isn't right, but Yao reaches down and grasps the hard steel of the breech and lifts the gun from the carelessly stacked multitude. Even as he starts to lean out over the tail gate, the kid has launched himself over the heads of the others and has grabbed the AK 47 by the wooden stock. Jerking it from Yao's hand, he turns and dances away, shaking the weapon above his head.

"He looked at least sixteen to me," says Diop grumpily, no doubt wanting to get this over with so he can get back into the shade.

"You reckon? The kid didn't even think to wait for ammunition."

He looks across at the sea of hands. The kids had surged in after the men were given their guns. He can see the men now in

236

the alleyways and on the shaded side of the road checking out their weapons. Some poke at them gingerly, clearly never having held an AK before, never mind fired one.

Again, Yao feels the queasiness.

But not all the men are novices. The country had been squeezing the life out of itself in civil wars for many years before the brief period of stability provided by Olomo. The Kalashnikov has always been the weapon of choice. He can see some of the men, better versed in its use, starting to help and instruct others.

Some comfort, but not much.

"Well," says the old soldier. "Our orders were to give all these out before returning. I think we should just dump them in the road."

Dumping the AKs in a pit might be better, thinks Yao. There must be ten million or more of them in Africa, but the quality varies and these look like the dregs. The wood work around the rear part of the barrel, the stock and the handle are deeply scored.

And the irony is that he was the one who'd bought some of them. A job lot, discards from a Ukrainian army upgrade, they'd gone for only $150 each, less than half the usual going rate in Africa. Supposedly all of them the Serbian Zastava M70 variant, he'd spotted some originals in the heap that could be over forty years old.

As they'd driven out here he'd gone over as many as he could, discarding those with bent barrels and loose fire selectors. Several didn't even have triggers.

Even for the ones he kept, he isn't sure which end of the barrel it would be safer to be on.

Diop, not waiting for his response, is already picking up more guns.

"No," says Yao. "I'm not giving these out to children. We'll head back."

"We'll get in trouble with Justice."

"Let me handle him."

The soldier shakes his head in displeasure but jumps down. The light-fingered kids, guessing what is happening, try to surge over the sides and the tailgate. Not able to stop them all, he knows he must set an example.

One little bundle of energy, already over the side and beginning to stand upright, is the unlucky one. Yao's hard military boot catches him dead centre, punting him away like a football.

The kids step back as one. The truck's engine fires and Yao just has time to crouch down behind the tailgate as it takes off.

Shuffling some guns aside, he sits back on the wooden boards.

The kids are running after them, leaving behind their little pal squirming in the dust.

'Lesser of two evils,' he thinks, but it doesn't make him feel any better.

The shanty town abuts onto the grass on one side of the airport's runway. The fence has been cut down, repaired, then cut down again, and now huts are encroaching remorselessly onto the grass. Periodically these are bulldozed by airport security but it's like fighting the desert's drifting sands.

As the truck drives straight across the grass to the terminal, Yao checks the remaining guns. Aside from the pile of eight weapons he's considered too demonstrably dangerous to distribute, there are about twenty-five still left out of the hundred or so they'd been given.

The airport's grass covered ground is smoother than the road and the guns stop rattling around. To the south he sees a 737 coming in, one of the four that Ligandan Airlines has in service. The only airline flying in at the moment, the plane will taxi to join one of the others in the fleet by the hangars. The only other plane in the airport is by the terminal, an East African Airways Boeing that has been here for a week now and isn't going anywhere soon.

He shades his hand and looks around. There is always at least one in sight and, sure enough, he finds it over to the west doing a big circle round the airport perimeter; close enough that he can see its little down pointing fins.

Close enough also to make out that it has under slung pods rather than Hellfires. After the slaughter of Olomo's family, the Americans have backed off on drone and cruise strikes, though Yao knows this won't last.

But at least today that means he and the flat bed aren't a target of opportunity.

'Target of opportunity'! How mealy mouthed the language of the American military is. What it really means is dead human beings, shattered bones, torn flesh.

The truck gets to the runway and follows the 737 in. Even at a hundred metres, he can feel the hot back wash from the jets. As the plane joins the other parked in front of the big hangar, his truck heads to the right and the staging area. To his dismay he sees that all but two of other trucks are back, their soldiers lying against their vehicles wheels on the shaded side.

So, it doesn't look like they've been as discriminating as he. He shudders to think of all those powerful weapons in the hands of the wild children of the slums scattered around the airport. Once you gave them out you never got them back. They would continue to do their mischief for generations to come.

Yao picks up his own AK that he's secreted at one back corner of the flat bed. A modern AK 12, its Picatinny rail has been fitted with laser sights. A BMW compared to the old 47's Skoda; Olomo let him buy it for himself as a treat.

He jumps over the tailgate and walks round to meet the corporal who's got out of the cabin. Diop is a veteran of many of Olomo's campaigns. No obvious ambition, just a three-meals-a-day soldier.

But he knows the score. "Here comes trouble," he says.

Yao follows his gaze and, sure enough, Justice, hands behind his back, is sauntering towards them. From a distance he doesn't look too bad, but when he's up really close in broad daylight it's a different matter; when you can see what the bushy beard is trying to hide. Bayoneted in the mouth by one of the old guard, a livid scar lies across one cheek. The blade had taken out the whole lower set and gum on the left. The prosthesis Justice uses to bulk out this side of his face comes in three bits, and he has to get them all in his mouth. Watching him assemble this in the early morning, all ten fingers in his mouth manipulating the pieces, is both grotesque and comical.

"Took your time." Justice's voice is always a deep threatening rumble. Then he spots the weapons still in the back.

"Didn't you understand the General's orders?"

"We gave the guns to all the men and women who would take them."

"Bullshit! You go into Crap Town offering free guns and you can't even give them all away?"

Yao shrugs.

"I don't believe you." Justice is close now. He's been eating goat.

"And do you think I care?"

"I'm going to tell you this just once so even a gutless little shit like you can get it. Your sweet little deal is over. No more travelling, no more fancy hotels, no more white women you can stick your shrivelled little dick into. That's finished. You're not even a 'Special Commander' anymore, whatever the fuck that is anyway. Now you're just a soldier.

"The General may have tried to spare your feelings by not making it explicit that I was your commanding officer, but he did say you had to follow my orders. Right?"

Yao doesn't say anything. Out the corner of his eye he can see the old soldier edging away.

"Right?" Justice is so close his hot breath roars across Yao's face.

Wild horses couldn't make Yao speak, but he slowly blinks.

Justice must realise this is the best he's going to get. "Good," he says. He seems to become aware of the old soldier's absence and he spins round. "Hey Fuck Face! Get back here!"

Yao has never seen the Diop move so fast. In a twinkling he's standing shoulder to shoulder beside him.

"New orders! For both of you." Justice turns and points back at the hangar.

"The white people. All they do is shit. Deal with it!"

Turning back, eye to eye again with Yao. "Understand?"

"Yes," says Yao putting as much contempt into the word as he can.

Justice sneers, then turns and heads off to the control tower, a couple of hundred yards away towards the terminal.

Yao realises the old soldier is looking at him. "Well?" he asks.

"You were right. You handled him. Now we get to clear up white peoples' shit. Thanks."

"Come on," says Yao wearily.

The big hanger doors have been sealed so the only way in is by a side door. Ten soldiers are ready around it. Sooner or later the captives may try to get out and will have to be discouraged.

A rusty stairway has been wheeled up to the newly arrived 737 and already the passengers are disembarking. Stunned and zombie like, men and women and kids blink in the sun and look round as though for help. None has any hand luggage. Some still seem to be in their night clothes.

"Let this lot go in first, then we'll follow."

Diop nods approvingly and gets out some cigarettes. Yao waves away the offered pack.

As they get to the foot of the gangway, soldiers shove the people into a ragged single line. At the front a soldier is dragging the first passenger towards the entrance to the maze of upturned vehicles and metal debris that blocks the front of the hangar. More soldiers are waiting there.

A cloud of smoke passes over Yao's face and he smells the harshness of the cheap tobacco.

"Now the fuckers know what it's like," says Diop approvingly.

Not really understanding what he means, but too tired to do anything about it, Yao keeps quiet.

The first passenger, a man, is told to raise his arms. Two soldiers move in close and start to feel in his pockets then pat him down from neck to feet.

The second passenger is a stout woman who squeals with shock at the soldiers lay rough hands on her. The man, perhaps her husband, shouts something and tries to turn back. A gun butt smashes into his teeth and he slams back against an old refrigerator.

Hands up to their faces, the rest of the women in the line began to scream and the children began to weep.

Meanwhile the searchers, fully warmed up now, are frankly molesting the next woman in line.

Yao opens his mouth to shout and takes a step forward but something grabs his upper arm and stops him. He turns around to look in surprise at the old corporal.

"Don't, sir! Really! I don't know what you and Justice have against each other, but I've never seen him as angry as he was just now. Usually he's ice cold. He's capable of anything, believe me."

Yao tries to shrug him off but the man holds fast. "You have no authority now, that's why they sent you out on that rubbish job in the slum," he says urgently. "Those men will not listen to you. They will beat you and you will stop nothing."

By now the other soldiers are clamouring for their turn to search the passengers. Just then their CO emerges from the maze and begins lashing out at his men with his knobbed stick. It doesn't seem to have enough effect so he draws his sidearm.

Insubordination by the common soldier is dealt with harshly in Olomo's army. Some semblance of order is quickly restored and the first passengers are dragged off into the maze. The searches, though still brutal and intrusive, become less overtly sexual.

Slightly reassured, Yao looks at the hangar and the work that has gone into preparing it. A simple chain link fence has defined a new perimeter surrounding the back and sides of it. A clear space of fifty metres lies between the fence and the hangar's thin walls. Razor wire delineates this zone. It's not somewhere to wander for a casual piss.

At the front, on the apron where the planes would normally pull in, is the metal maze like a cataclysmic multi-vehicle car cash. Scrap cars, so old and worn they were beyond repair even by the ingenious local mechanics, have been dragged from their rusty roadside graves and deposited here. Old white goods and filing cabinets, broken pylons and rusty lengths of rail have been used to cover any gaps. Barbed wire and any other metal fragments that are sharp and spiky have been strewn over everything so it looks like a covering of rusty grass.

It looks solid but he knows the cars, the biggest objects, will have been stripped of anything salvageable, maybe even the engines. They'll not be as heavy as they look.

"Wait here, corporal!" Yao walks back to the passenger seat in the lorry's cab and lifts out the knapsack that he's stashed in the foot well. He opens it and checks the canisters, each containing a nasty mixture of tear gas and pepper spray, and the launcher are all still there.

Would twenty canisters be enough? Would he need them at all? He has no idea. He knows well enough that the General plans to the point of obsession, though not with a view to controlling every action. Olomo has carefully explained the futility of that. Rather it is a matter of trying to foresee as many eventualities as possible and making sure options to deal with them are available to the men on the ground.

It's all about flexibility. Which is why, one minute, he's giving out AKs and the next he's clearing up shit.

Yao collects the corporal and they walk over to the maze entrance. To Yao's chagrin, the men guarding the entrance barely glance at them and make no attempt to stop them going through. There are plenty of black Americans who could pose as Ligandan soldiers, could infiltrate and cut their silly throats.

The smell of corroded metal is intense and the little defile is pressed in between rusting columns of dead cars. Dropped down without any particular care, some vehicles overhang the twisting path, making Yao worry that any shift in the structure will bring them tumbling down to crush him like a bug.

Between the overhangs he sees the top of the hangar and makes out the heads of the snipers looking down on the maze. Not a job he would like himself, even though it is unlikely the Americans would shoot down on the thin roof from planes or helicopters. The rounds would go straight through and hit the foreigners beneath.

But the Americans do have some of the world's best snipers and sniper rifles. From a few hundred metres back, it would be easy to take the top off any head incautious enough to pop up over the edge of the roof.

Which is a pity as the hangar roof is where he will be spending the next few nights.

Behind him he hears the corporal yelp. Looking back, he sees the man clutching his upper arm. "Caught myself on a bit of metal," the man whines.

"Is it bleeding?"

The man pulls his hand away and the palm is bright red.

"Better get that seen to. There are first aid materials in the hangar."

Eventually the path opens out to show a clear semicircle around the closed hangar doors. Three machine gun nests have been set up facing the maze, the muzzles poking out between sand bags.

The hangar doors are closed so the only way in is through the side entrance. At least this time the men there make some effort to establish their identities.

As they enter the hangar, the smell of shit hits him like a brick.

At least it's cool. The high ceiling allows the hot air to rise. Even though there are already hundreds there, the hangar's size means the thin blankets that are their bedding are still well separated. Most of the people are lying on them, though some of the men slouch against the hangar walls. He feels their baleful eyes on him and the corporal as they walk through the vastness.

Apart from some low-level chatter, the only sounds are the shrieks of the children. Having got over their shock, they're already chasing each other around the blankets.

Guards with machine guns line the inner sides of the big hangar doors.

"Where do you think they're shitting?" asks the corporal.

"From the way the blankets have been pulled clear, I'm guessing in that far corner. The old metal tubs will be behind those sheets they've strung up. We'll need to empty them."

"When you say we..." says the corporal hesitantly.

"With that sort of intelligence, I'm surprised you're still just a corporal. Get a couple of the guards to help you."

Yao looks round and finds the flight of metal stairs leading up to the first gantry. This forms a stage round three sides of the hangar at about wing level. More soldiers are stationed on this.

"I'm heading up to the roof. Join me when you've finished."

He heads to the left, trying to skirt the foreigners, but as he gets to the sidewall a very tall fair-haired woman gets up from her blanket and covers the ground between them in long strides. Looking back, he sees a couple of grim faced soldiers start to move towards her but he holds up his hand and they edge back.

As she comes close, the disparity in their heights is almost absurd. Having to crane up at her makes him feel very uncomfortable.

"I'm sorry, but do you speak English?" He catches the American accent but can't place it. Not Deep South anyway.

"I do."

"Can you help us? My husband is on medication. High blood pressure. 'Volcanic' the doctors call it. We were taken away so quickly we couldn't take anything with us, even his meds. Can we see a doctor, please?"

He looks away, his neck already beginning to hurt. "No," he says.

"He could have a stroke. He could die."

"Look Mrs. ...?"

"Fisher. Sam Fisher."

"Mrs. Fisher. You are in a very difficult position. These men..." he indicates the soldiers, "... do not like foreigners. They are men who have been oppressed all their lives, who have fought in brutal civil wars. Much of their problems they blame on people like you. Do not ask them for anything otherwise..."

"...they will beat us. Yes, I've seen that already." She points towards the other side of the hangar where kneeling people are clustered around some prone figures.

It must have taken some bravery for her to approach him like this.

She looks back at him. "But my husband might die. We have young children."

There's nothing he can do.

"Tell you husband to lie down. Tell him not to worry. That's all I can say."

"Will we be released soon?"

"Yes, tell him that. That would be for the best." He makes the mistake of catching her eye again, but looks away quickly at the fear and disappointment he sees there.

He turns and makes his way up the rickety metal steps. The height gives him a better view of the hangar floor. It can take another few hundred people, which is just as well as there are many more to come.

Looking round, he spots the ladder going straight up to the roof. Moving the knapsack round so it's across his back, he starts to climb. The higher he gets the hotter it becomes. By the time he reaches to the roof it's like a steam room.

A metal trap door now blocks his way. He pushes at it but it doesn't give, so he slams his palm against it several times.

Above him he hears someone clomping across the roof, then light stabs in and he reflexively strengthens his grip on the ladder.

"Come on then!" says a voice.

Clambering out onto the thin roof, he feels it bend under him and he freezes.

He hears the man chuckle. Gingerly twisting his head around, he sees the man is a sergeant and has the shoulder flashes of a shooting instructor.

"It won't give way," the man says with authority. "Though best not jump up and down too hard."

The man is taller than him and even more thickset, so as Yao watches him stride away, his own confidence grows.

But it still worries him the metal is so thin, not much thicker than corrugated iron. He guesses that thicker roofs on these huge hangars would make them too expensive and too heavy to support.

The roof is gently ridged and, at the end facing the runway, he can see a number of prone figures. As he gets nearer he can make out the snipers' rifles lying beside each.

Finding a clear spot, he sets down his knapsack and starts to unpack it.

"What the fuck?" says the man next to him. Looking up he sees all the snipers are looking round.

"Are those gas shells? Tear gas?" the man says disbelievingly.

"Nastier than that," replies Yao.

"Lethal?"

Yao hesitates. "No. Not by themselves."

"Then what the fuck use are they going to be?" Murmurs of agreement come from the others.

"You'll see," says Yao. "Maybe. Anyway, my corporal will be bringing up our guns later. Mine is an AK-12. Is that OK with the rest of you?"

"Not really," says another. "The whole point of the maze is

to slow them down so we can pick them off. Accuracy is what it's about. So that means rifles not modern-day Tommy guns."

'Definitely shooting instructors' thinks Yao. The rest of the army would just point and shoot whatever they had to hand.

"You do your business and I'll do mine."

Settling down, he notices that the sun is getting low on the horizon and he's grateful. This roof is still hot and must have been scorching around midday.

Checking back, he sees a couple of men at the back of the roof and one on each side. To the front, the steps are being pulled back from the 737. Far away to the right across the airfield, he sees the mass of tents where their headquarters have been set up.

Scanning round the whole perimeter, he can see clusters of vehicles and soldiers. Across at the terminal the single jet remains marooned. Yao wonders why it hasn't already been pressed into service. Did planes have keys like cars? Had the pilots hidden them away when they realised they were to become captives?

The sniper next to him grudgingly offers a smoke but he turns it down. They all watch a sturdy looking land tug haul the 737 back from the hangar doors and round, so it's facing the slipway leading back to the runway.

"Wonder where the Americans are now," says the sniper.

Yao makes no attempt to answer but it doesn't seem to put the man off. "How long do you think we'll be here for? What's the General going to do with all these foreigners anyway?"

Yao turns to look at him. Lean, skin as dark as Yao's, the guy has sharp, intelligent eyes.

"How would I know?"

"With these scopes we see everything from up here. We saw Justice himself talking to you, over there by the trucks."

"He was giving me a hard time."

"He certainly was. It looked personal. And yet here you are still living and breathing. You know him well, don't you?"

"We're not close but, if you like, I'll get Justice up here to explain our complex relationship."

"Oh, I definitely wouldn't like that," says the man and goes back to scanning the airfield.

"Whoa," says another sniper. "Looks like another fresh meat delivery."

Coming in from a side gate, Yao can make out a convoy of mini buses cutting over the grass. They pull to a halt before the maze and another bedraggled group of westerners stumbles out, shielding their eyes from the low sun.

Yao watches them wend their way through the maze. Several of them, like the corporal, start back as their arms touch bits of sharp metal. One woman, her thin dress catching as she walks by, is suddenly stripped to her underwear.

Beside him, the men roar in appreciation.

"A floor show as well," says the sniper. "Can this get any better?"

But it doesn't. Darkness falls and the only event to break the monotony is the arrival of the corporal, reeking of shit.

"Oh for fuck's sake," says a sniper holding his nose. "Get the fuck away from me!"

Laden with the two guns and ammo, eyes still wide from his clumping walk across the flimsy roof, the corporal ignores him and sinks down beside Yao.

"Mission accomplished, Corporal Diop?" Yao asks.

The corporal holds out a stinking arm for Yao to smell. "What do you think, Sir?"

Far to the East, the lights of the English District high on the hill are coming on. There are few other working lights in the city. With just a feeble sliver of moon as competition, the stars of the tropical night are having their way with the heavens.

"It's a good night for the Americans," Yao says.

"So, you think they might come tonight, sir?"

"The western prisoners are all pretty much here at last. Our troops don't have anywhere near enough night scopes and the night is dark; the moon will only get bigger from now on. It would make sense."

"What chance do we have? They could blow us all to pieces with their smart bombs and their drones. Their Delta Forces and their Navy Seals and ..."

Yao cuts him off. "If they blow us up then the hangar goes too, and all they rescue are corpses. So, they won't do that. Anyway, you should trust the General, he knows what he's doing."

"I meant no disrespect, sir."

"I know. Have a cigarette! Relax!"

But relaxing isn't something he can do himself. His hands tremble and the bile from his gut brings an acid tang to his mouth. These are signs of a sickness whose only cure is vengeance.

Apart from a handful who had been away, the missile strike had killed every man in Zinzi's village. A woman and three children had been crushed to death by collapsing huts and many more were burned or had broken bones.

He hopes the Americans will come tonight. He will happily slaughter them all.

The surviving villagers had soon realised that he had been the target. Zinzi had thrown in her lot with him and so she had been cast out as well. He had taken her back to his accommodation at Olomo's plateau HQ.

He cannot forget the pain on her face as she had to leave her injured, devastated mother.

Across the airfield he watches the flickering of the campfires, like a glittering necklace around the airbase.

Beside him he hears the Corporal start to snore and he reaches across to...

The 737 at the terminal erupts into a hemisphere of fire. Flattening against the roof he feels the blast wave ripple over him. A diminishing yell tells him a sniper has gone over the side.

The control tower has turned to matchwood and fragments patter down on the roof around him.

"Ahhh!" Diop yells in shock and stands upright.

"Get down!" Yao reaches across to grab him.

One by one, the little necklace of fires erupts into balls of flame as the missiles impact. His eardrums are buffeted by the blast waves.

He doesn't see it coming down, but he feels something hit the roof behind him. Swinging round, he sees a monstrous shape towering over him, illuminated by the flames from the burning 737. Then the monster starts to collapse.

Scrabbling frantically for his AK-12, he sees the snipers bringing their big guns round.

They're too cumbersome and it makes the men too slow.

Already the paratrooper is firing as he dives to the roof. Yao pushes himself upright. The para sees the movement but even as he brings his gun to bear, Yao pulls his own trigger. A line of holes punches across the roof and the man's head kicks back.

Then they're all frantically scanning the heavens. Even with the light cast by the flames, the black parachutes are tricky to spot. No more are coming down on the roof, at least.

The snipers recover and start to loose off at some of the paras who have already come down on the airfield.

The paras are descending in two long strings, one behind the hangar, one in front.

There'll be C-17 Globemasters up there somewhere, Yao thinks. Not much else would have the range nowadays. Each can drop just over a hundred paratroopers.

A huge bang makes the hangar shake and the people inside scream. Shrapnel tinkles down onto the roof. One fragment comes down on the back of his hand: not hard but he yelps with its scalding heat.

"A para must have landed on one of the mines," says Diop, then jerks his head down as the first bullets zip overhead.

All the snipers are crawling back from the roof edge. Lying as flat as they can, and with the height of the roof in their favour, the paras down on the field will need to be very far back to even see them. The front facade of the hangar is solid brick. Not so easy to shoot through.

And at least the snipers have night sights. Every few seconds, one attempts a shot. He hears one grunt with triumph.

Away to the side, something big moves. At the end of the runway, its whale-like belly illuminated by burning huts and vehicles, he sees a Globemaster gliding ponderously in. It comes down hard and quick and the sound, when it gets to him, drowns out the small arms fire.

This'll be bringing the heavy stuff. Once they've secured the airstrip, empty C-17s will come in. Engines will be kept running as the released captives are thrown on board so they can take off as soon as they're full.

Yao hopes they'll be in for a surprise.

More sticks of paratroopers are landing, some even in the path of the C-17. Yao watches as one deflating canopy is run over by the nose wheels, the paratrooper releasing himself and rolling clear just in time.

Now the C-17 is off the runway and taxiing towards the hangar. Below him he hears the machine guns in the front of the hangar open up and guesses the first paratroopers have got through the maze.

The plane stops a couple of hundred metres short of the hangar but its massive bulk is still overwhelming. The snipers try to get off shots at the cockpit but the fire above their heads intensifies.

Another mine explodes and more shrapnel rains down. This time it brings body fragments with it. The mines are dense around the hangar and the Americans won't be getting through them soon.

"Where are they?" says Diop, "With all the guns we gave them. Are they fucking their wives instead?"

Yao shakes his head. "Airports are big. Even this one. It takes time to get yourself together, get through the fence and then cover the distance."

But he doesn't feel as confident as he tries to sound. If a slum dweller sees hell breaking loose somewhere, would he really run towards it even if he did have a gun?

Then again, he thinks, it's not as if they have so much to lose.

He pops his head up for a brief look. The Globemaster isn't quite end on to him, so he can see the big ramp has come down.

Maybe, at last, he's going be of use.

New explosions come from the northwest towards Ribeo. That's where Olomo has hidden his 4th Brigade amongst the shacks and warehouses. Assuming they haven't got too drunk in the *shibeens*, they'll have started up their vehicles and should be heading this way. By now the F/A-18Es and the Super Hornets will have gone over to target of opportunity mode, and that's probably what they're hitting now.

"Mother of God," says a sniper. "What the hell is that?"

Three monstrous shapes are already stumping away from the plane. These pick up speed as they barrel towards the hangar.

Watching them is suddenly like stepping into a nightmare. Beside him he hears Diop whimper.

"Devils!" he says.

"No. Inside those things are just men. Everyone, try to bring them down!" But already the braver ones are popping way.

In response a shit storm of bullets zips over their heads while many thud into the brickwork just below the roof. The top of one sniper's head comes off and skull fragments skitter across the metal.

The things are loping along quickly in big smooth bounds. They're dark coloured so they'll will be tricky to hit in the dark. At least the petrol engines in their backpacks will be like a big glowing bulb in the night sights.

Even so, he knows they're well armoured and anyone shooting will need to hit the right spot to have real effect.

Grotesquely cumbersome, but freakishly smooth in their actions, the powered exoframes have even Yao trying to blink away this fever dream. He's seen videos sure enough, but nothing has prepared him for the inhuman quality of their motion: the *wrongness* of them.

Already they've come close to the other side of the maze and the snipers are having to rise further up.

Another head explodes and the snipers bury themselves back down on the metal.

Yao takes the extending mirror from his knapsack and twists the rod until he gets just the right angle. He's just in time to see the last exoframe disappear behind the piles of scrap metal. Purposefully, he puts the mirror down and fits the first grenade into the launcher.

"What use is that...ah, I get it!" says the sniper next to him.

"No you don't," says Yao.

He looks across at Diop. "I'll be as quick as I can but I need a couple of seconds when they're not shooting at me."

"Oh shit," says the Corporal. "Do I have to?"

"If you run quickly enough you'll be fine. Anyway, they'll never hit anyone as skinny as you."

"That's very funny," says Diop grimly.

"Look, when I say 'now' sprint that way then dive down. Got it?"

Diop nods reluctantly.

"God save us," breathes a sniper and Yao looks back as a rusty old car sails into the air away from the maze. Then an industrial fridge, several hundredweight at least, follows it in a graceful arc.

All the snipers are talking now and he hears the rising hysteria in their voices.

The monsters are getting into their stride and they can hear the shrieking of metal as the creatures tear the maze apart.

"It's just men in metal suits," Yao shouts. "Hold your ground!"

Where would they go anyway?

Chancing another quick look, Yao sees that already a defile is being cut through the maze, wide enough for the three suits to work together side by side. Metal arms swing up, hurling things to the side.

He takes a deep breath and looks at Diop. "Now!" he says.

And, God love him, the man is immediately up and running. The zipping sounds of the bullets wash across as the paratroopers try to track the running figure.

Yao gets to one knee, sights and pulls the trigger then flops back down as the canister arcs over the maze.

Looking back across the roof, he sees Diop dragging himself back round so he's facing Yao again. Diop nods.

Yao fits another canister and, as he does so, the first wisp of acrid gas comes to him.

"Now," he shouts and Diop is sprinting back. Yao isn't sure where the first shell has come down but, if anything, it'd been short. This time he gives it more heft.

He hears Diop yell then feels him crash painfully down across his legs. Looking round he sees the man grimacing and clutching his thigh. Yao kicks him off and fits another grenade.

"They're dancing," says a sniper in wonderment.

Looking up, he sees all three machines struggling out of the defile they've been creating. It's like a tribal dance he saw in the mountains once. Their whole bodies are shaking wildly, arms scything back and forth. 'Getting rid of the devils' is what the tribesmen called it.

The flailing arm of one catches another in a brutal uppercut, flipping it up and over to land with a crunch on its back. The one on its back convulses, like an upended turtle. The other two, their retreat degenerating into confused random walks, are reeling drunkenly around, their torsos jerking forward and back.

Now the snipers have clear shots and they open up with a vengeance despite the rain of bullets over their own heads.

Three huge curtains of light rise up from the airport, the burning phosphorus munitions Olomo's men had set up earlier revealing everything in their harsh radiance. Yao sees ragged waves converging on the runway. The light makes the waves falter but they recover quickly, more quickly than the paratroopers blinded by their light enhancing goggles.

And when they do recover, and see the rag tag army advancing, wildly firing their ancient guns, the paratroopers turn and flee back towards the C-17 already cumbersomely turning on the hard-baked dirt.

Now the snipers are whooping exultantly, turning their rifles on the retreating paratroopers, forgetting the exoframes whose paroxysms are now subsiding.

The C-17 has got around now and men are stumbling up the ramp even as the plane begins to slowly accelerate.

"No man left behind," says Yao grimly.

But of course, many are being left behind, over run by the wave of angry Africans. Brought down at last by fire so poorly directed it's almost random, they disappear under a mass of punching, stomping figures.

The ramp is producing a shower of sparks now and, as the plane gets back on the runway, he sees it start to rise. Behind it, a dozen or so paratroopers hold up their arms in supplication but it's too late. Everyone can hear the mounting roar of the engines.

Movement to the right catches his eye and he sees three pickups racing across the grass. Sighting with the AK 12, he can make out the tall figure of Justice in the back of the first one. He's struggling with something long and thin, and trying to get it up on his shoulder despite the bumping of the truck. On the backs of the other two trucks, trailing like wings behind the first, are mounted machine guns. As he looks, the muzzles flash. A second later he catches the chattering sounds.

The paratroopers straggling behind the retreating plane have dived to the ground and are firing at the trucks. Alternate tracer rounds from the machine guns streak towards them, raising lines of erupting divots as they track in.

Justice's pickup is gaining on the lumbering C-17.

By now the snipers have realised what's happening and are laying down fire on the unfortunate paras. Even so, some of the Americans are still bravely shooting at Justice's pickup. But the man is ignoring them, intent on bringing his RPG to bear on the accelerating plane.

It's going much faster now and, just as the distance between it and the pickup starts to increase, Yao sees a bulb of flame erupt from the RPG. Surely the plane is too far...

Flame belches out of a heavy under slung engine. Shattered fan blades rip up through the wing, shredding it and sending twisting metal confetti, red with reflected flames, high into the air. The pickup swerves away so fast Justice is almost thrown overboard. Scrabbling for a hold he disappears below the tailgate as the plane's ruptured fuel tanks explode. A vast fireball expands and gouts of flame curve up over the airfield.

The explosive force sends the plane crashing off the runway, tipping it over so the other wing scythes into the earth, slewing the plane round and thrusting the nose deep into the dirt. The whole thing flips over and the fuel in the other wing erupts. The tumbling ragdoll that has once been a plane is lost in smoke and flame.

A tongue of flame catches the fleeing pickup and turns the flat bed into a cauldron. The truck screeches to a halt and men jump out, dragging Justice off the back and covering him in something. The driver falls on him, smothering the flames as best he can.

Now the snipers are picking off the remaining paratroopers, though they soon have to desist as the mob gets there first. Soon wild, jubilant firing fills the air and spent bullets begin to tap down onto the hangar roof.

"Let's get down off this," says Yao. Diop has managed to tear a strip off his shirt and has bound his own thigh. Yao's mortified to think he'd been too busy watching the spectacle to help.

Looking closer he sees the bleeding isn't too bad. "Do you think you can make it down?"

"I can give it a try. Starting to get cold, though."

Yao strips off his shirt and puts it round the man's

shoulders. Better to get Diop down before he really goes into shock. Supporting the wounded man, they stumble across the roof towards the hatch. Around them it looks like the whole world is bathed in flames. The 737 and terminal building are being consumed. Nearer, flames are licking out of the truncated top of the control tower. Further away are the volcanic remains of the C-17, and all around the perimeter are petrol fires from burning vehicles.

From far above it must be a spectacular sight, though there will now be only an EA-6B Prowler to see it. Already, the fleet of Globemasters will have turned back to whatever staging post the Americans have been able to cajole or bribe out of other countries.

Yao leads the way down the ladder, always looking up as Diop hops awkwardly down from rung to rung. He feels he has to do this, though he isn't sure what would happen if Diop loses his grip. If he falls he'll probably just take Yao with him.

But the man is tough, as all the older soldiers are. A lifetime of fighting has done that to them.

Looking down, he sees the multitude huddled in one of the front corners. He sees the far wall has been perforated by shrapnel from the detonating mines. Though he'd heard at least one grenade exploding in front of the hangar as some paras had made it through the maze, the captives have decided that the front is safer than the back.

All look stricken. They can't have had a clue what was happening; all they would have been aware of was the dreadfully loud explosions and the almost constant gun fire. Gun fire that's still going on, though by now all the foreign soldiers will be captured or dead.

A sea of hate filled eyes bore into them as they get to the bottom of the final ladder. Supported by Yao, Diop hobbles over to the far side where the single doctor is to be found. He's been assigned to deal with the captives' medical problems, but his patients silently slip away as they approach. The doctor, a grey haired old guy, steps forward as though trying to be professional, but he can't help himself asking: "What's going on? The soldiers don't seem to know."

Trapped in here, how could they?

"We are victorious. Please attend to this gallant soldier."

Before he leaves he grabs Diop's hand. "Thank you," he says. "For everything."

"It was my duty," says Diop simply. "For Africa."

"For Africa," says Yao.

The soldiers either side of the hangar door are looking at him expectantly.

"Battle over," he says. "Just look after the captives."

Out of the side entrance, the stench of cordite and burning jet fuel rolls over him. The three machine gun nests are still intact, though at one a soldier is being attended to by another.

He starts to walk towards the entrance to the maze.

"Be careful, sir," a soldier calls from one of the nests. "They may not all be dead."

Yao turns and nods his thanks. No need to get careless. He unhitches his AK and jacks a round into the chamber.

He aims the gun as he advances. All he can see of the enemy is a single arm on the ground protruding from the first bend in the maze. Leaning to the side and edging along the inner wall of the maze, he sees several bodies.

Once he might have taken his time, pulling the guns away from them before checking if they were still alive. But he's seen firsthand how indiscriminate the Americans can be

So instead, slowly, methodically, he makes his way through the maze putting a single bullet into each head or chest, making sure they're all really dead.

By the time he gets to the clearing the machines have made, the firing from around the airstrip has subsided, though whether because order had been restored or the slum dwellers have run out of bullets, he doesn't know.

He carefully steps over jagged metal fragments on the floor of the clearing and gives a wide berth to a car hanging precariously above him. Now he can make out the two statues silhouetted against the Globemaster's pyre. To their left is the other prone exoframe. Gun in hand, though convinced now he doesn't need it, he carefully approaches.

Suddenly he hears the sound of screeching brakes. Looking to the right, he sees Justice's phalanx of pickups pulling up on the tarmac.

Justice leaps down easily and strides towards the exoframes, ignoring Yao. He's lost much of his thick hair and, though the light from the flames is too inconsistent to get a good look, Yao guesses the exposed skin of his neck and head will be red with burns.

Justice strides fearlessly up to the first exoframe and Yao, suddenly ashamed of his own caution, hurries to catch up.

"Let's see what's inside," says Justice.

Easier said than done. They wait while the men try to find catches to open. Yao casts a glance at Justice.

"What you did: that was brave. Spectacular too."

Justice shrugs and Yao sees him wince as his uniform moves over the skin of his neck.

"Are you OK?"

"Minor burns," says Justice dismissively.

Something clicks and one of the drivers standing by an upright exoframe leans forward eagerly. After a bit of tugging, the helmet comes off and they all cluster round as torch beams shine in.

He hears Justice's men gasp.

The blood and the shape give away what's revealed as being a head, though all the features have been pulped to a smooth curve.

"Get the rest off!" says Justice.

While the men struggle, Yao leans in to touch the suit. Most of the jointed panels are cold; carbon nanotube based, they don't drain the heat from your fingers like metal. Only the housing of the internal combustion engine, part of the device's backpack, is still radiating heat.

Manhandling off some of the chest plates reveals a flexible Kevlar sheath. Yao takes a torch from one of the men and shines it across the fine chain links. Sure enough, he sees where a couple of rounds have impacted but not been able to penetrate.

So, the pepper spray has done it all.

The Kevlar is secured by velcro and a few big buttons and the men open it out. Yao can see a couple of ribs sticking out of the battered flesh.

One of the men is shining a torch down into the suit. From the waist down it's full of blood pooling around what is left of the man's legs.

"How does this thing work again?" asks Justice.

"Haptics," replies Yao.

"No, Professor" says Justice firmly, "For simple soldiers."

Yao thinks back to what Altukhov had told him. As ever, the Russian had been ahead of the game. Yao wonders where he is now. Probably a very long way away and soon to go under the knife again.

"If you're inside a robot suit, to get it to move ahead, for example, you lean forward so your chest and leading leg touches the front. The suit senses this, using haptics, and directs the servo motors to move accordingly. Pull your body back a little and the suit stops."

"And if you don't mind me asking, sir," says one of the soldiers. "How did we kill it? These bullets don't seem to have got through."

"Pepper spray and teargas. Mixed to make the person sneeze uncontrollably. The head and body jerk forward, hit the front of the suit and make it move forward. But your head and body have bounced off the front and hit the advancing back of the suit. The suit stops and moves back, just as your head bounces off the back and hits the front coming back. The oscillations build. So, it's like a pea in a whistle, except the pea in this case is soft," and he points at the bloody mess of the occupant's face.

"So, every time a soldier sneezed this would happen. But people sneeze all the time!"

"And the computer in the suit can handle one or two, damp things down. But our... adviser... figured that it couldn't handle repeated paroxysmal sneezing, that the suit itself would batter the occupant to a pulp. These things have never been used in battle before. They're still testing their new stuff out on us. Still not taking us seriously."

"Not after tonight," says Justice, silhouetted against the flames.

Chapter 22. *USS Benjamin F. Sands, Gulf of Guinea*

War had started right above her head.

She'd become used to the regular take-offs and landings of the Forward Guard: their Hornets and Prowlers seeking out threats for a hundred miles around. Somehow, she'd become habituated to the brutal screams of their engines as they surged to high power to get themselves into the sky.

The landings were harder to get used to. At least with take-offs the engine noise would recede slowly as the jet banked away. With landings the damn things would crash to the deck then scream like a T. Rex with a Stegosaurus up its ass. Full power, so that if their hooks hadn't caught on one of the arresting wires, the plane could just blast across the deck and have enough energy to struggle back into the sky to live another day.

In some ways the sudden absence of the noise as the pilot, convinced the hook had caught and so cutting the engine, was even worse. It was like *you* were the one who'd crashed into the sea, all the noise and fury of the air becoming the oppressive silence of the deep.

All these things would awaken her but, once she'd identified them, she could always fall quickly asleep again.

But tonight, the noise had become almost continuous and sleep had become an impossibility.

Not that she missed sleep much. The execution of the three women hostages had brought her nightmare back with a vengeance.

Giving up on trying to get any rest, she swung her legs over the side of the bunk, fished out the coveralls from her locker and shrugged them on.

Making her way through the metal labyrinth, she could feel the buzz. After midnight things usually quieted down, but now the commotion was like a change of watch.

Emerging into the heavy air, she found the viewing platform full with cooks and administrators craning over the rail to look down on the hell of the flight deck. Deck crew were all over it, running around waving torch batons as fighters appeared on the huge elevators. Rolling off these immediately, they'd make their way clumsily to the launch point, avoiding all the parked aircraft and their bristling, angled up wings.

As each fighter powered up she had to clap her hands to her ears. The crowd to her right obscured the 'Crotch' where the angled deck met the main one, making the carrier's feats of legerdemain even more awesome. Now you see the jet safely on the deck, now you don't: the catapults seemingly whisking them out of existence.

And it kept happening. At least a whole wing was being launched.

"What's going on?" she yelled at a steward next to her in a brief interval as the next plane was being hooked up.

"How would I know? They tell us nothing!"

Not quite true: the internal TV stations did little else, but she guessed that when a real fire op went down, they kept it need-to-know. Too big a fleet, too many men, electronic communications now too good. Just one bad apple with a satellite phone could undo any hard-won element of surprise.

Her visits to the JIC had always been at Macik's invitation, but she'd been there so often they might not challenge her now. At least down there it'd be quieter.

But when she got there, it wasn't so quiet either. The engine noise may have subsided but Blue Tile Country was boiling with life as crew darted in and out of the various command centres. The Combat Information and Carrier Air Traffic Control Centres were roiling with hurrying crew. The JIC too was humming.

Lewis was leaning against a table and, as she entered, a quick smile flashed across his face. She winked and headed for him.

"So, what's happening?"

"Hostage rescue," he said. She wanted to reach out and touch him, brush his arm lightly at least, but she held back.

"At the Cleft?"

"No. Seems our friend Olomo has been clearing out three whole countries of westerners and busing them to Tembe airport. There's a thousand or more there now."

"Yeah? I never saw anything about that on the cable channels."

"It's starting to come through. Most of the expats worked way out in the bush or the deserts: teachers, missionaries, oil workers, geologists, whatever. Looks like he's been rounding them up over the last few days. It's only when he started to take bankers and administrators and lecturers from institutions in the big cities that the news got out."

"So, they're all at the airport. What're we doing?"

"All the Prowlers have been in the air for a while, plus an AWAC they managed to get there by means of a circuitous route and a shitload of air tankers. Targets have been identified; the radar at the airport is pretty much all they have in that line so it'll be the first to go. The advance wing of F/A-18's will be there in minutes. They'll take out troop concentrations and clear the way for the paratroopers."

"And where will they be coming from?"

He was trying to sound cool, like this happened every day, but she could tell he was excited. Times like this were what military careers were all about.

"An Armada of Globemasters is coming in from Malta. The leading ones will drop a few hundred paratroopers in to secure the airfield and free the hostages then the rest of the Globemasters will roll in to pick them up. Quick turnaround and then back home before Olomo can even get out of bed."

She felt a cold finger tickle her heart. "That sounds a little too easy. It's right in the heart of enemy territory. Won't Olomo be expecting this?"

"No, everything appears rushed, like he's reacting to the cruise strike that hit his family. We think he's lost it." He laughed. "Not that he really had it to begin with. The guy's nuts."

She shook her head. "But this doesn't... I mean you're forgetting The African and all his attempts at sabotage. Olomo knew we'd be coming here."

Lewis shrugged. "He had some insight about what would happen but he's just bit off more than he could chew. Anyway, what choice do we have? We've seen what he's been doing to the group of hostages he's got in the Cleft. Imagine what he could do with all these others. Just now they're all in one place, but we don't know for how long. We've got to strike now."

For once, the JIC was the nexus of Blue Tile Country. Information was streaming in from CIC and CATCC rather than the other way around.

"Air traffic control and all ground aircraft destroyed at Tembe," said Terni at his central terminal. "Second wave engaging ground targets."

Around her she saw high fives and could just about smell the testosterone.

But it just didn't feel right. Olomo had some mad ideas but he wasn't a fool.

Lewis must have sensed her doubt. "Look," he said reassuringly. "Olomo is just a Hitler wannabee. Monomaniacs: they can't be reasoned with. All we can do is nip them in the bud before they can do more damage. Once we've freed the hostages, and taken out what little military capability he has, his power will just wither away. Maybe we won't manage to kill him ourselves, but sooner or later someone else will. Someone the rest of the world can deal with."

She watched as explosions blossomed in night sight green on the big monitor. She knew there were shanty towns all-round the airstrip and she hoped the Superhornets' aims were true.

A Globemaster, already taxiing in, lumbered across the

field of view, but then the viewpoint swung away to take in a conflagration over towards the terminal and hangars. Lewis moved up to the screen and pointed at a little patch of burning hell. "That's were Olomo's forces had set up temporary headquarters. Any reinforcements would have come from there. Not anymore though," he said with relish.

She watched as missile after missile streaked in, each time the explosion blanking out the screen for a few seconds. It seemed to go on forever.

"Nobody could survive that," she said.

Lewis was nodding vigorously.

Then a multitude of hot objects, so many they looked like a single mass on the night sight, was moving across the airport from the west. The view zoomed out and she saw several other huge waves of the things washing in from other directions.

She pointed. "What...?"

"Whoa!" said Terni suddenly. "There's been a recall on the Globemasters. They're turning back."

Lewis' eyes widened in alarm. "But did they get the hostages?"

"Not enough time. Only one Globemaster landed."

The viewpoint from the AWAC or Prowler changed and she could see the one Globemaster coming back along the airstrip, trying to build up speed. She saw a wing erupt and the screen went white again. By the time the image was restored, the plane was just a trail of burning wreckage.

The room went quiet. She held her breath waiting for someone else to say it, but nobody did.

Finally, she said it herself, just to make sure she'd really understood, desperately hoping she was stupid and had got it wrong. "So we've just blown the shit out of his main airport, and killed God knows how many of his men, and now we're leaving this bloodthirsty tyrant with over a thousand Westerners to do with as he likes."

Nobody answered.

An hour or two later the videos started to hit YouTube. Shot from the ground, with the restricted perspective that entailed, they were confused affairs. Nevertheless, the exploding C-17 and the tide of African's washing over the American troops, drowning them under stamping boots and slashing machetes, made for gut wrenching television.

She was watching this in the little common room near her rack when a worried looking lieutenant found her. She was to report to the bridge.

She, Lewis and Lundt, now returned from the Aegis, waited on the Bridge wing. She looked out on the now gentle swells of the Gulf of Guinea. Macik was near the centre of the bridge, surrounded by anxious junior staff who would come and go as instructions were issued.

Joey took the time to look around. Getting up to the Bridge was an honour in itself and some crewmen never saw it in their entire naval career. As with the rest of the ship, the technology had a 70's patina interrupted here and there by a modern piece of contemporary equipment, like high tech medical implants patched into some old lady to keep her going.

Already sunlight was peeping over the horizon and it was going to be another clear day. From inside it, the *Sands* could become the universe itself, but from the Bridge, seven stories above the deck, it all looked easier to comprehend. Suddenly it wasn't so all-consuming.

Looking down, she saw a bunch of broke winged aircraft, mainly Greyhounds and Vikings, being herded forward. They were being pulled by tractors onto the bow facing runway, making space for the returning aircraft to land on the stern. With so many aircraft, and not enough space on the hangar deck to stow them all, the stuff that wasn't useful for any given situation, like the cargo transports and anti-submarine aircraft, had to be moved around to make way. It was like one of those puzzle boxes, where you had to shuffle around bits of wood to open it.

A glint of light to the south caught her attention and she saw a line of white rising from the horizon. Looking closely, she could just make out the Aegis destroyer that it had come from. Another streak of light appeared further west, too far to make out the ship it came from.

Then another missile leapt out of the first Aegis. As she watched, more and more condensation trails became lit by the sunlight. It looked like people were letting off streamers; like it was party time.

"What are they shooting at now?" she whispered.

"Anything and everything, is my guess," said Lewis.

"But he has the hostages. He'll kill them all!"

"Truth is, they're pretty much as good as dead anyway. I guess the Pentagon wants to try some shock and awe. One last attempt to shake Olomo's confidence. Bastard must be cock-a-hoop after what happened at Tembe."

"So what will they be shooting at?"

Lewis shrugged. "Army bases; whatever shipping he might have; vehicle depots. Terni could have told us what kind of targets were up."

"But I thought Olomo had fuck all in the way of facilities. In these places army barracks shade into towns, shanties build up round them to supply the soldiers' needs. Like barnacles on a rock. Put cruise missiles down in those and you'll kill more civilians than soldiers."

Lewis opened his mouth but she held up a warning finger. "Don't use the phrase *collateral damage* with me. It's a mealy mouthed, gutless term for murder."

"What else can we do?"

"I don't know but killing even more non-combatants can't be the answer."

Lundt had been quiet up to now. The NCIS office was deep in the bowels of the ship so she'd probably slept through the caterwauling of the jets. She looked groggy, like she'd been woken from a deep sleep. She pointed a finger in the vague direction of the coast. "I may just be a civilian, but this is war now. It's not just a few missionaries that got executed. How many of our soldiers died on that airstrip? Hundreds at least. Some of them chopped up like steers in an abattoir. Aren't you angry? Don't you feel that someone's got to pay?"

Joey opened her mouth to retort but saw Macik with a phalanx of senior officers coming towards them. It looked like they were having a knitted brow contest.

But this time, behind Macik's cold and calculating eyes, she thought she saw anger. Behind the cologne and deodorant, her keen nose picked up the tang of his masculine sweat.

"Thank you for coming to the bridge," he said, the professional civilities coming automatically to his tongue. "I presume you've been following what's been happening in Tembe."

"Yes, Admiral," said Lewis smartly, no trace of his usual cynicism evident.

"I want your assessments. I can't move for people giving me information yet we've wound up in this...position. Maybe a non-military view might help. Special Agent Beck: you've been there right from the start with this Yao character. What do you make of it all?"

She blinked in surprise. Standing a little straighter, she met his penetrating gaze. "I think we've underestimated these people from the start. The African...Yao, has tried to suborn at least three of your crew, and succeeded with two of them. He knew the CSG would be on-line when he made his move and he wanted to negate it by sabotage. And at the airport, that wave of civilians who overran our troops. A lot of them were carrying guns. It was like they'd been primed for this."

"Humiliation," said Macik emphatically. "That's what he's dishing out. He can kill the hostages by the dozen and all we can do is watch. The question is: why is he doing it?"

She realised he didn't seem to be listening at all, despite what he'd said at first. Maybe saying he wanted an outside view had just been another little internal box he felt he should tick. Maybe he was as much a victim of the box ticking mindset as his crew.

A tall young officer she'd seen in JIC leaned forward a little and Macik swung round to look at him. "Prohost?"

"Our analysts back at the Pentagon have been going through Olomo's history with a fine-tooth comb, including all the stuff he wrote as an academic. Looks like he's hung up on Sonni Ali."

"Never heard of him," said Macik.

"Few have," said Prohost softly. His voice was deep and she doubted he could shout loudly even if his life depended on it. "And that's kind of revealing in itself. Africa's fragmented, partly because of it being carved up by imperialistic nations like the British and the French. They used divide and conquer as easily as they used bullets. But Africa wasn't always a patchwork of countries. At one point, about 1200 years ago, there was one huge empire that covered half a million square miles, encompassing parts of Mali, Guinea, Niger, Benin, Nigeria and Liganda. And its first emperor was Sonni Ali: a conqueror in the Chinggis Khan mould. A brilliant military strategist and also, incidentally, a Muslim. His was one of the largest Islamic empires in history. Lasted over five hundred years in one form or another."

"Surprised I've never heard of him. Has anyone else?" asked Macik.

Plenty of shaking heads and, if her own lack of knowledge was typical, probably quite genuine. Then again, she doubted any of his men would dare even hint they knew more than Macik.

Prohost shrugged. "Anyway, Ali seems to be a hero of Olomo's. Someone he perhaps wants to emulate. His writings certainly make it plain he thinks Africa, at least sub-Saharan, should be more united. That it has the potential to be a superpower."

"So he's like a Black Hitler. An Islamic Black Hitler. Hadn't we guessed that already?"

Something was paining Prohost though he tried to hide it. Joey saw Macik's eyebrows twitch as he caught this too.

"You don't agree," said Macik with a hint of ice in his voice.

"Olomo isn't a Muslim. If anything, his philosophy, idiosyncratic as it is, is too exclusive. It's a kind of Black African centred Christianity and there's not much room in it for Islam."

"Hitler wasn't Muslim either but that didn't stop him being... well ... Hitler," said Lewis.

"We seem to be wandering off the thread," said Macik tightly. "Prohost. Why us? Why is he deliberately taking us on?"

"Because we're the most powerful nation on the planet. If he wants to unite Africa, and good luck with that by the way, then he maybe thinks humiliating us will show the potential of African power."

Macik was shaking his head. "But Africa's a hotchpotch. It's not just different countries: its different tribes, different religions. He'd be crazy to think he could do it."

"Our reading of his papers shows he has some awareness of the problems. For example, his ambitions don't extend north to the Sahara and beyond. The Muslim Arabs in the north are too far beyond the pale in his eyes. Olomo's main rallying cry is about throwing off the hands of the imperial oppressors. The Arabs, the old slave trading middle men, he sees as part of the problem."

"But the US hardly has any imperialistic pretensions for Africa. What about the Chinese? They're the imperialists nowadays." Macik was sounding exasperated.

Prohost was looking nervous. "Well... maybe not."

"Just spit it out," snapped Macik, "Don't try to spare my feelings!"

Prohost was looking very unhappy. A knobbly Adam's Apple slid up and down under the thin skin of his throat. "The Chinese are not like the imperialists of old. They're not interested in ruling African countries. They pay for the natural resources their own country lacks. They pay in hard cash or they invest by sending in their engineers and miners and medics to build roads and mines and hospitals. But they're not really spreading their ideology, other than perhaps by example. Plus they don't have religion to foist on the Africans like the old colonialists did.

"But also, they don't interfere with local politics, and maybe that's where they're different from us. The US waged proxy wars with the Soviets in a long list of African countries. We armed some seriously bad people here in the 60s, 70s and 80s. And the US is regarded as basically killing off African leaders we didn't approve us, such as Lumumba in the Congo.

"More latterly we've aided and abetted some unsavoury regimes for the purposes of obtaining natural resources, taking a more interventionist line than the Chinese, though more by using money than guns. Oil in Nigeria, rare earths in Tanzania..."

"Get to the point," said Macik crisply.

"So, we're the top dog on the world stage and we have form when it comes to Africa. So, he's teaching us a lesson. Presumably he's going to milk this situation for all it's worth. Keep us waiting out here powerless while he kills the hostages. It'd take us months to get enough boots on the ground, even if a neighbouring country lets us build up our forces on their territory. And they're probably too afraid of Olomo to do that."

"Can I ask a question?" asked Joey.

"Of course," said Macik.

"Why are we firing off cruise missiles at the Ligandans? What can that achieve?"

"We can degrade their infrastructure."

"What infrastructure is that? Are we talking military infrastructure? I keep hearing that militarily they haven't got a pot to piss in. They don't have much in the way of roads or railways or shipping. The one airport they've got has a burning C-17 splashed all over the runway. Why are we doing this?"

Macik looked at her in silence for a few seconds. Finally, he took a deep breath. "Special Agent Beck. Scores, maybe hundreds of your compatriots are dead. We can't stand by and do nothing. Then we really would look powerless."

"But we *are* powerless. Those cruise missiles will kill civilians. And that may make Olomo kill more hostages in turn. This can only make things worse."

"We can't do nothing," Macik repeated, more slowly this time. "At the very least we must make sure that he *personally* cannot get away with this. Otherwise there would be no deterrent for some other tin-pot dictator or religious group to do this elsewhere in the world."

"Does that mean you're sending the missiles into his plateau base? Even though it'd kill the remaining hostages there."

"It's an option. If we knew for sure he was there. Which, at this point, we don't."

Far away she saw another missile rise on fire and smoke.

The mess was almost empty. They still had an electronic mountain of crew files to go through, so a quick coffee wouldn't make much difference.

"This is so bad," said Lundt and then bit at her lip distractedly. "We're at that bastard's mercy."

"Which one? Is Macik any better than Olomo? He'll kill more civilians than even Olomo has so far."

"Come on, Joey," said Lewis, giving her a disapproving look. "We've got to do something."

"Would everyone please stop saying that! Killing more innocent people isn't doing *something*. It's committing murder!"

"I'd keep your voice down," said Lundt quietly. "This is a warship. Liberal breast beating doesn't play well here."

"Liberal? Nobody's ever accused me of that before! Not wanting some dirt-poor Africans getting blown to bits doesn't make me a liberal. It makes me a human being."

"This is irrelevant," said Lewis irritably. "Even if Macik wasn't up for it, which he most certainly is, then Tridens would make him do it anyway. New Democratic President, close fought election where the Republicans tried to paint her as weak and drove the message home advert after advert. She's got it all to prove."

"And being a woman as well," said Lundt, "We're always having to prove ourselves in what's still a man's world."

Joey could feel a blood vessel pulsing in her temple. "So what this is, it's all about overcompensation. We're blowing up Africans to prove a point? A US domestic political point? That is so fucking sick."

"Oh, come on," said Lewis. "After all those troops were killed, there'll be hardly anyone back home holding Tridens back. They want to see the bad guys punished."

"Hey, I got into this whole business just to see the bad guys brought to justice. But not at the expense of killing the innocent."

"Try taking the long view then. If we weaken Olomo, whether we kill him or not, there's going to be regime change. That's got to be better for the Ligandans and the Niassans and the Bukanians."

"Really, and how do we know that? Deposing the Taliban in Afghanistan, Hussein in Iraq, Gaddafi in Libya. How well did all that work out? In some ways those bastards kept things together. We're always so sure we're acting for the greater good, but history shows we haven't a clue."

"What about Hitler?"

"Hitler threatened world peace and had the military might to have a shot at European domination, at least. Olomo has fuck all going for him."

Lewis flicked his hand dismissively. "And if we let him beat us then we'll look even weaker than him. And then that really would be the end of the American century. Sooner or later China will be more powerful than us, then maybe India. Maybe we'll slip down the league table. But neither Tridens nor Macik are going to let it happen on their watch and I, for one, support them."

Joey looked away from their angry eyes.

Chapter 23. *USS Benjamin F. Sands, Gulf of Guinea*

Something was shaking at her shoulder. She pushed her arms up to ward it off and her hands crunched into something hard. Again.

This sleeping in a bunk was getting old.

"Jesus," she muttered angrily and struggled to see in the gloom.

"Hey, calm down," said Lewis, taking his hand off her shoulder.

"What the fuck are you doing here?"

"Waking you up. There's something you'd better see."

"For fuck's sakes." Irritably, she jerked off the blanket and put one foot on the floor. She saw his eyes widen and she realised her panties would be stretched tight over her crotch.

She pushed the flat of her hand up hard against his chest, making him stagger back. He could look at her pussy all he liked, but only on her terms. That bout in the NCIS office would do her for a while.

She made a circular motion with her forefinger and then shrugged her way into her coveralls as he turned to look the other way. A couple of heads were peeking out from other bunks but then retreating. Men here were unusual but not unheard of. People had to be fetched quickly from sleep all the time, and sometimes there wasn't always a woman available to do the fetching.

"Where's your Rec room?" he said.

She pointed back behind him. "Twenty feet, to the left."

"Come on!"

The little space was empty and the sound turned down on the screens. She saw him looking round.

"Remote?" he asked.

She couldn't see it and they had to crane over coffee cups and shift books aside until they found it under a *Sports Illustrated*.

"What's this about?"

"Olomo's going to do a telecast."

"Well that's stupid. We'll trace the feedback and shove a cruise missile up his ass."

"Pre-recorded apparently. Probably downloaded to a server in Portland or somewhere. Sent to all the main cable networks just in time to appear on the hour. Even if we did trace it all back, he'll likely be long gone. Guy's mad to take us on, but he's not stupid."

"He certainly isn't. But I'm sure we'll bomb wherever he was anyway and kill a few more innocent fuckers."

Ignoring her, he found CNN where a strapline was promising Olomo's broadcast in a couple of minutes.

"Coffee?"

"Yeah, thanks," he said.

She poured out some percolated stuff that had stewed too long. Fingers touched embarrassingly as they both reached for the little pots of cream and the sugar. She felt his eyes on her and, turning, she found his head only inches from her own.

"What?"

"Yesterday. That was...nice."

"Then you must have been doing it with someone else, because there was nothing *nice* about it."

She could see he was hurt. "I didn't mean it wasn't good. It's just *nice* isn't the word. Maybe..."

"Passionate?"

"Primitive is maybe better. Savage. Brutal."

He couldn't seem to work out whether he should be pleased or not.

"Worth doing again?" he asked finally.

But at that point, Olomo's elegant head appeared on the TV. He seemed to be at a desk with a plain plaster wall behind him, not like the wooden planks in his makeshift studio back at the plateau. Not enough reason to send a cruise missile there. Yet.

The man looked haggard, his eyelids heavy and the wrinkles more evident now around his eyes. His forehead was deeply furrowed. His battle fatigues were the browns and greens for jungle fighting.

He looked up at the camera. "Good day to you," he said slowly. "I am General Olomo of Liganda and I wish to talk to you all tonight about the foreigners arrested in Liganda, Bukana and Niassa. In this broadcast I am going to explain the reasons for these mass arrests." His tone was quiet, reasonable but seemed overlain by the terrible weariness of a man driven close to breakdown.

"You may be aware of how the United States military murdered my wife and children. You may also be aware of the attack they launched on a peaceful civilian airport in our capital city. How they bombed it, killing many innocent people. How the people of the city rose up and, despite the overwhelming firepower of the Americans, they triumphed and drove the invaders out. The Americans killed many of my people: poor people living in the shanty towns near the airport. That is something the Americans always do. For them the death of innocent people is a price worth paying for whatever selfish goal they are pursuing. And it was all so unnecessary, as you will see.

"But first I would like to give you some perspective on Africa and its history. You will need this to understand what is happening here."

Even as she watched, she could see the compelling old lecturer in Olomo, hidden under the stiffness of his military manner, begin to re-emerge. It was like the man was pulling on a comfortable pair of old gloves.

"Africa is the cradle of mankind. Nearly two million years ago, and only in Africa, *Homo Habilis*, the first maker of stone tools, our ancient ancestor, wandered the Serengeti Plains and the Great Rift Valley of East Africa. *Homo Erectus* followed and then finally *Homo Sapiens*. And, of course, we are all *homo sapiens*. Your ancestors *all* came from Africa. You are *all* Africans."

He sighed. "And that is something the rest of the world always forgets. Once your ancestors were black Africans just like me. And it was only 40,000 years ago, barely 1600 generations, when *homo sapiens* first left Africa. And from those brave ones, who first left the cradle of their birth, sprang all the peoples of the world.

"And it is not just mankind's DNA that came from Africa but its very spirit as well. The spirit that imbues our greatest religion. Jesus was not white. How could he be? What is even less appreciated is that Mary herself was a black African, as the work of Albert Cleague Jr has shown. Part of a tribe that had migrated from Nigeria, she and Jesus spent his childhood in Egypt. Ethiopian Christianity, which predates European Christianity, has always portrayed Jesus as black.

"So, Jesus was half black and half God. Yet the white people stole him, made him look like themselves. Stole him, just as they have stolen everything else from Africa."

"Oh, come on!" said Lewis.

"Not so fast," she said. "Ever been in a church which showed Jesus as anything but white. They're *all* wrong. At the very least he'd be Middle Eastern in appearance. Being at least part black isn't so much of a stretch. I'm not religious, but I was made to read the damn Bible in school. Never once mentioned what colour he was."

Lewis was looking at her like she was an idiot.

They'd missed some of what Olomo had been saying. "...Africa is the mother of you all, physically and spiritually. And how have Westerners treated their mother? How have they rewarded her for nurturing them?"

The heavy-lidded eyes were now baleful. "They murdered and enslaved her other children. Stole her possessions and smashed her home. Africa the bountiful, plundered by foreign hands, broken and left for dead. How the world, both the Arab as well as the Western worlds, have treated Africans is an infamy.

"First it began with slavery back in the seventh century and the expansion of the Arabian Caliphate into sub-Saharan Africa. Over the next thousand years nearly twenty million African men, women and children made the journey as slaves through that terrible expanse. Millions died on the way, their bodies abandoned for the jackals.

"Then in the 15th Century the Europeans came, searching for slaves for Europe and the New World. And of these, the British were the worst and it is they that have profited most from the human misery their greed created. Ten million souls taken from their homes, herded together more densely than cattle in the dark holds of stinking ships for months at a time. Made to wallow in their own filth. Dysentery and ill treatment alone killed over four million. Young women routinely raped by the sailors because the half caste children produced could be sold at top prices, the white blood thought to ameliorate the effects of the primitive African blood. Though not enough to make them as good as whites, of course." Bitterness was cutting through his weary tones now.

He stopped and swayed a little, as though the enormity of his words was becoming too much to bear.

"And then the Europeans came for our land and what it contained. Many thousands of Africans, from small tribes to mighty kingdoms, came under the heel of the white man. Africa was cut up like a chicken at a feast with European nations greedily tearing it apart.

"Belgium ravished the Congo for its rubber and copper, brutally treating the Africans who they used as slaves, killing ten million. Italy invaded Abyssinia, dropping mustard gas on civilians, murdering a hundred thousand and blinding and maiming countless more.

"And where the Africans rebelled, tried to push the invaders out, they were met with savage repression. The Dutch coming for their diamonds and gold in South Africa and Rhodesia and enshrining their filthy racist differentiation in Apartheid. The British killing fifty thousand, mostly children, in their crackdown following the *Mau Mau* uprising in Kenya.

"And it goes on. Portugal and the forced labour it instituted in Mozambique, lasting until the 1960s.

"And even when they left, or were thrown out, the colonialists left a legacy which would yield bitter fruit in the years to come. For the colonialists to rule, they had to ensure the Africans in their different tribes did not unite against them, for they were few and the Africans many. So, they set one tribe against the other. Germany in Rwanda, France in Mali and Algeria. They seeded bitter rivalries whose poison would percolate down through the generations.

"And then, as the European Colonial powers declined, their place was taken by America and Russia, fighting their proxy wars and using Africans as their foot soldiers. They deposed and even assassinated democratically elected leaders, like the Americans did in the Republic of the Congo, or the Russians did in Somalia and Ethiopia. They supplied arms and military advice and training to opposing sides in countless wars. In Angola alone, this led to half a million dead and over a million refugees.

"And even now, with the Cold War long over, America and the Europeans still plague us. Their multinationals still come to drain the continent of its oil and gold and minerals. By corruption, and using private militaries as surrogates, they suppress local protest. They pay pittances but drain countless billions of dollars from Africa.

"And so, after hundreds of years, it is the colonialists who have grown rich and the Africans poor."

During this diatribe Olomo had been slowly leaning forward, as though under the terrible weight of these infamies, but now he sat up straight and glared at the camera.

"Enough!" he boomed. A finger came up accusingly. "The White Man has been a curse to Africa. A child that has become a man and then turned against its nurturing mother. Africa could be rich, the richest continent on the planet, but to do so we must rid ourselves of this ungrateful son."

Ólomo's tone was implacable now, like the word of God himself. "The westerners we have arrested are not hostages, we are simply in the process of deporting illegal immigrants, unwanted aliens. We are ejecting them. We will cast them upon the waters where they may sink or swim. The scions of the colonialists are not welcome here. They never have been and they never will be."

"*Cast on the water?* Does that mean what I think it means?" she said quietly.

"So, I entreat the Americans to desist from raining down missiles on our heads to kill and maim innocent Africans. Not for simple humanitarian reasons; that has never cut much ice in their dealings with Africans in the past. No, they should stop because otherwise they may kill their own as we move them. We are expelling them."

"So, this is good, right?" she asked uncertainly.

"And I hope my fellow Africans, from Tunis to Cape Town, from Dakar to Bosaso, will follow our example. If we work together as brothers, we can drive out this evil forever."

"Ah," she said. "That part maybe wasn't quite so good."

Lewis was nodding in appreciation, like a centuries' old puzzle had just been solved. "Blame it on the white folks. Of course! Before we came along all the different tribes of Africa got on like peaches and cream. Guy's just a fucking racist. Stigmatising whites just like Hitler did the Jews. Classic strategy!"

The broadcast had ended and now the screen was showing an old picture of Olomo, back in his lecturing days. She looked at the dignified, intelligent face and wondered if it really was as simple as that.

Chapter 24. *Tembe Airport, Liganda*

The appalling smell lifted like morning mist as Sam stumbled out of the hangar doors, shoved forward by a heavy black woman in military uniform. She could feel her kids clutching madly at her long skirt, banging into her legs, as they hurried to follow. Gerry, she hoped, was close behind, though the men and the women had been separated right from the start. With her height, she'd managed to catch sight of him far off in a corner of the huge building.

It was quiet outside, quieter than an airport should ever be. She tried to keep up with the women and kids in front who were disappearing into the maze through the metal junkyard.

As they entered the shadowy walls of rusting metal, she heard someone scream.

Then Paul was tugging at her skirt, trying with his little six-year old body to pull her back. Women and kids were piling up behind them and people started to complain.

"No, Paul," she said urgently. "We can't stop."

But he was still pulling, so she grabbed his arm and dragged him after her. Laura had already squeezed round the two of them and was walking meekly ahead.

Too far ahead.

By the time Sam smelt the burnt flesh, it was too late to stop Laura seeing the thing on the ground. She was already rooted to the spot, hands up to her mouth, staring at the monstrosity of charred and broken flesh. One undamaged eye stared fixedly out of a jawless face.

"Christ, what's that?" said a woman behind her.

Laura's shuddering cries were coming between rapid intakes of breath. Sam got herself between the kids and the body, shuffling sideways to get them all past. She felt its toes slide across her ankle.

As she and the kids scuttled away, she glanced back to see the woman behind her go into hysterics. Frozen, she was blocking the narrow passage. Sam didn't wait to see what the soldiers would do about that.

The passage widened and they were out into the sun again.

"Mummy," she heard Paul say. Looking down she followed his pointing arm and saw bits of body scattered over to one side, a little yellow dog already dragging a length of slippery intestine out of a limbless torso.

She looked at the paper white faces of her children, their features stricken with horror, and decided she couldn't allow herself be sick. The broken line of prisoners was snaking out towards some parked vehicles and she quickly pulled the kids towards them.

Now the smell was of jet fuel and, far across the airfield, she could see a mountain of metal, palls of black smoke puffing into the sky above it.

"Is that a robot?" asked Laura, pointing to the left.

Sam couldn't tell what the hell it was. Metal certainly, but it was resting in a pool of blood already blackening in the tropical sun.

Keeping going across the grass, she became aware that the sky was full of big black birds looking for carrion. Now she realised little groups of vultures and buzzards had already landed all over the airfield. Their heads were moving, either high and darting looks at other birds, or down and diving into shapes on the grass.

Behind her she heard shots fired and looked back. Terrified people were tumbling out of the labyrinth, the blockage somehow cleared.

"Hey," said a deep male voice. Turning back, she saw a whipcord thin soldier gesturing angrily towards a brightly painted bus. Behind this she saw scores of others lined up.

Gathering the kids up, she hurried towards it.

"It's like the one in Manao," said Laura. "The one that brought the kids to school."

"Maybe it is that one," said Sam brightly.

"No, it isn't," said Paul, "the Manao one had a monkey on the side and it was sort of climbing onto the top. This one's just a got a crocodile."

"Is it going to take us back to school, mummy," asked Laura, the hope in her voice too painful to bear.

"Maybe it'll take us back to the States," she said.

"I do hope so," said Laura.

Other frightened faces watched as they scrambled aboard. Sam grabbed one of the remaining double seats and she and the kids crammed in.

"Is it far to go?" asked Paul.

Sam didn't know what to say and was too tired to lie.

"There's bodies everywhere," said Laura softly.

"Never mind," said Sam. "Never mind."

"Where's Daddy?"

"He's coming on another bus."

Just then there was a whirring sound and the engine gave a massive backfire before chuntering back down to silence. Another burst of whirring and, this time, the engine caught. She wondered who was driving. She must have passed right by them when she got on the bus but had been too distracted to notice.

Ancient shock absorbers, spongy to the point of insubstantiality, began to take a beating even on the runway grass. Holding onto the kids left her with no hands to secure herself and she was nearly bounced out of her seat. Around her she could hear mothers and kids crying in alarm.

Then they were onto tarmac and the wallowing of the bus damped down. She saw the shattered terminal and the skeletal remains of the 737 flashing by on one side then the bus slewed to the right as it turned out of the main gate and onto the road between Tembe and its airport.

She didn't know the city well. It was a place of transit, to be got out of quickly and into the purer air and kinder spirits of the country, where people appreciated you for what you did for them.

Then the bus turned right and they were passing through a shanty town. People, no doubt alerted by previous buses, were out in force. Out of the corner of her eye she saw something flying towards the bus and, behind her, glass shattered. A child began to scream.

Paul jerked back as something hit their window with a squelching sound. The window held, and whatever it was splashed out into a brown smear.

"Is that poo?" he asked.

The driver hit the horn and didn't give up. She felt the kick back as he hit the accelerator. Out of her window, she saw people staggering back as though the bus was producing a bow wave.

She prayed the driver wouldn't stop.

Then the town was behind them and the deep blue waters of the Gulf of Guinea came into view.

"I'm hungry," said Laura.

"Me too," said Paul.

"You should have eaten your breakfast," she said automatically, then remembered the gruel they'd been offered in the hangar. She hadn't been able to face it either.

"When are we going to eat?" At least his shock was being replaced by irritability.

Too enervated to answer, she watched as the bus rolled down the gentle slope towards what looked like the port. Dhow-like fishing vessels, hardly capable of venturing far into the Gulf, rocked at anchor in the lee of a headland forming a natural harbour. Along the wharf lay ratty little ships, wooden and like miniature galleons without the masts. She knew these served as coasters along the entire length of Western Africa and up into the Persian Gulf. Though they stayed close to shore, she shuddered to think of what the Atlantic must do to them sometimes. Sea storms in this latitude could be fierce.

Something wasn't right though. Not familiar with African ports, it took her a while to work it out. Then she remembered the bustle in the Old Creek in Dubai where they'd stopped over once on a cruise. On one side of the creek had been the hot maze-like bazaar, tiny shops crammed cheek-by-jowl, whilst on the other side the sleek variegated skyscrapers rose into the bright Arabian sky. By the dockside these same ancient little boats had been a hive of activity as cargoes of all kinds were hauled on and off. Mattresses, electronic goods in thick bubble wraps, stoves, bales of cloth and things which she couldn't even recognise, were being carried back and forth. Mountains of the stuff were lashed to the decks.

But here, even though it was still cool in the early morning, there was no activity. Groups of crewmen lounged on deck under the eyes of soldiers and watching their bus pass by.

Then the bus pulled to a stop beside a solid line of soldiers and they waited. With the bus now stationary the heat rose and with it the smell of urine. As time passed, Sam begun to wonder if she might have to piss herself as well.

The driver stood suddenly and made lifting signs with the palms of his hand. They all got up, Sam as ever crouching down so as not to hit her head on the infernally low ceiling.

Stepping down from the bus, a soldier grabbed her arm, then stepped back in a classic double take and looked up at her in alarm.

"Yes," she said through gritted teeth. "There are some tall women in this world. Deal with it!"

But he didn't reply and instead whistled through his teeth to attract the attention of the others, nodding his head in her direction.

"No giraffes," she heard one soldier say.

"She'd make two of you, Patire," said another.

The soldier who'd grabbed her grinned and nodded in agreement then he was pulling her down the dock, an absurd look of gratification on his face, proud that he was in charge of such an unusual specimen.

Looking back, she saw the kids had got a soldier each and were following behind.

The dock, usually an obstacle course of tottering stacks of cargo, had been cleared and she could see the way ahead. At the end of the dock, what looked like a river ran to the right and, over this, loomed a large ramshackle warehouse. From the stench she guessed it was the fish market, but now the big doors were open and she saw the whole place was crammed with boats. As she watched, one was pulled down a ramp by a group of soldiers. As she got to the end of the dock, she could look down to where prisoners ahead of them were being led. A ramp was taking them down to a lower jetty. The boats from the fish marker were lining up along this and the captives were stepping into them one at a time. In the first boat in the line were several African men who weren't wearing uniforms. They were crouching over some of the women and kids.

Her own soldier pulled her onto the ramp and she felt a tremor of dismay as her own substantial weight came down on it, and she felt it bow down and shake.

The soldier looked up at her. "Gently now!" he said.

Taking it easy, they got down to the jetty without being pitched into the filthy waters of the port and found themselves in another queue.

By African standards the operation was a smooth one. As she watched, the boats from the market were lowered on dollies into the waters then soldiers using ropes attached to the bows pulled them along the jetty to where the prisoners were waiting. The dollies were then hauled back up into the warehouse for other boats. To the left she could see a score or so of the boats already full with hostages, floating gently on the still waters of the harbour amongst several of the coasters.

"What are they doing, mummy?" she heard Laura ask.

"We're going for a trip. Won't that be fun?" she said lamely.

The boats were rubbish. Twenty feet or so in length, their decks were cluttered with makeshift superstructure cobbled together from odd bits of corrugated metal. Boxy and makeshift though the boats were, some had proper cockpits for the steersman whilst others were little more than a wheel exposed to the elements.

Some had tapering bows, others bows were snub nosed affairs that must surely impede their passage through the water. Lockers seemed welded almost at random on the decks. On all of them, big patches of rust had broken out through the oil and filth.

A boat with four men on it was hauled in front of them and it was their turn. The soldier called Patire handed her over to another man in the boat. Again, the pantomime reaction to her height. "Don't bang your head!" he said jovially.

A joke, of course, as none of the little boats had canopies. At the bow was some sort of big locker on which the soldiers were making the kids sit. At the stern some cargo netting was covering something bulky. Midships on this boat was a little half height cubicle for the steersman.

The man led her towards the bow and sat her down beside a red headed woman who was looking much the worse for wear. Wherever and whenever she'd been abducted, she'd been in full make-up. At some point she'd cried and her heavy eyeliner had run alarmingly. She was like something from a horror movie.

The man reached to his side and she saw a horse's tail of thin cords hanging from his belt.

"Excuse me," he said, and looped a cord round one wrist, then through an eyelet welded into the small rail running around the deck. He pulled it tight and she winced a little.

"Sorry," he said and loosened it by a fraction.

"Why are you doing this?" she asked.

He just gave a little smile and tied her free wrist to another eyelet. He was quick, his hands deftly tying the knots, and she guessed he was a sailor on one of the bedraggled coasters.

Now he was bending down and tying her ankles. She was

just beginning to wonder if boats always had so many conveniently placed eyelets, when suddenly she heard Paul shouting: "I want to be with my mummy!"

He was struggling with another sailor. Without thinking, she tried to go to him and felt the thin cords bite into her skin.

Paul was no match for the sailor. He put a knee across Paul's legs and quickly tied him down to the locker at the bow.

Laura dumbly let herself be secured next to him. Sam hadn't cried so far, but a deep sob welled out of nowhere when she saw the blank look on Laura's face. The little girl had gone into shock.

Distracted, she wasn't even aware of the other prisoners being secured. It was only when the three sailors doing the securing stepped off the boat and up onto the jetty that she realised something new was happening. Looking back, she saw the next boat along was already full too. A line of hostages ran all the way along the jetty and up the ramp. How many more of these awful little boats did they have ready?

Ahead, one of the old coasters was edging out across the inlet. The remaining man on their boat walked forward and reached to Paul's side, bringing up a line. Not even bothering to loop it first, he threw it towards the coaster.

The rope, ill prepared, snagged on itself and went down into the water well short of the other boat.

Behind her on the jetty, she heard the real sailors blowing through their teeth in exasperation. Then the boat dipped down as someone stepped on board, and she saw the sailor who had bound her stride forward to the bow. He hauled the rope back in, coiling it as he did so.

"Like this," he said and tossed it towards the coaster, the rope uncoiling in flight until the knobbed end dropped over its gunwales. A sailor on the coaster scrabbled for it then carried it back to the stern and secured it to what she supposed was a capstan.

Her own sailor had stepped back out of the boat and she

heard the rumbling of the coaster's engine as it started. Water bubbled up from its stern and it edged round towards the open sea. She felt their own boat tugged forward and away from the jetty. Then, not more than five metres out, she felt the boat shudder and, looking back, she noticed another line, now out of the water and dripping, connecting them to the next boat along. This followed them away from the dock until, a few seconds later, she felt another tug and realised there were three boats tied in a line behind the coaster.

Soon they were sailing smoothly out into the calm waters of the Gulf, the air flowing across their skin and soothing the heat away.

Beyond the harbour and further into the open waters, the boat began to roll a little. She saw the look of alarm on Paul's face and tried to smile reassuringly. They'd had worse on the lake near her home town in the Adirondacks. As long as they weren't at sea too long, they'd be fine.

But the gentle motion was more of a problem for her bony backside. There were no cushions and the plastic seating was unyielding. Funny about the plastic though. This boat looked too old and too African to have much plastic on board. Wood is what she would have expected.

Trying to make herself comfortable, she leaned back so the little railing was supporting her lower back. Looking to the side she noticed the fingers of one hand were over a rusty patch on the railing. For diversion, she ran them over its roughness.

Except it wasn't rough.

Surprised, she looked more closely and rubbed her fingers across it again.

It wasn't rust; it was paint.

That was strange.

Chapter 25. *USS Benjamin F. Sands, Gulf of Guinea*

The whole Command and Control complex was thrumming with analysts striding purposefully between CATCC, JIC, TFCC, CIC, SSES.

'Acronyms 'R' Us,' she thought as she walked through Blue Tile Country. She began to wish she'd paid a bit more attention to what these all meant. There'd been a handy glossary in her induction pack, but she'd got bored with it and tossed it aside.

Poking her head into JIC, she felt the tension right away. Lewis and Terni were bent over a terminal, and she eased herself through the thicket of busy analysts at their workstations until she reached them.

Terni looked up and nodded distractedly.

"What's going on?" she asked. Noises filtering down from the flight deck indicated that World War III was in progress again. Planes were taking off but none were landing.

"Boat people," said Lewis.

"Come again?"

"Olomo's kicking all the foreigners out. Putting them in little boats and dragging them out to sea. Right now. Lots of them."

"So, we've moved further in?" She'd been down in the NCIS office with Lundt and had heard the engines rumbling up. "So, we're going to pick them up, right?"

Neither of the men was meeting her eye.

"Right?" she said more loudly.

Lewis sighed. "We've got to be careful. Remember the Cole?"

"Err..."

Terni gave her a disapproving look.

"Gimme a break!" she said.

Lewis pursed his lips. "*USS Cole*. Guided missile

destroyer. In Aden at the turn of the century. Al Qaeda drove a little boat full of explosives right up to it. Bang. Great big hole; twenty sailors killed."

"Seventeen killed," said Terni testily.

"Right. So, we're a little hinky about letting small craft get close to our ships."

"But we're not going to leave all those poor people wallowing out there on the ocean?"

Lewis nodded. "We can't do that either. We're checking them out as best we can." He gestured to the screen.

At first glance, it showed what looked like a mummy duck with three little ducklings paddling after her in a line. Then she realised it wasn't that at all.

The chopper's downdraft made her filthy hair, sweat binding it into rat tails, slap across Sam's face. She jammed her eyelids closed to protect her eyes. If the damned thing came any lower it would chop all their heads off. Cracking open her eyes she saw that the man in the boat's makeshift cockpit, the one who even she could tell wasn't a sailor, was waving lazily up at the helicopter. On the coaster towing them she saw crewmen making rude gestures at the aircraft.

"That's an American helicopter, mummy," said Laura. "I can see the flag."

Air fiercely whipped over them as the helicopter suddenly slipped sideways. Then its nose dipped and, in seconds, it was above another string of boats. Hovering over these, the gently rippled waters were stirred into a frenzy by its downdraft.

'Checking us out,' she thought. Helicopters didn't have a long range so a navy ship must be nearby. For the first time since the airport battle, she let herself begin to hope.

The images weren't bad but the chopper couldn't get too close. The nearer it got, the more unstable the little boats became.

"Women and children," said Terni.

"And one guy in the cockpit. No uniform."

Terni reached down and the moving image froze. He moved the mouse and dragged out a square covering a couple of the women. Tickling the mouse wheel made the image expand. Lewis leaned in and pointed.

"They're all tied up. Secured to the boat. If the boat sinks, they go down with it."

Terni moved over to another terminal and started to tap away.

"How far away are they? In fact, how far away from land are we?" she asked. They'd supposedly been off the coast of Africa for days now but she'd never spotted land. They could be just off Coney Island for all she knew.

"They're already ten miles out, so they've got another ten miles to go before they reach us, give or take. But we won't let them get to the carrier. The cruiser and the destroyers will provide a picket. They're already dispatching their own launches and inflatables to intercept them."

This time when the helicopter came back, at least it stood off by a good fifty metres. No downdraft, but now salty sea spray was blown into their eyes.

"Heave to!" said an amplified voice. "Turn off your engines and come to a complete halt."

Sam saw their own boatman shrug and open his hands out wide. Maybe he didn't speak English.

"They want you to stop," she yelled in the Ligandan dialect she'd picked up. At least eighty percent of the population spoke or at least understood it.

But the man just smiled at her and waved her away.

"I repeat," said the American voice. "Stop at once."

They kept sailing on, the helicopter keeping pace with them.

The amplified voice said something incomprehensible. After three repetitions she guessed it was some poor co-pilot trying to read out a phonetic representation of a message in the main Liganda dialect, but it was coming out horribly mangled.

The man waved dismissively up at the helicopter.

Distracted, when she did look again at the sea, she was startled to see the grey shapes of warships ahead. The sky was alive now with condensation trails. Olomo didn't have an air force to speak of so they had to be American.

This close, they surely wouldn't let the fleet of captives turn back: wouldn't allow Olomo to imprison them again. She'd been looking closely, but unless the steersman had hidden something down beside him, the guy didn't even have a gun. All they'd have to worry about was if he sunk them.

Then he suddenly reached down and she caught her breath.

But rather than a gun, he brought up binoculars and trained them on the navy ships.

"Suppose they don't stop?" She felt stupid asking these questions but she couldn't help herself.

Lewis, leaning on the terminal desk, let his shoulders sag a little. "Then we'd have to stop them. The cruisers could sweep by at full speed, overturn them."

"But they're tied in. They'd drown."

Terni gritted his teeth. "Either that or get a RIM 116 up their ass."

Joey looked plaintively at Lewis. "Rolling Airframe Missile. Our anti-ship defense. Those matrix things you've seen on deck: look like R2-D2 from Star Wars but much bigger. The missiles are in the body which swivels and tilts on two sturdy legs."

She remembered them, but there'd only been a couple. There were a lot of little boats out there. A hundred at least, maybe a lot more.

"What about machine guns? Couldn't you at least use them to put a few warning shots across their bows?"

"There's a couple of light machine guns that can be deployed quickly. We used to have 20mm Phalanx cannons, mainly for putting up a shit storm of bullets to bring down incoming missiles, but those were replaced by the RIMS at the last RFO."

"Oh, please!"

"Refueling Complex Overhaul. The big refit all the Nimitz carriers go through at some point. The Phalanx was outdated technology and was superseded by the RIM system. A more elegant solution, though..." he paused and looked uneasy, "...what with the extra costs, the budget didn't allow us to get as many as the navy wanted."

"And would it be better for handling lots and lots of little boats? Wouldn't a super-duper cannon, low tech though it might be, be better in a situation like this?"

Terni gave her a supercilious look. "Those scows? Look how they're wallowing along! It'd be a turkey shoot whatever we used."

The helicopter was back yet again. The pilot had given up on the phonetics and was back to English. "Heave to now!"

But still they chugged on. They'd been at sea for over an hour and she felt the sun burning her scalp even through her hair. 'Poor Gerry,' Sam thought. Balding and red haired, his head would be as pink as a billiard ball in this sun.

She saw a finger of flame from the chopper, and a line of water spouts zipped across in front of the coaster. Above the noise of the rotors, she could just make out the roar of the gun.

At last their lazy steersman was paying attention and started signalling frantically at the men in the coaster. They were milling round on the deck and then the rumbling fountain of water over their propeller died away. The old scow's thick cross section slowed it down quickly, and soon the three boats behind it were bumping against its stern and each other.

One of the men on deck tossed the towing line back onto

their boat. The rope, heavy with water, lashed down over several women and making them scream with the pain and the cold.

Their steersman walked unsteadily to the back of their own craft and undid the rope towing the next boat in line. This time he coiled it up, but his throw was poor and the man in the next boat had to reach far out to pull it on board.

The coaster's engine had started again and it was turning. She felt a stab of relief. They were going to be handed over to the Navy.

As the coaster cleared her line of sight, she was surprised at how close the naval vessels were now. She didn't know much about ships, didn't know how big they were, so judging distances was difficult. But one big ship, a cruiser or destroyer perhaps, didn't look to be more than a mile or so away. Ahead of them, it was sailing across very slowly. Over to the right and quite a bit further away were another two ships. A long way off and directly ahead was a flat grey shape which even she could recognise as an aircraft carrier.

And all that stood between it and them was the shabby little man at the wheel of their boat.

Looking more closely, she could see just make out some little launches coming from the direction of the nearest ship. She started to breathe more easily.

A burst of white water erupted from their stern. The whole boat tilted, the bow coming out of the water. Brutal acceleration dragged her back along the bench, the chords digging hard into her wrists.

All the women were screaming now.

"What the fuck?" gasped Terni.

One of the little boats, nicely framed by the chopper's camera for the last several minutes, was suddenly gone. It took a few seconds for a surprised pilot to twist the chopper round. The damn boat was streaking away on a rocket exhaust of angry white water.

"Jesus shit..." Terni was typing rapidly away.

The sudden klaxon was ear splitting.

Around her, Sam could see a multitude of the little boats speeding across the ocean. Suddenly they looked so different from the clumsy, wide bellied wrecks they'd appeared. The speed was lifting them clear of the water and she saw the wider decks were a construct resting on sleeker shapes cutting the through the waters like knives. Within seconds the helicopter was well behind, but swivelling round to follow.

Already the naval vessels looked appreciably nearer. Were these Ligandan idiots trying to ram them? What good would these little boats do against steel armour? They'd bounce off like a squash ball against a wall.

The armada of racing boats seemed to be breaking into three groups. Theirs, in the middle, seemed to be aimed at the carrier still many miles away. One group was veering towards the two ships to the right.

The left group was streaking towards the ship that was much closer. It didn't look like any warship she'd seen in those old World War II movies. It had the sleek lines of the old warships but these were marred by what looked like a big boxy grey warehouse on deck. Top heavy, it looked like it would overturn easily.

"It says *Spencer* on the side," said a sharp-eyed kid.

"They're like...cigarette boats," Lewis was saying.

At least she knew what they were. Smugglers boats originally used in the Caribbean for smuggling cigarettes and rum but then later for drugs. Small boats with razor thin keels that could outrun any coastguard ship going. Not so good when the coastguards had helicopters and satellite tracking, but still used on smaller runs and often for illegal immigrants nowadays.

Not something you expected to see off the coast of Africa.

"Those things can do fifty knots or more," she said. "Can we out run them?"

"It's supposed to be a secret, but the *Sands* can do forty. At that speed we could pick them off at our leisure, what with the choppers and all our FA-18s already scrambled. Plus, the RIMs if all else failed." She thought she caught a trace of uncertainty in Lewis' tone.

"As long as Macik gives the order," said Terni grimly and she saw Lewis glance at him. "And he's got to do that *now*. The *Spencer's* much nearer. They can't get up to speed in time. They've *got* to start shooting."

"Shooting innocent American civilians? That's some order to give."

Like a new gravitational force, she felt something tugging her back into her seat.

"Ah," said Terni, "that's us taking off. They'll never catch..."

And then the whole compartment was jarred to the side.

It was the sound of the explosion that made Sam look round. Far away, a ball of smoke had puffed out the side of the carrier, just below the deck but far above the water line. As she peered more closely, she saw the flickering red of fires within.

"Christ, what's going on?" said a woman next to her.

Sam didn't answer. Looking back, she saw the chopper was keeping pace with one of the boats to their right.

"I think they're going to shoot," she found herself saying dully.

"But we're all American's," said the woman plaintively. "They can't do that!"

Looking ahead and to the left, she saw the *Spencer* had picked up speed but the arrow head of a dozen boats had altered course and were still trying to intercept her.

Seconds stretched to minutes and the distances between the boats and the retreating Spencer shortened.

Suddenly the helicopter that had been observing them was streaking over them towards the boats. To the right, she saw another chopper converging on these as well.

Sam began to pray silently but her eyes stayed open, drawn magnetically to the unfolding scene.

The little boats were fast and seemed almost on top of the ship when the firing began. A stream of bullets from a chopper picked a delicate line across the ocean towards the lead boat, but then struck with terrible violence, turning the stern to fragments. The bodies of the manacled prisoners looked like they were being punched by giants.

"They're trying to hit the engines," said the woman. Without thinking, they both glanced back at the stricken faces of the women at the bow of their own boat. Already they were screaming to be untied.

A heavy gun on the ship began to open up and she heard the chattering of machine guns. Huge geysers erupted around the boats but couldn't seem to get a direct hit.

Another explosion came from the direction of the carrier. It distracted her, so she almost missed what happened next, but, turning back, she managed to focus on the lead boat as a figure launched itself off the back and into the waves.

Then the boat piled into the side of the Spencer and a ball of light stung her eyes.

Blinking she saw big bits of metal thrown far into the sky.

Then something was racing across the surface of the ocean at them. The wave of white blasted over her, stabbing at her eardrums.

Steadying herself on the table after the explosion, Joey heard Lewis asking: "Did one of them get through?"

"No, they're still miles off," said Terni. "No incoming missiles. Nothing." General Quarters was sounding and she saw men scrabbling for their fireproof suits.

"A bomb," she said softly, crushed by the sudden sense of failure.

"We don't know that." He looked up at the ship's TV feed.

A strapline said: 'Explosion on stern hangar deck. Firefighting crews attend.'

Terni took a deep breath. "That was a big one. That means a big fire. And that means we can't go to full speed without fanning the flames. All we can do is turn into the wind."

Then he was on the phone, jaw clenched. "Terni, I must speak to the Admiral now!"

Seconds passed. Terni began to grind his teeth, then his eyes widened. "I don't care how busy he is. He's got to give the fire command on those boats vectored on the *Spencer*. They could have explosives on board!"

He looked round at them dumbly. She guessed he'd been put on hold again.

Then: "Yes, here! The President? I don't give a shit who he's calling..." Terni pulled the phone from his ear and looked at it dazedly.

Then, shaking his head, he went back to his keyboard.

A minute passed, then another. She watched as the boats ate up the distance to the *Spencer*.

The view from the helicopter was still framing one of the boats. Suddenly a cauldron of boiling water was surging towards the stern.

"Yes!" roared Terni.

The stern flew apart and she saw the carnage as cannon shells met soft flesh.

The bow dropped down and the boat slewed to a stop. Water was swirling in over the shattered stern. Women and children were thrashing around frantically, trying to free themselves.

"My God, it's going to sink," she said.

The view dipped and turned to the right. All she could see now was water speeding by. Then the view came up, the pilot cutting speed to bring the next boat into range and view.

"NO!" yelled Terni.

The boat was almost at the *Spencer*. As they, watched she

saw the steersman, curled into a ball, roll off the back of the boat. Travelling so fast he didn't cut the water; instead he bounced over it.

Everything disappeared in a white flash.

Joey felt the blood drain from her face and she felt faint.

The overloaded optics at last compensated, and she saw the view spinning crazily. "The chopper's been hit by the blast. It's going down," said Lewis.

The waves leapt at the screen then it all went black.

The *Sands* received another shove and documents cascaded to the floor.

"You're coming with me!" said Lewis grimly, grabbing her upper arm hard and yanking her towards the exit.

Chapter 26. *Gulf of Guinea*

"Where the fuck are you taking me?" She had to shout above the alarms.

"You're a civilian, Joey, and it's my duty to look after you."

She'd been trying to tug her arm out of his hand and she'd been gentle so far. This time she put some effort into it.

Suddenly relieved of her resistance, he staggered forward and almost tripped over a knee knocker but managed to get two hands to the bulkhead to stop himself. Breathing out hard, he turned back to look at her.

"I don't need looking after," she said, making an emphatic slicing motion with her hand.

"You're a Stranger in a Strange Land, Joey. And things may be going to shit in just a few minutes time."

"Why? You said we could outrun those boats."

He came back to her and gently grasped her hands in his. "Those hangar deck explosions may ...complicate things."

For the first time she thought about her life preserver, safely tucked away in her locker a couple of hundred metres away.

"How?"

Three more explosions, smaller than the previous two, made the deck shudder under them. Sailors were appearing from nowhere. They had to back into a space behind some stairs to stop blocking the passageway.

"Those big oval ports in the hangar bays, near the elevators. If they're open, or they've been blown out by the explosions, then they'll let air in. The crew may even have opened them so the blasts will have somewhere to go and not into the ship."

"So?"

"So, if we take off at forty knots, air will stream into the hangar, feeding the fire. Maybe the old AAAF foam system might have damped it all down but that was replaced with something nowhere near as good."

"Ah yeah! Environmental considerations, right?"

His eyes closed. He gave her an experimental tug to see if she would move, but she wasn't yielding. "The boat's metal Joey. Great conductor of heat. If the fire burns too hot, exploding fuel fanned by a roaring wind, then we're all in trouble."

"You're fucking joking! But wait a minute, why do we have to do forty knots at all? What about those RIM things, and the choppers and all those F18s up there?"

"I don't know how many choppers we've got in the air now. There were only two of them and we just lost one, at least. The F18s are great for what they're designed for, but those small boats will present a problem. They have, at most, one Harpoon air to ship missile each and I'm not even sure those could deal with boats so small."

"Don't they have machine guns?"

"20mm Gatling guns, yeah. But they have less than 600 rounds each and those boats make small targets. Fast moving ones at that."

"So, the RIMs?"

"Yeah, but there's only two batteries of 21 cells each. There's more boats than that. They can be reloaded but that takes time. Plus, they're mainly for radar emitting ships. The Armstrong's combat system can initially direct them at the targets, but then the onboard infra-red detection kicks in."

"And that'll work, right?"

He shrugged. "If the target's hot enough."

She gave a grim little smile. "OK. I think I'm beginning to get it. You said something a minute ago about looking after me."

He nodded. "I'll do what I can. Follow me!"

Over the knee knocker, he took the first corridor to port and they started to climb. All around them crew were moving quickly and purposefully, un-inflated life preservers round their necks.

Coming up one set of steep stairs brought them into a compartment several metres square. She saw the sign and number signifying a mustering point. She had one of her own but it was on the hangar deck.

Lewis was already opening a locker and bringing out something bright red with big floppy arms and legs.

"An exposure suit," he said. "Get it on!"

"What about you?"

"Orders haven't been given. It's different for you."

"Is it?" she said.

He didn't answer but waited impatiently as she stepped into the suit. Her holstered gun, which she'd taken to wearing all the time since the business with Trask, made it difficult to get the suit on. For a second, she thought of ditching it, but couldn't bear the idea of being defenceless at a time like this.

When she finally got the suit on, Lewis zipped her up. Then he hauled a life preserver out of a locker and put it round her neck.

Stepping back, he gave her one final check. He pointed at a ladder which rose to a hatch in the ceiling. "Up there and you're on the flight deck. Don't go up there until you hear the muster station alert. Otherwise, keep your head down as you don't want an F-18 landing on your head.

"Once you get up there, you're going to have to play it by ear. There should be sailors casting out monkey lines."

"Monkey lines?"

"Ropes with knots in them so you can shimmy down into the water. If things are really going to shit then life rafts'll be jettisoned. Get onto one and paddle away from the ship."

"And if there are no sailors to let out the monkey lines?"

"You'll find lockers, lids flush with the deck. You can deploy them but..."

"Oh God," she said. "After all this there's still a *but*?"

"If the boats hit, it'll be to starboard. If they do enough

damage, the water'll come in and we'll list in that direction. If we're going over too far, you'll have to get over the port side of the flight deck as it comes up and walk the hull down to the water. Whether there's any life rafts or not, get away from the ship."

He looked so earnest, so worried for her, her heart melted and she found herself holding his head and gently kissing him. His breath tasted sour but she didn't care.

The helicopter, tilted far to one side, slashed the ocean with its rotors. Shattered blades, moving sickeningly fast, scythed through the air.

Another blinding flash of light from the Spencer and a second blast wave almost overturned them.

But Sam couldn't hear a damn thing. She wondered if she ever would again.

Two seemed to be the trick as far as Olomo's men were concerned. The other boats aimed at the Spenser, those that had survived so far, were already changing course. Now all the ones she could see were making for the carrier.

And as she watched, the US Navy began to wage war on them.

With the helicopter gone, the sky had suddenly seemed clear. Then, appearing as though by magic, a jet fighter flashed over them. She saw Paul track its path with owlish eyes, jaw slack. Laura was looking at her, her mouth moving frantically.

Sam shook her head, raising her eyebrows. Would she realise she couldn't hear?

She didn't see it, didn't hear it, but angry air slapped at her back and head. She hunched up automatically and felt the boat kick up. Craning round, she saw heavy waves moving concentrically away from a section of ocean behind them.

Had that been aimed at them?

She saw a flash of light. A firefly trail arced up from the carrier and streaked towards them. She opened her mouth in a soundless scream.   Then, a hundred metres ahead, the missile dipped sharply and struck a leading boat.

Matchwood rained down on them.

Sam's world of silence was being filled with ringing and she realised her hearing was returning. "Please, turn back," she shouted at the steersman, but he wasn't listening.

Even through the ringing, she heard the next explosion. Looking back, she saw a massive fireball where the Spenser had been. The churning sphere of light was rising like a party balloon into the heavens.

The shock wave kicked the boat up, the little rail jabbing into her kidneys. The side of his little compartment smashed against the steersman, making him grimace in agony.

All that was left above water of the Spencer was the bow and the stern. Both tapered, they each rose out of the water, then slipped smoothly down.

A shadow blinked over them. A line of water spouts streaked towards their starboard side and slashed over the boat. One bullet, striking a woman dead centre, tore her body apart, and punched a hole through the deck.

The dead woman's arms were still held fast by the shackles, but the torso was split in two by a gaping bloody slash cutting up to the right side of her neck. The bit with the head, still intact, hung over to the other side.

Somewhere below the constant ringing, she began to hear the prisoners' screams.

Gouts of water were pulsing in from the bullet hole.

The carrier was getting big now and she could make out the planes on her deck. To the left, she saw another helicopter firing at the boats. More streaks came from the carrier.

Here and there, the little vessels were erupting as missiles hit. Others slewed to a quick stop as bullets took out their engines.

They were being steadily whittled away but there were still so many little boats skimming across the waves.

A last, feeble, disgraceful hope tugged at her mind. There were at least ten boats ahead. If enough hit the carrier perhaps their pilot would turn away, try to make it back to land. Her time in the airport hangar was suddenly like heaven itself.

She prayed for forgiveness for harbouring such selfish thoughts.

The boat ahead of her erupted in flame and their own steersman had to swerve round the wreckage. He might not be a real sailor, but he'd clearly been trained to handle this craft.

Laura was lying back, her eyes closed, and Sam hoped she'd fainted. Paul was turned around, looking in wonder at the carrier, now less than half a mile away.

Another boat was torn apart by a line of bullets from a jet then two more succumbed to missiles streaking in from the carrier.

She started to count. She could only see six boats ahead now. They were fanned out, trying to strike the mighty ship at different points. Looking back, she could see a few other boats coming in after them.

Another jet streaked by and the steersman in the boat ahead jerked at the wheel, trying to avoid the bullets, but he was going too fast. The boat flipped over, tumbling end over end across the surface of the sea and coming to a splashing stop.

As they whipped by, she saw it'd turned turtle. Everyone's heads would be under water.

Two more explosions and now only three boats remained ahead of theirs.

Then came the downpour. All around them the ocean was kicking up as though from a deluge. One concentrated shower came down on the first boat and little explosions tore into it and its passengers.

The carrier was so close now she could see a line of men on the deck, guns firing.

Now another boat received the downpour and her own steersman swung the wheel hard over. He'd been aiming directly towards the bow but now they were cutting across diagonally towards the stern. The bullet cloud tried to follow but he'd caught them out.

He vaulted over his little wheelhouse and was at the bow in three strides. Leaping over it and curling himself up, she watched him bounce across the surface like a ball: slowly quickly, being left safely behind.

Swinging her head back she saw Paul. He'd turned back and was looking at her, his face empty as though he were already dead.

Behind him, the carrier's side was looming high, the protruding lip of its flight deck almost overhanging them already. Looking up she saw men leaning precariously over the lip, desperately trying to bring their guns to bear.

Bullets pattered down on the boat but it was already too late.

She watched as it slammed into the carrier's grey wall.

Chapter 27. *Gulf of Guinea*

Lewis was gone; for some reason he'd felt responsible for Lundt as well. He'd gone to phone down to the NCIS office to try to get her up on deck.

He'd handed Joey a helmet. "Put this on! And remember: keep your head down until you hear the alert, or if we start to list," had been his last words.

But if she cracked the hatch open just a little, what harm could it do? Since the two big explosions from the hangar deck she'd heard no planes either coming in or taking off.

The rungs of the ladder had that slippery-sticky feel of salt water drying. Crew must be up and down here all the time so it couldn't be used just for abandoning ship. Even as she thought this, the idea of this whole damn gigantic thing doing down or otherwise being destroyed was just too hard to take on. Lewis had kept saying how this was just a precaution; with all their sealable compartments and watertight doors, Nimitz Class carriers were virtually unsinkable.

And he'd said it all without any apparent irony.

There was a simple latch and she turned the handle and gave a little push. The hatch moved easily, pivoting on a hinge on one side. She raised it only enough so her eyes were just above with the deck.

Except it wasn't the deck, the Flight Deck, anyway. Two short walls of grey metal pointed to the horizon.

It took her a second to figure it out. The hatch must be in the base of one of the runnels running the length of the flight deck. This was one of those metal ditches where the deck men dived for cover when planes were landing or taking off, so the jet blast wouldn't send them flying over the side.

That fucker Lewis had lied to her. The Flight Deck maybe one of the most hazardous environments in the world, but inside one of these runnels you were safe. He hadn't even trusted her to keep her head down, so he'd given her the bogeyman tale of a plane landing on her head.

'Bastard,' she thought, and eased the hatch up enough to let her crawl out. There was nobody ahead, just about thirty feet of runnel and then the sea.

Squirming round to look aft, she saw there was nobody there either.

Then she looked up and found the sky was gone. She nearly pissed herself.

A boiling mass of black smoke and flame was lifting up and covering the sky before drifting to starboard in the light wind. Putting a hand up to grasp the lip of the Flight Deck, she pulled herself up to get a better look.

Where the middle elevator brought planes up to the deck, there was now an evil cauldron. Swirling, serpent like coils of filthy smoke, shot through with fire, belched out in spurts. The wind was blowing it across the deck, allowing her to see further down the port side. Here another volcano, somewhere over the side of the ship, was sending flames and smoke up and over the deck.

The aft hangar must be on fire too!

Standing upright now, she saw that, aft of the middle elevator, the deck had become a rippling sea. Water was blasting out of pipes set into the deck and was sending a deluge into the burning elevator opening. Forward of where the wall of water started, she saw scores of men in white fire-retardant suits directing the jets of powerful hoses up into the air to arc down into the burning Hangar Deck.

In fires on ships you wanted the smoke drifting straight off the deck and out to sea. You didn't want it covering the whole ship. They'd been lucky and the Captain hadn't even needed to bring her round, the prevailing wind doing the job for him.

A gout of flame lashed out of the elevator opening and she heard the crump of an explosion from below.

All that fuel, all that ammo. If it all went off at once they'd never find enough of anyone to bury.

Loud gunfire to one side had her ducking down into the runnel. Automatic weapons were firing almost constantly but no bullets were zipping above her head. Tentatively, she raised her head up. On the other side of the deck, almost opposite her, a long line of marines was firing down at something in the water. Whatever it was, it was getting closer as their barrels were rapidly tilting down.

Something clanged at her feet and she started round to see Lundt's doughboy head looking up at her from the hatch down to the Muster Station.

"Everything OK?" asked Lundt.

Joey didn't know what to say. Her gaze flicked back to the marines who were now leaning so far forward they were almost shooting straight down.

A mighty hand, like God's but bigger, slammed into the side of the ship. The sharp lip of the runnel barged into her ribs. She saw the marines disappear, every one of them going head over heels, as the deck went out from under their feet.

She rebounded and now the other side of the runnel gave her a kick, sending jolts of pain radiating up her back and side. All breath left her and her ass thumped down hard on the deck.

Then the carrier rocked back again and she banged her head on the metal.

The hatch was at her feet and she saw that Lundt had disappeared. Bending over, she looked down into the gloom. As her eyes adjusted she saw a mass of arms and legs.

Badly winded, and unable to say anything, she could only peer down.

Blood was spreading from the mound of flesh. She made out Lewis spreadeagled under Lundt's lumpy body, both in survival suits. She saw him grimace and manage to get a hand out to hold his shoulder.

She tried to shout but all she managed was a faint wheeze.

Then the carrier kicked again and she ricocheted off the runnel, elbow and head impacting hard.

Now she was prone and the world was spinning fiercely. Reaching out both arms and legs, bracing herself against the metal walls, she waited.

The boat kicked again, then again.

Looking up, all she could see was billowing smoke.

Who'd mourn her, she wondered? Weiss, maybe. He was a nice guy. Her mom maybe also. Not right away but give it time. Perhaps that would bring her a little more perspective, a little more charity.

Enough breath back now to start blubbing.

"Joey!" The voice was faint and echoey.

She gave herself a few more seconds then gingerly hooked a leg over the lip and onto the first rung of the ladder. Taking her time, she made her way down, her hands tightly clutching the sides.

The lights were still on. The noise from countless klaxons was deafening.

She took a big step to get off the ladder and avoid stepping on them. Bending down over Lundt, she went to touch her but then jerked her hand back. One side of the woman's head was stoved in. A 'V' shaped trough ran straight along her head at eye level. The force had broken the skull so that jagged bone had pivoted up and broken through the skin. Unbidden, the thought of stepping in a puddle layered by ice came to mind.

Where the brain should be exposed, there was only blood.

A rattling sound was coming from Lundt's throat. Still alive, but not for long.

Stepping round Lundt's head and outflung arms, she got to Lewis who was looking up at her.

"Are you OK?"

"Not so much," said Lewis, but managing a smile. "Wouldn't put her helmet on; said it didn't fit. Lost her grip and came down on me like a sack of potatoes. Head hit the side of that

313

locker there."

He winced. "Think she broke my collar bone."

He paused to take a deep breath. "Had my hand on a rung. Think maybe her boot came down on that too. Hurts like fuck anyway."

Joey kneeled and heaved up Lundt's body to get a look. His trapped hand flopped free, a couple of fingers bent way too far back.

She took a grip on Lundt's exposure suit. "Sorry, Marcy," she said, hauling her off Lewis. It was like shifting a ball of jello.

Lewis managed to roll over and push himself upright on one elbow.

"Can you climb up the ladder?"

He didn't answer and she guessed he didn't know.

Standing upright, she felt dizzy and put a hand flat against a bulkhead. Then she realised she wasn't dizzy at all. The floor had gained a tilt.

"Yeah, she's listing," he said.

"Still think the *Sands* is unsinkable?"

"Criticism? At a time like this!"

She helped him to his feet. "How are we going to do this? Are your legs OK?"

He shuffled them experimentally. "Yeah, at least poor Marceline didn't take those out." He looked up at the ladder. "I think I can do it by myself."

"Yeah? ' Always have one hand for the ladder'. Isn't that the doctrine? How are you going to do that, exactly?"

"I'll just have to try."

"I'll be behind you, in case you fall."

"Well that's a bad...."

"Just fucking do it, OK?"

He shrugged and winced with the pain.

He got himself against the ladder and she crowded in behind him. Reaching round him, she grasped its sides. It made it difficult for him to move but he slowly climbed it, her feet always just one rung below his.

"Marcy definitely dead?"

"Definitely soon will be," she said.

When her head was almost at the hatch lip, she stopped and let him crawl clumsily out. Maybe she was imagining it, but the list seemed to be getting worse.

Climbing out, she found him already upright, one hand on the Flight Deck. From below she heard the Muster alert sound out at last.

It was difficult to see in the stinging smoke but more people were on deck now. Others were emerging as though by magic from hatches she hadn't noticed before.

"Why so few?" she asked.

"It's a big place to get out of quickly. And there's lot of edges, lot of stairs, lot of sharp objects. And those were big bombs. There'll be broken bones even on those not hit by the explosions or caught in the fires. And the list, already it'll be difficult to move across the ship."

"What about you? How easy will those monkey lines be now?"

"Forget about me! Just do like I told you!"

"Fuck off! You need a boat. Something that can be lowered with you in it."

"The only life boats going into the water will have to be on the starboard side. Already the list is too much to launch from this side. And if you launch from starboard then you risk the whole ship rolling over on you."

"Then we'll just have to get the boat out of the way before it does. Where's the nearest one?"

"There's a stage, just below the outboard weapons elevator." He pointed almost directly across the deck.

"C'mon," and she was pushing him ahead of her. Within seconds she'd lost her bearings in the smoke, but he seemed to know where he was going.

The deck juddered under her and she nearly lost her

footing. It was becoming a hill.

Suddenly something massive and bird-like was right above her. "Jesus!" she yelled.

"It's just a Greyhound."

"A what?"

"It's a little passenger plane, for transfers to shore."

Something inhuman groaned nearby, then came the sharp rasping of metal on metal.

"Not sure the securing lines will hold it. Sooner or later they'll give and the damn plane'll skitter across the deck and over the side. Yet one more thing to come down on our heads."

A vision of dead birds cascading into the water came to her mind.

The stench of smoke was becoming unbearable and she was struggling for air. Distracted, she almost stepped into the void but he jerked her back in time.

"It's OK, just another runnel. The real side is just a few feet over."

Looking carefully, she saw the other side of the runnel and her long legs took her over it in one long step. Lewis managed it too. Less elegant, less athletic, his leading foot came down hard and he grunted in pain.

Another edge and this one dropped much further down. The smoke was so bad she couldn't see the ocean. She couldn't even see any 'stage' one deck below.

"There should be a ladder, just over there," he said, pointing.

The top of the ladder curved up and round before meeting the deck.

She started to climb over. "Like how we came up, but in reverse."

Crumpling to his knees he shimmied round then shuffled back, his boot catching her in the mouth.

"Hey," she yelled.

"Sorry. Kind of tricky."

And it was. Even with her arms at full stretch, there still wasn't much room for him between her body and the ladder. To get on the ladder he had to turn to face her, his lower legs down between them. Then he had to sort of turn and fall so he was facing the other way.

His boots scrapped painfully down the front of her thighs and his full weight came down on her instep, making her roar with the pain. His feet scrabbled quickly and managed to find purchase.

"You fucking piece of fucking shit!"

"This was *your* idea. I was happy just to jump off the side."

"And fucking drown? Serve you fucking right!"

As they got below the level of the drifting smoke she could make out the 'stage'. Stepping away from the ladder, she saw a mounted machine gun and a missile rack. The rack held a couple of big two-by-two matrices connected together by a thick crossbar. Crewmen were manning the gun but the missiles weren't doing anything.

Lewis must have seen her puzzlement. "Sea Sparrows," he said. "Anti-aircraft, anti-missile. Not much help in this situation."

She indicated the crewmen. "None of these guys are abandoning ship," she said.

"And neither will we until and unless it's absolutely necessary. This list though... Hey I can't hear any firing! I guess all the threats..." he hesitated and she guessed he was remembering these included women and children, "...have been eliminated. Now everyone can concentrate on saving the ship. They'll be sealing the watertight doors, blowing ballast to raise any holes up out of the water..."

That didn't sound convincing, even to her. Anything strong enough to kick the carrier like that would have made a very big hole.

More explosions came from further aft and flaring gases glimmered through the smoke. Either the wind direction or their bearing was changing. Obscuring smoke started to drift away towards the stern, revealing more of the deck.

Far aft, she saw the sideways volcano of the aft hangar. Flame was roaring out and smoke curling up into the heavens. Holding onto a railing, and looking carefully over the side, she saw four foaming cauldrons strung along the length of the ship. All were already below the waterline.

The sound of tearing metal made her duck. Barely twenty metres aft, two aircraft rolled off the deck and smashed down into the sea.

The men on the machine gun exchanged mute glances.

The water should be twenty metres below, but it was looking a lot nearer now.

"Shouldn't we be getting the fuck off this thing?"

"Abandon ship hasn't been called," said Lewis.

"Maybe it never will be," said one of the machine gunners.

She put her hands on her hips. "If we leave it too late, then even if we get into the water, the damned things going to tip over on us."

Lewis looked at the gunners. He nodded at her. "Civilian," he said.

The men exchanged glances again. "We ain't looking," said one. "One way or another we're not goin' to need all these life rafts anyway."

"Joey," said Lewis urgently. "At the leading edge of this platform there's a rack of cylinders. Untie the two lanyards holding the first. You'll see a catch at the back. Make sure you know where it is but don't touch it yet."

She made her way quickly to the end of the platform and the rack.

The thing with the lanyards was a simple task but it made her realise how badly her hands were shaking. She heard him shuffling along the rail behind her.

"OK," he said. "Little locker, down at your feet. Open it and you'll see a monkey line, one end firmly secured."

The line wasn't much thicker than a finger but had baby

fist sized knots every metre or so. She was surprised at the weight as she hauled the coiled rope out of the locker.

She tossed it overboard it. Where the line met the water, it floated. Six knots lay across the surface.

"Now listen!" he said. "We've got to drop the raft before you shimmy down. Don't want it coming down on your head."

He stopped and blinked. "You can swim, right?"

"I may have been brought up in Denver, but we did have swimming pools there."

"Good. The current's weak so you should get to the raft. As soon as the capsule hits the surface, the cover'll split open and the raft will self-inflate. Don't take your time going down the line and, as soon as you hit the water, strike out straight for the raft."

"Then you jump and I'll paddle to get you."

"I can't," he said. "I've got to stay."

"What fucking use are you? You can't even open a door handle."

"It's my duty. Anyway, what use would I be to you even if I came?"

"I'm not going without you."

Over his shoulder she saw the Island, now like a high tech Leaning Tower of Pisa. A big, yellow mobile crane stored at its base began to move. Slowly at first, stopping and starting as its tyres lost and gained traction, it juddered across the deck then over into the sea. Several little tow trucks followed.

"Ma'am, I'd go if I was you," shouted one of the gunners.

She looked at Lewis. "But suppose they put out the fires, plug up the holes? Off you'll go and I'll be left behind."

"Even if we managed all that, we won't be going anywhere. Not for some while."

He nodded towards somewhere a few degrees off the bow. "Head north. Twenty miles'll bring you to the coast."

"Where they'll be very pleased to see me."

Without thinking, he shrugged and winced with the pain.

The ship roared and kicked and they fell against the tilted

railing. Joey, on her back, saw the plume of debris arc into the sky. Rolling over on top of him, shielding him, she felt metal pattering down on her helmet and plucking at her exposure suit.

Something hot seared into her lower back. Frenziedly she reached round to get hold of whatever it was and flick it away. Then she was licking the burned pads of her thumb and forefinger.

"That was very touching, shielding me like that" said Lewis, still under her. "Now get the fuck off this boat!"

"Ma'am," shouted one gunner. "I'm going to throw you over myself."

"I'd like to see you try," she said, but grasped the line and began to crawl over the rail.

"Wait a minute!" said the man, picking his way towards them along the 'v' between the tilted deck and the railing mounts. "Let me get the life raft released."

How could she have already forgotten that? The man clicked something and the squat cylinder rolled down the short rails and over the side.

"Hurry!" said Lewis.

Metal screeched above them, soaring in volume, coming closer. She ducked her head as a shadow covered them. Out of the corner of her eye she saw the nose of a plane crash down on the machine gun. The man who'd been there vanished under it.

"Vince!" shouted the remaining gunner and started to shimmy his way back, but then hesitated as the wreckage shifted. The crumpled nose had flattened the railing and it and the machine gun were canted over the void.

Lewis leaned in close to her. "FUCK OFF!" he yelled.

The rope, a stiff blue polypropylene job, was sore on her hands, but she managed to get a grip on the knots. Clearing the railing, the sea looked a long way down. Already the raft was fully inflated and almost directly below. Hand over hand, her feet clamping above each knot, she made her jerky way down.

The water was cold even through the suit. It held plenty of air so she figured she'd be quicker striking out for the raft before inflating her life jacket.

Her style was wallowy but in less than twenty strokes she grasped at the little ropes strung around the raft's side. Struggling to pull herself up and over, she felt like a marshmallow man, and was doubly glad not to have inflated her vest.

Flopping down, the suit digging deep into her armpits and crotch, she rolled over and then gasped in shock. The *Sands* seemed like it was falling on her. Lewis' worried face was looking down. She realised with dismay she was directly underneath the jet and the machine gun.

"Get away!" shouted Lewis.

"Not without you," she yelled back.

"Please!"

Bizarrely, a beefy arm suddenly protruded between Lewis' legs. His eyes widened in surprise as the arm rose and him with it. For an instant he was spread eagled against the sky, then he was plummeting, turning just enough in mid-air to hit the water feet first.

The spray blinded her for a second. Glancing back up through the stinging haze, she saw the remaining gunner waving down at them.

Lewis had gone under but he popped back up, the air in his exposure suit making it balloon out.

Paddling wasn't easy, and it took a while for her to reach him. Leaning out, she got a hold of his suit and pulled him close to the side. The she reached her hands under both his armpits.

"Gentle now!" he warned.

She hauled with all her strength and he howled in agony.

Only about a third of his body was out of the water.

She heaved again and his legs dragged over the lip.

His scream cut out. Looking down, she saw he'd passed out.

Somewhere, amongst the alarms and klaxons and exploding ordnance, she heard something else: something they'd played to her during her induction.

The water exploded beside the raft and it wallowed hugely. Then the gunner's head broke the surface and he was stroking quickly to the raft's side. He was a thick set man and she struggled to help him over the mattress-like side.

"Abandon ship signal at last," he said. "Now we can all go."

Metal tore somewhere above and the dangling plane scraped over the side. The port wing, like a huge guillotine, chopped straight down towards them.

Then the tail fin clipped the platform, swivelling the plane round.

The wing scythed cleanly into the water just a couple of feet off their bow.

Instantly the whole plane was gone.

The buffeting of the water sent them both down flat. Scrambling upright, the gunner unhooked something thin and flat that had been secured to the fabric of the raft. He pulled at it and a handle telescoped out.

"Paddle," he said, handing it to her.

"That way," he said, pointing straight out to sea.

And she did paddle, frantically. Still in the shadow of the behemoth, she glanced up to see the overhang had become so pronounced it was surreal. How could something so big and so unbalanced hang in the air like that?

The hail storm began. Crew men were appearing like magic on the side of the flight deck, and on all the platforms along the side of the ship. Some were scrabbling for monkey lines, others were hurling themselves into the water.

"Should we...?"

"Paddle for your life!" he muttered grimly.

But she couldn't stop looking over her shoulder and up at the grey mass looming over them. It was going to turn turtle, the whole flat mass of the flight deck flipping over and swatting them like a fly.

Then she realised something more complicated was

happening. The thing was still turning over but here, nearer the bow, the carrier was also rising. Away to the stern was a different matter.

"She's going down," she said.

"Keep paddling! Don't look back!"

As if.

At last they well beyond the line of surf made by falling crewmen and mushrooming life rafts, and she thought they might be clear.

"We should stop now," she said. "We should help these men."

"No! She'll make a hole in the ocean as she goes down. Water'll gush in to fill it. It'll get rough and there may be an undertow."

So, they kept going as a skyscraper seemed to haul itself out of the water, the whole deck turning. Planes still clung to it where lines had held, like mounted butterflies in a collector's case. Some butterflies shifted like they were still alive, swinging back and forth across the almost vertical deck.

"Oh, shit!" said the gunner. "She's gonna flip before she goes down. Keep paddlin' for fuck's sake.

Something caught her eye. It was descending from the Island, like a spider on a line of thread. It was one of the Rigid Hull Inflatables. As soon as it splashed down, the lines were cast off and the engine kicked in, propelling the boat out from under the overhanging structure.

"That'll be the Admiral," said the gunner. "He cut that fine."

On the tilted main deck, two huge burning eyes blazed balefully out at the world. Both aft hangar elevators were fully open now and the fires inside were intense. Small explosions kicked blackened metal out over the water.

The end came quickly. Top heavy with the Flight Deck, the carrier's list reached the point of no return.

The whole thing came over, accelerating quickly,

323

nightmarishly, like it shouldn't happen in the real world.

"Hold fast!" screamed the gunner.

Transfixed, she watched the huge flat deck swing over and down, crushing the puny humans in the water, slapping down with a bang that could be heard around the world.

It missed their little raft by many metres, but the blast of displaced air and water took them, giving her wings, sending her tumbling high above the blue waters of the Atlantic.

Chapter 28. *Gulf of Guinea*

The old ship was tough. For half a century she'd taken all that the oceans of the world could throw at her: typhoons in the Pacific, hurricanes in the Atlantic.

But now, four gaping holes had been punched into her side below the waterline. Explosions had torn through many compartments and water was gushing in hard, weighing her down on one side, making her twist. Inside, frantic crewmen closed water tight doors, tried to staunch the cold Atlantic seeping into her bowels. Men, caught on the wrong side of closing barriers, hammered with bloody fists as water filled their lungs.

But still there was not enough water to sink her. Not yet.

Her tilting was getting faster. As the heavy ledge of her Flight Deck neared the vertical, her fate was sealed.

When the flat top smashed down on the ocean, the Old Lady's undersides were revealed: the rudder and props like genitals, shockingly exposed for all the world to see.

And inside the Bridge, the dying Captain looked out in wonder at his suddenly inverted world.

Now the water could gush into the Hangar Decks, pushing the remaining air out, making her heavier and heavier.

Finally, stern first, she began to slip below the waves, the bow section of the flight deck inverted but rising into the air for one last time.

Just enough for its weight, now unsupported by water below, to break the old ship's back with a clap like thunder.

Backwards, her broken body slipped down into the depths.

Behind her, drifting up to the surface came a long trail of objects, some still alive and kicking desperately. Long trails of bubbles, condensing into vast pockets of air, exploded when they reached the surface.

Into the depths she fell, the Bridge windows imploding.

Deeper now, and the lighter bulkheads buckled and ripped with the pressure. More and more water pushed the air out, making her denser, increasing the speed of her fall.

The continental shelf dipped sharply here and she fell through miles of empty ocean.

Inside, still alive in watertight compartments, men and women prayed.

At last, stern first, she drove deep in to the sea floor. The bow section, attached still to the stern by lengths of weakened steel, like a slashed arm held on only by tendons, swung round like a hammer. Smashing down, it split open the hull, revealing the reactors in all their savage glory.

The water, terribly pressurised at this depth, poured into the reactors, moderating the neutrons, bringing their energies down to levels favourable for reactions.

Allowing the ship's fierce twin hearts to glow brightly for a century to come.

Chapter 29. *Tembe*

Looking down over the city, from here on its highest hill, everything looks so calm. Far out to sea he knows there is death and destruction but the only evidence is a trace of black smoke peeping over the horizon. That alone means some success.

Yao should feel jubilant but his heart is heavy. The General has explained it all, time and time again. He understands the motives: sees that, from their position of weakness in the face of overwhelming strength, that their options were limited; that they have been forced to be ruthless.

But he has also seen the prisoners, back at the hangar: seen their humanity.

He sighs and spits into the dust.

Glancing round, he automatically checks the positions of his men. He should be chivvying them on, trying to make them focus despite the oppressive heat. Behind tree trunks or cars, he sees them scanning the sky, starting at every bird that flies.

As well they might. Yao loves Olomo but he cannot understand why they are here; yet this is where he was sent straight after the raid on the airport. There's nothing to guard here. The family that once lived here are for the most part dead, slain by the Americans. Would the Americans regard the old palace as a symbol, something worth smashing for its own sake?

The Americans still have the evil birds at their disposal but they'll be out looking for Olomo. He knows the General is on the move up country, far from here and the Plateau. At least with him gone from the Cleft, everyone there will be safe from American attack.

And this gives him great comfort. The village had been no place for Zinzi anymore. Her husband had brought death down on them. The survivors might have clubbed her to death.

His own family is long dead so the Cleft is the only place

he could put her. She's in a small tented enclave, near the entrance to the valley, with all the other wives and servants, and well away from Olomo's headquarters. Far enough for the heavy trees to soak up even the blast from a cruise missile. Close enough to the exit if this set the trees on fire.

At least that's what he hopes.

A flicker to the south makes him blink. Whatever it is, it's silver and moving too fast to be a drone.

The thing banks and begins to descend. He feels alarm as he recognises a Super Hornet. He opens his mouth to warn the troops, but then stops himself. The plane is coming down miles to the west.

It is trying to land at the airport and that can mean only one thing.

He punches the air in triumph.

"The General's plans have worked," he yells to the men. "The American's aircraft carrier is disabled, perhaps sunk!"

Their AKs chatter into the sky as he watches the jet come in.

'Out of the frying pan into the fire,' he thinks to himself.

What choices for that poor pilot! The nearest non-hostile airport is hundreds of miles away. Some of the planes from the carrier might have enough fuel to make it, but others won't. They can ditch into the sea and hope to be picked up in a war zone of sinking ships. Or they can land amongst their enemies.

If he was in that position, he'd rather eject over the Atlantic. Many slum dwellers are grieving for friends and relatives killed in the abortive attack on the airport. The airmen will be hacked to pieces unless the soldiers can whisk them away to a less certain fate.

He watches as the plane lands and disappears behind a small hill blocking the view of the runway.

His eyes flick back nervously to the sky, scanning for drones.

He sees only a second fighter arcing in over the Gulf for a

landing. He checks his watch. The grounds are big and he can't keep his eyes on all his men at once. Many are behind the building at the gate. They've been here three hours; enough time for some of the soldiers to start wondering about any pickings there might be in the big house. Enough time for greed to overcome the fear of what would happen if they were caught.

And they'd do anything to avoid being caught, so every time he checks, Yao does so with caution. He jacks back the slide on the AK before turning and striding towards the main entrance.

The facade is too ornate, too flowery for his taste. It reeks of colonialism. Why the General allowed his family to live here he will never understand. It is the General's one fall from grace in his eyes.

Checking the door handle, he makes sure it is safely locked. Then he gets the ring of keys out of his pocket and finally finds the right one.

The heavy doors swing open under his light push and he enters the sudden cool of the interior. The ceilings are high, impressively so, and they suck the hot air upwards.

He tries to soften his tread, but his boots still clop over the marble floor. Careful to avoid the brightly patterned rugs strewn over the lounge area, each is unsecured and slips easily from under your feet, he checks behind couches and armchairs for hiding figures.

Then he makes for the kitchens, though there is something about the stillness of the house that makes him almost certain he is quite alone.

And, sure enough, the kitchen is clear. The stink of spoiled food hangs in the air. If things ever calm down, he must get the staff back in to clean it all up.

Padding round the kitchen, he sees something he hasn't noticed before. At the back of one pantry, what he had taken to be a wall is actually a door. There is no handle, just a keyhole almost hidden by a bunch of dried chillies hanging from the ceiling. Yao goes through the keys on his chain, trying each one without success. He goes through them all again, carefully and systematically, but still none works.

Stepping back, he looks at the door and thinks about the layout of the house. It's big with several extensions and it takes him a while to orient himself. Finally, he realises the door leads to a windowless extension abutting onto what once had been the stables. Maybe there'll be another door there. He'll check later.

He goes back into the lounge and up the stairs to the bedroom area. He tries not to think ill of the dead, but he can't help pursing his lips at the opulent beds with their extravagant bed clothes and the myriad overstuffed pillows.

The kids' rooms are like toy stores. He notes the expensive toys strewn round. That's the first thing a light-fingered soldier would have taken.

But he checks in all the cupboards anyway. Finally satisfied there are no intruders, he heads downstairs and out the front door, carefully locking it behind him.

The heat, as ever, is a shock after the coolness of the house and he feels beads of sweat prickle on his back.

Scanning the air for drones, he makes his way to the left and along the long front of the house then turns towards the stable block. The stables are longstanding and are overgrown by an aggressive ivy that, back in the forests and jungles, relentlessly strangles the mightiest of trees. Here it is masonry that's falling to its attack.

The extension that connects the stables to the house is newer, less than ten years old he guesses from the ivy that has colonised only a third its length. The roof has a gentle pitch but isn't as steep and imposing as the house or the stables. Flat roofs here never worked. When the rains came, they were fierce and rapidly overwhelmed leaf clogged drainpipes, bringing flat roofs down on their unwary inhabitants.

At least his keys get him into the stables. Horses long gone, the place has been cleaned out and now holds go karts and quad bikes and two big Mercedes SUVs. Racks of tools line one long wall and the air is tainted by the smell of lubricating oil.

To the left of the entrance, he comes to another door leading into a small room where grooms, in the time of empire, would have eaten and snoozed and polished horse brasses.

And there's another door in this room, much the newest in the whole place, and it must give access to the new extension. Again, he tries all the keys but none fit. Stepping back, he looks at the door, pondering whether to break it open. He's supposed to check there has been no theft. It's possible there's something precious in there. A man could have climbed onto the roof of this single storey building and kicked his way through.

He decides to walk around the other side of the stables and make sure the roof is intact, but then he notices a skylight above the door. It's hinged and looks big enough to crawl through. He'll have to check it.

Back in the main body of the stables, amongst the hedge trimmers and chain saws and motorised mowers, he finds an aluminium ladder lying on the floor.

It proves to be too long, so he has to rest it at a shallow angle. He pulls a heavy tool case over and puts it at one end to stop the ladder slipping down when he puts his weight on it.

Gingerly, he makes his way up it. The skylight is firmly closed. Peering through it, he sees only pitch black and remembers this room has no windows to the outside. Cursing himself for his stupidity, he makes his way back down and goes to hunt for a torch.

The tool case is well equipped and he soon finds one.

Back up the ladder, he shines the beam through the glass, moving it round, trying to build up a composite image of what's in the room.

It's difficult to understand. Everything looks so old. The inside walls seem to be made up of logs even though he knows the outside is brick and stone. The floors are wooden and rough with planks that seem to have been walked on by generations of dirty boots and feet.

There's nothing here that fits in with the splendour of this house, but there is something about the furniture, old and well used, that seems strangely familiar. A desk, in particular, plucks at his memory as does the lines of plain wooden chairs lined up facing it.

He shines the torch on a wall again, moving it down its whole length. There's a break in the logs were the surface flattens out. The torch beam at this distance is weak, and it takes him a while to make out this is supposed to be a window. On this is stuck a large photo showing the thick trunks of trees.

Even more puzzled now, he shines the beam into the further corner.

Then he sees it. At first, he thinks its looming shape is that of a man, but then he realises the profile is too rectangular. Aiming the beam more carefully, and squinting harder, he can see that it's an old clock: a grandfather clock with something below the hands on its face. Is that a cow and a crescent moon?

By the time his conscious mind finally recognises what this is, some subconscious part of him has long since made the connection. He finds he's already left the stables, has sprinted to the front of the house and is frantically climbing into his SUV.

Chapter 30. *Gulf of Guinea*

She came out of a dreamless sleep. She found herself floating on her back, the bright tropical sun now dim. For a long time, she hung there like a pond floater, inhabiting a thin surface world above a yawning deep.

A deep that had easily swallowed just about the biggest object she'd ever seen.

Body aching from injuries and strains she'd picked up over the last couple of hours, first masked by adrenaline and fear but now more strident, she gathered what little energy she could. Turning her head to the side, she fully opened an eyelid sticky with salt.

Her nose had already told her there wouldn't be much oil to see. In old war films ships went down trailing oil slicks and, as they cracked apart, thousands of gallons of fuel oil would float to the surface to cover men there with black ooze.

But a nuclear-powered ship didn't use fuel oil.

Nuclear reactors: underneath her right now. She wondered how they were doing.

In the dimming light the surface of the sea looked like the ground after an open-air rock concert. It was covered in detritus for as far as she could see: life rafts and preservers, pillows, documents and clumps of clothing which she guessed were men and women. Lots of them. The *Sands* must have split open, God knows how far below her, releasing the bodies to rise from the depths like ascending souls.

But there was some life amongst the destruction. She could pick out several life rafts with people on board scanning through the wreckage field.

As long as she didn't move she felt comfortable and relaxed and would have been content to float like this forever. But finally, against her better judgement, she raised a faltering arm and croaked: 'Hey!"

She swallowed and moved her tongue, trying to work up enough saliva to lubricate her mouth. "Hey!" she said again.

A head on a raft about twenty metres away snapped round and she waved. The man pointed and yelled: "Over there!"

As it got nearer, she saw six or seven of them in the raft, though only a couple seemed to be capable of any activity. The others just leaned against the pillowy sides, not even sparing her a glance.

The raft hit her gently, the bow marshmallowing her aside. She looked up into the worried face of an earnest looking man.

"Going my way?" she asked.

"Ted, gimme a hand here!"

Another head appeared beside the first man's then hands were reaching over, grabbing the arms and the lapels of her exposure suit.

They heaved her up and landed her clumsily onto the watery floor of the raft.

The first thing she saw was Lewis, lolling against the side, eyes half closed and face ashen with shock.

"Ivor," she said, touching him lightly on his one good hand. He didn't seem to notice.

"Do you think there's any more of them around?" said one of the men who had hauled her on board.

"I don't think so," said the other. Both were in exposure suits. They seemed to be barely more than boys, just like most of the crew on that damned thing.

"Then maybe we should risk a flare. I'm pretty sure that's the *Farragut* over that way. That over there," and he was pointing in the direction of the sun, "I'm pretty sure that's the *Merrivell*. At least they're not high tailing it out of here. That means there's no more of those suicide boats. Right?"

"I'm a fucking cook," said the other guy. "I don't know what the fuck's going on. Come to think of it, last time I looked, Marshall, you were a cook too."

"We've got at least a dozen flares here," said Marshall. "I'm gonna risk it. We need to get picked up before it gets much darker."

Ted checked around. "Nothing else moving so I guess it's all over. Why not?"

After some fumbling, a bright light whizzed up into the sky.

She was beginning to feel a little more human. Looking round, she saw the three other occupants, two men and one woman, all staring blankly at the horizon. Their world, huge and noisy and crowded and bustling, had suddenly disappeared.

She touched Lewis' hand again. "Ivor! Can you hear me?"

She shook his hand gently. An eyelid twitched and his eyes focused on her. "Joey?"

"Yeah. How you feeling?"

"Fine. You?

"Just swell. Are you in a lot of pain?"

"It's not so bad if I don't move." His voice was little more than a whisper.

"They're signalled the other ships. We'll be picked up soon."

His eyes began to close then flicked open. "*The Sands*?"

"Gone."

Moving slowly, like a hundred-year old turtle, his head swivelled round and he looked out dazedly at the disappearing horizon.

"You mean completely?"

"I'm afraid so. Lots of wreckage, but otherwise..."

"The other ships are never going to be able to take us all. Not all six thousand. There just isn't room. Any other ships are still days away. Maybe if the *Farragut* emptied all its stores, tossed them over the wall..."

"There isn't six thousand," she said gently. "It all happened so fast. I can only see a few life-rafts."

"Shouldn't have happened. Damn thing was supposed to

be unsinkable."

He lapsed into silence and she looked round again. Ted and Marshall were tending to the woman who was alive but wasn't reacting to anything.

"Hell to pay," said Lewis suddenly.

"What?"

"Thousands dead... military and civilians. Hell to pay."

"How?"

"Macik. He'll move heaven and hell. Even if he didn't want to, Tridens would make him. Too much loss of face."

"What can he do? His carrier group doesn't even have a carrier anymore."

"He has the *Farragut*. He still has the power to level cities. Tridens'll give him the codes. Fire from the sky."

"Nuclear missiles?"

Lewis didn't say anything.

"You think he'll go nuclear?" She must have been loud because, out the corner of her eye, she saw Ted and Marshall turn to look at her.

"After what's just happened?" said Lewis, "Might be tempted myself."

Ted kept sending a flare up every half hour, but they weren't the only survivors and she was afraid their flares were lost amongst all the others.

After a few hours the other flares started to die out and he started to send them up more frequently. She checked her watch. It was 3am already.

Finally, it must've been their turn for rescue and one of the Farragut's Rigid Hull Inflatables made its way towards them, nudging aside all the stuff in the water. Ted threw them a line and soon they were being towed behind the RHIB, along with another raft it had picked up.

When they got to the *Farragut* she saw a flotilla of life rafts drifting astern in the current. She hoped they'd all been full.

A sling was lowered to get Lewis up onto the deck. She climbed the pilot ladder and, as her head cleared the lip of the deck, her heart sank again to see how relatively empty it was. If there'd been hundreds of survivors it should have been full. The Aegis wasn't a big ship, with nowhere near the space of the *Sands*.

As she sloshed onto the deck and moved clear of the ladder, a junior officer with a tablet came up to her. Military grade, in the sense that the surfaces had camouflage design, it looked puny and incongruous after what had happened. Somehow a no-nonsense clipboard would have been more reassuring.

"Name?"

"Josephine Beck. NCIS."

The officer poked at his screen. "Welcome aboard the *Farragut* Special Agent. Are you injured? Need medical attention?"

"No. I'm fine."

He nodded. "This gentleman," he indicated a crewman who stepped forward, "will take you to your temporary quarters."

"Follow me, please," said the man gently, though his eyes regarded her sharply. He had the usual buzz cut through his sandy hair, and a thin intense face.

A few metres down the deck he turned into a hatchway.

"Have you picked up many?"

"Not so you'd notice." His tone was brusque and she guessed he was hiding his feelings.

"What about the Admiral? Do you know if he made it?"

"He's here and spittin' nails. 'Face like thunder'. Heard that expression before but now I know what it really means."

"And Captain Larsen?"

He shrugged.

The corridors weren't as cramped as on the carrier, though everything was painted the same dull greys and browns. At least this ship was newer and lacked the patina of age which sometimes made her think she was living in an antique when she'd been on the *Sands*.

The crewman turned left into a mid-sized compartment. About thirty people, sitting on blankets on the floor, all turned to look at them.

"The Rec room," said the man. "This'll be where you'll bunk for now."

"Thanks. What's your name, by the way?"

"Farris. And it's worth remembering names again. We're a much smaller crew, not the thousands you had on the Bird Farm."

Joey looked round. A young woman, blond and clean cut, beckoned to her then reached down and shifted her blanket over a little. "You can go here. Just get a blanket from the pile to your right."

Her name was Susan Melkowitz. She had high protuberant Slavic cheekbones which long hair might have softened attractively, but the short cut she had gave her face a much harder edge.

"Yeah I was in Pri-Fly. Once the fires and explosions stopped take-offs, I was freer than most. Meant I got a better chance to get off."

"Pri-Fly?"

"Primary Flight Control. 010 level in the Island."

"High up!"

"Not so high when I got off. Island damn near took me down when she flipped."

"High up like that, you must have got a decent view. Did many get off?"

Melkowitz hesitated and her tough features seemed to soften. "We've got to face it. We're the lucky ones."

"What now?"

"Good question. They don't tell us anything." Melkowitz turned. "Hey you!" she yelled. Everyone turned but only the guy underneath a big wall mounted screen found her looking at him. "Turn that damn thing on!"

"What for?" said the guy.

"News."

"Haven't you had enough news for one day?"

"The officers on the Bridge have got other things on their mind than keeping us up to speed, but that doesn't mean we've got to stay in the dark."

The man shrugged and found the remote on a little plastic holster attached to the bulkhead. He poked around for a while, flicking through some channels. "Different channel numbers than on the *Sands*," the man said apologetically.

"Stop," Joey yelled. The channel showed the tall, elegant figure of Olomo.

"Fucker!"

"Shitball!"

"Butcher!"

Too much to hear what Olomo was saying. Joey shushed them all.

"...delusional faith in the power of their military technology. And we have shown them their mistake. We are too many and too clever. Wars are fought man against man and the gutless American military have forgotten that. They hide behind their machines but, rather than making them strong, it makes them weak. We will cast them all down, just as we have consigned their vaunted carrier group, 'the most powerful military weapons system on Earth' as they love to say, to the deeps from which it will never return.

"I call upon all the peoples of Africa to rise and cast off their oppressors, both military and economic. We are the most important continent on the planet. We will not be held down any longer. Oppressors of the world: you are not welcome in Africa. Leave or we will send you to Hell."

Behind Olomo she saw a battered old grandfather clock and, beside this, a window showed the dark trunks of trees. He was supposed to have disappeared into the bush but was still in the same headquarters on the plateau where he'd held the kangaroo trials of the original hostages.

And even as she thought this, a deep rumble shook the

Farragut.

"Missile launch!" said Melkowitz savagely.

Chapter 31. *The Plateau*

His foot has been hard to the floor even through the villages. At such speeds the heavy SUV launches itself missile-like off every bump in the road before crashing down onto its brutalised shocks. Something bad has already happened to the driver's side shock absorber and the car has developed an appreciable list.

And Yao's body feels like he's been mowed down by a stampede of cattle, heavy hooves stamping down on his innards and lower back.

He's already had to swerve wildly, a village boy suddenly frozen in his spotlights, making him slew through some spindly corn before finally fishtailing back onto the road and trailing a slipstream of red dust.

But at least he's near now and can see the where the mountain's bulk is erasing the stars.

He slows as he comes to the first road block, otherwise they'll shoot him and the SUV to pieces. As he pulls up, the cloud of dust catches up and settles around the vehicle. Some sentries, AKs up and ready, mooch towards him. He's never seen them before but they must know him for they nonchalantly wave him through, while a couple of younger soldiers pivot the barrier round.

And he's off again, more slowly now as there are too many people about. This is where the servant women cook the food, where they wash the clothes of the men in the boisterous stream bouncing down the floor of the Cleft.

Keeping his speed down is a feat of will and he has to take colossal breaths, like an old man struggling for air. The SUV has stopped rattling but his hands still shake on the wheel.

A gaggle of women are blocking the way, all bunched up

in the middle of the path and talking animatedly. He flashes the lights and hoots the horn. Most ignore him, but others make dismissive, disdainful gestures with their hands.

The trees are pressing in too closely either side to go around. He clicks the central locking closed and eases forward. They see him coming but don't move but, as soon as the bumper taps the first well-padded rump, the women start yelling and screaming. Dirty clothes are thrown at the windscreen and hands bang at the windows and rattle the door handles.

But he keeps going and, when they see he means it, even the bigger ones find the energy to waddle aside and pour a cacophony of abuse at the SUV. A couple of rocks bounce off the roof but then he is beyond them.

The trees are like hulking beasts in the streaming headlights.

Taking the little turnoff, he heads up the short stretch to the circle of tents where he left her. Quickly reversing the SUV back and forth, he manages to turn it round between the heavy trunks. Then he's out the car and sprinting to her tent. Grabbing the flaps, he rips the coarse cow hide stitching apart and reaches into the dark.

Zinzi screams, deafeningly in the confined peace.

"It's me," he says. "Quickly, get out!"

"But I'm not..." but his fumbling hands have found her upper arms and he's dragging her out of the tent.

"Yao! Stop!"

His pulling has disarranged her shift, exposing much of her chest, but for once he doesn't care who else sees her body.

"I'm nearly naked. Let me..." But he locks his arms on her shoulders and marches her to the SUV.

"What's...?"

Yanking open the passenger door, he lifts her easily into the front seat and closes it quickly then hits the central locking button before she can get back out.

In a flash he's round the other side. Opening the lock, he's able to reach in and grab her arm to stop her climbing out in the moment her door is unlocked.

"Have you gone mad?"

Clicking the lock again, he puts the key in the ignition and the engine roars to life and the car starts rocking down the slope.

"Put your seat belt on!"

"Stop the car!"

"Put your seat belt on or you will get hurt!"

Then he has to ignore her as his speed increases on the winding, rutted road. If he hits one of these big trees then the SUV may be finished.

"What are you doing?"

"Trying to save your life. Put your seat belt on. Please!" This last spoken with more force and urgency and yearning than anything else he has said in his life.

He can't take his eyes off the track to look at her, but he hears her intake of breath. Then he hears the click of the belt buckle snapping into place.

The herd of women have displaced a little from the centre of the road but it's still going to be difficult to get by. Hearing the SUV, they start to shift back into the middle, making a point.

Yao puts his foot down hard and, in the side mirror, he sees a gout of dust fountain up from under the back wheels.

"Yao!" Zinzi screams.

And for a second the women hold their position. Then they're tumbling aside, big women rolling in the dust, and the car is through them with inches to spare.

Zinzi goes quiet but he can feel her eyes boring into the side of his head. Ahead he sees the soldiers' campfire. With a surge of relief, he sees they haven't swung the barrier back. The SUV blasts through and, in his mirror, he sees soldiers fumbling their guns to their shoulders.

Reaching across he grabs her head and tries to push it down, to get some metal between it and the guns. She yelps and fights. He sees a gun flash in the rear-view mirror but the bulb of flame is into the air: a belated warning volley.

Already far enough away to be safe, he lets go and she jerks upright and he feels an angry slap on his cheek.

"He's goading them," he says.

"What?"

"Provoking them; pushing them to react. To murder more."

"What are you talking about?"

Clear of the trees, the plateau spreads before them, dotted here and there by lights in the villages rich enough to own generators.

The road empty before them, he chances a look at her. She's as far back from him as the door and seat belt will allow, her eyes wide with shock. She almost doesn't seem to recognise him.

"I had to get you out! You see Olomo..."

A thunderclap. A cloud punches him in the face. The straps bite deep into his chest.

The dashboard lights appear again as the airbag subsides. Looking across, he sees the passenger side bag doing the same, revealing Zinzi frozen like a statue, hands clenched in fist. Her wild eyes watch as it flattens like a big piece of gum on a city pavement.

"We must have hit something," he hears himself say stupidly.

Zinzi's eye swivel round and she gives him a look of fathomless incomprehension.

Rather than face her, he fumbles at the door handle but it won't open. The door is stuck fast. The electric window gets down about a third of the way then sticks.

He looks back at her and points to her door. "Can you get out?"

But she doesn't seem up to it, so he reaches across and finds the door opens easily. He undoes her seatbelt and half shoos, half pushes her out the door. Then he crawls out after her.

First, he checks back in the waning light. He can just make

out the outline of the mountain and the forested cleft cut into it like a woman's crotch. It has to be a couple of miles away at least; too far for a cruise missile's blast to reach them. He breathes a deep sigh of relief and feels the tension start to drain away.

At the front of the car the passenger's side is almost undamaged but the driver's side looks like it's been stoved in by a black pyramid. A termite hill, perhaps?

But when he reaches out to touch it, he finds it soft and sticky. The driver's side headlight is dead, but the other is still working, and he realises that what he has touched is black pelt. He'd milked enough of the damned things in his time to work out this was a cow, a black cow that must have been waiting for him right in the middle of the road.

The impact has pulverised the tissue and shattered the bone. The cow's body has become unconstrained, gravity turning it into a loose pyramid of flesh.

Kneeling down, the mountain hidden behind the SUV, he looks across at Zinzi. She's stepped back a little, almost like she's considering running back to the Cleft.

"It's a cow," he says, as though that will explain everything.

A dazzling light sears his retinas. Just for an instant, before his vision overloads, he sees her, a shadow against the incandescence, bones revealed.

He gets to his feet and stumbles blindly towards her, arms outstretched. Already the light, though still bright, is fading and his vision is returning. He sees before him an angel: a being of flame. To her left, the sun is rising.

He's blinking hard now, hoping the water in his eyes will extinguish the flames that are covering her.

His groping hands find her and are seared.

Suddenly a wall of air hits him and he's flying.

He slaps down on the ground, tumbling end over end, punches pummelling his whole body, dragging him down into endless darkness.

But light finally returns, a flickering through his closed eyelids. A cool wind is blowing over him, raising goose bumps on the unclothed flesh of his forearm. Even opening his eyelids brings pain to his battered face.

Somehow it is no longer night. Turning his head towards the sun, he sees it is now on the earth itself.

But it isn't the sun, it's the Cleft. It's like the mountain has become a volcano again, sending out a spreading river of lava and filling the Cleft with flame.

Painfully he gets to his feet. Where is he? What has happened to the road?

Then he sees it, a ribbon cleared through the charred vegetation. Twenty metres or so away, something is lying on it. Puzzled at first, he realises it's the hulking mass of the SUV, bizarrely upright and resting on its tailgate. It looks like a dog begging. When he gets to it, he sees the sides are caved in and all the windows are smashed.

Looking dazedly around he sees, dotted over the plain, crowns of flames where once villages had stood.

What has happened to Zinzi? What could have done this?

It takes a long, long time staring dully at the SUV, at the road, at the burning mountain, before he understands.

The heavy body of the SUV has saved him from the searing light and radiation, its metal body shielding him. But Zinzi had been standing by its side with only air between her and the detonation.

He starts looking for her, though already he knows she's dead.

The blast had thrown him far so there's a lot ground to search. He crosses and re-crosses his path. He sees it soon enough but somehow it slides out of his thoughts. A tree trunk blackened by the searing heat of nuclear light, perhaps.

So, he skirts around it, shuffling through the dust, checking inside the shattered SUV again and again, even poking at the smeared-out bulk of the cow flesh, its bean bag softness impeding it tumbling far in the blast wave.

And finally, he cannot avoid it any longer. Turning back, he makes his way towards the thing with leaden steps.

Surface blackened and charred into lumps of cracked carbon, hair and shift burned away, there is nothing to recognise.

But what else can it be?

Chapter 32. *USS Farragut, Gulf of Guinea*

"I'm going to have to ask you to put the torch down." Joey could hear the tightness in her own voice.

Miller, a tall black guy with a boxer's broken nose, was swaying side to side, his head whipping back and forth in his agitation. "It was murder," he said, the agony in his voice sounding like nails scraped across a blackboard. "Pure and simple!"

But the torch was still waving, not that it was much of a weapon anymore. Miller had used it to smash just about anything breakable in the Rec Room, and now the bulb unit hung out limply on fragile wires. It looked more like a crushed soda can than a club.

"Put...the torch...down."

Miller looked at her angrily and her hand automatically touched the tunic of her camo gear to feel the solidity of the Sig underneath it.

"Thousands of black people dead. Doesn't that bother you at all, Aunty Thomasina?"

"The torch. Now!"

"Fuck you!"

With her left hand she raised the side of the tunic and with the other slipped out the gun. Two handed, she took aim. All the others in the room backed even further against the walls.

"Oh, so you're going to shoot me now. Black on black. Won't even make the evening news."

"Don't tempt me."

"Doesn't it bother you at all, 'Special Agent'?"

"What bothers me is a guy going nuts in a confined space in the middle of fucking nowhere."

"So, you'd kill me. Chalk up one more dead nigger to the CSG."

"No. I'd aim for your legs if I could, trying real hard not to hit your balls." She clicked back the hammer.

"You're fucking kidding me," he snarled but she could tell he was losing steam. No matter how smart the guy, their junk lay at the centre of their being.

"So now what?"

"The torch."

He threw it down contemptuously.

"Now turn around! Down on your knees! Hands behind your back!" Even as she was speaking she was moving forward, fishing the cuffs out of their little holster, not giving him time to do anything stupid. Placing the gun against the base of his skull, she clicked them on.

"Get up!"

Behind him, gun pressed into the small of his back, her other hand on the chain joining the cuffs, she steered him out the compartment and then left down some stairs. The so-called Brig, usually a storeroom, was full of *Sands'* survivors. It looked like they'd be needing somewhere else to bunk down.

"Doesn't it bother you?"

"Of course it fucking bothers me, you ape! Doesn't mean I have to act like a self-indulgent piece of shit."

"Sure, you keep on telling yourself that. Out there your brothers and sisters are charcoal briquettes, but you're keeping it tight. No self-indulgence for you, God forbid!"

She jerked the chain so he stopped. "Brothers and sisters, my ass! How many hundreds of years has it been since our ancestors left Africa?"

"They didn't 'leave'. They were abducted. Enslaved. And how proud they'd be of you now!"

She shoved him forward. The Brig was between the laundry and the food store. Slamming him against the wall, she used the hand that wasn't carrying the gun to open it. Three pairs of eyes looked up at her from thin foam mattresses.

"You'll all have to leave. Need this room again."

They started to object but then saw the gun and the

handcuffed man.

"Where are we supposed to go?" said one woman, but they were all reluctantly getting up.

"Talk to the XO! Not my problem."

While they took their time to mooch out, she checked the little key cupboard next to the outside of the door and found the key that fitted the lock. When all the others had got clear, she undid his handcuffs and shoved him into the room, then quickly closed and locked the door. A broad hatch, big enough to slide a mess tray through, was at eye level and she drew it back. He was in the centre of the room, hands on hips, looking back out at her.

"Ain't you going to take my shoelaces and belt in case I hang myself?"

"Be my guest." She slammed the slide closed and pushed home the vertical bolt so he couldn't get it open from the inside.

Then she leaned far back against the bulkhead until the top of her head was touching the cold metal and closed her eyes. Maybe Miller's freakout could help her.

Things had been fractious since the bombing. Macik had shut down all exterior comms after the missile launch. Even so, the launch of a nuke was news that would never be kept secret on this tin can. Finally, even Macik had grasped that his control freakery had failed and the exterior feeds had come back up.

Plugged in again, they found a world that was going nuts.

She needed air. Letting the hammer down, she put the Sig back into its holster and took the steps up three at a time. The antechamber to each deck hatch was still red light only, but by now everyone knew it was a waste of time. There wasn't a boat within twenty miles to see any light, and Olomo had never had any aircraft to speak of. They could light a bonfire on deck and nobody would see or care.

On deck, a good wind was blowing towards the land. The big flotilla of inflatables and RHIB's were now all along the length of the ship down the lee side. There was about fifty of the things tied together in chains of five or six. Considered too much of a shipping hazard to just let go, one of the crewmen had told her the craft would have to wait until another CSG arrived to take them on board.

And the *George H.W. Bush* CSG was only two days away.

It was now or never.

She looked down at the choppy water. The *Farragut*, still looking for survivors, hadn't moved in days. The *Merrivell* had soon taken on as many of the injured survivors as she could, including Lewis. Many needed urgent medical attention so she was steaming back to unload them at the nearest friendly port.

Which was a real problem. The whole seaboard was up in arms against the US. The US base on Ascension Island was the nearest place they had.

Back home people were more with the program. The loss of the *Sands* and thousands of sailors, and all the American civilians used as human bombs, had stoked a desire for vengeance. To many, the nuking of the Cleft seemed righteous.

But unsettling images were coming in. HD cameras were cataloguing the carnage. Burned children like kindling, bodies strewn around like matchwood.

And images of the survivors. Not old black and white photos of stunned orientals but exquisitely detailed studies of people not too different from herself huddling down on a blackened plain where every blade of grass had burned away. Sudden desert in the heart of tropical Africa.

In Niger, the airstrip they used for the drones had been overrun by a mob. The small group of marines guarding it hadn't stood a chance. Every single one had been lynched.

Amidst a tumult of world protest, the President's tough facade was beginning to crumble.

Only the third ever use of atomic weapons against a civilian population, and all by the same nation.

She made her way back down now, deep down to the stores. Dry goods, tins and bottles rapidly being depleted by all the extra mouths, still filled up half the space there. Behind a stack of cans was a box she'd emptied of tins. Inside was the knapsack, still undiscovered.

Nothing to stop her now.

At the top of the stairs she stepped into the corridor. To the left and back towards the stern were the Rec room and her bunk. To the right was the end of everything she'd ever known.

She stood for a long time. Vaguely, she was aware of crewman squeezing past, giving her odd looks.

She waited, letting the anger rise, then headed right towards the bow.

Maybe he wouldn't be in. Had he slept at all in the last few days? Would his conscience have let him?

What kind of dreams did he have?

It was like any of the other unremarkable compartments but for the Captain's name stencilled across the door. No blue tiles marked the territory here like it had on the Bird Farm; just one cabin in a line of four for the senior officers.

But the Captain was somewhere else sharing with the XO. Macik had the cabin now.

Walking up, like it was routine, she wrapped her knuckles on the thin metal. Maybe she heard a muffled *'Come'* and maybe she didn't, but she went in anyway.

He was sitting at the shelf that served as a desk and was hunched over a monitor. Two other shelves welded to the bulkhead held books and manuals. Ellory, the captain, had taken whatever personal stuff he'd had with him. Maybe Macik hadn't been able to rescue any personal stuff from the carrier.

She was glad. She didn't want to see any pictures of wife and kids.

Portholes were for civilian ships, so Macik's skin looked pale in the light cast by the recessed fluorescent. He sat back as far as the backrest allowed and turned to look at her. He raised a single eyebrow, perhaps too weary to say anything.

"Had a problem with Chief Miller, Admiral. Problems

with a few of the crew in fact. Thought you should know about them."

Macik motioned to the bunk which filled up most of the cramped cabin, and she sat down on the edge. The black and brown and yellow streaks of her camouflage gear clashed with the blank whiteness of the sheets. The camos had been all that was available to replace the overalls shredded by the *Sands* evacuation.

"Can't remember much about him, to tell you the truth. Big carrier group, or used to be," and he turned to tap on the keyboard. Miller's photo appeared on the screen along with some text she couldn't read.

"Good service record. Nearly twenty years in. What was the problem?"

"He's in the Brig. Trashed the Rec Room. TV screen, water cooler. Got into some pushing and shoving."

"Anyone hurt?"

"No. I took him in before things got out of control."

"Good, but why are you telling me this? Why not the Captain or the XO?"

"Well, because I guess you're responsible for it all."

"How?"

"Because you launched the cruise missile with the nuclear warhead. The one that killed all those Africans."

She waited to see how he'd react. Would he tell her to fuck off, or would he get angry and lash out?

Instead he just brought his arm up, resting his chin on the palm, forefinger straight, the tip touching his temple.

"Is this about Miller or is it about you?"

"Miller, me and maybe a quarter of the crew. Haven't done an audit or anything, but that's my guess."

"And what would you have done instead, Special Agent? Thousands of Americans dead, many of them civilians. Shrugged your shoulders and gone back to your Facebook and your Twitter and whatever the hell is the flavour of the month?"

"Villages were all over that plateau. Plus, God knows how

many camp followers, wives and children were in The Cleft. All vaporised or burned. And for those who survived: radiation sickness to come."

"You're a civilian, you don't understand about war."

"Miller and the others aren't civilians and, anyway, this isn't a war, far as I know."

"Come on, Beck! Not like you to be mealy mouthed. You sink a carrier and a frigate then that's war. Don't waste my time by pretending it isn't. Olomo caught us napping and brought us down. Can't let him, let them... because it's not like Olomo is alone, he's got the people of three countries behind him...we can't let them all get away with it. Geo-politically we have to show we're strong and have the will, otherwise it's a long way down."

"So, revenge had nothing to do with it?"

"Oh, come on, for God's sake. This is the real world. It's never either/or. Of course, I wanted revenge, the President wanted revenge, and most of the American people did as well."

He shook his head. "But don't go underselling the geo-political aspect. As a country we're going down and have been for years. China, Brazil, Russia; one day they'll all overtake us in GDP terms, maybe in other ways as well. The rollercoaster of empire. Some go up, some go down. It never stays the same. But it usually happens smoothly, over generations. This business was like a big step down: too much, too soon. We couldn't allow it. Couldn't allow some tin pot dictator to humiliate us like that."

"Tin pot dictator? Your arrogance was your big mistake right from the start. Olomo's had you every which way but you're still underestimating him."

"I'd remind you he's just atoms, spread over most of West Africa."

"Is he? I'd be surprised unless suicide was integral to his messianic plan. But I'm guessing he's still alive somewhere. This whole thing was planned right from the start."

"Sounds almost like you admire him." For the first time she heard a trace of anger in his weary voice.

"Hate the fucker! I see where he's coming from but I hate him nonetheless. Means don't justify ends. What he did was brutal and heartless and his idea of a united Africa is madness. But I'm not underestimating him. You could talk of David and Goliath but that doesn't even begin to do him justice. An ant against a tank is better. He planned to get us here, timed everything. The taking of the first bunch of hostages so the *Sands'* Strike Group would be the one that was sent to deal with him. He'd looked for and found the weaknesses in our technology. He provoked us to murder his family then provoked us to destroy his people. And we followed right along."

"Still not sure what you'd have done instead."

"Anything I'd suggest would just look like weakness to you."

"I bet whatever it was would look like weakness to anyone."

He sighed and glanced back at his terminal. "This isn't getting us anywhere. I have a lot to do. Goodnight Special Agent."

"Did it take much convincing to get the President to give you the launch codes?"

He looked back at her but she couldn't read him.

"Man on the spot. His views count," she continued. "A President with everything to prove. Overcompensating, trying to look tough."

"If you're trying to make me personally responsible for all this..." he waved his arm vaguely at the bulkhead, "then you're just looking for a scapegoat. That's weak, self-indulgent thinking, Beck. I'm disappointed in you."

She nodded. "Yeah, maybe I'm stretching it a bit there. Maybe she didn't need too much convincing. But one thing I'm clear on is that you could have talked her out of it. 'Man on the spot', the one who's been injured the most. He says 'Hold your fire'. That carries weight. Would have given even a belligerent President pause for thought, never mind a weak one."

"It's you that's weak, Beck. Putting all the blame on me.

But we'll see how it turns out."

"What do you mean?"

"There'll be investigations, more commissions than you'll know what to do with. They'll scrutinise every bowel movement we've all ever made. Justice will be done."

"Oh sure! President released the codes, so her decision ultimately. You're just a good soldier. Sure, you could never set foot in a foreign country because you'd be arrested and put on a charter flight straight to the Hague. For your crimes against humanity. But back in the States you'll be lionised by the right wing. You'll be a hero."

He just looked at her without expression and she couldn't tell what he really thought of himself. Good or evil, hero or villain?

But she didn't care.

Plucking a pillow from the bed she threw it at him. He started in surprise but caught it two handed across his chest.

In one smooth movement she brought the gun out. Shoving the muzzle deep into the pillow, she pulled the trigger.

Time must have passed. A wisp of smoke, curling up from the blackened hole in the pillow, brought her out of her reverie.

The gun was still in her hand. Mechanically, she de-cocked it and put it back in her holster. Macik's head was tilted back over the top of the chair. Eyes open and mouth wide, as though for a shout that had never come. Heart mashed by the single bullet, the lights had gone out quicker than she'd have ever have thought possible.

He was heavy but she'd always been strong. 'Wiry strength' her Dad had called it, even before she'd kicked the shit out of him. Macik was easy to heave over onto the bed.

She pulled a sheet over him and shoved the pillow under his head, making sure it was covering the hole. There was blood on the swivel chair back but she turned it away so it wouldn't show.

Not that it mattered. His staff knew he'd been working for

days without sleep and she hoped that, when he didn't answer, they'd keep out.

Cracking the door, she checked for any sounds of activity, then clicked the cabin's lights off and slipped out.

Collecting the knapsack, she was soon back on deck, starboard side, looking over the rail at the flotilla still tethered along the side and fanning out with the wind.

One more look around, and with a silent hope that nobody on the blackened bridge was looking down at her, she climbed over the railing and grabbed hold of a tethering line.

The current and wind were light so her weight on the line made the craft below draw in. There were two life rafts then a rigid hull inflatable. The rope was thinner than a ratline and bit into her hands, but she managed to trap the line between the sides of her feet and the strain eased.

Soon her feet found the edge of the first raft and she stepped down onto its billowy floor. Like a kid on a bouncy castle, she giant-stepped her way across it until she got to the mooring rope linking the next raft in line. Pulling on this was harder than she'd expected and she felt the sweat start to form on her brow. When it was close enough she stepped in and across it. Then she hauled in the rigid hull until it nudged against the inflatable's side.

Scrambling onto the craft's firmer floor, she took the strain on the mooring line then untied it from the cleat. As the boat gently began to drift away, she pulled on the line to stop it.

Then things got cumbersome, but at least there was little noise. Using the lanyards on the other inflatables she was able to pull herself around. Securing her own boat's line round to these, she was able to step into the other rafts and loosen their lines to the ship.

Getting back into her own boat, she was now part of a small flotilla drifting away from the *Farragut*. Feeling in the knapsack, she found the sheet of black plastic she'd filched from the stores: wrapping material that had been discarded in a waste bin.

Lying flat down, she pulled the plastic over her, but left one eye uncovered so she could scan the receding ship.

She'd drifted less than twenty metres when a bright light lashed over her. Whoever was using the light was darting it back and forth over the water. "Shit!" she heard someone say.

She was gambling they wouldn't try to recover the drifting inflatables by night, but she needed someone to spot them. Otherwise, when she drifted clear of the *Farragut's* own radar shadow, they'd likely mark her as a target. A shit rain of ordnance would come down on her head in seconds.

Another light flashed down from the starboard bridge wing. In the reflected light she saw a figure lean over the side, flat hands up to the sides of their face, and shout something down to whoever was on the deck. Both lights winked off.

Fifty metres now but still no other boats were being lowered.

She'd chosen the rigid hull because it had a motor, but she didn't dare use it, not yet anyway. Gently drifting boats they'd accept. Anything that suddenly accelerated and there'd be hell to pay.

Deciding when to turn on the motor would be tricky. Twenty miles from the coast and eight hours until light, current maybe only one or two knots. Perhaps they'd leave her alone long enough, not bother to retrieve any of the survival boats, so she could drift peacefully to shore.

But if they did come for the boats, she'd need to turn on the motor and make a break for the shore.

Maybe by then she'd be lost in the sea clutter or perhaps they'd figure she was just a fishing boat.

Then again, maybe not.

Chapter 33. *The Plateau*

It takes all night. In the back of the SUV, next to the spare wheel, he'd found a little shovel for extricating the vehicle when it lost traction in sand or mud. With this he's been working hard, harder than he ever has in his life. The ground, baked solid by months of sun, is unyielding at first. Afraid he might break the tool, he scrapes away at first. After several inches the ground becomes softer and the tool can scoop up little mouthfuls.

It has to be done before the sun comes up and shines its remorseless light. He has to get her under the earth before then.

The grave is not deep, there has been no time. But does it have to be deep? He thinks of the flash and the blast. Hyenas, wolves and foxes would have burned away. No scavengers would come digging here until after the rains. Rains that would soak through the ground, softening the charred flesh and melting her back into the earth.

Finally, his last token of love given, he turns his back on the fiery remains of The Cleft and heads south along the flash-blackened road. He doesn't know where he's going; he just needs to get away. Some part of him makes him do this: some part geared for survival, inured to his emotions, untouched by his loss.

This strange aloof part notes the wind is in his face, knows that it will blow the fallout north and east. Realises he will probably live; knows his fingernails wouldn't blacken and twist in obscene gnarled shapes as the cells that make them were kicked into overdrive by the radiation. Knows he won't start shitting blood, or lose his hair, or watch as whole sheets of his skin slewed off. That part of him, that core of selfishness, makes these calculations while the rest of his mind keeps carefully blank.

Along this road should be little villages. Even this early in the morning, stalls should be open selling fruit or water. But for a mile or so there's nothing. All signs of mankind have been scattered to the winds as though by the fiery breath of an angry God.

But further on, he does find remnants. Cropped circles of blackened, still burning wood mark out where huts have stood; debris trails like the tails of comets lie behind each.

Further on he recognises blackened logs as torsos, the thinner arms and legs entirely consumed by the fire.

Then he comes to a bigger village, and a brick building still stands but the roof is gone. And beside it is an SUV, untouched by the fire.

A movement to his left makes him spin round. Two soldiers are poking through the remains of a house. One suddenly points down and the other brings something up to his eye.

It's a camera.

Yao shuffles over towards them.

One of the men sees him. "A live one! Get a shot."

The camera swings round and tracks him as he approaches. Looking down in the debris of the hut, he sees the blackened body of a baby and realises this is what they have been filming.

"Are you OK?" asks one of the men. Their uniforms are neat, their skins undamaged. Sweat glistens on their faces and they keep glancing north. Smoke rises from the whole plain, but above The Cleft rolling clouds of darker smoke puff into the sky and form a tilting column as the wind pushes it away.

"You look like a zombie. I wasn't sure if I should shoot you with this camera or with my gun." The soldier is young, maybe only eighteen, and he seems to be using the camera with some facility. Yao doesn't know him but the other soldier looks familiar. Older, maybe thirty, broad shoulders but with a paunch that erupts between the buttons of a tunic that is too small for him.

"I am Yao, Special Commander to General Olomo.

The older guy steps closer, screwing his eyes up to get a better look. "My God, so it is! Were you in that?" and he points north.

"Not in it, but close." The talking makes him aware of how dry his throat is, of his sudden terrible thirst. "Have you any water?"

The older soldier nods and races back to the car. The bottle of water he brings back is tepid but it's the best thing Yao has ever drunk. He slowly bends his knees and sits back, letting his backside thump down on the road.

"What are you doing here?" he asks.

"Filming," says the younger guy. "We're a Special Unit. There're teams of us, all over the plateau. Taking pictures, like we've been trained."

"Trained?"

"Yes," says the younger man a little hesitantly. He looks enquiringly at the older guy who just shrugs. "We were sent to study at Cape Town. Media course."

"When?"

"Six months ago. We just did the film maker module really, not the whole thing."

"And who does this unit report to? Wait, let me guess! It's Justice isn't it?"

"Special Commander Nyere. Yes indeed."

"Look," says the older one. "We're nearly finished here and we're heading back. We could give you a lift. Can't stay longer anyway. The Colonel says we have only two hours within six miles of the epicentre. Otherwise the radiation might be harmful."

Yao's no physicist, but even he knows this is bullshit. It's all about the wind direction. They've just been lucky.

But, he reflects, why disturb their ignorance? Then he thinks about the steersmen on the cigarette boats. Had there ever really been a plan to pick them up after the attack?

He follows the men back to the SUV. "Whoa," says one suddenly. "Look at that!"

Yao is swaying a little and finding it difficult to focus, so it takes him a while to understand what he's seeing. On a wall of the brick building is the silhouette of a man riding a bicycle. He can even tell the man had been thin and with rather a long nose.

The sight transfixes him and he doesn't see the other thing until the men move in for better close-ups. Below the shadow made by the flash is a blackened pile of debris.

It doesn't make sense at first. There are man-made shapes in there: some straight, some circular. But there's also bone and teeth.

Man and machine fused together in a nightmare of metal and flesh.

Yao's universe sweeps round in a quick, vicious swirl. He's unconscious even before he hits the ground.

The jolting of the SUV brings him round. He opens his eyes and sees fresh, unburned countryside going by.

"Back in the land of the living," says a voice. "Thought we'd lost you for a while there."

It's the younger guy, in the front passenger seat, but turned around to look back at him. "Here, have some more water. By the way, I'm Corporal Diawara, and this is Sergeant Bankole."

Yao gulps the fluid down rapidly.

"Want some food? We've got some rations."

Yao shakes his head. "Where are we going?"

"We're heading back to our station near Ellana. We'll take you to the city hospital."

"Forget it! Take me back to your HQ."

"Not sure that's wise," says Bankole. "There's the radiation you'll have been exposed to, plus you look like you've taken a battering. One side of your face is purple and you're not walking well."

"I wasn't that close and, anyway, I was down behind a car, right behind its engine block in fact. That's why I'm not burned and it would've stopped a lot of the radiation too. Haven't eaten or drunk anything from round here since the blast and the winds are taking the airborne stuff north. So maybe I got a few x-rays worth of radiation, but I'll live. Took a bit of a tumble in the shock wave, it's true, but nothing's broken. So, forget the hospital."

Most of this has been for his own reassurance but Diawara sticks his lower lip out, apparently impressed with Yao's knowledge. Good job cameras are pretty much point and click nowadays, Yao thinks.

"But there's going to be a bit of a walk at the end," says Bankole. "Are you up to it?"

"Walk?"

"Yes. To confuse the Evil Birds. We park the car in the city then make our way on foot. Too many people, too many little alleyways for them to follow us. About half a mile."

"I'll be fine."

He must have drifted off because the next time he wakes the sun is passed its zenith and they're on tarmaced streets.

Calling Ellana a city is shooting a little high even though it's the second biggest conurbation in Liganda. Big enough to be jammed with traffic, anyway. Showing a cavalier disregard for pedestrians, Bankole doesn't hesitate to mount pavements, nudging aside the boxes and trestle tables of makeshift stalls, leaving a trail of fist waving proprietors behind.

Turning down a side alley, barely wide enough to take the bulky machine, they emerge behind a big block-like building with no windows. A large makeshift opening has been knocked into the brick wall and Bankole drives through this, passing a couple of armed soldiers to one side, and comes to a halt. He turns off the ignition.

"OK, we're here."

Yao climbs out, joints and back protesting strongly. Straightening himself with some difficulty, he looks around. The size of the interior space gives this place away as an old abandoned cinema. Nothing else in this country is as big. Seats have been stripped out to clear a big floor space. Several SUVs are parked to one side.

"This way," says Diawara. "We'll take it slow. If you need

help, just say."

They head away from the ragged hole they'd driven through and towards what must have been a fire exit. Through this and they're into an alley so narrow the bottom may never see the sun. This takes them further from the main road and into the broader warren of a bazaar with striped awnings overhanging raggedy little shops and cafes.

It takes about half an hour and Yao has to get them to stop for five minutes to let him rest. His thigh is aching and, without looking, he knows it will be badly bruised.

Finally, the little shops give way to modest office blocks, no more than four storeys high. In a back alley behind one, the two soldiers come to a halt and Bankole bangs on an unmarked door.

The door opens and they find themselves looking down the barrel of an AK.

"Who's this," says a gruff voice.

"Special Commander Yao. Don't worry, he's one of us," Bankole says.

The muzzle withdraws and they all enter. Yao hears the door slam and lock behind them.

The corridor they're in takes them by small offices, then they're into a bigger area. Large windows on one wall have their blinds drawn. To the rear of the space is a line of high counters.

"This used to be a bank, right?" says Yao. He sees the *Schneider* logo and wonders what has happened to the German staff who ran this place.

"Yeah, there's a whole row of them here."

"Ah, I know where we are now. Cissokho Street."

"Yeah."

They're crossing the bank floor where customers once queued before the tellers. Somewhere to their left a deep voice rumbles into life.

"The deserter returns."

Justice is lounging at a desk, his arms resting on piles of

papers. He beckons to them. "Where'd you find him?"

"Becke, a mile or so South of the Cleft," says Bankole. The two men are rigidly at attention in Justice's malign force field.

"And did you beat him?" Justice sounds genuinely surprised, though not displeased.

"The blast did that," says Yao.

Justice nods. "Go away," he says to the men. "Upload your stuff! The world is waiting."

His big horse head turns to watch them go.

"Blindfold?" he asks.

"What?"

"Do you want a blindfold when we shoot you? Because that's what we do when people run away. When we catch the cowards we shoot them. I know you're not much of a soldier, but even *you* must know that."

Yao drags over a chair and sits down facing him.

"How much of this did you know was going to happen?"

"What the fuck are you talking about?"

"The nuclear bomb. The blast has barely died down and you have those guys out filming. Guys trained to shoot film. Since when did the Ligandan Army have a film unit?"

"There seems to be much the favoured son did not know. Perhaps he is not so favoured after all."

"Zinzi was in The Cleft."

Justice's head goes back just a little before he stops himself. He hasn't known.

"Stupid place to put her. Big target."

"I didn't have anywhere else to put her. My village is dust now and has been for over twenty years. Just like yours. I have no family I can send anyone to. And I didn't know we had places like this." Yao waves his arm to encompass the bank.

"So, your wife is dead?" Yao senses no sympathy; Justice is just after information.

"I got her out of the valley but the blast caught us before we could get clear. Yes, she's dead."

"So, you did know what was going to happen. Otherwise why would you have tried to get her out?"

"I didn't know, but I guessed. I saw what was in that extension at the Palace in Tembe. A mock-up of where we held the trails in The Cleft. I could only think of one reason for that. The General wanted the Americans to think that was where he was. One more provocation. Did you know they would use a nuclear device?"

Justice shrugs. "It wasn't certain. The General thought that the Americans would consider carpet bombing the place, maybe use their Daisy Cutters, but he figured the Americans wouldn't consider that emphatic enough. Plus, the Cleft is a big place. It'd take a hell of a lot of munitions to make sure they got the General.

"If you think about it, they used all that conventional stuff with Saddam Hussein and he never really did them much direct harm. He just pissed them off. With the hostages and the carrier, what we did to the Americans was far, far worse. We showed the world the American's weakness, forcing them to demonstrate their strength."

"What about Bin Laden and the Mujahaddin? They killed thousands of Americans?"

"And they might have nuked them too, in the early days at least, but they didn't really know where they were. In this case the Yanks thought they did."

"Thousands, maybe tens of thousands of our countrymen have died. Why did the General do this."

Justice shrugs again. "You know the strategy, at least I thought you did. Accelerating provocation. Except rather than us provoking the Americans, this last round has the Americans provoking the whole of Africa. Not everyone in Africa likes Olomo, but they like a nuclear attack by Americans on their continent even less."

"I want to talk to him."

"Oh, you will." Justice beckons to one of several soldiers who are standing around the bank's foyer.

The man double times over and salutes.

"Tie-wraps?" asks Justice.

"Not on me, sir, but there's a police station down the road. I could see if they have any handcuffs."

Justice nods. "That'll do nicely."

"You're kidding," says Yao.

"Oh, I know the General has a soft spot for you, and he probably won't have you shot, but I've got a good excuse to lock you up, for now at least."

He starts tapping the papers like he's doing a drum solo.

"And that's much too big a chance to pass up."

Chapter 34. *Gulf of Guinea*

It had been a long night, lying down looking up at the gently swaying stars. Plenty of time to review what she'd done: to meditate on her folly.

Too hung up on fairness and justice, or just plain suicidal? A rebel against authority or just a destroyer of order? An assassin or a closet anarchist?

Certainly, a bridge burner *par excellence.*

Whatever way you looked at it, 'fucked up' pretty much nailed it to the mast.

And then finally, to one side, the sky started to lighten and she knew at least what direction to take. Bringing the engine to life at the lowest revs, she turned the boat north. A couple of extra knots on top of the current shouldn't excite too much attention, not unless they'd already discovered Macik. If they had, then there were plenty of smart people in the navy to connect the dots.

As the stars were washed away, the horizon to the north was turning lumpy. Working up to all this, she'd got a good look at some charts, studying the coast intently then checking inland on some internet maps. Hills on the coast were small so she couldn't be far off. There were no reefs.

Looking back, it was still too dark to see the *Farragut*. She strained for the sound of rotor blades. What was left of the CSG still had one helo.

She could hear nothing but the lapping of the waves against the hull.

The light was building quickly now and ahead she could see a tree fringed shore. It couldn't be more than a mile or so now.

Looking back again, she saw something in the sky. Ramping the motor up, the front of the boat rose out of the water, and she had to stand to see over the bow.

She still couldn't see the *Farragut* but the thing was coming from that direction. It had to be the helo and it was coming fast.

She saw white water ahead now as the waves gently broke on the beach. Grabbing up her knapsack, she crouched, like she was about to start a race. As the bow ploughed into the soft sand, she pedalled her long legs, hurdling the hull then pumping up the beach. She could hear the helo coming but didn't look back. Ten yards shy of the first trees, a big shadow flitted over her but then she was amongst them and zigzagging between the palms.

Maybe they'd try and land, drop off a couple of marines. She kept running, a hard jog but not flat out, enough to soon put miles between her and the beach. The going was easy, the undergrowth sparse, though sometimes she felt thorns nipping at the bare skin of her arms.

She gave it fifteen minutes then stopped. Leaning back against a palm, she slid to the ground and closed her eyes. A faint wind was whistling through the foliage but there was no sound of pursuit, no sound of rotor blades.

The feeling started deep in her gut but blossomed quickly, lightening her. She felt the exultation before she understood why she felt it.

Total freedom. Her entire life history cast off: shed like a snake does its skin. She was up Shit Creek but she was as free as anyone ever could be.

And in darkest fucking Africa of all places. Couldn't speak the language, the only cash she had was little more than fifty dollars, doled out to the survivors by the Quarter Master for buying sundries. At least she'd hoarded food, candy bars and other snacks, plus a few bottles of water. That was all in the knapsack along with her gun.

Time to change: the camos she threw into what looked like a mass of rhododendrons. Out of the knapsack came some bluer coveralls she'd managed to find in a broken locker on the Franklin. She'd cut them off at the waist, leaving only the trousers, and had ditched the top with its Navy insignias. She'd cut holes around the waist and threaded a length of rope through them as a belt. She put the trousers on but kept on her white tee shirt.

People in this country seemed to wear any old shit. They wore, basically, what they could get their hands on. Out in the boondocks, true enough, the women seemed to wear those voluminous dresses covered in weird zigzag patterns, but for the more urban dwellers along the coast it seemed anything went.

Her boots might be a problem though. They were military grade and brand new. Getting out the knife she'd got from the RHIB's locker, she worried away at them, scoring the surface. Then she scraped them over the ground trying to ingrain blackened vegetable detritus.

Now what? She had a plan, hatched on board the *Franklin*, which looked increasingly flimsy now she was on this new continent.

Ghana had seemed her best bet, about three hundred miles to the east. At least their official language was English. She had a watch, gold ring and necklace plus the canned stuff she'd snaffled. Maybe she could trade for enough local cash to buy tickets on the little buses that made their way up and down the long coast. She'd have to use gestures to communicate. American accents wouldn't go down well here.

In Africa, borders were porous to the point of virtual non-existence, but on the big road there'd likely be some checkpoint at the border. She'd need to get off early then head out into the bush, then rejoin the road once she was in Ghana.

And once she was there...well, who knew? Maybe some little village somewhere would let her teach in return for food.

That was the trouble with freedom. You just didn't know what it would bring.

The forest was thinning so it was easy enough to navigate north by the sun. She must be four miles inland now but still she hadn't crossed even a path, never mind a road. For the first time since she was sure she wasn't being pursued, a feeling of unease nibbled at her euphoria.

She couldn't even recognise a single tree in this... was it forest or was it jungle? What was the difference?

What the fuck was she doing here?

Then, suddenly, she was out on a rutted track, the vegetation muscling in closely to it either side. She looked up and down the track as far as the jungle would let her see, but there was nothing. Turning east, she slung the knapsack over her shoulder and started off.

A cap would have been nice, something to shade her eyes, but the only ones on the ship made no secret of which navy they belonged to.

A sharp pain on her forearm, like someone had driven a nail in, made her yelp. A fly the size of a quarter was eating her. She shook it off and watched it fly away, bumble bee heavy, and leaving behind a fat globule of blood glistening in the sun.

Then she saw the snake. The flattened bits were mashed up to form tread marks but the rest was already swollen in the heat, the size and colour of an inner tube. The fucking thing must have been ten feet long.

She'd never liked snakes and had tried hard not to think about them on her run through the trees. Giving the corpse a wide berth, she scratched absently at her arm and felt skin coming off under the nail. To her surprise, she saw a patchwork of little bites across her forearm. They were already starting to swell. The touch of nail immediately made them start to itch.

Looking carefully at her other arm, she saw the underside had a whole bunch of little dots trailing along a vein. Putting down the knapsack she ran her hands up and down her arms, like she was washing them.

Was that how you got Sleeping Sickness, or Leishmaniasis or any of the other awful things you could get here?

"Calm the fuck down," she said to herself. "It can't be that bad, otherwise there'd be nobody on this damned continent."

Then again, she hadn't seen anyone yet.

Twenty minutes later, around a bend fifty yards ahead,

came a woman and a couple of little kids. They were laden down with sacks. She watched all three heads come up to look at her.

Should she greet them as they passed? Smile? Nod her head? What was the protocol? Even on a country road in the States you wouldn't ignore a passerby, not like you would in a city.

They all stopped dead in their tracks, watching her approach. As she got nearer she saw their eyes were open in amazement.

She smiled and waved. The little girl waved back. The mother hesitated then nodded.

Joey walked by and didn't look back until she was round the bend, then she slipped off the road and into the undergrowth.

What was it about her that made her stand out? She tried to think of the newscasts about Liganda that'd been playing on the news channels, or anything about Africa she could remember.

People weren't well dressed. They were too poor to pick and choose. She looked down at her clothes. The tee shirt couldn't be it; they were ubiquitous. The boots might be the giveaway but she couldn't do without them. The mother and her kids had been barefoot but she couldn't walk like that. She'd be limping within thirty feet.

Trousers maybe. Too long? Men often wore them long but when she thought about it, she couldn't remember seeing any African women wearing them.

Yeah, that'd be it. Taking the trousers off, she cut them in ragged lines a couple of inches below the crotch. Shorts; she'd definitely seen some women wearing them.

But it was still worrying. She got her gun out of the knapsack and stuck it down the waistband of the shorts at the back, where the loose tee shirt hanging down would cover it.

Another thirty minutes and still nothing but the jungle and the red dust track. She wondered at the family carrying those sacks so far. She'd expected to come across some sort of village or town pretty quickly.

And then there it was. Round one final bend and she saw the track opening out ahead. A handful of huts, conical shaped, and a couple of fires burning unattended amongst them. She saw nobody until she saw the pickup, then the two soldiers in camo gear leaning against the sides. A third one was standing in the back, leaning on the machine gun mounted on the flat bed.

And they'd seen her. Now was the real test.

They didn't move as she approached, though their eyes were all taking her in closely, making her feel like a model under scrutiny on a catwalk. She glanced at them once then looked lazily around. Not another soul was to be seen, just a couple of dogs rooting at something by one of the huts.

Another glance at them. One soldier had an AK 47 over the crook of his arm like a shotgun. The other had a holster and she saw the butt of an automatic pistol protruding. The guy in the flat bed didn't seem to have anything but the big gun.

The AK guy would be the one to go for first, if it all went to shit. He was thickset, meaty. He was grinning at her, a gold tooth glinting in the sun.

The truck was to the side of the road just where it spread out into the clearing. If she kept walking, she'd pass them by five metres.

The guy with the AK beckoned to her but she smiled, waved a hand dismissively and kept on walking. She saw the two of them push themselves off the side of the truck and walk in front of her.

Stopping, she put her hands on her hips and looked at them sternly. The guy with the pistol raised his hands. What he said was incomprehensible but was clearly a question.

She turned to look at him. Out of the corner of her arm she saw the AK start to swing. Too fast for her to do anything, the butt smashed into her jaw, twisting her whole body round and sending her crashing down into the dust.

Chapter 35. *Ellana*

"Yao, my son. What were you thinking of?"

Yao rouses himself and looks out at the endless rows of little boxes and gleaming steel. A tall, bald man is looking through the bars at him. He is dressed in light cotton shorts and a stained green tee shirt with a shoulder holster under one arm. Justice is smirking at his side. He realises with a start that the man is Olomo, but he's bald now, the dome of his head looking too big for the slenderness of his face. He looks like a new species of man. He seems tired but his eyes burn.

Rising slowly to his feet, Yao brushes at the new uniform they've given him, though the bank vault is about the only place in Ellana that is clean. Straightening himself up, he steps to the bars so they are barely two feet apart. The General's clothes look like they had been slept in and Yao guesses he's been travelling around, making himself less of a target in case the Americans realise he is still alive.

"Desertion is a very serious charge. We have executed men for less."

Yao stands at attention but says nothing.

"Can you explain your actions?"

Yao's mind is reeling. Confusion hides within confusion.

"Zinzi," he finally says.

"What about her?"

"She was at The Cleft. I took her there after her village was bombed."

"Is she...?"

"Dead. She burned like a candle before she died."

Olomo's eyes widen. "I am very sorry to hear that, but it does not explain your desertion."

"I saw the mock-up of your Cleft HQ, at the Palace, in the annex."

Olomo begins to nod a little. "I did not know she was there. I would have warned you."

Yao says nothing. There were many others at The Cleft. Olomo had made no attempt to warn them. Just more bait for the Americans.

The silence stretches.

"Let him go," says Olomo finally.

Justice's brow creases in irritation but he doesn't look surprised. "This sets a bad example."

"Which is known only to us. His men think he was just called away. Yao has been of great service. We could not have done what we did without him. And he has suffered. I will give him this one chance."

Justice shakes his head but brings out a key and unlocks the door.

"Come, my son," says Olomo and turns back for the stairs up to the ground floor. Yao follows sheep-like, not sure what else to do. "We will take you to my doctor. He will dress your wounds. He is in the bank next door seeing to a prisoner, an American spy."

All the soldiers click to attention as Olomo steps out onto the tellers' floor. A little metal fence, barely up to his hips, had been wedged open so he strides through and towards the exit at the back of the building. Just before they enter the gloom of the alley, shielded from the sun by the bank on one side and a tall fence on the other, Olomo fishes a baseball cap out of his back pocket and puts it on his head.

The vault had been cool so the heat and humidity are a hidden force that assaults Yao and he wonders yet again if the rains will ever come. Barely twenty metres down the alleyway, they stop at the unmarked back door of another big building. Justice raps on this and a hatch slides open, then another guard is quickly fumbling at the lock.

And again, they are in a bank with an almost identical layout, though here the colour scheme is softened by a hint of yellow. He sees the *Bank D'Agricole* logo. The French are always

375

just that little bit less clinical than the Germans.

Down into the vaults, they come to another room full of security boxes. More barred doors form little cells, so you can see any prisoner inside easily enough.

One door is open and all he can see is the back of a man bending down over a chair.

"Doctor," says Olomo. "I have some more..."

The doctor stands up and steps to the side, revealing a woman on the chair.

"It's her," Yao blurts.

The tall, lean woman is tightly strapped to the chair, tie wraps securing her arms to the chair arms, her legs to its legs. She is naked and he can see the lips of her sex through a thicket of black hair.

"What?" says Olomo, irritated at the interruption.

"The woman in Norfolk. In America. The one who nearly caught me. The government agent of some sort." She's looking at him venomously.

"That's intriguing," says Olomo.

"Why is she naked?" Yao finds himself asking.

Justice nods his head up. "Couldn't risk her having a tracker on her clothes. My men stripped her and checked her cavities carefully. She's clean."

"And they beat her?"

"She had a gun. They hit her just once. Why do you care? As I remember, she shot at you. Tried to kill you."

"Even so, women should not be mistreated. Not when they are helpless."

"That's the best time," says Justice and snorts.

Olomo holds up a hand. "Enough of this! We need to talk to her. *I* want to talk to her, but I have not slept for days. Doctor, see to this man!" He points to Yao then checks his watch. "Yao, be back here at 11pm. We will begin the interrogation."

"And what about me?" asks Justice.

Olomo claps a hand on his shoulder. "My son. You must

continue to keep us all safe."

But Yao does not sleep, or for no more than a few minutes at a time. Soul freezing images snap him back to consciousness and eventually he finds himself fighting sleep like a man fights his own death.

Lights are off in the ground and upper floors of the bank lest they attract the attention of the Americans. He hears someone coming in from the back entrance and he sees a torch beam lancing across the room, illuminating chairs and desks and other obstacles.

"Yao my son!" Olomo's voice is soft, as though not wanting to wake the soldiers sleeping on the floor.

Yao's mind is dull, zombie-like. He rolls off his mattress and feels for the gun belt reluctantly returned by Justice. Getting to his feet, he secures it round his waist then makes his way towards the door down to the vaults, catching up with Olomo as he gets to it.

Olomo lets him through first then closes the heavy door behind him. The stairway curves down and round but the windowless vault below is lit and enough light reflects from the walls to show the steps clearly.

As they get to the bottom, Olomo flicks his finger at the little makeshift cell and the sergeant waiting there opens it and steps back.

"You can go, Sergeant," says Olomo. "Leave me the keys!"

The man salutes and is gone. Yao hears the door at the top of the stairs open and close.

Olomo walks into the cell, hands behind his back. He starts to circle the woman, still bound in her chair.

"This," he says, "is a travesty of a black woman."

The woman is sneering up at him, a picture of defiance, but he sees the creases in her forehead and the way she sits so immobile in the chair. She must have been bound like this for many hours and, even though the chair is padded, there will be

377

pressure sores and she must be in agony. Looking round, he can see no signs of food or drink. Her lips are chapped and the bruised side of her face is even more swollen now. He sees traces of white around the purple bruise and he guesses it is the remains of some ointment the doctor has administered.

"She is neither one thing nor the other. Neither black nor white. Mistreated in her own country, she is still the lap dog of the Americans: the white Americans."

"Condoleesa Rice, Colin Powell, white people like that" says the woman. "Oh, yeah, and who was that other guy...Barack Obama? Those'll be the white people you're talking about."

"As good as white," says Olomo, still circling.

"Black," she says. "They're all black."

"Really? And how much did they do for other black people, either in Africa or even back in America."

"So that's your criteria for blackness. Not the colour of their skin but what they do for Africans."

Olomo's hand slaps her hard across the bruised side of her face. Yao sees her try not to flinch; probably more pained by any movement of the sores on her arms and bottom and legs than by the blow itself. His scrotum tightens at the thought of her agony.

"I will not be lectured to on doing good for Africans by someone whose nation just dropped an atomic bomb on my countrymen."

"Don't be so modest! The nuke is as much down to you as anybody. Credit where credit's due."

Olomo's clawed hand grabs one of her small breasts, twisting hard. She yelps with surprise and her body jerks then she howls with the pain from raw skin moving against the chair.

"You sick fuck," she says through gritted teeth, her face a mask of misery.

"Let me tell you what offends me the most about you. It's your arrogance. Because your skin is black you think you can just melt into this country. That you can walk amongst us, confident in your disguise, sure you will never be detected as the spy you are."

"I'm no spy."

Olomo snorts in derision. "You thought you could pass amongst us. You thought you were an African. But you have *never* been an African. I doubt there has been an African in your family for generations. It doesn't matter what skin colour you might have: in your heart you're white."

He looks back at Yao. "They found her walking along the road fifty miles west of Tembe. What would you think if you saw her? What could you instantly tell?"

Yao just wants to go away, to have more time to think, but he still cannot refuse the General. He looks at the woman who is regarding him with pure hatred.

"You could never pass as an African. Your walk, your hair, your whole attitude is the product of a different culture. And your body: too tall, too lean, too well muscled. Your ancestors came from far north; they were Nubian I would guess. Not West Africa. There is no one like you here."

"I wasn't spying. I was here because I had no choice. There was nowhere else for me to go."

"And why is that?" asks Olomo.

The woman goes quiet, apparently lost in thought. Yao gets the impression there's something she could say but can't work out if she should.

Olomo slaps her again on the bruise.

"Fuck off," she says through gritted teeth.

Olomo stands back a little, regarding her.

"I could give you to my men," he says. "Would you like that?"

She looks up at him. "Sexual threat? Is this the way of the Black Messiah II? Black or white, is that what Jesus would do? Rape women?"

"I am not the Black Messiah, I or II."

"Really? I mean I'm surprised. Here you are resurrected before me. Risen from the nuclear fire. What else could you be?"

He punches her hard in her flat stomach and the chair tips

over and crashes to the floor.

"Get her up!" says Olomo.

She may be skinny but she's tall and he guesses she weighs as much as he. He manhandles the chair upright then looks closely at where her leg is strapped to the chair leg. The chair is indenting hard into her muscle, secured tightly at points just above and below the calf. Like a penumbral shadow, even the skin just clear of the bindings is inflamed and there's a smear of blood on the chair leg. The thought of putting a bullet through her brain to end her agony flashes through his mind.

Olomo is bending down in front of her. "What's your name?"

No response.

"Who do you work for?"

Still the woman gives him the baleful look.

Yao shifts a little. "I know you're a government agent. You were in that bar in Norfolk."

"Oh, I know you, you nasty little shit. Shame I missed."

"So, are you CIA, NCIS maybe?"

She shakes her head then looks back at Olomo.

"You murdered your own family."

"Your country murdered my family. Their blood is on your hands."

"Not so easy. You led us to believe you were with them, or at least in a building near them. You wanted us to kill them. Same with the Cleft, I'm betting."

"That's nonsense."

"Wife and children. Pawns for your own mad ends. Africa will never unite. All this death has been for nothing."

Olomo doesn't seem to feel it necessary to debate this with her.

"Are you here to kill me?" he asks.

"No but, believe me, I would if I could!"

"Then why are you here?"

Again, Yao sees indecision in her face. There's definitely

something she's not sure she should say.

"There are men in my army, men whose souls have been crushed by the oppression of others. Men who follow without question. I will fetch them and they will cut you. Bit by bit, they will cut you until blood loss or shock will carry you away to your white Heaven. Spare yourself this!"

She tries to spit in his face but only a few pathetic droplets emerge from her cracked lips and weakly spatter down onto her breasts and legs.

Standing in front of her and getting a good swing, he slaps her again. Her chair rocks back. Yao sees her feet spread as they push hard on the ground, tilting the chair even further back.

Then it rocks forward and he sees her feet flatten again, then push hard, impelling the chair towards Olomo. He tries to yell a warning but it's already too late. Helpless, he watches as her mouth opens and her neck arches back.

Strong white teeth snap shut on Olomo's groin. Eyes wide, he staggers back but her bite holds and she's dragged along with him. Batting at her head, his face wracked with pain, his legs give way and he goes down.

With the fronts of her legs now against the ground, she has real leverage. Her head wrenches back and forth, worrying at his groin like a terrier at the guts of a cat.

Then, with the sound of cloth tearing, she flicks her head to the side and spits out a gobbet of blood and tissue.

Olomo's mouth is slack with shock but he's scrabbling at his holster.

Yao doesn't know how the muzzle of his gun gets into Olomo's gaping mouth, but he feels himself pull the trigger.

In wonder, he watches a fan of blood and brain tissue slap onto the floor.

He looks down Olomo's body and at the woman's head resting against its groin. She's staring up at him, her teeth still bared, blood plastered down her chin.

Feral.

Yao listens intently. The gunshot was muffled but still sounded like the crack of doom. It's a big vault and quite deep. The door at the top of the stair is heavy and closed.

But it's night and all should be quiet.

"What...?"

"Shut up!" he whispers.

The woman is breathing heavily, and a couple of sibilant rattles came from Olomo's dying body, but otherwise there is no sound.

Holstering his gun, he tips her chair to the side so she's no longer taking her weight on her knees. He digs out the pocket knife he always carries and she gasps.

"I'm not going to hurt you," he says. The tie wraps are resilient, and he has to saw away at them, but finally her legs are free. Before he does the same for her arms, he looks her in the eye. "I'm trying to help you. You do understand that, don't you?"

"Yeah," she says, "I've got that. I just don't understand why."

"Neither do I," he says.

Finally, her arms freed, she rolls clear of the chair, twisting them round so she can see their backs. They're terribly inflamed and must hurt like hell.

"I've got to get you out of here." He looks at her nakedness. "Did they bring you in like that?"

"No. After they stripped me and searched me they put me in a wrap-like thing before they drove me here. Then when we got here, your singed friend with the nasty scar took it off again. I think he tossed it somewhere over there."

Yao rises to leave the cell but then stops. Bending back down he fishes Olomo's Glock out its holster and sticks it in the belt of his pants. The woman gives him a sardonic look.

"Hey, African," she says, "What Olomo said was true. About me sticking out like a sore thumb. You're my only hope. I get it!"

The vault is big but there's really nowhere to hide Olomo's

body. He finds the balled-up wrap in a corner by some filing cabinets and brings it back to her. He watches her struggle with it, then irritably snatches it from her and winds it around her, ignoring her winces. He isn't expert, but it's a good enough job.

Bending down, he feels through Olomo's pockets and finds a wallet and quite a bit of currency. Pocketing this, he finds Olomo's little torch clipped to the side of his holster. Taking this, he stands and faces her.

"We'll go upstairs. You'll be my prisoner. Limp a little, look like you're in pain."

"I think I can do that."

"Do exactly what I say." He draws his gun and sticks the muzzle into her back. "Move, but not too fast, remember!"

They get to the top of the stairs and he opens the door. He whispers: "Forward through the little gate then diagonally across to the right-hand side corner. That's where the exit is."

He clicks the torch on and they set off. Glancing round, he sees men sleeping on camp beds or on the floor.

But there's a sentry at the end of the little corridor leading to the exit. He sees them approaching and clicks his own torch on.

"I'm taking her to the bank next door," Yao says. "Open!"

The man seems to recognise him. He just nods and does as he's told.

"Left," says Yao as the door closes behind them.

"Do you know what you're doing?"

"At the end of the alley, go right."

They edge their way through the boxes and bottles that litter the alleyways. Some light filters in from roads at the other end of side alleys, helping some.

"Jesus, I think I just stepped in some shit."

"Welcome to Africa."

"Just so you know: I can run some but not on bare feet. Not on anything but sand."

He remembers her long, limber strides back in States. "I've seen you run," he says. "You're fast."

There are some lights on in the old cinema. Three identical black SUVs are lined up. They find a soldier sleeping at a desk, some keys spread out before him.

"Sergeant!"

The man comes to, blinking. "I need a car, for Tembe!"

"Yes, sir," says the man, grabbing the first key then apparently thinking better of it. Yao tenses but then the man chooses another. "This one's nearly got a full tank: the one in the middle."

Yao prods her towards the car and opens the passenger door for her. Holstering his gun, he gets into the driver's side and starts the engine.

It's tricky manoeuvering the big brute through the narrow alley but eventually he's able to turn right onto one of the few paved roads of the city.

"Where are we going?" she asks, shifting uncomfortably on the hard leather.

"I don't know. North and East. Ghana, maybe. Somewhere with an American Embassy or consulate at least."

"No thanks."

He glances across at her and she turns to look at him.

"Confession time," she says.

A row of several little shops still has lights on and he pulls over. "Stay here!" he says and takes the key out of the ignition. The sleepy owner sits upright when he enters. He scoops up water, dried meat and the sickly candies all Ligandan's so relish. Finally, he chooses some antiseptic cream and a Lancôme skin lotion knock-off. The name isn't even spelled right. He takes this all to the wooden plank that's a counter and uses Olomo's money.

Tossing his purchases on the middle row of the SUV, he gets back in and they're off again.

"Why did you kill him, the Admiral?"

"Maybe I'm blacker than you think I am."

They drive in silence. Tarmac peters out and the bare

bulbs over some of the shacks become less frequent.

"Ditch me!" she says finally.

"What do you mean?"

"Ditch me. Dump me. I'm a fish out of water. Can't speak the language. Can only draw attention to myself. I'll drag you down. You've a better chance on your own."

"No." Already ruts are showing and he slows down to reduce the vibration. Every bounce makes her wince.

"How come?"

"Means and ends," he says. "I've spent too much time and effort justifying both. And it's all ended in evil. A terrible evil. I must make amends. Why not start with you? You're all I have."

"All you have?" she says disbelievingly.

"All my country, all the people I know, will now think me their enemy. I must flee so I cannot help them. You, I can do something for."

"Don't you have family? What about your wife...what's her name...Zinzi."

"All dead."

He hears her swallow.

"There is some cream in the back, for your skin."

Now there is only darkness except for the light from the dashboard. She retrieves the cream and starts slathering it on her skin.

"So, what is the plan?" she asks.

"Like I say: I think Ghana is our best bet. The official language is English, so we will both be able to communicate. I will help you try to fit in, try to make an African woman of you."

"But we can't use anything that can identify us. Even if we get out of Liganda, the CIA is after both of us and, believe me, they'll be looking real hard."

"Again, you haven't grasped the nature of this continent. A tiny fraction of one percent of people have a passport. There is hardly any social security so there are no identity cards. Borders stretch for hundreds of miles and leak like a sieve. We stay away from cities; change our appearance as best we can. We are educated, we can teach. Perhaps we will be able to build up new identities. Maybe you will be able to leave Africa."

"That's never going to happen, not for travel to the developed world anyway. Facial recognition software is too good now."

"Perhaps not. Anyway, I have an idea for that we can talk about later."

Keeping a low profile for a lifetime would be a tall order, but already he is starting to dream.

"And what about whoever takes over from Olomo? What do we have to fear from them?"

He shrugs. "Justice, the horse faced man with the scar you talked of, has a special place in Olomo's command structure, as indeed did I once. But there are generals in the army who resent both of us. They will not accept his orders easily. Justice will be busy with his own problems for a while to come, even if the Americans let him live."

"But what about right now? Can they catch us?"

"Our own military communications were the first things the Evil Birds...your drones...took out. They took out quite a bit of the mobile network too when they hit the central relay points. Our pursuers could try contacting some of the units stationed around the country, if the landlines still work, but I'll be avoiding the population centres. There are no planes or helicopters to search for us."

"What about satellite tracking?" She's looking around the interior. "This is pretty new. It may have a tag."

"Believe me, there is no tag. Olomo was paranoid about that. He knew that's how you would have tracked him."

She turns to look at him. "I don't think you should use the word 'you' like that anymore."

He nods.

Chapter 36. *The Bush*

The burning wood casts flickering light over grass shrivelled by months of unrelenting sun. The fire is a pinprick of light in the black bubble of a moonless night. Far off, something howls in rage.

Yao sits facing her. Both are kneeling. His knife is heating in the flame.

"I'll do this quickly," he says.

She takes a deep breath. "There'll be blood so I'd better..." Reaching down she pulls off her tee shirt and tosses it aside. Then she shimmies out of her cut-off pants.

"Shall I start?"

"Yeah."

Dabbing some rotgut whisky onto a clean piece of cloth, he wipes it over her cheek. Concentrating on this, he nevertheless feels her eyes on him. He touches the knife to the skin an inch below her eye and she gives an involuntary start.

"Sorry," she says. He takes another deep breath.

The knife point touches her flesh, indenting it a little before the skin breaks. He draws it down a thumb length towards her mouth. She's breathing quickly and tears have formed in the corners of her eyes.

"Did that hurt?"

"Keep going."

The next cut, a fraction below the first, is angled into it to make a shallow 'v'. A sliver of flesh rumples up but doesn't fall free. Gently pricking both ends of the sliver, it comes away and he flicks it into the dark. The cut forms a runnel and beads of blood drip down from the lower end and onto her left breast. He watches one bead slide down the top until it gets to the nipple, where it hangs like a dewdrop.

He blows out a breath held for a long time and looks back

into her eyes. They're glazed with pain.

"Keep going," she says.

Two more slashes, half inch between them on this cheek, then three more on the other. He doesn't use a straight edge to guide him as it isn't the custom. Perfection is not what he is looking for.

Gently wetting a cloth with more alcohol, he dabs it on the wounds and, this time, she gives sharp little moans with the pain. Her eyes are closed and her breasts rise and fall with her rapid breathing.

"We'll give it a minute or two then I'll pack your wounds with clay. As you heal, the clay will be pushed out, making the scars prouder, more conspicuous. I have heated the clay, made it sterile," and he nods towards a tin can resting on a rock, one side licked by flames from the fire. "I will rehydrate it with the bottled water so it will be free from germs."

The intensity of her gaze is unsettling and again he has forgotten how to breathe.

She leans back, her hands supporting her arched back. "Clean me!" she says.

The blood makes her hard nipple taste coppery. Carefully he licks every trace from her breasts.

She lies fully back now and brings her knees up. Leaning over her, he starts at her neck then runs his tongue down over her honed, washboard stomach then cleans small splashes of blood that have dropped to her thighs. Then his tongue moves up into the valley between them.

When water is scarce, and the natural oils of the skin aren't antiseptically washed away, they accumulate and give people a smell, an aroma authentic to them.

He notes with exultation that she's already tasting like an African woman: a taste that is deep and rich and ancient.

When it comes to lovemaking, she's as fierce as he. At first, she's open to him, but when her blood starts to burn, she rolls over and is on top of him, tearing at his clothes, taking his manhood urgently in her mouth, consuming him.

And it becomes a fight. He's strong, but her leanness gave her a wiry strength. They roll over and over, each trying to find purchase for their thrusting loins.

A violent roll bumps them against the rock and it nearly topples the can into the fire.

She laughs and put a hand flat on his chest. "Relax! Let me take the lead first."

As she rides him, he feels blood from her wounds drip down on him. He hasn't tried to kiss her, fearing it would be too sore for her, but she leans in and their tongues find each other. Again, it's a fight, but with softer weapons that will not leave a bruise.

She's frantic now and he's pushing up as best he can. Angrily she's rubbing back and forth across his groin and her fingers dig deep into his shoulders.

When at last she's finished, he rolls on top and takes her in his turn.

Afterwards, side by side, they look up at a sky whose stars have been washed out by their little fire.

"You make love like a man," he says.

"You've fucked a man before?"

"No, of course not. But you make love the way I do. The way other men say they make love."

"We can sort something out. You can take the lead next time," but then she hesitates. "There is going to be a next time, isn't there?"

This first sign of vulnerability tugs at his heart. "Yes, please," he says.

She smiles and lies back.

"The clay," he says.

He dabs again with the alcohol then, with the flat of his blade, he presses the newly sterilised clay into the wounds. The clay is red and makes it look like congealed blood.

She's leaning back looking up at the sky. "How long has this got to stay in?"

"You shouldn't talk," he says. "The movement of your skin may dislodge it. I have bandages here and we'll put them on overnight. They'll keep the clay in place until the inflamed skin closes over it enough to hold it in place. Over the next week or so it will be pushed out from within. After we've taken the bandages off, the wound must be open at all times."

After the bandages are applied, he looks her over. "You did a good job with the eyebrows," he says. He guesses she may not have done much to trim them in the past, but now she's plucked away at them determinedly with tweezers, reshaping them, converting a gently curving tear drop shape into a shallow inverted 'v'.

At a stop in a little village a few miles inside the Ghanaian border, he'd got a woman to cut her hair. With rusty scissors, she'd massacred a hundred-dollar hair style into something more authentically ragged.

Henna, and a gooey hair substance that is more like a fixative, complete the effect.

And all her clothes are second hand now.

"Look at me and practice the eyes," he says.

Her immediate reaction is the piercing gaze that is still such a problem. He watches her struggle to kill the life in her eyes, to make them look stunned and dulled by years of hardship under the tropical sun.

He shakes his head. The tribal scarring was much easier than this.

"Perhaps if you focus on a point a little behind my head, then it wouldn't look like I was being probed by a searchlight."

Her eyes narrow in annoyance then they defocus, but it still isn't quite what he's after.

"You need to look blank, incurious. And your actions as well. The way you walk, the way you do things. You need to be slower, less...calibrated. You're like a machine sometimes.

"And try and keep the annoyance out of yours eyes," he adds quickly, afraid she will hit him.

"I've had enough for now," she says and he lies down beside her and they look up at the sky.

"Tell me what you did. For Olomo." She's trying not to move her lips too much and it sounds odd and strained. "Take my mind off this shit you've ground into my face. It's stinging like fuck, by the way."

"Good. It means your body is already rejecting it." He turns on his side and puts his head in his palm and looks at her. Despite the danger, she looks less severe, less stressed than he has ever seen her.

"Olomo raised me. The last regime was a hangover from British colonial times. The British used a divide-and-conquer approach throughout their empire, favouring one ethnic group or tribe over another. It's how those brutal old imperialists got away with it so long. Once they left, then the time was ripe for ethnic cleansing. That's what happened to my people. But the cleansing didn't happen almost overnight, like it did in Rwanda. It wasn't fast enough so it would be noticed and excite the attention of the world. A rolling program, out in the bush, with no one to see. My village was burned, my family killed. Olomo scooped me from the ashes of my past life and raised me like his own son. Educated me here in Africa, in Germany and..."

"Edinburgh."

"Yes. I was trained to deal with businessmen in the west. Trained to understand how the arms trade worked, introduced to all our contacts by what was left of the old military after Olomo took over. A few were spared but the other senior soldiers were punished for what they did."

"Suspended sentences? Open prisons?" she asks wryly.

He smiles weakly. "There was a degree of suspension in some cases, yes. But, anyway, I was groomed to buy what we needed when we went to war with the Americans. And, yes, even then it all seemed so bizarre, so ambitious. After what the

391

Americans did in Afghanistan and Iraq; the way they toppled regimes that seemed invulnerable. 'Shock and Awe' seemed to work, at least at first.

"So, anyway, I thought Olomo was crazy at first, but then he gave me a history lesson."

He turns onto his back. The fire is going out and he can see some hazy stars. "Throughout the ages some armies, some militaries, have looked invincible. The earth always seems to be theirs. Then suddenly, unexpectedly, they're defeated. Ancient orders are overturned overnight. Sometimes it's a new technology possessed by their opponents that does it. Like when tanks were introduced to traditional battlefields. Infantry based armies didn't stand a chance.

"And this isn't just a modern phenomenon. Archers mowed down infantry, guns mowed down archers. Horse cavalry and chariots were the big thing thousands of years ago and swept all before them.

"But there's another factor. It's not always new technology that makes the difference. In the ancient world, cavalry and chariots became vulnerable when the infantry started to use long sharpened sticks to bring down the horses. Once the horses were gone, the charioteers and the horsemen were cut down easily because there weren't many of them. All the expense had gone into horses and chariots and not into increasing the numbers of boots on the ground.

"And that was the American's weakness that Olomo, in his genius, understood. Instead of chariots, the Americans had carriers strike groups costing so many billions of dollars each. That meant that even they couldn't afford lots of them. Their love of technology made them invest more and more money into fewer and fewer military units such as ships and planes. And that made them vulnerable." He thinks of the absurd powered suits taken out by pepper spray, and the hawks bringing down the little flying robots and the dogs catching the crawling things. "But it isn't just a lack of numbers. The fetish of technology breeds a blindness to the simple defences that can be mounted against them."

He takes a deep breath. "You asked me what I did specifically. This is a poor country and the money we had for our military was in millions, not billions. We had to direct our funds wisely, to leverage it, as you would say. Those boats that attacked the Strike Group and the high explosives in their bows, for example. I got them in little deals struck all over the world. Explosives from the Chinese. Some of the boats from them too but also South America and India. Not too many purchases at one time. Nothing to alert your intelligence services."

"Your?"

"Sorry, I keep forgetting."

"The nuclear attack. Did you know that was coming?"

"No, I would not have..." He stops. He still cannot talk about her, not yet.

He shakes his head as though this will rid him of her memory. Not remembering is the only defence he has. "According to Justice, Olomo did think the Americans would go nuclear, or at least considered it a reasonable possibility."

"OK, but even without the nuclear strike, what did you think would happen next? What was his vision?"

"Africa would unite and cast out all the foreigners, including the Chinese. Their gifts are like the Trojan Horse. Olomo would show the imperialists could be beaten, that they were nothing to be afraid of. He would draw them into escalating violence on both sides.

"But, of course, I was being naive. He was like a father to me and I had been under his spell. It would need something else to bring the disparate and often warring countries of sub-Saharan Africa together, and the nuclear bombing of African soil might do just that. Olomo may have been crazy, but I think he knew exactly what would happen. And, who knows, it may even precipitate the end of the United States."

"Perhaps. Things must be crazy back there. Half of them waving their fists in righteous fury, half appalled by what their own country has done."

"At the very least America will be a pariah state." This is only his guess as they haven't seen any papers or TV in their slow back roads progress across the West African bush. "The only certainty is that whatever's happening out there, neither of us can go back."

"How much of Olomo's money do you have left?"

"Hardly any, but I have an idea how we might get some more. It'll be risky."

"How did I guess?"

"We'll talk about that more when your scars have healed and you learn to stop looking at people like a cat at a mouse."

She slaps him on the chest back handed, but then she burrows into his side.

She's sniffing at his armpit.

"What are you doing?"

She doesn't look up. "It's your smell. When I first picked it up, in that hotel room in the States, it alarmed me. It was alien. It hinted at things...at a life...that I didn't understand. A life that, at some stage, my ancestors had lost."

"And now?"

"It's not alarming, but it's still overwhelmingly...sexual." She kisses his chest.

Gently he puts his arm on her raised shoulder and, pushing her back down, he rolls on top of her. He eases his legs between hers.

"You must stay still," he says. "Doctor's orders."

Chapter 37. *Kumasi, Ghana*

She has her back against the stairway wall and looks out onto the madness and mayhem of the city streets. And here, where a number of busy roads meet around a big central square, it is Africa to the power of two. Crowded, noisy, chaotic.

Countless little tables, stacked high with fruit and items she doesn't even recognise, make the sidewalks treacherous, forcing everyone to step out into the traffic to get by.

Not that the traffic is moving quickly, as the multitude of blaring horns testify.

The stairs she's sitting on give access to an apartment building and she has to keep shifting back and forth to let people in and out. Next to her, on one side, a substantial woman is selling what she suspects is cow dung, pressed into disks and piled up into an impressive pyramid. The woman is much favoured with customers though, without exception, they are scandalised by her prices. Each transaction is a tiny war.

Joey tries not to look as the customers touch the stuff without gloves or bags or paper. Back home, people would handle it like it was plutonium.

On the other side, a larger table holds a tray of guts with a pig's head as a centrepiece.

At least it keeps the flies off her.

And all the time she's trying not to look too closely at anything, trying to do what he's taught her. Look into the middle distance, appear unconcerned, incurious. A tired woman in a dishdash with faded crimson stripes, resting for a while with a pile of clothes beside her in the cut-off bottom of a white plastic drum.

To her right, on an adjacent side of the square, the modern facade of the Pan African Bank rises out of the chaos.

A big yellow minibus pulls up in front of her, blocking her

view. She tries to keep the worry from her eyes, and starts to slowly shift her position, but then it moves off.

It's getting late here in Kumasi, one of the larger cities in Ghana, and the street life will go on until late in the night. The banks, however, follow European hours. This branch of PAB is due to close in fifteen minutes so Yao will have to be out by then.

And if he isn't, what the hell will she do?

She slips her hand through the slit in the side of her dishdash, as though to scratch unhurriedly at her side, but really to feel the hard butt of Olomo's absurd pearl handled Glock.

She sighs heavily, then stands and puts a hand on a thrust-out hip. She glances idly round, her gaze sweeping the square, looking for any signs of them. It's like looking for a bee in a hive where every single bee looks different. Sensory overload. Already sick with tension, she has to close her eyes for a second as dizziness washes over her.

He'd had to give notice. You can't just walk into any branch of PAB and ask for the equivalent of nearly three hundred thousand dollars. The last of Yao's money float for his international purchases for Olomo, it must be like a flashing light in a poor country like this. It's been a month since the loss of the *Sands,* and the CIA will have been busy checking back to find exactly how the boats and explosives were purchased.

Yao says he used a string of accounts in different names and this one hadn't been accessed at all. Olomo had a wild idea of sending scores of men in wingpacks, the gliding ones with micro turbo jets motors, swooping down on the carrier, again in the hopes of large numbers overwhelming the defences.

The account had been set up to buy one, to try it out, but then Olomo had gone cold on the idea. Flying the damned things took a lot of specialist training in Germany and that would have excited way too much attention.

So, the money was still there, waiting. Would the CIA have tracked it? Would what was left of Olomo's people be after it too? Yao thinks Olomo kept things compartmentalised and this account was a secret between him and Yao, but he doesn't know this for certain. Justice, it turned out, had been privy to many more secrets than him.

She curses her weakness, curses her western fussiness. He could live without money; he's done it before. He's used to hardships she couldn't even imagine.

But she's not. He's getting the money for her so she can live something like a comfortable life.

She knows that looking after her is his way of atoning for what he's done, but it's not enough for him. Sometimes watching him thrashing about in his sleep, she thinks his dreams must be as bad as hers.

And as for the whole business of Zinzi...he just clams up. He's shut the lid, locked it down. It's how he's coping but she knows people can only do that for so long. Then they burst.

To her left, she catches some movement higher up and sees a man climb precariously onto a wobbly trestle table in the paved central area. Holding a book aloft, he begins to harangue the crowd but his words are lost in the horns and the rumbling of the traffic and the chatter. Uncaring crowds eddy around him.

'You get them everywhere,' she thinks.

Then she sees him. Tall and thin, elongated face turned at an angle. Without thinking, she reaches in and touches her gun.

And then her heart sinks as she sees another man: a big American, ten metres to the right of Justice. Black, as any operative would be for this job, his sharp eyes give him away. A wolf among sheep, his eyes flick here and there, drinking in every detail.

She scans the roof tops but the buildings, remnants of colonial times, are all well pitched, their roof lines unbroken. But there are upper windows all around the square and many are open, their interiors hidden in shadow. Would they sanction snipers to shoot into this crowd?

After what had happened to the *Sands*, why not?

She looks back at Justice. Stock still, he's about five metres from the bank, near the corner it makes with the road beyond. Is he waiting for reinforcements or are they already here?

Back to the American, and he's leaning against a doorway now but still looking out into the square. Jeans and shirt: too new, too clean. Pathetically obvious.

Like Justice, he'll have back up.

If there'd only been one bunch of them she might have had a chance. She could have opened up as Yao came out of the bank, become their focus, taking their bullets, giving him the chance to escape.

Too bad, but she still has to give it a try. Anyway, her choice of target is clear, she'd much rather kill Justice than any CIA people. She remembers his rough, groping hands as he'd ripped the burka like garment from her, touching her as he bound her naked to the chair. Killing him will give her one last pleasure.

Easing off the wall, she gives a desultory tug to straighten her dishdash, then begins a slow meandering walk, glancing at the tables, slowing drifting around the square towards Justice, coming up behind him.

Looking ahead, she sees the American's gaze still scanning around. For a second it seems to alight on her and there's the glimmer of automatic appreciation she's used to, but then his head kicks back slightly like he's seen something disgusting and his eyes flick quickly away.

The three parallel scars on each of her cheeks have healed a touch paler than her skin and she knows they look like the gills of a shark. They've revolted him.

That's not something she'd have expected a professional to show.

She slows, suddenly in doubt. Then the man gives a big smile and pushes himself away from the door he's been leaning against. He thrusts a hand out and another man appears out of the crowd and grasps it. Both start laughing and clapping each other on the shoulders. Then they turn and shuffle through the crowds, around the corner and out of her sight.

She hardly dares hope but it all looked so natural. Maybe,

just maybe, all she has to deal with is Justice and whoever he's brought with him.

But then maybe they'd already been in the bank waiting. Maybe Yao is already in handcuffs or even dead.

Justice is standing, hands on hips and she's less than five metres behind him now. People wander in and out between them, spoiling her line of fire, so she moves closer. He hasn't seen her and is still intent on the bank door where it gives out onto the street corner. She reaches in and pulls the gun free of the band of her shorts, but still keeping it hidden by the dishdash. The gun is already cocked so she's ready.

When... if... Yao comes out, she'll fire into Justice's back. Maybe it'll distract the others, make them turn their fire on her. Yao will have a chance and she knows he can run fast.

She still can't see the others. Olomo's secret policemen are heavy handed thugs, Yao has assured her. They should be easy to spot even in this garish fucking zoo.

A flash as the pane of glass in the opening door catches the fading light. It's Yao, bag in his hand, coming out. Something small comes with him and streaks by Yao's legs as Justice goes into a crouch.

She's tugging the gun out, elbowing a dumpy woman out of the way and sighting it on Justice's bent back, her finger tightening on the trigger.

The small thing cannons into Justice and he snaps upright and suddenly there is a child in his arms. He spins round, the little boy high above his head, then he sees the gun pointing at him and the look of joy freezes on his face.

It isn't Justice.

Then Yao's batting her gun hand down, the arm with the bag snapping round her back and pulling her away. "Run!" he hisses.

And then they're sprinting across the road, brakes squealing around them and horns blaring. Into the small alleyway and the labyrinth beyond, taking the twists and turns at full speed, palming aside shoulders and backs, sending people spinning.

"How many?" she hears him ask.

"I don't know. Maybe...maybe none."

But he doesn't slow. Away from the centre, the little alleyways become more deserted and darker, the few bare bulbs already the centre of fly storms. The SUV is waiting for them by a grove of trees on the river just beyond where the city finally peters out. Twenty minutes and they'll be there.

But he slows and pulls her aside into a small side alley. He puts his finger to her lips and they listen. Far off, they hear the cry of the muezzin and, looking up, can see the blood red sky of sunset. They wait but there are no shouts, no running footsteps.

They look at each other and she sees the puzzlement and disbelief on his face. Like her, he seems unable to countenance hope.

"Come on," he says finally.

This time they walked unhurriedly, like Africans, as the buildings become more spaced out and the ground dustier.

Finally, the lights of the city give out and they are embraced by the African night.

If you enjoyed this book then please consider writing a review for Amazon or Goodreads

Other books by Fergus Bannon

The Heretic

Dan Erlichmann, the son of a psychopath, is a man brutalised and alienated by his upbringing and by his experiences as an MI6 operative in Chile in the '70s. After his mission there fails, and the woman he loves is killed by military torturers, the traumatised Erlichmann is reassigned to 'turning' Soviet Cold War scientists. Incidents in Hawaii and Prague produce a vendetta that lasts for decades with Lev Stepunin, a KGB security officer. Then, in the present day, a disaster at a Russian research facility reveals catastrophic flaws in mankind's understanding of reality. Erlichmann and Stepunin suddenly find themselves forced to work together to ward off the possible extinction of the human race, their lives torn apart as they resort to the most violent outrages. Labelled as terrorists, their motives and characters are questioned by everyone, not least by themselves.

Judgement (foreword by Hal Duncan)

Like an episode of CSI scripted by Timothy Leary and filmed by James Cameron – Gary Gibson, author of Stealing Light and the Extinction Game

A tight fast-paced, Bournesque thriller wrapped around a science fictional core that shifts scale so rapidly it gives you vertigo. Heartily recommended – Neil Williamson, author of The Moon King and the Ephemera.

It started with a few isolated incidents: a mob shootout in Las Vegas, a firefight in the Central American jungles - one apparently unconnected event after another hinting at a worldwide conspiracy of unprecedented proportions. CIA computer geek Bob Leith realises it's something much more than global terrorism, something literally not of this world. His understanding of the nature of reality, and of what it means to be human, will be challenged to the very core in this dazzling novel of intrigue and espionage.

About the author:

The Truth is NOT out there

Fergus Bannon is the pen name and alter ego of a scientist who has become heretical about all we think we know of the universe. He believes the universe is far more dangerous and unpredictable than the comfort blankets of science and engineering suggest. He explores these concerns in his latest books, the fast-paced thrillers **The Heretic** and **Leviathan's Fall.**

Scottish by birth, he was brought up in the south east of England. Following graduation, he ran away to sea, his merchant shipping line taking him to some of the choicer trouble spots around the world. Rich though the seafaring life was, it could also be rather dangerous. After a run-in with a death squad in South America, and then nearly getting his throat slit in Jamaica, he began to harbour doubts about his long-term prospects. A hurricane in the Atlantic, and a major fire on board ship in the Pacific, only reinforced these concerns.

Nursing an ambition to live until the age of forty, he therefore came ashore and eventually became a Professor of Clinical Physics. He now lives in Glasgow with his wife and two daughters.

He still travels extensively and has recently returned from a paranormal (no, he doesn't believe in that either) investigation tour of South America with a famous psychic. This will be the basis of a novel called **Life and Other Shadows** to be published in 2019. He has also just written a non-fiction book **Science for Heretics** (under his real name of Barrie Condon) that seeks to show how profoundly hollow our understanding of just about everything actually is.

Made in United States
Orlando, FL
04 December 2022

25485556R00222